Still

Book one in the Still Series

Eniola Prentice

Copyright

Still is a work of fiction. Apart from well- known actual people and events in the narrative, all names, characters, places and incidents are the product of the author's imagination or are used fictitiously. Any resemblance to current events or to living persons is entirely coincidental.

Scripture quotations taken from the New King James Version of the bible.

To everyone who nurses invisible scars in the heart that are seldom talked about, there is a soothing balm of Gilead that has made all things beautiful in His time.

Psalm 46:10

Be still and know I am God
I will be exalted among the nations,
I will be exalted in the earth!

Chapter One

Sola

I confidently opened the white twelve by fifteen inch envelope with *Stedman College of Medicine* emblazoned on the middle in big bold letters. The large envelope was always a good sign, since rejection letters were sent in smaller envelopes. The letter said what I hoped for and expected: "Congratulations Fadesola Cardoso, you have been accepted into Stedman College of Medicine."

I stepped into the next four years of my life with a little trepidation, naivety and optimism. I wonder what I would have told a younger Fadesola at that moment. Truthfully, I don't know what I would have told a younger me.

She would not understand anything I had to say.

But that day, prodded with the excitement of an uncertain but certainly bright future, she took a leap of faith.

We all took a leap of faith.

Chapter Two

Tayo

I walked past the pulsating, gyrating bodies in the club and bumped into a couple of girls jumping excitedly to the blaring techno music. "Hey, watch it!" I called out while trying to maneuver with the three drinks in my hand.

I made it past the dance floor and took the empty spot in the VIP section couches with my boys Trey, Harry, and Toby. Each had managed to acquire a girl to make out with in my absence. Trey was sucking face with a brunette girl that looked barely legal, while Harry was being straddled by two women and somehow managed to make out with both of them at the same time. Tobi was passed out next to the line of cocaine he was doing. I adjusted my position on the couch so I was directly opposite the straight coke lines and rolled my dollar bill into a tube.

I inhaled the first line with the rolled bill and exhaled quickly, then I did the second line in quick succession.

I began to feel the euphoria almost immediately. The pulsating music, with the alcohol and cocaine, created the perfect synergy for a pleasurable experience.

I felt my phone vibrate. I pulled it out of my back pocket, which was difficult, considering that I was high as a kite.

It was a text from my brother:

Mom just opened your mail this morning. You got into Stedman College of Medicine! I am surprised you actually did it. I am proud of you bro! Call me tomorrow!

So I found out that I had been accepted into medical school in an intoxicated and drug-induced euphoric state.

But in the next four years, any ounce of residual euphoria from my drug-fueled lifestyle would be wiped out. I would be confronted with a past I was not ready to acknowledge.

The symbol of my wasted, hopeless and unruly years lay in medical school… waiting for me. The truth is, I was never going to be ready to confront this past until it stared at me squarely in the face, like a mirror, projecting who I was to me.

But through this ordeal, I found real love, the hard kind.

Then I found the type of love that would forgive me for anything. I found the love that set me free forever.

Chapter Three

Nikky

I casually looked through my mail after I retrieved them from the mail room in the hostel.

Yes! It was another large envelope! *Please, God, let it be from a school in the East Coast and not the West Coast!*

I glanced at the large bold letters in the middle of the envelope: STEDMAN COLLEGE OF MEDICINE.

"Yes!" I exclaimed and leapt for joy in the elevator, ignoring the quizzical glance I got from the woman standing beside me.

I ran into my dorm room and tore open the envelope. It said exactly what I expected it to say: "Congratulations Nikky Abe, you have been accepted into Stedman College of Medicine. We are also pleased to announce that The Office of Financial Aid will also be offering you a full year's scholarship from the Leslie Dorme Fund."

"Yes!" I screamed. I screamed again and did my happy dance, which was a cross between the running man and the moon walk, in my dorm room.

So for me, that's how medical school began—with a happy dance—but in the next years the happy dances would cease. Some days, on the really bad days, I would come to regret my decision.

But in my despair and regret I would learn how to love and be loved unconditionally.

The hard way.

Chapter Four

Ladi

"Ladi, it's a big envelope. Open it," my mother said, smiling at me and thrusting the envelope into my hand.

I eyed the envelope cautiously, and my heart leapt with joy. It *was* a big envelope.

Mommy stepped back in an attempt to give me some privacy while I opened the envelope, but I knew she would be standing right outside my door. I stopped her with a wave of my hand. She might as well know now.

Her eyes gazed at me with hopeful anticipation as she watched me open the envelope.

"Ladi Adeoti, we are pleased to announce that you have been accepted into Stedman College of Medicine." I read the words slowly, hardly believing what I read.

With those words, my four-year ordeal ended in success. I finally got in.

Mommy already had tears in her eyes, and I am quite sure I had tears in mine, too. She cradled my head in her hands like she used to when I was a boy and whispered in my ear, "See, I told you. God is faithful."

Indeed He was. We stayed together for a moment in that position, savoring this moment.

Suddenly my mother said, "I have a feeling that you will meet a woman in medical school."

I glanced at my mother in alarm. Mommy always had the gift of prophecy and, when she made statements like this, we took her very seriously.

I smiled and simply replied, "We will see, Mommy."

She smiled back at me like she had a secret that I wasn't privy to.

"You just wait and see, Ladi Adeoti," she replied.

I would often wonder how my mother could have been so astute and what she had seen in my future that made her so sure of her prediction, because in Stedman College of Medicine, I would not only meet the love of my life...

I would meet the woman that would change the course of my life forever.

Nothing can recapture the magic of freshman year of medical school. It's the magic of unbound potential and limitless possibilities. It is the stuff dreams are made of.

Enjoy these days because they will not last forever.

Vaneessa Pope, MD
Class of 1994

The first few days of freshman year were the most exciting for the Class of 2012.

Those were the idyllic days of bliss.

Ladi Adeoti, MD
Class of 2012

Chapter Five

Sola

As the taxi cab driver drove the luggage-laden car towards the airport, I glanced at the passing cars and the buildings of downtown Michigan and vowed never to return. My only regret was leaving two people that I absolutely loved behind; but one way or another, I was Stedman-bound. I closed my eyes and pondered on my relatively short twenty-two years of life. For some reason, I began to think about my parents.

I grew up believing that, after a certain age, the choices of the parents cease to affect the child. I was wrong. My parents' choices, mistakes, and decisions have shaped my life and certainly almost destroyed my life. Even now, it is almost impossible to break free of their influence. It started on the day I decided to become a physician. I was six years old, maybe seven, and my mother was joking with my two aunts, discussing what I would become in the future.

"What does Fadesola want to become when she grows up?" Aunty Bola asked.

"She probably wants to become a supermodel like Naomi Campbell or Claudia Schiffer. You know she's always reading those Cosmopolitan and Vogue magazines you have in your room," Aunty Blessing said.

They all laughed.

"And dressing up in her mother's clothes and high heels," Aunty Bola continued.

"What about an astronaut? Remember you wanted to become an astronaut, Sola," Aunty Bola said.

"No," my mother finally said. "She will become a doctor just like her father," she said with finality and smiled.

I smiled back at her, exposing the huge front gap in my six-year-old teeth.

There was something about the way my mother said it... Was it the awe or respect in her voice, the inflection of her voice or the way she smiled approvingly at me after she said it? There was just something about the way it was said.

At that moment, something clicked in my heart. I decided I was going to become a physician. So every grade, every class, every school I attended in my life was to accomplish this goal. I think in some ways I was also unconsciously trying to please my father. The man ignored me for most of my childhood and my six-year-old self reasoned that if I became just like him, I would get more than a side glance when he decided to visit our house in Lagos.

The few minutes my father was around, I comprehended the fact that my little brother and I were the spare family, that there was another family with my father, and, although we lived in an enormous house, they lived in the even bigger house as a family unit. This was the family that my family and I were inferior to. At six years old, I grasped these concepts and accepted them. But I still craved his acceptance, whatever he would offer, even the little moments of his undivided attention. So when the marriage ended, and I was shipped off to my grandmother's house in the summer holidays, I was devastated.

Slowly but surely as I grew older, I realized he would never become the father I needed, and so I said to myself *You don't miss what you never had.*

In retrospect, his grand exit heralded the beginning of the mental decline of my mother. She had accepted her role as the spare and wasn't quite expecting to be disposed of so easily. When she began to exhibit signs of mental illness I thought to myself *Yes, it serves you right.* I was not in the least bit sorry for her. My cruel assessment was my revenge for her ineptitude in fulfilling her role as my mother. I did not develop my attitude overnight—it was due to a progression of events which finally culminated in a visceral disdain for her and her decisions. I will never forgive her for not protecting me when she was supposed to.

She had enough sense to move to America with my twelve-year-old brother and me after the debacle of her marriage. But even before we left for America, I knew that I had become what I feared: I had become my mother.

I was exactly seventeen years and eight months old and recognized that like my mother, I too exhibited signs of mental illness. I was good at keeping mine a secret and did not lose my mind totally. But when I began to exhibit signs of mental deterioration, on the days I questioned my own sanity, I realized what my mother really went through.

My mental illness was simultaneously sudden and gradual but before I could even recognize what was going on I, who was once alive, died. My death did not require a non-beating heart but a nonfunctioning mind. It rendered me inconsequential, a walking, breathing, and talking collection of functioning biological systems, in a dummy.

This was the cost of losing my mind.

I never let my wounds show, but a thorough examination of my life would reveal the cracks covered with paint, the filth suppressed with perfume and the flaws covered by displaying the best of me at all times.

But my mother's continual mental decline terrified me; I looked at her and saw my own inevitable future. This terrorizing thought cuddled me until it choked me, provoking me to leave Michigan. I wanted to be as far away from her as possible and chose to attend the first medical school that accepted me, regardless of where it was, almost as if I could out run my future.

"Ma'am…ma'am…ma'am…we are at the airport." The impatient tone of the cab driver broke me from my reverie.

"Thank you so much," I replied and quickly rummaged through my purse for the cab fare and handed it to him. He grunted an unintelligible reply and quickly went to the truck to unpack my luggage. I went through the unusually quiet Michigan airport security checkpoints relatively fast and boarded my plane.

As I buckled my seat belt tightly, following the instructions of the flight attendant overhead, I exhaled, filled with a sense of elation.

I finally did it! It felt like I was flying towards my long-awaited destiny.

I had the same feeling of elation in the cab ride after the plane landed in Ronald Reagan airport in DC. I sat quietly in the backseat of the car, eagerly watching the unfamiliar landscape of the state capital that was to be home for the next four years.

"The White House!" I called out and pointed excitedly as the cab passed the familiar building.

The cab driver smiled and nodded politely, probably used to the sight of the familiar white building and the reaction of excited tourists to it.

I could barely contain my excitement and was anxious to see the apartment I would be calling home. I hoped I made the right decision, considering we all decided to live together after a Facebook conversation. I had answered a Facebook ad posted by another freshman named Irene enrolling in Stedman that year. She sounded sane and, most importantly, friendly. I didn't get any serial killer or psycho vibes from her. I hoped I was right...

My heart sank when the driver made a right turn into a questionable-looking street. It was a stark contrast to the modern and expensive-looking neighborhoods we had driven past.

We stopped at a traffic light, and my eyes caught sight of someone dancing.

I turned and saw a tall, thin woman with a bad weave holding a cigarette and dancing at the entrance of a record store with two large speakers blaring loud music.

"Yeah!" she screamed as the pedestrians ignored her and crossed at the traffic light. I made a mental note to avoid that street, Georgia Avenue.

"Are we close by?" I asked the cab driver.

"Yes, ma'am," he answered.

My heart sank again. I didn't want to live in the suburbs, but I wanted to at least feel safe in my neighborhood. A drunk, dancing woman in the middle of the street was not my idea of a safe neighborhood. I breathed a sigh of relief when the cab took another turn into Elm Street where Irene said the house was located. The area looked relatively safe in comparison to the questionable parts of town we had previously passed. I especially liked the fact that the neighborhood was so colorful. Each row house was packed closely but neatly to the next, and each house had a unique color:

orange, red, blue. The street was tiled with red brick. I craned my neck in anticipation as we neared the house and hissed in irritation as we got to yet another stoplight. There seemed to be a lot of stoplights in Washington DC!

"We are here, ma'am," the cab driver said as he pulled up next to a grey house.

"Thank you," I replied and climbed out of the car.

Well, the house looked nice.

The cab driver helped me remove my luggage from the car and drove off, leaving me with four oversized bags.

"Well, here goes, Sola," I said to myself as I rang the house bell and waited.

"Please God let her be as nice as she sounds," I said under my breath.

"Hey, you must be Sola. Hold on," I heard a voice call out.

The door was opened noisily and I was quickly enveloped in a hug.

"Hey! You must be my new roommate. I am Irene! You must be Fadesola."

I was a little taken aback by her hug but decided instantly that I liked her.

"The other housemate isn't here yet, but I made some jollof rice and cupcakes."

I was amused. We had barely moved in, and she was already cooking.

"Wow, so you must have really settled in," I said.

"I didn't have to settle in. I already live in DC."

She stepped out of her foyer and surveyed my bags. She placed her hand on her hips and said, "Now, we live on the second floor, so how are we going to haul these four bags upstairs?"

I shook my head in confusion. Irene scared me a little but looking at her with her hands cocked on her hips just felt right.

I knew right there and then that I had made the right decision in choosing Stedman.

Chapter Six

Ladi

Right before I got accepted into Stedman, I made up my mind that this would be my last round of applications to medical school. The first time I applied I was optimistic, eager and, in retrospect, a little unrealistic. I was in my third year of undergraduate studies at the University of San Diego. I remember the meeting with my college advisor, Mr. Browne, and displaying my arrogance.

"I didn't waste my time applying to second-tier medical schools, because with my record and abilities I am a strong candidate for top-tier colleges."

Mr. Browne shifted uncomfortably in his chair and seemed to choose his words carefully. "I understand you have this perfect GPA, and your research experience, plus your awards, which will certainly set you apart... How can I put this? You may look exceptional here in U of San Diego, but all the applicants to medical schools like Harvard, Yale or Vanderbilt have your identical record. You will not be exceptional to them but the norm."

I cleared my throat and said, "I respectfully disagree with you, sir. I don't want to waste my time or money applying to schools I will never attend."

Mr. Browne sighed and said, "Well, I hope you know what you are doing, Ladi."

"I do," I replied and stormed out of his office, dismissing his concerns as the ramblings of a white, prejudiced man who couldn't believe a young black man could make it into an Ivy League medical school.

Well, it turned out that Mr. Browne was right. He was right three times over. I applied to med schools for three consecutive years and was rejected by schools at different levels. The first time

I applied to Vanderbilt I was waitlisted in the interview stage, the second time I was sent the generic rejection letter and wasn't even offered an interview. I didn't apply to Vanderbilt the third time.

Frustrated, angry, and quite frankly, scared after all the rejection, I questioned my decision to attend medical school. A decision that was made for me the day my brother died in my arms in Lagos, Nigeria. That day has become imprinted in my mind. It was an idyllic sunny day; Lagos's intensely hot weather was pleasant, the sky was spotless, that day was perfect. I was wearing a black cotton tee while my brother was wearing a white button-down shirt and jeans.

One minute my brother and I were having a trite conversation, the contents of which I don't remember, then I heard a loud bang and almost instantaneously the driver's seat, where my brother was just moments before, was destroyed and unrecognizable. My brother's now lifeless body was entangled in the heap of metal while the passenger's side of the car, where I was sitting, remained perfect, creating a stark yet horrifying contrast. I would later find out that the car had been hit by a truck whose brakes had failed. Although emotionally and mentally shaken, I was physically okay. However, my brother was unconscious and was bleeding from a deep gash on his forehead. We were rushed to the hospital by motorists who had witnessed the accident.

That was where it became apparent that my brother's life was not going to be saved in the hospital. The hospital staff refused to admit him until we had paid the admission fee. A pretty young woman who accompanied me to the hospital promptly paid because I had no cash. After paying, I was informed by the same nurse that the doctor on call couldn't be reached and we had to wait for him or another doctor. She quickly added that the phone lines and electricity had just been cut so it would take some time. Time was exactly what Femi lacked and with every moment wasted, my brother's chances of living diminished.

I felt completely powerless.

So I did the only thing I could to provide some comfort to my brother as he slipped away from this world into the next. I wrapped my hands around him with his head on my lap and prayed. I cried out to God to let my brother live.

He didn't.

Femi died in my arms, and in that moment of feeling completely hopeless, holding my dying brother in my arms, my destiny became apparent to me. I made a promise to myself that another family would not lose a child so senselessly.

I made up my mind to become a trauma surgeon.

The second hardest thing I had to do was to tell my parents that their son was dead. Femi's death almost destroyed my family. My parents, who I believed had an unwavering and unbreakable faith in God seemed to crumple, especially my father. With the passing of time the wounds became less painful, and we all healed individually and accepted that Femi was gone. My family's faith in God became even more strengthened and the memory of my brother fueled a stubborn tenacity to pursue my dream despite three rejections. The memory of holding my brother's lifeless body did not allow me to give up, and I halfheartedly tried again the fourth time, choosing Stedman at random.

My high school friend urged me to come for an informal visit before I was even offered an interview. The school was situated in an urban-congested neighborhood, in stark contrast to the picturesque campuses of Harvard and Yale that I had daydreamed about. Stedman College of Medicine, however, had an interesting and unmatched history. The school tour guide, a third year medical student, enthusiastically recited the history of the school to me.

"Stedman College of Medicine was built in 1868 by a charter headed by General Drewes, a celebrated war hero and humanitarian, with Deacon Tascott, Deacon Maurine, Deacon Branson, and Deacon Paul. The original idea of the school was a seminary school, but the five men are unsure of who brought up the idea of a medical school. The school history archives claimed that there was some argument before a compromise was reached. The basement of the school is the seminary school while the medical school and hospital are the top floors. The basement also has the old chapel and a post office."

"Are they still there presently?" I asked curiously, the history buff in me awakened.

"Yes, the rooms still stand. I never have time to go down there though, with med school being so busy."

He led me upstairs and past an office with bold letters that said ADMISSION OFFICE.

"The admission office is closed right now, but you will probably go there when you are offered an interview."

I nodded.

We walked past the admission office to a winding old corridor. He pointed as he talked. "Here the school puts the pictures of all past alumni on the wall, but of course, we don't have picture from as far back as 1881. It starts with pictures of Stedman's five founding fathers," he said, pointing to grey pictures of five men on the wall in a church.

"Legend has it that there is a piano somewhere in the basement which all the five founding fathers signed." He added conspiratorially, "No one has been able to find it."

I studied the wall, fascinated.

It was interesting to see the pictures capture the changing eras. At first, the pictures were grainy and unclear and the medical school class was made up of only men. Then I spotted the lone female in the class roster of one of the classes. The '80s was characterized by both male and female afros and the '90s by colored pictures, all the way to the 2000s where I saw alumni that looked more like me.

"See, we have a quite a legacy," the tour guide chimed in, breaking my reverie.

"Yes, you do," I replied, thinking to myself that every person in these photographs, regardless of time, was linked by the common dream of becoming a physician. Though some of them may be dead, they spoke to me from the walls of Stedman College of Medicine, and in that they lived on, encouraging me to pursue my dream and earn my place on my wall. Stedman had not been my first, second or third choice for medical school, but at that moment it seemed like the only choice.

The next week I received an invitation to interview at the Stedman College of Medicine and made the cross-country trip from San Diego to Washington again. On the day of the interview, I signed in to the admission office and spotted the group of young, eager interviewees making small talk in the reception area. I wasn't feeling particularly friendly so I kept to myself and hoped the rest of my interviewees would get the message. The shrill laughter of a fat boisterous guy put an end to such notions. "What school did you go for undergrad?" he screamed to an uncomfortable looking woman who was right next to him.

"University of Michigan," she answered quietly.

"I heard you guys have about 300 people in your medical school, must be really competitive," he replied.

It seemed like the woman was not interested in a conversation with him, but to be fair to him, he really was just following medical school interview protocol. All the student forums advised everyone to appear "friendly" because "you will be observed throughout the interview day for any verbal and nonverbal cues that might provide clues of your potential for being an excellent candidate for the medical school." Considering the fact that this was my fourth interview season, I was a little jaded. But I was also intrigued by the woman, and my radar, which was historically accurate in picking out Nigerians, was going off. She had to be Nigerian.

I decided to intervene on her behalf because she now had a pained "please, get me out of here" expression on her face.

"Why did you apply here?" I asked him and caught the eye of the woman. She looked exasperated, then looked my way and smiled.

Honestly, this is my backup school," he replied.

There was an audible gasp from the group. Obviously, he had not gotten the memo from med school interview protocol and the student forums. This was a gross violation, a cardinal sin even. You never ever told fellow interviewees your true feelings about the school. Never! You answered the question with a generic "I like what the school offers." The student forums talked about actors who posed as interviewees and were planted by the school to observe and report back to the school. I really doubted the validity of that story, but I admired this guy's guts and suppressed a laugh as other medical school hopefuls edged away from him like he had a communicable disease. The woman used the opportunity to change seats and she took the empty seat next to mine.

"Hi," she said. "What's your name? I am Fadesola, but most people call me Sola." She offered her hand.

"I am Ladi," I said and shook her hand.

And that's how we began, with a handshake. Only it wasn't just any handshake, it was a handshake with the woman who would change the course of my life forever.

Chapter Seven

Nikky

"Daddy, stop it! It's not that far away," I screamed and stared down at my parents.

"But, Nikky, you have never lived so far away from home." Mom nodded in agreement with my father.

"Mommy, I talked to you about this. Medical school is very competitive. I couldn't get into a school close to California!" I screamed back.

That wasn't exactly true. I could have chosen a medical school closer to home, but I was determined to be as far away from home as possible.

Let me put it this way: my parents were a tad overly protective.

Fine, I will be the first to admit that at nineteen, I am quite young to be going to medical school. I mean, it's not my fault I was allowed to skip a few classes! Why did I have to get punished for it with my parents monitoring my *every* move with the comment, "You are too young Nikky. You need guidance!"

Okay, maybe my parents were not as bad as I made them seem.

I adore Mommy because she is the most loving and caring human being I know. Period.

She's also the funniest person I know, and I get some of my charming, playful personality from her. Unfortunately, she also gave me her body which includes a ginormous butt on a petite frame. In fact, I look almost exactly like her. People refer to us as sisters sometimes, and Mom beams with pleasure whenever anyone says that. This is where daddy makes a silly comment with his booming voice of how he "shined his eye to choose a wife." This phrase in normal English means that he chose a good wife. And my mommy is a good wife indeed to Daddy, because she is the opposite of him in every way. He is big, tall and round just like a teddy bear, while Mommy is short, and petite. The only thing he had in common with my mom was his playful personality, which I think was genetically passed on to me. I am fun to be with. It's true! If you took a random poll of all my friends they would all mention my adorable gift of making people laugh. Well except for Lala, because there was that little incident in the chemistry lab when I almost set her on fire. But, seriously, I have the coolest family ever!

We laughed at everything, my parents and I.

We laughed when daddy informed us he was uprooting us from the familiarity of our lives in Lagos, Nigeria to move to America because I got accepted into the school for gifted children in America. I don't know if laughter was the appropriate response, but we laughed nonetheless. It's mindboggling to think my parents flew half way across the world because I got accepted to a school, the Stanford School for the Gifted run by the famous Stanford University. Applications were open to students around the world and the school selected just 100, so it was a big deal in Nigeria when I got in. I remember I applied because my secondary school principal urged me to because "I was extraordinarily brilliant." Whatever that means...

My academic career in America was pretty much the same as in Nigeria, but my parents became so much more overly protective. They always said, "These American children and their ways are not like ours back home, Nikky. We have to watch you so you will not go astray. Look at the Fadare's children. Deola even had the audacity to call their parents by their first name." Then Mom would go on a diatribe about the latest ill-behaved teenager she encountered. I endured this for nine years, and so escaping from my parents' overly protective nest was a motivating factor after high school. I purposefully applied to only East Coast schools and got accepted into Yale University. Obviously, my parents, or more specifically my mother, sabotaged my plans by no fault of hers really.

She had a heart attack (non-medical speak) or myocardial infarction (medical college debt-loaded speak) the night I was packing for Yale in Boston.

No, it's not a joke. She literally had a heart attack when she thought of losing me, her only child. My dad also started making frightening comments about DVTs (deep vein thrombosis). This was medical speak he had picked up during my mother's stay in the hospital. Big sigh...

I had no choice but to stay in California.

However, my mother's little crisis was the genesis of my choosing a career in medicine. I had several reasons for choosing medicine and in no particular order:

1. The cardiologist was hot.

2. The cardiologist was very, very, very, very hot.

3. He helped save my mom's life.

Number three is the type of thing you would encounter when reading medical school applications, but in my case, my story was true. Of course, when I wrote my med school essay, I made the story a bit more melodramatic. I think I added a bit of crying and screaming next to my mom as they applied the defibrillator on her dying heart. But, seriously, that day shaped my life. Watching my vibrant, crazy, and tiny mother looking deathly ill and close to death shocked me. I wanted to be part of this profession with hot men...and women who saved lives.

But because of Mommy's health scare, I was forced to stay in California and attend Stanford.

Do you know what my parents did?

My parents visited me every *single* weekend in college.

They became better friends with my roommates than I did because Mommy bribed them with homemade food.

They had a horrifying fight with the security guard about visiting hours that almost got them banned from the dorms. The security guards actually have a BEWARE OF TROUBLE MAKERS sign in their main office with my parents' pictures, looking every bit like troublemakers.

The mortifying horrors my parents put me through in college are really too numerous to recount. To cut a long story short, I choose Stedman College of Medicine to be as far from my meddling parents as possible, but my parents were not done with convincing me to stay.

Just when I thought my well-laid-out plan had worked and I would be escaping,

they brought out the big guns.

Aunty Nike, my namesake and Mommy's twin sister.

You see, Aunty Nike did not look the least bit like my mom. Aunty Nike was often mistaken for Mommy's older sister because she was taller and bigger than Mommy.

However, Aunty Nike more than made up for her lack of physical similarity to my mom by being the extreme version of my mommy.

If mom was dramatic, Aunty Nike was histrionic.

If mom made people laugh, Aunty Nike had people peeing in their pants from laughing at her jokes.

If mom could cook up a storm, Aunty Nike could cook up a hailstorm.

In fact, my cousin, Aunty Nike's daughter, was my age and was my mommy's namesake, Elizabeth. Yeah. They both thought they were hilarious for naming their daughters after each other.

Rolling eyes.

Anyway, they summoned me into the living room drug intervention–style one week before it was time for me to depart for Stedman.

Aunty Nike started with, "Nikky, please don't kill my sister. Don't destroy my family. You will kill your mother, which in turn will kill your father and I, and leave your cousin an orphan. Do you want to do that?"

They both stared at me silently with my mom nodding in agreement and saying, "Ehen, tell her."

Aunty Nike began crying while Mom began consoling her.

I watched them silently and held back my laughter.

Aunty Nike continued, "You are your parents' only child. It is not easy for them to see you go halfway around the world. Why won't you stay here?"

"Please, Nikky," she said, clutching her heart with tears streaming down her face.

Wow. It was an Oscar-worthy performance.

I would have been moved if I hadn't seen the very same performance for my cousin Elizabeth when she planned to attend a college that was just four hours away.

Mommy and Aunty Nike had joined forces and convinced her to stay in the Rancho Cucamonga area where we lived.

But that was Elizabeth, and I was Nikky.

Elizabeth had somehow missed the genetic imprint for sass and wit that was passed along to the other women in my family. Lizzy, as we all called her, took after her father and was mousy, quiet, and easy to guilt-trip.

I was not.

It would take more than an Oscar performance to convince me to stay.

I began by kneeling down and putting my face in my hands.

They watched me silently.

I hid my face in my hands and thought of all the orphans and dying children in the world.

This method always worked for me when I had been caught doing something naughty as a child and needed to cry. Soon the thought of all the poor hungry children brought tears to my eyes, and I turned to my aunty and mommy.

"Mommy, Aunty Nike, I understand where you are coming from but this is the opportunity of a lifetime. I have been given a full four-year scholarship for Stedman. Do you know what that means? I will barely have any student loans and as a medical student, that will be such a great help to me."

My mommy and aunty watched me with a blank stare.

Okay, it was time for my big guns, the kryptonite for any Nigerian mother with a daughter close to marriageable age.

"And Ada my friend said that well-behaved Nigerian boys from good families are much easier to find on the East Coast."

My mother's head jerked up when I completed my sentence.

She and my aunty exchanged looks.

Aunty Nike said, "So you guarantee at the end of medical school you will come back to us with an engagement?"

Oh, what have I gotten myself into?

"I can't make promises Aunty, but I don't want to be an old maid forever. I think my chances will be better there. Mommy, you are always saying I should start looking for a husband early," I added.

  I was good.

 And when Aunty Nike and Mommy smiled simultaneously and exchanged glances, I knew I had won.

 I was Stedman College of Medicine–bound and nothing would stop me.

Chapter Eight

Tayo

"What do you mean I don't have housing! I called to confirm," I screamed at the harried-looking man on the reception desk. The scene was chaotic. It was moving day in Morgan Complex, the graduate school housing on campus. Several students were pulling bags towards packed elevators. A long line curved round and past the open doors and people pushed past one another in the crowded atrium. Finding Morgan Complex itself was a complicated process to begin with. Apparently, the complex is in the middle of a block of buildings nicknamed the quadrangle containing the graduate schools, medical, dental, pharmacy and law school. I was given this information by an overly flirty and friendly blonde chick whom I had asked for directions. She also used the opportunity to ask for my number. What can I say? I am hot, rich and connected; these sort of things always happen to me.

Med school, like everything else in my life, sort of happened to me, too.

After graduating from college, I really wasn't motivated to do anything. What is that saying again? Why work when you can party? So lacking ambition and direction, I dodged the questions of future plans from my parents by taking a gap year and travelling the world to "discover" myself which really was an euphemism for getting wasted in London, Lagos, or L.A. I dodged questions from my girlfriend at the time by promptly dumping her and ending the relationship, giving her the usual "it's not you it's me" speech. I dodged questions from my two older brothers with stable and responsible jobs with my father's company by ignoring their persistent calls. Until one day, I found myself in the ER of Stedman Hospital in Washington, DC with a broken leg, the result of a night of drunken debauchery gone wrong. To cut a long story short I was beyond wasted when Sean (who was equally or slightly more intoxicated) urged me to jump off the VIP platform in the Lush Club. Being very foolish and very drunk, I complied. Well, the last thing I remember was an excruciating pain in my thigh and waking up to find myself in the run-down, slightly weird-smelling emergency room of Stedman Hospital with no recollection of the events of the prior night. But during my unfortunate stay in the hospital, I met the gods of medicine…

Orthopedic surgeons.

In the totem pole of medicine, ortho (as referred to by the medically inclined) was the "almighty," regarded above all and any specialty. The most competitive, vicious, and brightest minds in medicine were ortho surgeons. Every day the medical team, which was made up of the attending surgeon and resident, would round on the patients, and I would observe a "boys only club" branded by unparalleled swag, alpha manliness, and machismo. No one needed to tell these dudes they were the best, they knew they were the best and made no apologies about it! My mere admiration turned to worship after a conversation with the head doctor, the attending Dr. Halston. Dr. Halston was a legend not only in orthopedic circles, but in surgery at large. He was one of the most accomplished doctors in Stedman College of Medicine. He had numerous groundbreaking research publications and scientific grants to his name. The new surgical techniques he created revolutionized the field of orthopedic surgery. With all his accomplishments, he was the coolest and most humble dude you would ever meet. The residents would all but worship him if they could but he was cordial and polite to everyone, from me his patient, to the nurses who adored him, and the medical students who hung on his every word.

"T," he said one day, using his nickname for me because he didn't want to butcher my name as Americans usually did. "So what's next for you, man? Not getting drunk and jumping off platforms, I hope."

"No, I certainly hope not," I answered sheepishly.

He rubbed his hand through his grey hair then replied, "Son, your story is disturbing. Getting drunk and engaging in risky behavior is inadvisable. In fact, I think we should keep you here until you decide what you want to do."

For some reason that I have yet to fathom I asked, "Can I be an orthopedic surgeon?"

"You can be anything you want to be, son. I think Dr. Charles Grey, the greatest surgeon I have worked with, said: the only thing that can stop you is you. If you want to become a surgeon, young man, the only thing stopping you is you."

After I was discharged from the hospital, I ruminated on my conversation with Dr. Halston and decided he was right. The only hindrance to taking the next step in my life was me. It seemed like my biochemistry degree from Oxford University in London was not going to be wasted after all. I took my MCAT, applied and was accepted. I got in to Stedman!

But after my eight-hour drive to DC and the debacle in Morgan Complex, I was almost second-guessing my decision to attend medical school. I had driven all the way from West Virginia, my parents' vacation home in the States, with the notion that my housing was paid for and set up. Apparently, it was not.

"Sir, step aside. Your issue is being dealt with by staff, and I need to attend to other students," said the Asian man with a tag that read "Property Manager."

I sighed and moved away from the line. That was when I felt a tap on my shoulder and turned to the biggest brown eyes I had ever seen.

"Hey, you look stranded too," she said, offering her hand and smiling excitedly.

I shook her hand and answered slowly, "Yes, I am. I am Tayo."

She replied, "I am Nikky. Nikky Abe, first year medical student and Nigerian. You are Nigerian, right!?"

She looked flushed and excited, just like a little child and her enthusiasm was infectious.

I laughed then replied "Yes, I am Nigerian. And hello, Nikky Abe," I added, my eyes lingering on her brown ones.

I did not know it then, but I would take the girl with the big brown eyes on a roller coaster of a lifetime and that girl I met...with the big brown eyes...would become the greatest love my life would ever know.

When we were medical students, we were a different species separated from the human race. A species that spent twenty out of twenty-four hours studying.

Amanda Brick, MD
Class of 1984

The most commonly used phrase a medical student will utter is, "I have to study."
Another is "Is this material going to be on the exam?"

Thad Brown, MD
Class of 1999

Yes, medical school was a journey of a lifetime…filled with stressful days and sleepless nights. The sheer will, pure ambition, and sometimes the terrorizing possibility of a loss of the dream was the constant fuel propelling you never to give up, even when you wanted to.

Supo "Soups" Folaranmi, MD
Class of 2012

Chapter Nine

Sola

"You ready?!" Irene asked as we walked towards the registration booth in the middle of the lobby.

"I think I am," I answered. It was officially the first day of medical school and, though it was just orientation, I could feel the butterflies in my stomach.

"I am so excited girls," Tina, our third roommate, squealed, mirroring my internal feelings. Irene looked quizzically at Tina and caught my eye before covering her mouth to stifle her laughter. I quickly turned away so I wouldn't laugh too. It was quite apparent that Tina was going to be an interesting housemate. She was a tiny Asian girl with big expressive eyes who moved her hands theatrically whenever she talked. She also had the most interesting things to say. For some reason, she knew half the class already. As we ate the delicious food Irene had prepared on our first night together, she quickly opened up her laptop to the class page on Facebook and began her personal assessment about everyone.

"That girl, her name is Spencer...Spencer Cook. I hear she's very smart. She got top honors in her class in UCLA."

She would continue, again pointing at another person. "He is kind of the big man on campus at his school."

I was astonished that she had gathered all this information in so little time, but she seemed nice...a little talkative, but nice.

"Hello, last names from A to J sign in here and K to Z sign in at the other table!" a beautiful, dark-skinned woman standing in the middle of the lobby called out.

We quickly headed towards her.

"Here you go," said the woman as she handed me a name tag and a registration packet after she located my name on her list. The registration packet contained the financial aid documents, demographics form, and other miscellaneous documents.

"Do I fill these out now?" I asked

"No, the documents are due later in the day. You guys should have fun, mingle, get to know one another. Trust me, you will miss these stress-free days," she replied with a smile.

"Okay," I replied.

I turned towards Irene but she had spotted a couple of students I assumed were upper classmen and screamed "Hey guys, I haven't seen you guys in forever!" She quickly began to chat with the group. Tina, my interesting roommate, had also somehow disappeared into thin air.

I was unsure of what to do next. However, the book *100 Things You Need to Survive in Medical School,* which I had studied thoroughly the night before, mentioned that "during orientation, all potential students should try to make connections which they would utilize for a lifetime."

The problem was that most of my new classmates were in groups or pairs talking to one another. I noticed a line of equally lost-looking students next to a table packed with bagels, juices, cookies and tea, and I headed that way. I figured I could start a conversation with somebody in the line. I took a place at the back of the line.

"Hey, I am Fadesola, everyone calls me Sola," I said to the girl standing directly in front of me.

She turned around and replied, "Yes! You are Nigerian! I am Nikky. There is another Nigerian here. His name is Tayo. I don't know where he is right now," she said in a rush.

I laughed then replied, "Yeah, I am Nigerian. So—" I continued but was interrupted by Nikky's phone ringing.

"Please, Mom, I am fine," she answered quietly.

"Yes…we just started orientation," she answered impatiently. "Mommy, I told you I am fine," she said again. "No, I am safe here…No, I have not found any potential husbands! Please stop embarrassing me!"

I listened to the one-sided conversation in amusement.

"What college did you go to?" she asked as soon as she got off the phone.

"University of Michigan," I answered. "What about you?"

"Stanford," she replied. "I am so excited to be here. Medical school!" she screamed and a few people in front of the line turned to look at us curiously.

I laughed as I shooed her quiet. "They are staring. Don't confirm the stereotype of Nigerians being loud and obnoxious."

"Yes, you know that's true. So do you think med school is half as bad as people say it is? I met some juniors yesterday in a bar, and all we got were horror stories. It made me a little depressed actually," she said as she piled croissants and bagels on her plate. It occurred to me that for a petite girl, she seemed to be eating quite a lot. She probably was just nervous. Considering the fact that it was the first day of one of the most important times of our lives, I couldn't blame her.

"You already met a few upperclassmen?" I asked.

"Yes, I live in Morgan, and some upper classmen helped Tayo and me with our housing. Can you imagine there was a mix-up with our housing? It was such a nightmare. The administration finally got us our rooms and room keys after we almost died of starvation!"

"Well, thankfully, you didn't die," I said, amused.

"Anyway, Tayo was so helpful. He bought me McDonalds and had quite the talk with the building manager."

"Really? He sounds like a good guy. Will you introduce him to me?" I replied.

"Oh, I will!" she exclaimed, nodding her head vigorously.

"He should be here now. I wonder where he is," she said, turning her head to look around the foyer.

"He is probably running late," I offered.

"That's odd, I called him this morning to wake him up. He should be here by now. Maybe I should give him another call."

"I don't know, but it's 8:30 already. Maybe he is running late. Morgan Complex is really close by so he should be here soon."

"Well, I don't know," she said as she closely examined her bagel before taking a bite out of it.

"I met another Nigerian during my interview," I continued. "His name is Ladi. I wonder if he chose Stedman."

"Really, we have another Nigerian! I am so excited, we all are going to be such great friends!"

"Wow," I said as I chuckled. "You do love your Nigerians, Nikky."

"I do! Stanford was really…white. Stedman is different. So many different cultures, backgrounds, people—" She was interrupted by an announcement from a stern-looking man who stood in the middle of the foyer.

"Students, welcome to Stedman College of Medicine," he started. "I am Dean Roberts, the Dean of Academic Affairs. We will begin the orientation in Room 1007, our recently renovated, state-of-the-art freshman lecture hall."

The din of conversation was cut short as we all headed to the lecture hall. Together, Nikky and I grabbed seats at the far back of the class. Dean Roberts walked to the microphone on the podium and announced, "We will begin shortly. I will give the latecomers five minutes only."

"Where is Tayo!?" Nikky said again, twisting her head round to survey the lecture hall. "He will miss everything!"

Chapter Ten

Tayo

Why do I find myself in situations which always includes a hot chick? I thought to myself. The tire jack fell on the floor with a loud clang, and I exclaimed loudly.

My day started out typically, except of course it was the first day of medical school.

I promptly got out of bed at seven in the morning with Nikky's admonition ringing in my eyes. "You can't be late, Tayo. We need to make a good impression in medical school. I am so excited!" she screamed. I held the phone away from me so she wouldn't damage my eardrums.

I liked the kid. I mean I really liked the kid.

After we got our apartment situation sorted out, she insisted we do some grocery and room shopping. I wasn't really keen on grocery shopping, but Nikky fixed her brown eyes on me and practically demanded we go shopping together.

I couldn't refuse, especially because she looked so beautiful when she pouted and said, "We have to! You don't want us to starve, do you?"

Ladies and gentlemen, boys and girls, my name is Tayo Smith and beautiful women are my kryptonite. Her pursed lips and her brown eyes were enough to convince me. Nikky and I spent most of the weekend prior to orientation together, even going to happy hour with a few upperclassmen. She was talkative, witty and animated, in a child-like innocent way.

I found her refreshing.

She made me laugh, a lot, whenever we were together. I really liked her...I mean liked her as in "I would like to get to know you" like, not "I would like to hook up with you" like. That alone made her a keeper—I rarely met girls in the former category.

But how did my carefully laid plans, which included looking dapper in my pink Armani shirt with my Ralph tie, and spending most of orientation with Nikky fall apart?

A beautiful woman? Yes. Another beautiful woman with panic and stress etched on her face on the street next to Morgan Complex, trying to change her tire and swearing rather loudly. Wait. Did I say woman? I meant sea goddess. She was, simply put, the most exquisite creation I had ever set eyes on. She was quite tall, long hair in a ponytail, cat's eyes. She was dressed in a form-fitting pant suit which, as a full-blooded male, I appreciated.

The gentle man in me was moved (it had absolutely nothing to do with her pretty face and hot body). "Hey, do you need any help?" I asked and walked to her parked car.

"Yes," she answered breathlessly, turning up to look at me as she fiddled with the bolts of her tire.

"Hey, let me try," I said and knelt down next to her.

"Well, there goes the notion of the independent woman," she said, laughing.

"My name is Ego. What's yours?"

I cleared my throat and put on what I hoped was my sexy voice and replied, "It's Smith. Tayo Smith." (I loved doing that.) It worked.

She laughed and offered her hand "As in Bond. James Bond. Well my name is Osere, Ego Osere."

"You are one of the few girls that actually gets that," I replied as my hand lingered on hers.

"What are the chances of meeting a gorgeous Nigerian guy to help me fix my tire?" she said flirtatiously.

We held our gazes for a moment.

She suddenly broke the eye contact and said, "I hope I am not late!"

"I am working as fast as I can so you can make it to the school on time," I answered.

"No, it's not your fault. It's mine. I should have checked my tire this weekend. I have a donut in the trunk, but the thing is, today is my first day in medical school. I really don't want to be late."

I dropped the wrench in surprise and said "Don't tell me you are going to Stedman College of Medicine!"

"I am," she answered slowly. "Don't tell me, it's your first day too! It's my first day there as well!"

I nodded with a grin on my face. What were the chances? I hoped she was thinking of spending most of the orientation day with me.

"Really? What are the chances!" she said. "It's such a coincidence."

It was a convenient coincidence indeed. I owed Cupid one.

"I will hurry up and fix the tire so we won't miss our first day of medical school," I replied as I quickly undid the last bolt of the last tire.

We hurried into the lecture hall in the middle of Dean Robert's speech and hurriedly grabbed two front seats. As soon as my butt touched the chair, I heard a hissing sound and someone scream, "Hey! Tayo!"

I turned back to see Nikky waving excitedly. She was sitting next to a chick who looked embarrassed by all the ruckus Nikky was causing. I waved quickly and turned my attention back to Dean Robert.

Ego laughed and said "You are quite popular, Tayo. I think I should stick with you."

I opened my mouth for a sure-to-be-witty retort, but I was interrupted by a woman with dreadlocks clearing her throat at the podium and introducing herself loudly. "Good morning Class of 2012, I am your dean of student affairs, Dean Clarion. I am sure we will get to know one another very well these upcoming months. I would like to welcome you again to Stedman College of Medicine. Our first order of business is the traditional roll call."

She began to call out the names of all the people in the class from a list in alphabetical order.

She then proceeded to butcher my full name.

"Aaa-de-tao Fol-or-so Smith," she called out.

I only recognized my name because of the Smith at the end.

All one hundred and twenty-five freshman medical students were present.

"Ladies and gentleman, turn to your left and to your right." We all obeyed and chuckled as we did so.

"These are the people you will spend the next sure-to-be challenging four years of your life with. Welcome to the journey of a lifetime, Class of 2012."

Chapter Eleven

Ladi

The journey of a lifetime…it certainly felt like it! The excitement in the air was palpable, tangible even. This was the beginning of a bigger picture that we were all a part of. It seemed unfathomable that just a few years ago, Stedman College of Medicine was my third choice for medical school.

Dean Clarion continued, "The curriculum is broken into each organ system of the human body. Then each organ system is broken down into divisions called units. Your first unit will be Molecules and Cells One, which is your basic cell biology and biochemistry; Molecules and Cells Two is immunology. You will round off the year with three units of Human Anatomy."

Dean Clarion paused then continued, "Failure. Failure is sometimes inevitable. Failure is simply an unsatisfactory grade, scoring below seventy in an examination. Listen carefully folks, hopefully I won't have to go over this with any of you because we certainly hope that everyone succeeds. If you fail a unit, you can take a retake exam. If you fail the retake, you will be required to attend summer school. But remember, you can only take summer school for two units. Failing more than two units results in an automatic dismissal from the medical school, or repeating the year if the curriculum council gives you another chance."

Her clear voice rang out in the lecture hall and was met by silence.

"You don't want a merely satisfactory grade either. You never want to be satisfactory with anything in life. A new study found out that the number of residency training spots remains the same while the number of applicants is on the rise. Your academic record from your first day of medical school counts. Ya'll are not average. You were picked from over two thousand top applicants."

I felt goose bumps rise on my hand. It was a privilege to be chosen from a pool consisting of extremely intellectual future doctors and, considering how difficult it was for me to secure my spot in medical school; I owed it to myself to be the best. I would strive to be at least in the top ten in the class.

"Eighty-five is Honors or an A," she continued. "This is what you should strive for. You should always go in to that examination hall of 3019 prepared for battle. I remember as a medical student sitting right where y'all are sitting and I used to walk into 3019 thinking they really can't ask me anything I am not prepared for. That's how prepared I was."

"This med school thing is going to be intense," whispered the woman sitting next to me.

"It certainly sounds like it," I replied.

"Hey, I am Ronke," she said, offering her hand.

"Nigerian, huh? My name is Ladi," I said, shaking her hand.

"Yes. Born and bred in Lagos," she replied and smiled. She continued, "Here I was thinking having a masters in genetics would give me an edge. I am really scared. Medical school is a whole new different, crazy, intense ball game."

"A masters, huh? You are not alone in that respect, Ronke. I am scared, too. It seems like we have a diverse class though, a couple of people with masters, PhDs, some coming back to school after careers, fresh-out-of-college undergraduates. It's a good mix."

"It is," she replied.

"I hope we all survive this," she continued

"We will," I replied softly.

Or at least I hoped we would, that all 125 of us would be graduating in May 2012.

I turned my head silently to analyze my new classmates.

We really were a diverse bunch and this was not surprising. Stedman College of Medicine was known for diversity. There were many Caucasians including Americans and international students, quite a lot of Indians, Asians, Latinas also. Another major racial group in the class was undoubtedly black, which included African Americans, Africans and Caribbeans. I spotted a woman who looked familiar seated at my far right.

I racked my brain for a moment then recognized her. It was Sola, the woman I met during my interview. We had both promised to keep in touch after the interview, but we never did. I remembered her witty commentary during the interview and smiled to myself. She certainly made the long day more bearable.

I waved to catch her attention. Her face lit up with recognition, and she waved back.

I turned my attention back to the podium where Dean Clarion was droning on and on about examinations and failure. I perked up when she said, "Ya'll are dismissed for lunch. We will meet back here at two for a meet-and-greet with the upperclassmen."

There was a bustle of activity as the students all headed towards the exits. I quickly caught up with Sola.

"Hey, stranger," she said and smiled warmly as we hugged.

"Hey," I replied.

"So you ended up choosing Stedman."

"Yes, I did. I didn't see that fat, obnoxious guy though. What was his name again?"

"Raymond!" she exclaimed, her eyes lighting up with laughter.

"He was probably ratted out by the planted spies," I replied.

She chuckled loudly.

"Don't tell me you believe that folklore, Ladi?"

"Hey! Raymond's absence here proves it!"

"Planted actors? Really? This is not the CIA Ladi, it's just medical school," she replied.

"Yeah, it's just medical school, and we are just future doctors who will save a life or two. We are not that important!"

She laughed loudly and said, "Fine, you win Ladi. There were planted spies during our interview."

"I am not sure you really believe that," I replied, walking alongside her.

She shook her head at me then. I laughed, catching her eyes again.

We fell into comfortable silence

The woman standing next to Sola, whom I hardly noticed, cleared her throat loudly. "So! I haven't met you. I am Nike, everyone calls me Nikky."

"Oh, I am so sorry!" Sola exclaimed. "Nike, this is Ladi. We met during our interview."

"Hey, nice to meet you," I said and shook her hand.

"So lunch…We could try the school cafeteria?" Nikky said.

A couple of the students seemed to be heading that way, so we joined the crowd. I introduced myself to some of my other classmates as we made our way through a labyrinthine path past the pictures of alumni to the walkway with transparent windows.

"Girl, you missed what happened last night! It got buck wild!" said a tiny, interesting-looking Asian girl who ran up to Nikky. She was dressed in stylish, masculine clothes that looked oddly feminine on her tiny frame. Her jet black hair was cropped short and combed into a short bob above her forehead.

"What?" Nikky asked, taken aback.

"Apparently, Lenny and Dee in our class had a lot more fun than we did…." she said, her voice trailing off suggestively.

"Girl! What! It was a fun night out, but I didn't think anyone got that drunk!" Nikky replied.

"Wait, you guys, hold on. A couple of you guys went out last night?" Sola chimed in.

"Yeah, a couple of us from Morgan went out last night for happy hour, and I met Tina," Nikky said, pointing to Tina.

"Sorry I didn't introduce myself to you. Of course I know Sola because she's my housemate. I am Tina." Tina moved her hands to emphasize each word as she talked. Tina continued, "Are you guys coming to the welcome party tonight?

"There's a party tonight?" Sola asked.

"Yes. Apparently it's a Stedman tradition. The second years talked to a couple of us about it so the guys are having the party at someone's house close by," replied Nikky.

"I hope you guys make it, but Nikky, let me tell you more about last night," Tina said as she dragged Nikky away, deeply engrossed in conversation.

"Wow. Parties and hookups? Already?" Sola said, shaking her head.

I laughed and shook my head also.

I wasn't surprised though, because the first two weeks of medical school had the highest percentage of romantic entanglements in the freshman class. I had read a scientific report on the online student doctor forum. The suggested hypothesis for this phenomenon was the extremely short attention span of the average medical student. After the first two weeks of school, medical students quickly lose interest in the most readily available dating pool, which was one another. However, because fellow medical students are the only available dating pool to the average med student and due to the need for emotional support during the intense midway point of the school year, there is a spike in romantic entanglements during this period, making an analysis of the phenomenon a two-bell curve.

It was quite a detailed report.

Sola and I wandered through the cafeteria looking for something good to eat as Tina and Nikky quickly left us behind, deeply engrossed in their gossip.

"The spaghetti and meatballs looked good," I said, stopping at the food counter.

"Too many calories. We are in medical school. I remember someone telling me about saving lives just a moment ago. Let's look for something healthy," Sola replied, leading me reluctantly to the salad bar.

We got our food and headed to the crowded dining area of the cafeteria, where we found a table with a few freshmen.

"You went to undergrad in Michigan?" I asked and pretended to eat the leaves I had no interest in.

"Yep, U of Michigan. I took one year off and applied here and got in."

I remember on the interview day you said you went to University of San Diego for undergrad," she continued.

"Yes. It was a good four years there."

"Well, at least you had good weather in San Diego. On the other hand, I was stuck in the harsh winters of Michigan."

"That's good though! You are probably used to the cold by now. I am not! The northeast winter is going to be so tough on me."

"It's not too bad. You will get used to it," she replied, smiling.

"I think not. I absolutely hate being cold. It was one of the reasons I avoided coming to the northeast for medical school, but here I am."

"So what changed your mind?" she continued, pushing her salad away.

"You really want to know?" I smiled mischievously.

"Yes, I do actually." She smiled too, meeting my eyes.

"History."

"History?" she asked.

"Yes, history. Stedman's history is intriguing. The five founding fathers, the city beneath the school, the wall of the alumni was all very fascinating to me. On that day something just clicked for me; I just had to be a part of it."

"I barely listened to the history part during the interview," Sola said sheepishly. "But I am glad that it all convinced you to come here and here we are again," she said, meeting my eyes.

"Here we are again," I repeated, catching her eyes and smiling at her.

The first med school party in Stedman was traditional but the connections formed were often short-lived. The biggest, most lasting connections were formed with whom you studied with, not whom you partied with.

Christopher Braun, MD
Class of 1975

The most interesting and most gossip-worthy events happened in the parties. So I never missed one party in my four years in Stedman. Hookup, breakups, almost hookups and everything in between happened, and I knew it all.

Tina Hong, MD
Class of 2012

The Class of 2012 studied hard and partied harder!

Tayo Smith, MD
Class of 2012

Chapter Twelve

Sola

The loud music blaring from the white row house on Fifth Street made the party location impossible to miss.

"It's here," said Tina.

All three girls in the car turned their heads to get a better look at the house.

"Is that Bryson? He looks fiinnne! I think he wants to do ortho, too," Irene suddenly screamed. I followed her gaze and watched a striking and certainly handsome guy walk up the steps into the house.

"Ortho! Girls, we better try looking for our future boos tonight," added Tina and then she stepped out of the car.

I applied some lip gloss and straightened my blouse then got out of the car too.

I hope I didn't overdress, I said to myself. Nikky's text from earlier mentioned someone called Ego who had a tight mini dress.

"Dress to kill girl! I am riding with Tayo and his new friend Ego who has on a too tight mini dress."

I looked down at my sheer white blouse with a bubble skirt and hoped I was dressed to kill as Nikky so aptly put it. We walked the few blocks to the house from where we parked.

"I hope we have fun in this party," Irene said.

"I hope so, too," I replied.

The rhythmic clicking of our high heels and the loud music from the house were the only sounds on the relatively quiet street.

The door to the house was unlocked, and we walked in through the kitchen to a dimly lit house. I slipped through bodies packed like sardines and made sure I held on to Tina and Irene. There was beer, wine, cranberry vodka and rum bottles on the kitchen table in the center, where a few people were gathered around the table mixing drinks. We slipped past a pool table in the adjacent room with a few people playing pool. The din of the music, which was loud in the kitchen, was two decibels higher in the main living room where most of my classmates were socializing in groups. A few were dancing with one another. I shook my head at Fred, a guy in my class whom I had met yesterday. He was slumped on the chair, snoring loudly, holding a bottle of beer.

Irene pointed to an empty couch not occupied by an inebriated adult and screamed to be heard above the din, "Hey, let's sit here!"

"I will get some drinks for us," offered Tina, who hurried off in the direction of the kitchen.

We settled into the couch and surveyed the party. Everyone seemed to be having fun.

My eye caught a curvy woman in a short red mini dress, and waist-length hair with a drink in her hand, singing along with a group of freshmen to the lyrics of the rap song that just came on.

Was that Ego? The one Nikky was talking about? She looked interesting…like the kind of girl you didn't leave your husband alone with.

I texted Nikky immediately

I see the Ego girl. I am not sure about her. Are you here? I am sitting on the couch closest to the door.

Right on cue, Tina came, barely holding on to three questionable-looking drinks with Nikky right behind her.

"Look who I found," Tina said.

She squeezed herself in the small space between Irene and me, and the space fit her petite body perfectly. She looked even more beautiful with makeup on which accentuated her perfect doll-like features, especially her brown cat's eyes.

"Nikky!" I screamed. "You look really gorgeous."

"You look nice too," she said, hugging me tightly.

I hugged her back half-heartedly. I hate the physical interaction required for embraces. It was an invasion of my private space and a breach of the invisible line I let few past.

But I liked Nikky, so she was allowed to breach that line. She glanced at the woman in the red dress and her posse dancing in front of our couch and said, "They seem to be having fun."

"Is that Ego you told me about?" I asked, edging closer to her.

"Yep, I don't know about her. I haven't decided if I like her."

I chose my words carefully and replied, "We don't know her, Nikky."

"I mean, where did she get her outfit from? Whores 'R' Us? That dress is too tight and too short."

We both giggled like naughty school girls.

She continued, "I am just good with the auras of people. I am an expert actually and I am not sure about her..."

"What exactly is an aura?" I asked, amused.

"Well, an aura is the vibe someone projects. It's almost a spiritual, emotive thing. If we have time I will tell you of my history of spotting bad auras of bad people."

"Hmm, I look forward to this conversation," I said holding back laughter.

We were interrupted by Damien, a classmate I met previously during orientation.

"Hey, mind if I join you girls?" He squeezed himself between Nikky and me without waiting for an invitation.

Nikky whispered in my ear, "Tina warned me about Damien. He's a weirdo. I will leave you two at it." With that, she grinned and quickly slipped off the couch.

Damien turned to me with a smile and said, "So, Sola was it?"

I nodded, and he continued, "How long do you think the average man can hold his breath?"

"I don't know."

"Two minutes." He grinned like he had just made the funniest joke in the world.

I sighed inwardly. Tonight was going to be a very long night.

Damien didn't seem to notice that I quickly lost interest in our conversation. He subsequently tried to engage Irene, but she ignored him also. He finally gave up and bid farewell to both of us.

Irene said, "Wow, he was so weird, and his breath stinks. He smelt of garlic and onions!"

"I feel bad for ignoring him, but I couldn't take it anymore," I replied.

"It was horrible—" She stopped mid-sentence because something caught her attention.

"Hey, isn't that Nikky making out with that guy?"

I turned my head slowly and was astonished to see Nikky and her male friend plastered against the wall, kissing furiously.

Irene whispered in my ear, "I know that dude! That's Tayo, and he's in our class." I followed Irene's gaze and watched the couple, who were both obviously drunk, as they kissed passionately.

"I think we should keep an eye on Nikky so no one...takes advantage of her. She's a little tipsy," Irene said

I nodded and watched them silently.

The guy turned slightly and glanced at us on the couch, obviously gawking at them. He broke himself away from Nikky and then stared at us directly.

Then he grinned and pulled Nikky to a dark corner of the room away from our field of vision. A feeling of foreboding came over me, and I realized there was something vaguely familiar about him.

No! No! Sola, stop it, I admonished myself. But I couldn't let go of the sinking feeling. *God! God! It can't be him.* It was dark, and maybe I was tipsy. It couldn't be, but what if it was? I had to make sure.

"Are you okay?" Irene asked. "It looks like you have seen a ghost."

No. If he was who I thought he was, I had just seen a nightmare.

I composed my expression and replied, "Nothing, just tired. So this guy, Tayo, what is his last name again?"

"Tayo Smith," Irene replied.

Immediately Irene said the words I dreaded, it took every fiber of my being not to scream in pain and anger. It took every fiber of my being not to begin to shake uncontrollably.

"Okay," I replied, keeping my voice monotonous and biting my lower lip to prevent the tears that threatened to fall.

"Are you okay?" Irene asked again. "What did I say? Do you know him?"

"No, no," I replied quickly, but my tears were dangerously close to falling and unraveling secrets I had locked in my heart.

I got up from the couch abruptly, ignoring Irene's confused face.

Away from Irene's examining eyes, the tears began to fall uncontrollably. I heard someone crying, a guttural crying, and I didn't recognize my own voice. I bumped into dancing couples, boisterous conversation, and the roaring laughter of my classmates, all oblivious to the fact that my carefully constructed existence of normalcy was going to be ripped apart.

I made my way to the door with my eyes blinded by tears and my heart filled with a searing pain. I walked not knowing where I wanted to go, but knowing I wanted to be away. So I began to run, run as fast as my legs could carry me, away from the shame, pain, anger and regret in Tayo Smith. My barely recognizable sobs reminded me that I was indeed still alive.

Chapter Thirteen

Ladi

I did not want to attend the party tonight, but James, my British roommate and a sophomore medical student, kept insisting.

"Dude, man," he started with his British accent, then paused to apply a generous amount of gel in his hair. "This is the party of the year, man!"

"I thought you said the party after the white coat ceremony was the party of the year."

"Yeah, but this party will be the baseline for measuring the fresh meat!"

"Fresh meat?" I asked.

"Yep, the hot new freshmen in your class that will be joining Stedman and expanding our dating pool options!" he completed his statement with boisterous laughter.

He lowered his voice then said, "I think I may have spotted my future girl among your classmates."

"And who might that be?" I asked.

"My African Queen: Ronke," he answered, then blew a kiss to himself in the mirror.

"You don't mean Ronke Adefisayo?" I asked.

"Yes, I do. In fact, I was hoping that you could introduce me to her."

"Sure," I answered uncertainly.

I didn't know how to break it to James but from my meeting with Ronke and my subsequent conversation with her, but she would never date James. We bumped into one another once again after our dismissal from orientation and somehow the conversation led to spirituality. She was a Bible-believing, Bible-quoting Nigerian woman, the breed commonly known as the *spiro* or *spriticoco.* Her first prerequisite for a man would be his faith, and she would never just date anyone unless there was a chance it would lead to marriage.

James was out of the running by default.

I nodded in sympathy as he continued to ramble on about how beautiful she was and how he was going to woo her by singing the song "African Queen" by the popular Nigerian artist, Tuface.

However, his statement about women was one of the reasons I tried to avoid social situations, like the party. There would invariably be alcohol, music, and lots of women.

A powerful combination for temptation.

Another reason I thought it prudent to avoid the party was the mention of hot girls immediately brought Sola to my mind.

What is wrong with you, man? Are you going soft?

I barely knew the girl but I couldn't stop thinking about her and our conversation on the day of orientation. I had given Sola a lot of thought. In fact, I had given her too much thought. I didn't understand why I replayed my conversation with her over and over again in my mind. Or why I remembered the color of the top she wore when I first met her during the interview. Or why her dark close guarded eyes intrigued me.

With her smooth, chocolate-brown skin, long jet-black hair, and even longer curly lashes, she was undoubtedly beautiful. I even liked and analyzed the mole on the right of her face next to her full almond-shaped lips. But her beauty did not warrant my obsession with her. I had met beautiful women before, and I didn't come home analyzing their facial features. She would be one of the women I would characterize as temptation by no fault of hers really. I had to be careful. After struggling with sexual temptation and seemingly overcoming it, I could not regress spiritually.

Maybe I would sit this party out. I didn't think it would be my type of scene anyway, but James was not going to give up that easily.

"Sit what out? Dude, you just have to come for this party! Don't be lame!" he insisted.

"I really don't want to come out tonight, man. Maybe another night."

"There will never be another first freshman party for the Class of 2012 again! Don't be lame, dude! Let's go."

"James, you really don't need me to party. Just go have fun," I replied.

"But I need you to be the designated driver because I'm gonna get whiteboy wasted!" he screamed and pumped his fists in the air.

"Well, if it's to keep you safe maybe I will come," I said, jumping off the couch and heading to my room to change, not admitting to myself that the thought of seeing Sola was foremost on my mind.

For some reason, as I pulled my car out of the driveway with James on the passenger's side, my mother's words came back to me: "Put everything you do in Washington through the God filter. Ask yourself before every action, 'will He approve of what I am doing?' because He is the only one that matters."

I suppressed all thoughts of a God filter as I headed to the party. I did not want to feel guilty, but as we drove past the neat row houses of my neighborhood I recalled the last conversation with my mother.

"I am so overjoyed. You made it into medical school finally. The God who got you in there will keep you in there."

Thinking of my mother's prayer for me brought a smile to my face.

She was a woman that I will respect and love all of my life. Something told me that going to this party wasn't part of the "making mama proud" list, but what she didn't know wouldn't hurt her.

I parked my car in an empty parking spot a few blocks from the house, and James practically sprinted into the house party.

"See you in there," he said.

I sighed then made sure all the car doors were locked.

It is obvious I am going to be the parent in this relationship, I thought to myself as I headed toward the loud music.

Then loud sobs broke the relative stillness of the street. I thought I was mistaken and ignored the sound but heard the sob again. I looked down the street and spotted a familiar woman on the sidewalk hunched over, crying.

"Are you all right?" I asked uncertainly.

She did not seem to hear me.

"Should I get help?" I asked as I approached her.

She didn't appear to hear me but my noisy shoes seemed to catch her attention, and she stopped sobbing for a moment. The evening was uncharacteristically cool for the summer, and I pulled down the sleeves of my sweater. I wondered if she was cold because she was wearing a skirt.

"Hey, Ladi. What are you doing here?" she asked.

"Sola?" I replied. I knelt next to her on the street curb, disrupting a pile of leaves in the yard next to the curb.

"Hey, what's happened? Did someone upset you in the party?"

"No," she answered. "No, but I am so confused, Ladi. I don't know what I did to deserve this. I just wanted a fresh start. Why is this happening?" she said in a rush and broke into sobs again.

I was taken aback by the force of her emotions.

"Shh, shh. It's okay," I said and pulled her close.

But it seemed that only made it worse, and she cried even more hysterically. I stroked her hair as she cried and didn't try to stop her because it seemed like she needed to cry. The goose bumps on her shoulders reminded me of how chilly the night was. I removed my sweater and wrapped it around her, ignoring the cold wind.

"Thank you," she said in between sobs.

"You are welcome," I replied.

"Will you stop crying now?" I continued. "It's cold, Sola. If you want to cry we could at least go somewhere warm," I added.

She smiled at my comment, accentuating the mole on her face. "I am so sorry. Yes, sure. But I don't want to go back into that party."

"Did someone in there hurt you?" I asked.

She paused before she replied, "Yes, long ago."

"Do you want to talk about it?" I asked.

"No," she said firmly. "Ladi, please could you just take me home. I rode with Tina and Irene, and I don't think they are ready to go home."

The whole situation was odd. Finding her crying on the porch, looking so beautiful and broken at the same time, I wanted to know what hurt her so deeply. But I sensed that if I pushed she would retreat further behind the veil of secrecy in those intriguing eyes of hers. "Okay, I can drop you home," I said then pulled myself up from the curb and offered my hand to help her up. Her cold hands grabbed mine firmly as she pulled herself up from the curb. The rustling leaves were the only sound in the quiet night as we walked silently to my car.

"Here, take some tissue," I said offering her a box of Kleenex in my car.

"I look like a mess!" she exclaimed, using the tissue to dab at her eyes and cheeks.

"No, you don't," I replied.

"You are such a liar," she replied, shaking her head.

"Okay, fine, you look like a mess," I replied and pulled out of the street.

She laughed, a deep throaty laugh.

"That is two times I have made you laugh tonight," I added.

She sighed and replied, "Thank you so much, Ladi. You came right on time. I don't know why I am laughing really. I am just so…so…hurt."

I could see she was holding back her tears again.

"It can't be that bad. It will get better, whatever it is that is bothering you."

"You don't know, Ladi…I am not…I don't know…"

She turned to the passenger's side window and stared at the passing cars.

I tried again. "Sola, it cannot be that bad. I understand we just met and I will respect your privacy, but your tears…"

Her tears broke my heart; they were reminiscent of the helpless cry of a deeply wounded animal at death's door.

But she was immutable. She had put up a silent wall between us.

We rode in silence until I got to her street and parked the car.

"Thank you, Ladi. I appreciate this so much," she said, turning towards me.

I didn't want her go to an empty house, being so vulnerable.

"Sola, I don't want to seem forward, but you shouldn't be alone tonight."

She looked uncertain and replied very softly. "I am fine. I will be fine. It always turns out fine."

She seemed to be trying to convince herself that she was fine.

"Are you sure, Sola?" I tried again.

"I am fine, Ladi. Thank you so much."

She leaned in, almost reluctantly, to give me a hug.

I hugged her back, the sweet, fruity smell of her perfume enveloping me.

She whispered in my ear again, "Thank you, Ladi. Thank you so much."

"You're welcome," I replied. "Anytime you are crying on the street, just call me and I will be there."

She smiled again and, almost like it was a second thought, added, "Ladi, why is this happening to me?"

I didn't know what hurt her so badly but at that moment, I wanted to protect her from whatever it was. I doubt she knew what her hurt, vulnerable eyes and her pleading voice was doing to me.

"I don't know, Sola. But they say everything happens for a reason. Whatever it is happened for a reason."

"Not this," she replied. "I am so confused. So confused."

"Sola, will you at least tell me what happened?" I asked softly.

She immediately withdrew and replied, "I can't, Ladi. I just can't. Besides, my boyfriend will take care of me."

"Thank you so much, Ladi," she continued as she moved back slightly. Then she slipped out of the embrace and got out of the car. I watched her as she made her way to her apartment complex. She turned and waved at me before she closed her door, leaving me with an empty feeling, almost like I had lost something I never had.

Chapter Fourteen

Sola

I crumpled into tears on the floor after closing the apartment door.

I wailed unabashedly, grateful that there was no one in the house to hear my anguish.

This is not happening. This is not happening.

A million thoughts raced in my brain, and blind panic invaded my mind.

I began to shake uncontrollably.

God, this is not happening! This is not happening! God, why would you do this to me!

Where was this God that claimed to love His children and why would He allow me to suffer so senselessly?

Where was He?

I had to call Dare. Dare would know what to do.

With trembling hands, I dialed Dare's number.

"Hey, Sola," he answered groggily.

I tried to control my sobbing and screamed through my tears, "Dare! Tayo Smith is here!"

"Sola, hold on! Stop crying. What is going on? I didn't hear what you said," he answered.

I heard the background noise of the television.

"Here, let me turn down the volume of the TV," he said. "What is going on? Tell me."

"Dare…Dare…Tayo Smith is my classmate…he's my classmate…I saw him today!"

There was a pregnant pause on the phone.

'Sola. Are you absolutely sure it was him?"

"Yes."

"The Tayo Smith, *the* Tayo Smith we all knew."

"Yes, yes, *the* Tayo Smith."

"Oh no."

"What should I do, Dare? I don't know what to do. I just can't...I can't...I don't know what to do. How is this even possible?"

"I understand Sola, please calm down. I will think of something. Calm down for now, baby. Please stay calm."

"How can you tell me to be calm?! Dare, what if he tells everyone what happened? Med school was supposed to be my fresh start. I don't know why this is happening."

"Slow down, Sola," Dare replied slowly.

I was afraid to ask the next question but asked, "Do you think he remembers?"

"He doesn't. He won't remember."

"How are you so sure?"

"He won't. He can't."

I slammed my face into my palm in frustration and said, "Dare, this is not happening! This is not happening!"

"Sola...please calm down."

"How can you tell me to calm down!? How can I remain calm? Oh God!"

"Please just remain calm. He won't allow himself to remember. I know him. He just won't," Dare said.

"But what should I do now? I don't know what to do."

"Has he seen you?" Dare asked.

"No...well, yes...not directly. It was dark."

"But did he remember you?"

"I don't know. We were at a party, and he was probably half drunk already." I added hysterically, "Dare! Dare, what should I do?"

"Is it possible to transfer medical schools?"

"No! NO! I just got here! I like it here!" I screamed.

The thought of leaving Stedman filled me with dismay.

"Sola, be realistic, transferring might be a definite possibility. If he recognizes you, things could get messy."

"He can't touch me here. I am in America now."

"He can," Dare replied simply.

"No. Please help me. I don't want to leave. I like Stedman! I am just getting to know my classmates! Please help me. Help me…Please help me! Help me!" I began to scream.

"Shhh, keep your voice down Sola. Calm down, Sola, please!" he started.

I only sobbed louder.

"Dare, help me! Help me! Please help me!" I screamed like a broken record.

"Sola, please…" Dare started, his voice sounding slightly panicked.

He knew I was losing control, and he knew what happened when I lost control.

I was in pain; this was a very familiar pain, an emotional pain so tangible that I felt a physical pain in my heart.

I was still screaming, but then I realized I was screaming something different now, a cry that my soul cried every night, a cry that never brought the much-needed answer. "God, help me! God, help me! God, help me! Please help me!" I screamed, wailing in a bundle on the floor with my back to the front door.

"Hello…Sola…" I heard Dare's voice call from my cell phone that I had flung to the side.

I ignored his voice and rocked back and forth against the door.

"God, help me! God, please help me! God, help me!"

I was hurting, and I had to ease the hurt somehow. The warmth generated by the friction from the hard and rough carpets both comforted and bruised my body.

I was suddenly hit with a wave of nausea, and I rushed to the bathroom.

I retched violently into the toilet bowl. Then for a moment I was bent over the toilet bowl, with my hair stained with vomit. I flushed the toilet and pulled my hair back.

I was hit with another wave of nausea and vomited again. This time I didn't bother to flush because I knew that I would be vomiting again.

How did the promise of medical school end up this way?

I lay there crying with my head hung over the toilet bowl, vomiting until bile rose from my throat. Then there was nothing else to vomit.

So I became unnaturally calm, sobbing softly.

The pain was unbearable; I just wanted it to go away. I needed the hurt to go away.

I am constantly in pain.

Then I knew what I had to do. I knew what would make the pain go away.

I needed my blade.

I got up from the toilet bowl and flushed. Then I quickly turned to the medicine cabinet opposite the toilet bowl. I brought a clean blade with me from Michigan. I always carried an unopened clean blade…just in case I needed one. But where was it?

I carelessly tossed the drugs I had just carefully arranged just days prior into the sink. I looked over to the cabinet, where Irene's shampoo was neatly arranged in a row, and moved them roughly to the side, ignoring them as they rolled onto the floor.

Where was that blade!?

I looked under the sink in the drawer, moving the cleaning products around.

Then I found it.

The sight of a new packet of blades flooded me with relief.

I quickly grabbed the blade and slowly opened the wrap.

I slid down the bathroom wall to the bathroom floor, and I rolled up my sleeve.

I poised the edge of the blade over my left hand.

Sola, not this again. Don't do this to yourself again.

"I have to," I answered back. "It's the only thing that will make the pain go away."

I poised the blade up my arm in an angle, careful not to cut too deep.

Then I began to cut my arm, tentatively at first, then I increased the pressure, watching the blood trickle down my arm.

I felt it, the unexplainable easing of the tension, like a taut rubber band that had just been released. The emotional pain I felt no more, and the only pain I felt was physical.

But I knew it was temporary.

I would feel the pain, a permanent resident of my heart, again. It was always there, lurking in the dark, and it would come back very soon.

❖

When it was over, I grabbed a damp towel from the bathroom railing and put it over the cuts to halt the bleeding. Then I carefully bandaged my arm awkwardly using only my right hand making sure to conceal the cuts carefully.

Now I would have to wear long sleeve shirts for the next few days. I hated that. I would also have to constantly worry about concealing the cuts so no one would see them, but I was used to it.

I can never quite remember what gave me the idea to cut myself. All I remember is that I was sixteen and pinching myself hard to feel pain, and it wasn't working. Then one day I saw a clean blade in my bathroom and began to cut. No one ever found out, not my mother or John, my brother; it was my dirty little secret.

It was my way of coping.

It was my painful paradise.

Cutting was mine; it was my method of controlling my pain. I could not control every time someone had caused me pain in my life; it was beyond my control, and this was the only time I could control it. This time pain wasn't inflicted to my life without my approval or my control. I wasn't used as a plaything. This time I was in control.

I attributed this part of me to the flawed mental framework I inherited from my mother.

I have only ever told one other soul about my cutting and that was the love of my life, Dare. I love him because he never judges me. He understands that this is how I cope.

I glanced at the mess I had made in the bathroom and quickly began to tidy up, grateful for something to take my mind from Tayo Smith.

But it did not work; all I could think of was Tayo Smith.

My mind refused to believe that Tayo Smith was here, but the reality was that he was here. How did this happen? Maybe he wouldn't recognize me, and I would be left alone in peace.

But it was too dangerous.

I could not let what he knew become known. It was too shameful, and that alone would kill me.

But if I stayed and he didn't remember, then I would be...

I couldn't complete that sentence because I knew I wouldn't be fine. I would be in constant fear and emotional turmoil.

I returned to the living room and picked up my cell phone.

It had thirty missed calls from Dare, and immediately I felt guilty.

My poor baby had called thirty times. He was probably worried about me. I could picture him in his casual pants and ripped bare chest, pacing frantically in his living room, and immediately I missed him. I would have given anything in the world to be with him right at this moment, to lay my head on his chest while I listened to his heartbeat and hear him tell me everything would be okay.

Sure enough, my phone began to vibrate again.

"Hey, baby, I am sorry. I am just sorry. I lost control," I answered.

"Sola, don't do that to me again. I was so worried. I was this close to calling the police."

"Baby, I am so sorry. I am sorry. I am frustrated."And scared," I added.

"What did you do? Did you..." he asked.

"Yes, I did."

"Okay, Sola. As long as you are good now."

I sighed with relief. Every time, I feared Dare would make me feel like I was crazy, but he never did. There was no judgment with Dare, only acceptance.

He understood my madness because he knew everything, absolutely everything about me. I could be vulnerable with him. I was unashamed with him. He accepted me for what I was.

"Yes, I am good now," I replied.

"Sola, please calm down for now. I know it's difficult, but we just have to think of a plan."

"What plan, Dare? Just sit and wait to see if he recognizes me?"

"It's that simple, yet not that simple."

"So what do I do? He barely saw me today. It was a darkly lit room. What about when he sees me in the daylight, like in class?"

"He won't remember," Dare answered.

"Why do you keep on saying that!?" I answered, feeling frustrated at his refusal to accept reality.

"How are you so sure?" I continued.

There was a pause.

Then he answered, "Trust me, and take my word for it."

"Can you come and pick me from Ronald Reagan airport tomorrow? I have to make sure you are okay."

"Why?" I asked in confusion.

Then it clicked. He was coming! My baby was coming! Everything would be all right.

"Baby! Are you coming? I am so excited! What about work?" I asked in a rush.

Suddenly the situation did not seem so bad anymore. Dare was coming. He would take care of me and tell me what to do, just like he always did.

"I'll give them an excuse," he answered. "I can't leave you alone, Sola."

I immediately felt a rush of gratitude.

"Thank you, Dare, I appreciate you so much."

So my fears were somewhat allayed but not completely. Dare would come and take care of me. But what would happen when Dare left and I had to face Tayo Smith every day for the next four years? This notion was almost inconceivable to me.

Chapter Fifteen

Nikky

I, Nikky Abe, am a woman who knows what she likes.

In no particular order, I know that I like medical school already.

I know that I love Anderson Cooper, the CNN reporter also known as "the silver fox" in certain esteemed circles.

Finally, but certainly not least, I am absolutely and positively in love with Tayo Smith.

It could explain why at this moment, I was making out furiously with him in a nondescript corner of the party. Don't get me wrong. I am not the type of girl that makes out with random dudes at parties... Well, except for that one time in undergrad when I made out with that guy when I was slightly inebriated. What was his name again? Emeka or John. Anyway, I will have to say Tayo is a good kisser. He teased me with his mouth, little kisses, little nibbles here and there that left me wanting more.

He was a welcome change to most Nigerian guys I had made out with, whose kisses left my mouth feeling like it had gone through a paper shredder. In fact, I recall that the weekend after I made out with Emeka, I had to apply *Rub,* the Nigerian equivalent of *Vaseline*, on my lips because they were bruised.

Tayo was not like that.

He was gentle.

As I said before, I am not the type of girl that would ordinarily do this. However, it wasn't my fault. From the moment I met him, I knew he was going to become my husband.

It started in the foyer of Morgan Complex, immediately after he turned to me and said,

"Well hello Nikky Abe."

I immediately had a vision.

I know! I know! Stop laughing, but I did!

These types of visions are a part of my Extra Sensory Perception gift that no one, especially my parents, takes seriously! For instance, I once had a vision that our neighbor's dog would die in a horrible freak accident involving a lawn mower. I tried to convince Mommy to tell the Bakers that their adorable Alsatian, who everyone called Little Timmy, would die but did she listen to me? Nooooo.

"Nikky, stop this nonsense, my dear," she said. "You have an overactive imagination."

Well, though unfortunate for the Bakers, I am pleased to say I was somewhat right. Little Timmy did not exactly die, but the Bakers were robbed three days later. My visions are not a hundred percent accurate but they are pretty darn close to being accurate…sometimes.

So back to my vision with the future love of my life, Tayo Smith. I saw myself holding a very beautiful girl. She was about two years old, and she was the perfect genetic combination of Tayo and me. Tayo was dressed very casually in loose-fitting pants and a shirt, and he was smiling at me and the child.

I just knew, right there and then, that I had seen our future together.

Tayo Smith was going to be my husband. It was as simple as that.

So I wasn't such a hoebag for making out with him now! I mean we *were* going to have an adorable little daughter together.

I was a little confused after my vision, and I stared at him blankly for a moment.

In fact, we both stared blankly at each other for a moment, and I swear there is no other man who can look at me the way he does. He looks at me very intently, like he is totally absorbed in me.

When we finally tore our eyes away from each other, he said, "I am glad I have you as a partner."

He gestured to the chaos around us in the foyer of Morgan Complex and continued, "We need to find our apartments together."

Then he flashed that devastating smile of his and then…guess what he did…*he winked.*

I almost swooned right there on the spot, but I kept my composure.

"Okay," I replied nonchalantly, my heart beating a mile a minute.

I was thrilled and confused at the same time. Thrilled that this gorgeous specimen of a man called me his partner and wanted to be with me and confused at the vision I just had.

"Come on, let's go," he started, then he pulled my hand firmly and marched towards the now frazzled-looking property manager, Mr. Vinit.

"This is totally unacceptable. I have paid my school tuition and rent for my apartment in Morgan was included in the tuition." He glanced at me then said, "I assume that the young lady has paid her tuition too and there is no reason why we both should not have an apartment."

He paused, waiting for my assertion, and I silently nodded.

I hadn't done much talking since he grabbed my hand, as I had inadvertently become mute. It must have been the god-like good looks that had me mesmerized.

"Why are we being subjected to this?" he demanded

"Yes, sir. We understand your patience sir," Mr. Vinit started. "Let me locate your apartment number and get your key."

"Take care of the young lady first," Tayo commanded.

He sounded like he was used to giving orders, and I liked how he put my needs before his.

We watched Mr. Vinit's retreating back for a moment, then he turned to me and said, "So, Nikky Abe, what are we going to do together in the next few days?"

I screamed inwardly, but outwardly I gave him a demure smile, the one Mommy said men positively adored. "We can do whatever you want, Tayo Smith."

Then he smiled at me for the second time that day, and again I almost swooned. We basically spent the time before orientation together until orientation when he met that girl. What was her name again? Ego. The one he met when she had a flat tire.

But now he was making out furiously with me and all felt right with the world. I don't know how we ended up in this position. All

I remember was that he pulled me to dance with him saying, "Hey, you. I have been looking for you."

I think we danced for a total of fifteen seconds and then the next thing I knew we were pressed against the wall, making out.

I couldn't wait to tell Mommy about him because it looked like OPERATION BRING-A-MAN-BACK-TO-CALI wasn't going to be a total bust. Of course I would exclude this little making-out session in my story.

Tayo suddenly tore himself away from our embrace and said, "I think your friend wants you."

I turned slightly to my right and saw Irene with her arms folded, staring at me with a mixture of concern and disapproval in her face.

I sighed inwardly to myself and reluctantly turned to Irene.

"Don't worry. We can always continue where we left off," Tayo whispered in my ear before casually stepping back from me.

Didn't I say this man leaves me wanting more? I had to physically restrain myself from running after him.

I was also careful to simply smile back at him and not grin like an idiot.

Irene was at my side in seconds, and she said urgently, "Nikky, be careful, baby."

I rolled my eyes then replied sheepishly, "I am careful, Irene. We were just having a little fun."

"Nikky, I know we are classmates and all, but you don't know him that well. I feel I should look out for you."

The annoyance I felt toward Irene for bringing my make out session to an abrupt end evaporated. She was just concerned about me. Now that I could analyze the situation with a clear head, away from the dangerous tempting lips of Tayo Smith, that is, this wasn't a good look for me at all. A slightly buzzed Nikky Abe making out with an equally buzzed classmate of hers in the first official social function of my class did not paint me in a good light with my new classmates. I had without a doubt made sure that any gossip about Dee and Lenny was yesterday's news. I wasn't too bothered actually. After all, this was just my first official step to becoming his wife.

"Let's head out," Irene said.

"Okay," I answered. The party was winding down anyway, with only a few die-hard dancers remaining on the dance floor, and the previously packed kitchen was virtually empty.

I suddenly remembered and said, "Where is Sola?"

"She left already. She seemed kind of upset before she left though," Irene answered.

"What upset her?" I asked as we headed towards the door.

"I don't know…It was kinda weird really. She saw you and Tayo making out and she got upset."

"Are you serious?"

"Yes," Irene answered with a shrug.

"Maybe you misinterpreted what you saw."

"I don't think so. She saw you with Tayo, and then she rushed out of the party."

"Really. That's odd…" I answered with my voice trailing off.

Tayo and Sola had not met officially since orientation began, so it was unlikely that my make out session would upset her. Besides, she told me she had a boyfriend. It was apparent to me that Sola was going to be my *besto* a.k.a. best friend in medical school, and Tayo was going to be my boyfriend so I wanted them to get along.

Sola getting upset at the sight of Tayo and I together was not a harbinger of good tidings.

Chapter Sixteen

Tayo

I woke up with a splitting headache and a feeling of foreboding.
Crap! I don't remember anything that happened last night.
My eyes slowly began to acclimate itself to the bright rays of sun filtering into my living room.
What was that smell? It smelt like death.
Slowly I realized that the smell was coming from me; it was a mixture of alcohol and vomit. The vomit I certainly hoped was mine.
What happened last night?
I ignored my throbbing head and sat up on my couch, then quickly scanned through my cell phone. There was a text from James, whom I met during the day of orientation, that read:
Blimey Tayo, I knew Nigerians party hard but last night took the cake. Making out with not one but two females! Naughty boy! I hope you are sober now mate!

Making out with two females? Nothing he said made sense to me.
I was very afraid.
I had just begun a new chapter of my life, and it was happening again.
I quickly searched for James's number on my phone and called him with my heart pounding.
"Big T Smith!" he answered. "Finally gotten over that hangover ai! Last night was crrrrraaaaarazzzzy!"
I winced at his chirpy voice; each word sliced through my skull like a knife.
"Yeah…" I started uncertainly. "What happened last night?"
"Stop playing, man!"

I was almost afraid to continue, but I said, "I am not. I don't remember."

James chuckled then said, "You were more wasted than we thought." He cleared his throat and began, "Well, it all started when you made out with Nikky and then Irene acting as the DUFF, aka Designated Ugly Fat Friend, put a stop to that."

He laughed heartily at his own joke and continued when I remained silent.

"Anyway after Nikky, you started making out with Dee. I must tell you, man, she wasn't the most attractive of human beings. You must have had serious alcoholic beer goggles on."

He chuckled then continued, "You were so drunk, you couldn't even stand and me and a couple of guys had to physically carry you back to Morgan Complex. I've got to add that you are pretty mean drunk, Tayo. You were quite violent, cursing and spitting.

"It was hilarious really," he added.

My heart sank then I asked carefully, "After you dropped me in Morgan Complex, do you know if I left the apartment?"

"Well, you were pretty belligerent and kept talking about another party you were invited to, but we told the security guards at the entrance to be on the lookout for you. I seriously doubt they would have allowed you to leave the complex in that state."

I breathed a sigh of relief, then said, "Okay, thanks, man. I owe you one."

"No, thank you, man. That was pure comedic relief for me. I hope you can make orientation in one piece and you are not too hung over," he replied then hung up.

I couldn't believe it had happened again.

This was humiliating.

Panic rose in my throat like a tight vise around my neck, and I could hardly breathe. The fact that I may have done things last night that I had no recollection of was humiliating.

Calm down, Tayo.

Then I called the one person that might understand: my older brother, Temi.

"Hello?" he answered grudgingly after the third ring.

"It's me, Tayo," I answered breathlessly.

He sensed the panic in my voice and immediately his tone changed.

"What have you done now?" he asked, with an edge to his voice.

I told him the story quickly, leaving no details out.

"Well, that's not too bad. So you made out with a few girls. You have done worse."

His statement was met by silence.

We both knew what he referred to.

The contents of the blue folder locked in a vault in Nigeria.

The incident carefully documented in the blue folder started out as the typical story, but that day did not have a typical ending. The typical day always started with a wild alcohol-fuelled party and ended with feelings of shame and helplessness after the inevitable blackout. This time it did not end with feelings of shame and helplessness but with feelings of horror.

I remember Hassan's quizzical "yeah, right" expression when I told him I couldn't remember. He told me what happened that night leaving important details out of it.

"It's better you don't know all of it," he said.

When he was done with his sordid tale, I was shocked into silence.

"I thought you knew what you were doing," he said again, shaking his head in disbelief.

"Does anyone else know about this?" I asked.

"Yes. There's me and you then the three others who were there and another one. The one who instigated it."

"At least, tell me the name of the one who instigated it."

"It's better if you don't know that."

But I had to know. So I went to my brothers so they would help me clean up my mess.

I will never forget the disdainful looks my brothers gave me that day. I saw a reflection of what they thought of me in their eyes. *You good-for-nothing failure*, their eyes screamed.

"If not for our father's bad heart and the fact that this would kill mother if she knew, I would tell them. I would let them know what kind of son you are," Temi started, his eyes sparking with anger.

It was a formidable scene, with me sitting opposite Temi, who resembled an enraged bull at that moment, with my head curled in my hands.

"I am ashamed, horrified, and alarmed that I came from the same womb as you. You are a useless good-for-nothing mess up who will never amount to anything," he completed, his mouth curled up in distaste.

And Temi was the more sympathetic brother. Tade showed his disdain with silence.

You are not even worth my attention, his silence said to me.

He maintained this dignified disdain towards me even now. Whenever I was home, he barely acknowledged my presence and usually grunted in response to my greetings.

Even when I got accepted into medical school, he wasn't impressed.

"Let's see how soon you will mess this one up," were the first words he said to me.

Although royally pissed off at me, my brothers would do anything to protect the family name. They did what needed to be done to clean up my mess. Hushed conversations between my brothers, disdainful looks cast my way, and a burly detective are the fragmented memories I refuse to piece together in my bid for self-preservation, to try but fail to convince myself that it didn't happen.

Finally the incident ended with a blue folder, the contents of which are only known to my brothers and the detective. I was excluded from the secrets because my brothers echoed Hassan's sentiments:

"The less you know of this the better."

I could not even be trusted to keep my own secrets.

Temi warned me sternly, "If this ever comes out, I can rest easy, knowing you know nothing. This way you can't implicate yourself because you are foolish enough to do so in a drunken or drugged up state."

The aftermath of this event was a deep sadness that prompted me to give up alcohol for almost a year. However, alcohol is a demanding mistress, and she was soon back in my life in full force. So there were other incidents, other blackouts, other clean-ups by my now irate brothers, but none as disastrous as that contained in the blue folder.

There was also a brief stint in an alcoholic rehab center in the States and later in London, orchestrated by Temi. I lasted two days in both centers.

I reasoned that I was not an alcoholic. In fact, I *know* that I am not an alcoholic.

Do I get a little bit carried away with alcohol? Yes.

But am I an alcoholic? No.

Through the years I almost forgot what I did; if you can't remember what happened, then it is easier to convince yourself that it didn't happen. But I couldn't get rid of a nagging fear. One day, my secrets could literally and figuratively come out of the vault and on that day, there would be no brothers to clean up my mess.

Chapter Seventeen

Nikky

"Girl, Tayo made out with another chick right after you!" Tina exclaimed, right after I sat down in Room 1007, the lecture hall.

I struggled to maintain a benign expression on my face because I knew even my expression would be fodder for more gossip for Tina.

Inside, I was smoldering with anger though. I knew something wasn't right when I woke up this morning. It was a feeling I had, quite similar to the premonitions I usually felt before Aunty Nikky, my mother's sister, visited in California. Her visits were never good; it was like having a double dose of Mommy and the finding-a-husband-while-you are-ripe lecture. I ignored this unease and attributed it to my ESP acting up again, then I got a text from Tayo that said

I am sorry for what happened last night.

Sorry! What did he mean by sorry? Those were the best twenty minutes of my life! I had rehearsed how I would recount the story of our first kiss to our daughter. I mean, that was singularly the best kiss of my short adult life; in fact that was one of the best moments of my life and he was apologizing for it. I immediately came down with a stress headache and didn't trust myself to compose a suitable reply, just as I couldn't trust myself to reply to Tina's probing questions.

"So what's really going on with the two of you? Are you dating? Or was that just a drunken kiss?" Tina continued.

"I don't know, Tina," I replied.

"Well girl, you better know because you can't just be giving your cookies out of the cookie jar like that," Tina replied, rolling her neck for emphasis.

Sola quickly slipped into the seat next to me.

"Great, I am not late," she said and flashed a smile

I glanced at her in greeting but was taken aback by her appearance; she had dark circles under her eyes and her skin was blotchy.

"Oh, I didn't get much sleep last night," she quickly said when she noticed my expression.

"Well, I was talking to her about her naughty behavior last night," Tina continued.

Tina was sooooo annoying.

Sola glanced at me and said, "Nikky, you have to be careful with Tayo…he's not the sort of guy you want to get mixed up with."

Her eyes flashed angrily as she spoke, and I wondered why.

"Do you know each other outside of med school?" I asked.

"Why would you say that?" she asked quickly.

"I am just curious," I replied.

"No," she answered quickly, a little too quickly.

I considered probing further, but Sola's body language had changed; she had become taut and rigid.

"Let's just pay attention to the lecture," I replied, grateful that the security expert poised to give us a lecture on campus security was taking his place on the podium.

"My name is Nelson Benton," he started.

"As medical students, you will be doing a lot of studying late here till late in the morning. I urge you to walk in twos…"

I could not concentrate on the lecture; it wasn't like he was saying anything new anyway. My mind kept drifting back to Tayo and his antics. I felt literally like my heart had been ripped from my body when Tina told me he made out with someone else, fifteen seconds after me. I mean, this was the love of my life, the man I was destined to marry. I was hurt, more than I would ordinarily have been if he was just another drunken make out session. There had to be some reasonable explanation, and I would politely demand one when I saw him. I turned my head to scan the lecture hall for him but he was notably absent, and I hissed with irritation.

Mommy was right. Boys could be so annoying sometimes.

"Nikky, I am so sorry about last night. We were both pretty drunk," Tayo started. He looked suitably contrite. His hair looked unkempt, and he stuck his hands in his pockets.

He had sauntered into the lecture hall an hour late and refused to meet my eyes. I was forced to corner him in the lobby of 1007 when we were dismissed for lunch.

I regarded him for a moment and chose my words carefully before I replied, "So what happened meant nothing to you at all? You were drunk?"

"No!" he quickly answered. "It's just that…I don't…I don't…"

"Just say what you have to say, Tayo."

"I don't want to ruin our friendship. We have a great thing going here."

He caught my eye and said, "You are my Nikky."

He gave me the look again, and I almost screamed. How was it possible that with one look this man almost had me going mental?

He continued, "We hang out together, and we are cool. Things like this will bring in complications to our friendship. It was just a kiss, not a big deal."

Friendship? Cool? Just a kiss? These were not the words I wanted him to use! I wanted him to say he was madly in love with me, that he was drunk when he made out with Dee and perfectly sober when he made out with me.

"Well, we should be more careful then. We need to protect our friendship," I said.

"Thanks," he replied, then he did the absolutely worst thing he could do.

He ruffled my hair and put his arms around my shoulders, forever banishing me to friend zone.

He continued, "I am so embarrassed, you know. I was really drunk."

"Hmm," I replied distractedly.

I barely heard because the word *friend* kept replaying over and over in my mind. *He sees you as a friend. You are his friend Nikky, not his girlfriend or future wife.* But my inner monologue could not convince me. The vision I saw had been very powerful.

He didn't know it yet, but he was going to be my husband and that was that.

Chapter Eighteen

Sola

"Please, please guys, make sure you have paid all fees to the university. You will be expunged from the university if you don't," Mrs. Alfman began.

Orientation had not started on a good note today, and it did not look like it would end on one. Mrs. Alfman was talking about my least favorite subject, financial aid in medical school.

Then yesterday Nikky got into a fight with Tayo Smith's harem: Ego Boyo and Dee Marsen. Ego was the girl who danced provocatively with Tayo Smith at the party and Dee was the girl he made out with. Unfortunately, during orientation yesterday all four were in the same group for the scavenger hunt. Dean Clarion explained that medical scavenger hunt was a Stedman orientation week tradition: the students were divided into groups and had to follow instructions camouflaged as medical trivia until we found our "treasure" which turned out to be a textbook. Both Dee and Ego did not take the game too seriously; they both giggled and rolled their eyes with Ego complaining that she shouldn't have worn six-inch Louboutins for this. Nikky, on the other hand, took the game seriously and quickly became irritated with them.

"If you don't have anything positive to contribute then both of you step aside," Nikky hissed to them.

"That's rude. You don't have to speak to us that way," Dee replied

"I will speak to you whatever way I please," Nikky replied.

Nikky turned her attention back to the game by turning over the card with the clue and said, "The twentieth amino acid. I think that is...okay, the next clue should start with the letter H. Let's go find it. We won't need Dee. She may have more important things to do…like random hookups and make-out sessions.

We all gasped at her comment, and then I laughed nervously to make the situation less awkward. Laughing nervously was obviously the wrong thing to do because both Ego and Dee glared at me and have been giving me dirty looks since then. They obviously associated me with Nikky, and now they didn't like me. *Great.* I had a million things to worry about in medical school, and now I could add having classmates as enemies as another one.

Mrs. Alfman continued, "As you all know, when ya'll graduate from medical school, you will have loans of over a hundred thousand dollars, and that's a mortgage, you know. My assistant is passing around some tips on how to reduce your debt."

I barely glanced at the pamphlet when it was handed to me. I did not like to think about the student loans and the amount of debt I had. It made me too anxious—I had enough anxiety in my life to deal with.

I turned my attention back to Mrs. Alfman's speech about our bleak financial futures as future physicians. The words *subsidized loans*, *unsubsidized loans*, *private loans* and *FASFA* were overused as she spoke the lingo of broke, debt-ridden medical students.

When she was done speaking, Dean Clarion stepped up to the podium and said, "Thank you, Mrs. Alfman, for that…uplifting speech." There was a smattering of laughter from the class.

She continued. "Today's agenda is very quite simple. You will be divided into groups of ten for team-based learning sessions. Freshmen students traditionally enjoy it because gives you all chance to get to know one another."

She continued, "I also wanted to talk about the short white coat ceremony." She paused for effect. "The short white ceremony indoctrinates you into the esteemed career of medicine by bestowing to you the ultimate symbol of a physician: your white coats."

There was a stillness in the room. We were young, hopeful, future physicians filled with potential with an understanding of the gravity of her words. This was the beginning of the realization of dreams. After gaining acceptance into medical school, we had the ultimate reward: an opportunity to be a part of this noble profession of servitude.

Dean Clarion continued, "Some schools prefer that you earn your white coat in the third year, before moving to the clinical-orientated part of medicine. But at Stedman, we think differently."

She smiled then, and scanned the lecture hall with her eyes.

"We see you all as clinicians already and expect you to think like one. Everything you learn now or do now is for your patient."

Dean Clarion remained silent for a moment as her words sank in.

She continued, "The ceremony is very simple. Each member of the class is called to the podium, then you will be cloaked by a family member with your white coat. Remember to give me the name of the family member who will be cloaking you. The ceremony starts at four o'clock on Friday. That is all. Check the list posted outside the lecture hall for your team-based learning groups."

Nikky quickly joined the many other classmates who were talking excitedly as they rushed out of the lecture hall to check their groups.

"I hope we are in the same group!" Nikky exclaimed.

I smiled at her infectious excitement. I was okay with being in the same group with anyone except for one person. What were the chances that we would be in the same group, anyway?

"Yeah! We are in the same group!" I heard Tina exclaim to someone to the right.

"Let's check our group," Ladi said, leading me to the posted list. We had bumped into him standing outside the lecture hall next to the list.

I quickly scanned the names on the list and my heart sank when I saw the name directly under mine.

Tayo Smith

"What's wrong?" Ladi asked, searching my eyes.

"Nothing," I quickly replied.

"Are you sure?" he asked again.

"Nothing is wrong. Leave me alone!" I snapped.

I regretted my words immediately because he visibly flinched.

"I am sorry. I am sorry, Ladi," I quickly apologized. "I am just stressed out right now."

He regarded me for a moment then said, "Okay."

Sola, control yourself.

I was embarrassed at my outburst and feared that Ladi now viewed me as emotionally unstable. He had called me repeatedly after the "crying on the street" incident, but I screened his calls. He was persistent though, because the next day, he stopped me in the lobby of the lecture hall.

"Are you okay, Sola? You weren't responding to my calls, and I was a little worried."

"I am fine," I lied, not stopping to talk.

I wasn't ready or willing to give him an explanation for my outburst, so I tried to brush past him. This turned out to be a mistake because he held my hand firmly, pulling my long sleeve shirt in the process.

He held my hand carefully and examined the fresh cut marks then looked at me.

"I had a bad reaction to something," I quickly lied.

"Sola," he started. He pulled me in closer to him so I was staring directly into his eyes.

"Are you okay?"

The way he said it, the inflection of his voice, almost made me break down and tell him everything, but I couldn't.

So I lied again, "I am fine."

That was the last serious conversation we had, and we both carefully avoided the topic. I kept wearing long sleeved sweaters to conceal the cuts, which had become disturbing even to me.

I really wanted to tell Ladi what was going on, that my tightly wound emotions were in turmoil, but I couldn't. I spent my mornings physically forcing myself to come to class—trying to avoid Tayo Smith—and my nights cutting, to reduce the tension that had built up during the day.

Even today, I tried to skip the financial aid orientation.

I sent a text to Nikky asking her to make notes for me.

I immediately got a frantic phone call from her.

"What! Sola! Are you sick, and I mean throwing up and having diarrhea simultaneously? Are you dead in a ditch somewhere? Are you bleeding? If you answered no to any of those questions then there is no way I will allow you to skip orientation! This is medical school. The most important time of our lives!"

Of course, I could not tell her why I was avoiding class and she was quite insistent I come.

She then proceeded to tell me about statistics which showed a steady decline of grades when medical students did not attend class.

"But this is not class, Nikky, this is orientation," I answered dryly.

"Excuse you! That's even worse. You will miss this most essential bonding experience with your classmates. You know all the seniors told us we need a support system. How will you get a support system if you stay home all day?"

"I don't know, Nikky," I started.

"Please Sola," she whined. "Orientation will be boring without you!"

I sighed and replied, "Okay, if you promise not to get into fights with anyone."

"It's not my fault!" she protested. "Ego and Dee were being so disruptive!"

"Okay, okay! I will see you. I am on my way," I answered with a laugh.

I was almost regretting that decision now.

I was going to come face to face with Tayo Smith, and I wasn't prepared for it.

So I began walking towards the exit, opposite the steady stream of students walking towards the discussion rooms. I heard Nikky's loud voice, stopping me cold in my tracks.

"Sola! Discussion group is that way! Where are you going?"

I fixed a smile on my face and turned slowly, thinking of an excuse I would give her. My smile froze on my face because trailing behind her was Tayo Smith.

I contemplated turning towards the exit and running, but I couldn't. Nikky had caught up with me.

My knees became so weak that they almost gave way and I could barely control my shaking.

"Where are going to Sola? The discussion rooms are in the opposite direction."

Sola, control yourself, don't panic.

I fixed my eyes firmly on Nikky, ignoring Tayo Smith and said, "I am really tired. I wanted to head home."

Nikky put her hands on her hips, much like a mother would and said, "We talked about this, Sola. We need to bond with our classmates—you can't leave." She paused for a second and continued, "Why are you breathing so fast? You look very ill."

Her voice became infused with concern, "Are you really ill?" she asked, touching my forehead.

Control yourself, Sola, don't let her suspect anything.

I immediately reined in my emotions.

"I am fine, Nikky. I will just wash my face in the bathroom, maybe I will feel better. I will come for team-based learning."

"Yeah! Sola!" she screamed, hugging me.

"Anyway. I want you to meet Tayo Smith, my friend, the one we talked about," she continued, stepping back.

He smiled at me.

He actually smiled at me, and he said "Smith. Tayo Smith."

Time stood still, everything was in slow motion.

He offered his hand for a handshake.

Every fiber of my being recoiled against touching his hand, but if I didn't, there would be questions.

Questions. I couldn't risk that.

So I offered my hand gingerly to him, letting only my pinky finger touch his hand.

"So you are the Sola Nikky won't shut up about," he continued. "Well she goes on and on about you. It's nice to finally meet you."

"Anyway—" he started and was interrupted by a voice.

"Hey Mr. Smith, you want to walk me to class? I want to have a stern talk with you. You have been a naughty boy."

It was Tami, another classmate.

Tayo laughed and turned to us, "Girls, as you see, duty calls. Nice meeting you, Miss Sola," he said and made a beeline towards Tami.

Nikky rolled her eyes at his retreating back and said, "Let's go to discussion Sola."

"You can go ahead I will catch up with you. I need to use the bathroom," I answered.

Nikky turned round and looked at me quizzically, "Are you sure you are okay, Sola?"

"Yes, I am fine. I just need to use the bathroom quickly."

"Okay," she answered as she watched me walk away.

I stared at myself in the mirror in the bathroom. My beating heart and my perspiration-riddled body made me feel like I was preparing for a battle.

I stilled myself at the sink while breathing deeply.

He really could not remember.

He was not acting.

I was both grateful and enraged at the same time.

He really could not remember.

That night was just a typical night for him. I was so little to him that I had been deleted from his memory, like I never existed, like it never happened.

Was he pretending? Did he really recognize me but he didn't want me to know that he knew who I was? Did he have even more sinister plans up his sleeves?

I was worried, very worried.

I could barely stand the bubbling emotions within me. I needed to know for sure if he actually remembered who I was. I wanted so badly to call Dare but he was on a plane towards DC at this moment.

I would go to discussion group, then I would find out if he was pretending.

I walked out of the bathroom and each step I took was heavy with fear.

I stood at the doorway of the glass windows of the modern and newly refurbished discussion rooms. I was one of the last students to come in. There were ten black leather chairs around a grand wooden oak table with my classmates seated around it. A projector took most of the space on the table with a modern laptop in the corner of the table. A white chalk board was on the opposite side of the room. I quickly scanned the room.

Then I saw him...lazily looking through his cell phone.

I suppressed a physical wave of loathing mixed with fear and swallowed. Then I stepped into the room quietly.

He did not look up from fiddling with his phone.

I took the chair slightly opposite him, and he finally looked up and stared at me.

I held my breath...

He smiled broadly and said, "Hey, Sola. I didn't know we were in the same group."

He looked absolutely...guileless.

Wow. He really could not remember.

Chapter Nineteen

Tayo

I tore my eyes away from Nikky's friend, Sola. She had a peculiar expression on her face like she was afraid of me. It was odd to say the least. She was beautiful though, and I liked her dark eyes.

Her eyes were a stark contrast to Nikky's, a tempestuous one which mirrored her feisty personality. Nikky was keeping me very occupied during orientation. She called me out of the blue after a particularly long and boring day of orientation and said, "Let's go skydiving, Tayo. I googled a place near Maryland where we could sky dive!"

"I don't understand. Why do you want to go skydiving?"

"I just want to, but everyone absolutely refuses to go with me. Then I thought, who isn't a chicken? Tayo! Tayo is fearless!"

I took a big gulp.

"Nikky, there is no time to do this."

"There is! I Googled it. The location is thirty minutes away and it will only take fifteen minutes, so that's forty-five minutes back and forth."

"But I am tired Nikky. I really don't like the idea of dropping out of a flying plane."

"But we only live once, Tayo! Let's do this! Or are you scared? Even with all your Lagos boy swag, you are scared?!"

What did she mean by that? I was absolutely and categorically not scared and I said so. "Nikky, stop that! How can I be scared? My nickname in Kings College was Danger Mouse. Me, scared? Girl, stop!"

"Well then, I will come to your apartment, and you can get your car. Put your money where your mouth is, Tayo Smith."

"Okay," I answered softly. My arms got sweaty all of a sudden.

I was scared. No, scratch that, I was petrified.

Nikky looked maniacal in her skydiving gear smiling at me, taking pictures and, might I add, flirting with the instructor. On the other hand, I tried not to pass out from my anxiety. How exactly had she talked me into this? It was those big brown eyes of hers, I tell you. She was difficult to refuse.

The idea of jumping off a flying plane did not appeal to me at all. Trust me, I had tried to get out of it by trying to ignore her persistent phone calls, then her persistent banging on my door. It didn't work. She insisted that she would stay outside my apartment door until I stepped out.

Nikky Abe would be the end of me.

"Okay!" the instructor screamed over the roaring engines and wind.

"Let's go over the instructions again! You guys will be strapped to your instructors and there will be a countdown. Three, two, one. Then you will give us the thumbs up sign and off we go!"

"Yeah! This is great Tayo! I am so excited! Maybe we can turn this into a tradition!" Nikky screamed.

"Sure," I replied.

The instructors did a last minute check of the security straps and then Nikky and her instructor moved to the open door of the flying plane.

"One! Two! Three!" the instructor screamed.

Nicky gave the thumbs up sign and screamed, then the instructor leapt off the flying plane.

Oh heck na! What! This girl was cra cra as in crazy. I was not going to do this!

I turned to my instructor with the intention of telling him that I wanted to be taken back to the base immediately. But, to my horror, he also moved quite swiftly to the open door and started his countdown!

"No! No! No! Take me down! I am too young to die! Please take me down instantly!"

"Okay, calm down, sir. If you don't want to do it, we don't have to."

"No! No! I don't!

"Don't kill me for my mama!" I added with my Nigerian accent becoming more apparent in my fear.

"What did you say?" he asked, looking at me quizzically with amusement in his eyes.

I shook my head as I dismantled the harness, handed it to the instructor, and quickly crawled to a safer part of the plane, far away from the open doors.

If I thought I would get away with not jumping, I was wrong. Nikky had planned a special picnic for us back at the base. She proceeded to make fun of me for *not* jumping.

"Mr. Cool as Ice, Mr. Smith. Tayo Smith. Mr. Too Hot to Handle is just a chicken!" She laughed gleefully.

"Stop it, Nikky. I had a headache. That's why I didn't jump." I helped her set up the picnic.

"Yeah right, and goats have wings and can fly. The instructor told me that you absolutely refused to jump!" she said again, screaming with laughter at the end of her sentence.

The whole picnic could pretty much be summed up into that conversation. I don't know why I was still friends with her.

I knew the answer to my own question though.

The way her brown eyes watched me, her disappointed face when I told her I was actually inebriated during our kiss, and the way her eyes lit up when she saw me told me an all-too-familiar story. The problem was that Nikky demanded more than I was willing to give her. I am not a relationship type of guy and after a few disasters and stalkers, I am a little cautious.

After dinner, we lay quietly on the grass, staring at the cloudless sky.

"I miss my mommy," Nikky suddenly said.

"Aww, mommy's pet," I teased.

"It's true. You can't blame me. I am an only child."

"Okay, fine. You are allowed to be a mommy's pet," I answered.

"You are lucky to have brothers. I am quite sure you are close to all of them."

I hesitated before I answered, "Not really. They see me as…a good-for-nothing mess-up."

I chuckled at her shocked expression.

"Those were the exact words of my brother, Temi. I think that's why this whole med school thing means so much to me. It's like saying to them, 'See, I am not so bad after all.'"

"But why would they say such horrible things to you?" Nikky exclaimed. "You poor thing," she continued then touched my cheek.

"I am a mess-up, Nikky. I have messed up a lot of my life till this point and I hope and pray every day I won't mess up this med school thing."

"You won't!" she exclaimed with her eyes flashing. "I won't let you."

I chuckled and replied, "I know you won't, Nikky. You will be the Bonnie to my Clyde."

Chapter Twenty

Nikky

I hissed in irritation.

Ego was in my group.

It's not that I don't like her... Okay, fine, I really don't like her.

Especially since Tayo tries to turn our little duo into a trio by insisting we include her in every orientation-related activity. Like when he suggested we add her as a partner for the scavenger hunt

Sigh. My relationship with Tayo is quite...challenging. We spend the majority of orientation together. I mean he constantly texts and calls me so we can be together. He acts like he likes me by basically dropping those little phrases, "I was the Bonnie to his Clyde", "Juliet to his Romeo", "I was the only sugar in his tea", and "the only honey donut in his personal vending machine". He says things like that, constantly, yet he *flirts* with every female within a one-mile radius of him. I wish he could act more like the Tayo I saw in my vision or more like my imaginary boo, Anderson Cooper.

My obsession with Anderson started when I saw him on CNN when I was seventeen.

No, I didn't get a vision that he was my future hubby.

But my mouth hung open when I first I stared into his piercing blue eyes and dignified grey hair. From then on, I began to store all things Anderson, every poster, every news clipping. I even had a bookmark of Anderson. He is my idealized, well-behaved boyfriend, and the age difference does not matter to me. Of course Mommy did and does not appreciate my obsession, and she immediately called Aunty Nikky for a serious prayer conference to save me from "bringing any white boy to the family". Honestly, why couldn't Tayo be more like Anderson? And why was I in the same group as Ego for goodness' sake?

Ego and I were too different to be friends really. I really tried to ignore the bad aura I detected when I first met her on the night of the party, but I couldn't.

I am very good at detecting bad auras, which I have defined as the spiritual frequency of individuals. This is another gift of mine.

Some people just have good auras while others have evil-no-good auras.

Ego definitely had an evil-no-good aura.

For example, I had warned Mommy that the man who lived down our street back in California had a bad aura. She ignored me and invited him into our house for dinner. He was hauled off to jail for bank fraud the next day. Some people even said he murdered someone.

Next, I warned Daddy about his secretary's bad aura, and she was fired the next day for chronic lateness. I had warned Daddy about our gardener also. He was eventually fired because he stole some silverware from the kitchen.

My parents still refused to acknowledge my gifts and chalked it up as "coincidences."

I was right about Ego. I just knew I was. There was a disconnect with her immediately when she stepped into the car with her nauseatingly fruity perfume on the night of the party.

She looked slightly everything, slightly sluttish in a too tight, too short skirt, slightly gaudy with the shiny wristwatch she had on, and slightly fake with her obviously fake Brazilian weave.

Do I sound like a hater right now?

I will be the first to admit that sometimes I do have some *haterade* tendencies, but that did not for one moment make my assessment of Ego Boyo incorrect.

She was definitely trouble.

Then she whined throughout the scavenger hunt, complaining about feet hurting in her Louboutin heels. *Then* she started flirting with Tayo, suggesting that he carry her because he had "well-defined" muscles. Her friend, Dee, who seemed to be a little on the slow side, was equally as exasperating.

I was right about Ego, and it had nothing to do with Tayo. It wasn't as if Tayo had any chance of dating her anyway. Tina told me Ego liked another classmate, a guy named Ben who was almost as hot as Tayo. Tina added that, from her Facebook investigation, she found out that Ben had a fiancée or girlfriend. If that was true, it was going to be very interesting watching Ego's love life in medical school.

As usual, I was right. Ego Boyo did not have a good aura.

In the discussion room, Ego Boyo, with the support of her little minion Dee and her annoying Midwestern accent, insisted on contradicting every single suggestion I made.

"We could write down every idea for a diagnosis on the chalk board," I said.

"No, we don't need to. It will waste time. Adele will do that in her notebook," Ego answered sharply.

"No, it won't. It will keep us more organized."

"There is no point in writing twice."

"There is if it will keep us more organized."

"Maybe we should just stick with the notebook," Dr. Baker interjected.

I wasn't surprised. Dr. Baker had been smiling at Ego like a Christmas goat since she walked into the room. Of course he would side with her.

I smiled graciously while boiling with rage inwardly and contemplated retorting but was interrupted by my buzzing phone.

It was a text from Tayo.

Hey, how is your discussion group going?

He was doing it again, acting like he was concerned about me, just like a boyfriend would. I got texts like this on a daily basis.

Bad. Ego Boyo is annoying.

I turned my attention back to the discussion.

"I think she would be alkalotic," I said.

"I don't think that's the point, Nikky. We have to discuss the biochemical consequences of vomiting in the patient," Ego replied.

Huh? Who died and made her queen? Furthermore, I was right: the patient *would* become alkalotic. I had a case like this in my advanced biology class I took at Stanford. Alkalosis *was* a biochemical process. It took everything in me not to tell her what I really thought of her in that moment, so I settled for telling her what I really thought about our patient.

"Alkalosis is a biochemical process, Ego."

"It is, but according to the discussion notes, we are supposed to focus on the consequences of vomiting on the glucose metabolism of the patient."

Well, thank you, Miss Chemistry but acid-base disturbances is a biochemical process.

"Yes, but her acid-base status is important."

"Maybe we should choose a discussion leader," Dr. Baker interjected quickly again.

"I would like to be the discussion leader," we both said at exactly the same time.

The discussion room became silent.

"Well, both of you could work together," Dr. Baker said.

Ego and I both eyed each other silently.

"Well, I could work with her...I guess," Ego said, looking directly at me, not flinching.

OH HECK, NO!

This girl was looking for trouble! I immediately saw a flash of red in my eyes; this was the number one danger sign that the incredible hulk inside of me was about to be unleashed.

What exactly did "I guess I could work with her" mean!?

I immediately heard an inward voice that sounded uncannily like my mother's saying *Nikky, calm down. Don't say anything you will regret.*

I plastered a careful smile on my face and said, "Of course, thank you Ego, for deciding you could work with me. You are too kind."

I turned to Dr. Baker and asked, "Can we begin?"

"Of course," Dr. Baker said quickly, sensing the tension in the room had eased.

I gritted my teeth in irritation as Ego began assigning duties to me and the rest of my classmates like we were her underlings.

Ohhh, this girl was so annoying. I glanced at her again and imagined snatching her Brazilian weave off her head. I am sure she was bald underneath.

The single thought brought a smile to my lips.

Chapter Twenty-One

Sola

"Fine, Nikky," I said, trying to cut the conversation short.

"Do you think Vice President of Education is a good position? You know I need time for other activities, especially studying," she continued.

Nikky had arbitrarily decided to run for a position in the student body class elections and insisted on analyzing her decision with me. I wanted to tell her that I couldn't care less about student elections, but as usual she wouldn't get off the phone.

"Nikky," I started. "I will call you back, later."

I hung up when the airport cab parked on the opposite side of my street. I ran out of the door towards Dare; immediately he stepped out of the cab. He smiled at me with that sexy smile of his and dropped his bags quickly so he could accept my hug.

He looked gorgeous, as usual. He was just a few inches taller than I was, but he carried himself like he was six feet. He was my dark chocolate king with black brooding eyes and thick bushy eyebrows. His sideburns stopped at an angle on his face just the way he liked to shave them despite my complaints.

I stood there, enveloped in his embrace, touching him, kissing him, smelling his cologne, with my head on his chest. I felt safe.

I knew I was a woman; that was worth something.

What I had with Dare was indescribable, and I knew that no man would ever make me feel like he did. I was loved, cherished, and wanted by him. He understood me utterly, the big things and the little things. I loved the fact that he knew the big things and the little things, like how I liked my Indomie noodles prepared.

I was secure in his love for me.

I began to cry, overwhelmed with emotion.

"Sola," he whispered softly in my ear. "Don't cry. Don't cry, baby. I will take care of you."

"I know. I am just so happy you are here with me.

"I needed you so much, Dare, you don't even know how much," I continued.

"I am here now, everything will be fine."

I led him towards my apartment door, grateful that my housemates Irene and especially Tina were not at home.

I watched him affectionately with a smile on my face as he scanned my bedroom with his eyes.

"Your room is beautiful, Sola."

"Thanks, babe," I replied.

"Are you hungry? I made jollof rice," I quickly added.

"No, I had some breakfast, and being with you is enough for me," he said, then he flopped into my bed.

I smiled then lay next to him with my head on his chest.

"Tell me everything," he began.

So I did.

"So we can conclude that he doesn't recognize you," Dare said carefully, when I was done.

"Yes, I think so Dare. He can't be that good of an actor. He doesn't remember."

"Good. I told you he wouldn't."

"So what is the next step? What should I do?"

"Baby girl," he started and I instantly knew I wouldn't like what he would say next. He only said *baby girl* when he wanted to say something unpleasant.

"I have done some research online. Second year is actually a good year to transfer medical schools. I can't have you here with him for four years."

I lay silently on his chest, and the tears slowly began to fall.

I had barely gotten to know Nikky and the rest of my classmates, and now I would have to leave.

"Sola, answer me please. What do you think?"

"I don't know what to think, Dare. I am tired. I don't know what to do. Your plan sounds good in theory, but honestly I am frustrated," I said and pushed myself off his chest.

"I can't take this mess of a life anymore. Like seriously, why me? Why would this happen? Why would he even choose to go to this medical school? Wasn't he a party animal? Why the sudden change in him?" I asked angrily.

Dare pulled me back towards him.

"Sola, please calm down. Don't lose control. It's just how life is, that's just how the cookie crumbles sometimes."

"Well, why does my life have to be that way!?

"Why?" I continued with tears streaming down my face.

"Shhh, shh, Sola please don't cry. You know what your tears do to me. I can't take it when you cry."

"I am just tired, Dare. So very tired. Why is this happening to me?"

"I know, Sola."

"No, you don't," I answered sharply.

I was tired of his meaningless platitudes; no one knew what I went through, not even Dare.

He looked stunned and hurt by my retort.

I immediately regretted my words and said quickly, "Baby, baby, I am so sorry. I am sorry. I am just on edge."

"I understand, Sola," he answered quietly.

We lay in the bed silently for a while, then the relative silence was interrupted by the Stedman Tower Clock. It rung eight times signaling that it was eight o'clock.

"We don't have to talk about transferring today," Dare said.

"I know. I don't want to," I answered.

"We have a long time to talk about that. I will be staying till the white coat ceremony."

I searched his face to see if there was a hint of a smile.

He looked at me and smiled.

"What about your job?" I asked.

"I took my vacation now so I could be with you for the whole week."

"Oh, Dare," I said and hugged him tightly with tears in my eyes.

Then for a reason I could not fathom, while I was in Dare's arms, an image of Ladi came to my mind. That was puzzling…

Chapter Twenty-Two

Ladi

"Hey, Ladi, you definitely should run for class president," Ego said in the lecture hall.

"Class president? Really?" I replied and laughed.

Ego was in the same orientation group for HIPAA training, the mandatory privacy information training every medical student had to go through. Orientation, which had seemed exciting, was now tedious. We half listened as the heavyset man droned on and on about keeping patients' records private. Many of my classmates now skipped many of the activities because it was getting repetitive. There was orientation from every single department in the school, from campus security to technical support, and finally a completely useless orientation on how to use the library like we medical students would not know how to use a library by this time in our education careers. However, students attended events like the Freshman Fish Fry and Pizza Social because of the free food. A few students still attended the monotonous events, but I was reaching my wit's end.

I turned to Ego and replied, "I will think about it."

"You should," she said and smiled.

Ego was an extremely attractive woman who looked confident and well put together. We formed an easy camaraderie when we met one day in class.

"Think about it, Ladi. You do have leadership qualities," she continued.

"How would you know that?" I asked, amused.

"You have good Christian mommy's boy written all over you! Christian mama's boys always have leadership qualities."

I laughed and said, "You're not the first person to tell me that. Do I have it plastered on my forehead?"

"No, but you just look dependable and trustworthy. You know, like how I seem to have bad girl stamped over my head," she replied and then laughed.

"No, you don't!"

Ego laughed and said, "You are a guy, and all guys like me. The girls are the ones I have trouble with."

"Have you tried talking to the girls about it?"

"You are so cute, Ladi. You know girls are vicious!"

"Not all are, Ego."

"Hmm," she nodded, not looking fully convinced.

She continued, "Did you get the email about financial aid? I wanted to know if I was the only one who got it."

"No," I answered.

She immediately looked worried, then said almost to herself, "It must be because I haven't paid all my tuition yet."

"What did you say?" I asked.

"Nothing," she quickly replied.

"Ego, are you sure everything is alright?"

"Yes…" She was distracted when Ben Odojie, another classmate, quickly walked out of the room.

"Excuse me," she said and quickly rushed after him.

"Okay," I replied looking at her retreating back quizzically. I turned my attention back to the tiresome lecture but my mind drifted back to the conversation I had with her about student elections. *Class president? What position would I run for?*

Chapter Twenty-Three

Tayo

"No, I am not running for class president!" I insisted to the fifth classmate or so who asked me on my way to 1007 where the student election was being held. The class buzzed with excitement, and speculation was rife about which students would run for what positions. Positions like president and vice president seemed to be sought after, and a few names had been mentioned including mine (obviously), Ladi's and Ben's, another classmate of ours. My class student government really wasn't a concern of mine, but Nikky had kept me up all night talking about her desire to run for Vice President of Education.

First, she had weighed the pros: great leadership position, and she really wanted to change policy, she said, or something to that effect. Then she weighed the con: this position would cost her time away from studying. She went back and forth between deciding she wanted to run and then changing her mind. By the end of the conversation, I was so exasperated with her, I assured her I would show up to the student elections for morale support so I could get off the phone. Nikky was seated at the far right of the class with Ladi and Fadesola, with her eyes shining with excitement. I was seated next to my boys, Lenny (of the infamous Lenny-and-Dee-first-week-hook-up and Dee of my infamous drunken make-out) and TJ a.k.a. the man with the two first names, Thomas Jacob. When I wasn't with Nikky, the three of us always seemed to hang out together, and I liked the dudes.

They were a lot of fun.

The excited chatter in the class was interrupted by members of the Student Government body walking into the room. My eyes were immediately drawn to a tall, slim woman with a long neck that made her look regal. Her dark eyes were accentuated with what I was certain were fake lashes, since no human being had lashes that long. It wasn't only the fact that she was so beautiful, it was the way she carried herself that attracted me. There was no haughtiness; she just had a self-assuredness that a lot of women lacked.

The beautiful woman went to the podium and then adjusted the microphone for her height.

"Hey guys, my name is Belinda Belfonte. I am the student council liaison officer. I am in the Class of 2011. I will let everyone else introduce themselves," she said then passed the microphone to the other members.

Belinda Belfonte...

I watched Belinda run her tongue over her glossed lips and smile.

I turned my attention to Tami, the motherly and bubbly student council president.

"Class president?" called Tami.

There was a quiet silence in the room. After all the gossip and speculation, I thought this was going to be a sought after position.

"We need a class president...please," Tami continued.

There was a commotion in class with a smattering of applause. I turned and saw Ladi quietly raising his hand.

"Yes! Thank you! A round of applause for this brave man, please. Come forward please," Tami said.

Immediately, I was on my feet and began the slow clap while gesturing widely for my classmates to join in the applause.

I am so proud of my boy!

"Ladi! Yeah! You go, Ladi! That's my boy!" I screamed.

He shook his head and laughed as he made his way to the front of the class.

Soon the hesitant slow clap I started had evolved into a thunderous applause and a standing ovation with calls of "Ladi! Ladi! Ladi!" and much laughter.

"Your name please," Tami asked with chalk poised over the black board.

"Ladi Adeoti," he replied.

"Any other takers for class president?" Tami continued.

Tami's call for other candidates was met by silence.

"Well, he is running unopposed, Class of 2012. Why don't we give a warm welcome to your new class president, Mr. Ladi Adeoti!" Tami continued.

"You are the man!" I yelled, leading Lenny and TJ to catcalls and whistles to the class's amusement.

Tami called for a few other positions like vice president and a few other boring positions and I summarily tuned out. I think vice president went to Ronke, another chick in my class.

I returned my attention to the student elections when Tami said "Vice President of Education?"

Nikky calmly raised her hand. I could tell she was resisting the urge to run to the front of the class, probably because she remembered my advice that she act cool.

I immediately stood up with the same slow clap again.

"Owwwww! The hotness! Go, Nikky! Vice President of Education in the hizzhouse!"

She smiled gratefully at me.

I smiled back and winked.

Lenny and TJ immediately joined in with more catcall and whistles!

"You go, Nikky!"

"Go, girl!"

Soon the whole class was applauding loudly and screaming Nikky's name.

"Any other candidates for VP of Education?" Tami asked.

Her statement was again met by silence.

"Okay," Tami continued and scribbled Nikky's name on the chalkboard under "vice president of education".

"Welcome, Nikky Abe, the new Vice President of Education for the Class of 2012!" Tami said, and Nikky bowed her head slightly, accepting the applause.

"Next is VP of Social Activities," Tami continued.

Lenny and TJ began to chant, "Big T! Big T!"

"All the ladies love Big T! Go on with your bad self, Big T!" TJ called.

There was a smattering of laughter in the class with more catcalls and whistles. The atmosphere seemed more like one of the alcohol-induced rave parties I had the pleasure of attending in Europe than a serious, professional student election.

Soon, another section of the class led by Ben began to chant, "Big T! Big T! Big T!"

Soon the whole class was cheering loudly.

I stood up and opened my hands up in acquiescence and walked over to Tami in front of the class.

Well, I had to give my audience what they wanted.

It was Big T time!

Tami said, "Judging from the response of the class, I am not going to call any more candidates for this position! Welcome, Tayo Smith, a.k.a. Big T. You are the new vice president of social activities."

I smiled broadly, accepting the applause of my classmates and peers.

I don't remember much of the white coat ceremony, but I remember I recited the words of the Hippocratic Oath with no clear understanding of the words yet with an understanding of the weight of the words and of the mantle.

Dana Ramirez
Class of 1986

The best past of the white coat ceremony for me was taking pictures in the lawn in front of the Matthew Rice building which had the words "STEDMAN COLLEGE OF MEDICINE, WHERE DREAMS BECOME REALITY."

Nikky Abe
Class of 2012

Chapter Twenty-Four

Nikky

The white coat ceremony started out so beautifully, almost as if God knew we were celebrating. The auditorium had been beautifully decorated with balloons, and despite its colossal size, the room was filled to capacity. The din in the room rivaled that from a soccer stadium. The freshman class talked excitedly with one another in the aisle reserved for us. Our freshly starched white coats were laid carefully on each reserved seat, arranged in alphabetical order, each white coat representing the potential of a future physician. The deans of the college of medicine and invited speakers were seated opposite us on the stage. There were hugs, screams and squeals, and lots of flashing cameras.

Dean Clarion, dressed in a very slim-fitting yellow dress, walked to the podium, interrupting the hubbub of activity in the room.

"We will begin now. Please could you all take your seats…thank you. Welcome to the 111th white coat ceremony of Stedman College."

There was thunderous applause from the audience and a few hoots and catcalls.

"This ceremony is a tradition of the Stedman college to welcome our future physicians into the Stedman family and the beginning of their formal education to become physicians. Our guest speaker, Dr. Robert Halston, needs no introduction. He revolutionized the field of orthopedic surgery and general surgery with his techniques. After completing his residency in orthopedics, he returned for a five-year residency in general surgery. Every attending physician in this room knows that is a remarkable feat. He was the first African-American to become an orthopedic surgeon, the first to become the president of the American Orthopedic Society. Also he was the first African-American to become the president of the General Surgery Association of America, a position he held for ten years. He is a proud alum of Stedman College, and we welcome Dr. Robert Halston."

Every person in the room stood to applaud Dr. Halston, who really needed no introduction. He was one of those figures in medicine that had been elevated to a god-like status. He was celebrated in Stedman College of Medicine. His dignified yet humble walk to the podium as he all motioned for us to take our seats illustrated what type of man he really was.

He started with "Dr. Charles Drew once said 'Excellence of performance will transcend artificial barriers created by man...'"

I listened to Dr. Halston's words and felt goose bumps.
Please, God, make me half the physician that he is.

Tayo was lucky enough to have met this man after he broke his leg. However, I never could get the full story about the incident from Tayo. He became very dodgy whenever I asked him. I glanced back and spotted Ego and Tayo. Tayo whispered something in her ear then they both laughed. I rolled my eyes in annoyance.

I cringed when I heard a booming voice from the corner of the room, "Bravo! Bravo! Dr. Halston. So inspiring!"

A few of my classmates tittered in response. It was Daddy being rather embarrassing again. I sighed and shook my head in amusement. My parents were characters.

First, Mummy insisted on meeting all my floormates so she would know "the company I kept." She also came armed with an assortment of pepper spray of different strengths and sizes. She then proceeded to demonstrate how to use them, accidently spraying daddy's eyes in the process. This almost made us late because I had to wash out all the pepper from daddy's eyes. His eyes still looked slightly red. *Sigh.*

Mommy brought enough food to feed a small kingdom with her. Jollof rice, chicken, *obe efo*, *obe ata*, fish stew, meat pie, suya.

I obviously wasn't going to be cooking for my first few weeks, and I loved my mummy for that. I loved my daddy, too. Well, sometimes I did.

I don't think there were prouder parents in that room. My parents practically beamed, and though I tried to hide it by shooing them away as they fussed over me, I was happy that I could make my parents so incredibly proud of me.

Dr. Halston concluded his speech to great applause.

"Wow, that was so inspiring," said Ladi, who was seated next to me.

I missed the last part of the speech, but I am sure it was, so I nodded in agreement.

Dean Clarion walked back to the podium and said, "Ladies and gentlemen, the moment you have all been waiting for. Our future physicians will be cloaked."

I moved to my place in line with butterflies in my stomach. I was first to be cloaked, because my last name was Abe. We all moved to line up in alphabetical order on the steps to the right of the stage. In Stedman College tradition, we had to choose one family member and one physician to cloak us. I chose my mommy because Daddy insisted that he was better at "getting the crowd hyped."

Sure enough, I could hear his booming voice in the audience screaming, "Yeahh! That's my daughter Nikky Abe! Alleluia! God is good!" The audience laughed, and this time I laughed also. I could barely hold in the emotions. I was going to become a physician, a doctor, and the decisions I made would help save or hurt a human life. I was humbled and overjoyed all at once. Dean Clarion announced my name, and I walked carefully up the steps, making sure I didn't fall. I walked to the boldly marked X in the middle of the stage. My mommy walked towards me, beaming proudly, with an attending from the hospital, a Dr. Francis, who was assigned to cloak me. I held back my tears as she hugged me and placed the white coat on me, carefully, almost with reverence, assisted by Dr. Francis. My father's hoots and hollers were infectious, and soon the audience joined him in his applause.

God make me worthy of this white coat, I thought to myself as I walked off the stage.

Chapter Twenty-Five

Ladi

I walked to my place in line with Dr. Halston's poignant words still fresh in my mind, "Take care of every patient like you would take care of your mother."

In my case, I would take care of every patient like I would have my dead brother if I had been given the chance to save him. My mother's encouragement and prayer that morning was still fresh on my mind: "I know your brother is with the host of heaven cheering you today, my son." Even my father surreptitiously wiped tears from his eyes, and my father was usually inscrutable. I had never seen him show much emotion except when my brother first died.

But today was extraordinary.

I remembered the nights I stayed up in bed and wondered if indeed this dream was going to be realized. If indeed, my destiny was to be a doctor. It was, and I got in. God made it possible. I glanced back at Sola. She looked excited and animated, a stark contrast to the night I found her weeping. I met her boyfriend briefly prior to the ceremony. I felt slightly irritated by his simpering and eager-to-please manner. Something about him rubbed me the wrong way. I focused my attention back to Dean Clarion who called my name.

I walked to the marked X in the middle of the stage and stood proudly. I saw my father, back straightened in his impeccable suit, at 6'3" slightly shorter than my 6'4", walking towards me with a smile on his face. Overcome with emotion, I let tears of joy and accomplishment fall. Father hugged me and whispered into my ear, "My boy. Congratulations. I am so proud of you. Your brother is, too." He placed the white coat on me with the doctor assigned to me. I searched for my mother's face in the audience as we posed for pictures, and sure enough she was wiping silent tears from her eyes. With my white coat on, I felt the weight of its responsibility.

At last, I was a part of the chosen few.

Chapter Twenty-Six

Sola

I watched Ladi, posing with his dignified father on stage, before taking my place in line to be cloaked. The emotions I felt were indescribable.

We did it! We all did it!

I glanced back at my younger brother and felt a rush of love for him. My mother did not come and I was glad. I did not want her here anyway. Since she started declining mentally, she stopped taking care of herself. It was sad, really. My mother, who had been a drop-dead gorgeous former beauty queen, a woman who could turn the head of every man in the room, now had unkempt hair and wore baggy, ill-fitting clothes. It was difficult to contemplate. However, the change that was hardest for me were her eyes. Her eyes that had once sparkled with life had become dead. I never looked at her directly even when we spoke because I did not recognize who this woman was. It hurt me very badly, and so my mother was hidden in a place in my heart where I did not go.

But today was a different type of day, it wasn't about my mother. Every single aspect of today culminated to make me feel a foreign, almost rare emotion in my life: happiness.

I was delirious with happiness.

Dare made me deliriously happy. He made breakfast for me every morning and took me out to explore DC every night. We were definitely enjoying our time together because we avoided the subject of transferring medical schools. I knew sooner or later we would have to talk.

But for now, I was enjoying this wonderful accomplishment. I glanced at Dare on the opposite side of the stage, ready to cloak me, smiling broadly. He caught my eye and winked at me. I winked back. I was so happy, so very happy today. I had set out to be a doctor, and my dream was coming true. Nobody was going to take this day from me, not even Tayo Smith. Each step I took was a symbol of defying all odds that said I wouldn't make it. I climbed gingerly up the stairs and I heard my brother scream, "That's my sister! That's Sola!"

I smiled brightly as I stepped on the boldly marked X.

Dare embraced me and kissed me affectionately, "I love you Sola. You did it. We did it."

"Yes, we did," I replied, smiling.

He cloaked me with the help of the physician, and I walked off the stage wearing the white coat, a mantle of my calling into medicine, hands intertwined with the love of my life.

Chapter Twenty-Seven

Tayo

I felt a little uneasy watching Sola and the guy who was obviously her boyfriend on stage. There was something vaguely familiar about him, and it made me uncomfortable. *There is something very odd about Sola. Something doesn't feel right.*

I turned my attention back to the white coat ceremony and replayed Dr. Halston's speech in my ears.

He was such a humble and dignified man, everything I hoped to become as a doctor.

His parting words to us were, "Keep God first in everything to you and seek not any glory but to glorify God. Pray He uses you as a vessel of healing. Remember the words of the Hippocratic Oath you will say today; adhere to them so you can become excellent physicians and diagnosticians and most especially healers."

I loved this man! He needed a church dedicated to him. I was going to do everything in my power to become a doctor like him even if it killed me. Even my parents were impressed by his speech. I glanced at them as he spoke and watched with amusement as they nodded vigorously and applauded during his speech.

It was a stark contrast to their reaction when I first told them I was going to medical school. I might as well have told them I was going to a finishing school. They both sat rigid in their chairs, trying to figure out if I was joking.

My father looked like he was holding back his laughter, and then he burst out laughing. "I am sorry, I am sorry Tayo. You do realize medical school is work, very serious hard work. It's not a degree in partying!"

Wasn't that obvious? I was hurt and annoyed by my parents' response. Did they ever stop to think that because they had such little expectations of me, I in turn had little or no expectations of myself? I angrily walked out of the living room that day ignoring my mother's pleading voice and my father's mocking voice saying, "Leave him. Next week he will beg us for money to throw a party. He will come crawling back."

But I didn't come crawling back. Instead I was here, taking my place with my future colleagues. Today my parents beamed brightly at me, and my mother snapped pictures furiously as I walked to the middle of the stage to be cloaked by my brother Temi. For the first time in a long time, Temi smiled at me with approval and hit me on the back lightly, saying, "Finally, you are becoming the man I knew you could become. I am proud of you."

I couldn't even pretend the tears that were rolling down my eyes were due to an allergy (my default excuse when my friends caught me crying while watching *Titanic*).

Chapter Twenty-Eight

Sola

We skipped the school reception after the white coat ceremony and headed back to my apartment at Dare's insistence and to John's disappointment.

"Did you see all that food in the reception?" John asked with his eyes widening in disbelief. "Why are we going back to your house? We are missing that delicious spread in the reception," he continued.

It *was* a delicious spread indeed. Curried chicken, lamb, goat meat stew, fried plantains, coco bread, meat pie, rice, fruit punch, and a chocolate cake with "CONGRATULATIONS, CLASS OF 2012" written boldly on top. The line for the food quickly formed in the lobby of 1007 with hungry medical students and their elated families eager for some good food. My mouth watered as I eyed the food but I also eyed the lobby dreading an encounter with Tayo Smith, especially with Dare here. Dare, who was usually calm, also looked around nervously.

Our eyes met after John's comment.

Dare said slowly, "John, we are going to a really nice restaurant. I made the reservation long ago."

"Well, they better have really good food if we are skipping this meal," John said, walking towards the exit with his six foot frame towering over everyone.

As John retreated, I turned to Dare and asked, "What restaurant?"

"I don't know, but that was the only thing I could say that would make your brother leave," Dare answered.

I chuckled and shook my head.

When we got to the packed cars I cast a quick glance to my classmates and their families and saw Nikky, Tayo, and Ladi posing for pictures under the Stedman College of Medicine emblem in the lawn. Nikky's father kept fiddling with the camera, which apparently was not working, and Nikky's mother kept insisting they "smile for the picture!" and telling Nikky to "stop looking so cross." Of course, Nikky was rolling her eyes in exasperation as the guys chuckled.

I sighed inwardly. I would love to share this moment with my classmates, to be carefree and take pictures, but I couldn't.

I had secrets that had to be kept.

After lunch, we drove to the airport so Dare and John could catch their flights back to Michigan.

"Sola," Dare started, when John was out of earshot.

"I know."

"You have to leave Stedman, you know that, right? If you want to…function normally. If you want to stop our secret from getting out."

"I know."

"I am sorry, Sola. I wish it didn't have to be this way. You don't have to give up on your dream, just endure this year, and then transfer."

"I know."

"Shh, Sola, stop crying," Dare said, pulling me closer.

But Dare could not understand. Stedman was the much-needed new beginning for me and to see all my hopes get dashed because of a coincidence was difficult. The half-formed connections and friendships I had formed would always remain as such, half.

"Tayo Smith will one day burn in hell," I said through my tears.

Dare said, "He will. If I can help it, he will."

I clung tighter to Dare in the airport terminal for a moment with taxiing planes as the back drop of our melodrama. "I love you."

Those words stemmed from my desire to be protected by him. I always told him that, but I don't know if he realized how strongly I felt about him.

"I know. I know, but I will try to visit often," he replied and surreptitiously glanced at his watch because he was running late for his flight.

I clung to him tighter, burying my head on his chest. He smelled so familiar, like Davidoff, the one I bought him for his birthday last summer. It was a smell I was used to, and its familiarity reminded me of what I would be losing when Dare stepped into the plane.

"Fadesola," he started.

I knew he was getting exasperated. He only called me by my full name when he was.

"We talked about this. I will visit often. Think about the frequent flier miles we will acquire," he said, searching my eyes for a smile.

"I know. But I will miss you nonetheless. I am scared, Dare. Tayo Smith…"

"I know but when you transfer, our lives will go back to normal."

"But I will still miss you."

"By phone, email, Facebook…we will keep in touch somehow, Sola. I should be more worried about you getting a new boyfriend from one your classmates."

I hissed sharply, "Dare, be serious."

"It's true, Sola. I was reading some scientific research online yesterday.

"On the student doctor online forum," he continued, as an answer to my quizzical expression.

"A student-run website collecting surveys from bored medical students is not scientific research!"

"Okay, baby, he said laughing then he kissed me slowly.

I felt the tension in me slowly dissipate, but I could not shake off the uneasiness I felt. For some reason his joke immediately made Ladi come to mind.

Long after John and Dare had boarded their flight back to Michigan, I lay in my bed at three in the morning in a cold sweat, unable to sleep. The events of the past days were surreal, from getting into Stedman to Tayo Smith and then having to transfer schools.

I was frustrated with my life.

"When is all this going to end?" I asked aloud.

Then I felt the familiar vise-like pain in my heart and tears began to fall. This time I was too tired to even think of cutting.

"God, where are you?" I asked aloud. "God, where are you. Why have you abandoned me?"

But you believe He doesn't exist, I gently reminded myself.

I laughed bitterly. Yes, that was true.

God did not exist to me.

Normal people got angry or upset with God.

I was enraged with God.

How can a God who claimed to love His creation allow all the horrible things in my life to happen to me?

What exactly was He doing?

Where was He?

I have all these questions for Him, but He never answers back.

So, to let go of my pain, I have convinced myself He doesn't exist.

It did not appear that I was convinced tonight though, because as I lay in bed and cried silently I asked Him over and over again:

God where are you? Am I not worth something to you?

Do you not love me?

I ALWAYS attended all the classes and lectures regularly in the freshman year. I can't say the same for the rest of my one hundred and twelve classmates.

Rakhi Patel
Class of 1974

Class was more of a social event for me. I could catch up with my friends. Did people go to class to actually learn?

Tola Roger Federer
Class of 2000

Chapter Twenty-Nine

Sola

I made my way to class the next morning, making sure to come early to grab a good seat. I turned on my laptop in the lecture hall, opened the PowerPoint for the lecture, and waited for Nikky and Ladi.

Nikky had sent me a frantic text message that morning.

Make sure you keep a seat for me please! I can't be late for our first official day of class!!!

My classmates walked into 1007 lecture hall, some hurling book bags, with the more fashionable ones with stylish tote bags. I glanced around the lecture hall, hoping to catch a glimpse of Nikky inside, hopefully without Tayo.

As if on cue, Nikky came rushing with Tayo close to her heels. "Thank goodness, you kept two seats."

I swallowed my irritation; the dynamic duo were together again.

"Thank God, we made it here on time," Nikky said as she slipped into the seat next to mine.

"Hey, Sola," Tayo said to me.

I mumbled something in greeting, avoiding eye contact with him.

He watched me silently for a second, and right before his stare got downright uncomfortable he turned to Nikky. "Okay, I am going to sit with Lenny and Thomas."

"Is that wise? Lenny and Thomas can be very distracting. We really need to concentrate and learn, free from distractions," Nikky completed with her eyes widening like she was giving an impassioned speech.

He smiled and then said, "Trust me, Niks. You would be a distraction to me if I stayed here with you. You know I can never stop staring at your pretty brown eyes."

Nikky had the good sense to reply, "Yeah right," but I knew she was pleased with his blatant flirtation.

He grinned then gave her a hug.

My goodness, they act like an old married couple already.

Then he swiftly walked up the stairs to the back of the lecture hall.

Nikky rolled her eyes at his retreating back and said to me, "Tayo can be such a guy sometimes."

"He can."

"But he makes me laugh, so I keep him around."

"Hmm."

"He doesn't have that effect on you. You are the only female immune to his charms. Whenever I talk about him, you don't seem interested, unlike other girls in our class."

"Well, I have a boyfriend. Women with boyfriends are immune," I answered dryly.

"Not with how good-looking that boy is. No, women with boyfriends are not immune!" Nikky turned her lips upwards and looked pointedly at me.

I did not want to continue talking about him. Those were dangerous waters so I changed the topic. "Hmm that's interesting. How are you feeling about the first day of class?"

"So excited! This is huge! I have decided to color-coordinate my notes and organize by subject matter," Nikky said, with her eyes shining brightly.

I chuckled and shook my head. I turned my head and saw Ladi slipping into the seat next to mine. He looked well rested and quite handsome today.

"Hey," he said smiling. "Excited about our first official class?"

"I guess," I answered.

"That doesn't sound too promising," he replied. "Nikky is obviously more excited," he said and high-fived her.

"Nikky is always excited for stuff like this. She is a geek," I said and winked at Nikky.

"Whatever guys, I am a proud geek. Geeks change the world. Albert Einstein was a geek, and he changed the world." Nikky answered matter of factly as she arranged her multicolored pens on her desk, separating them by color.

Ladi's eyes caught mine over Nikky's head, and we both smiled...with our eyes. I noticed we were good at that, smiling at each other with our eyes.

Our conversation was interrupted by an older woman with grey hair announcing on the podium with a crisp Irish accent, "I am Dr. Potts. Welcome to Biochemistry, your first lesson in medical school. I hope my class is the first of many intriguing classes."

Well, it certainly seemed that the class would be interesting, judging from Dr. Pott's outfit. She was wearing a revealing low-cut blouse and a long red skirt, which accentuated her long legs. But then she wore hideous fishnet stockings underneath and yellow high-heeled boots that had spikes.

Ladi turned to me and said, "Did she get dressed in the dark? What is she wearing!?"

I shook my head slowly and replied, "I have no idea, Ladi."

Dr. Potts continued, "This class is the building block of every medical term or principle you will learn. Right now this class might seem tediously boring, but don't underestimate the joy of knowing the little enzyme in the Krebs cycle."

She droned on and on about the importance of biochemistry, and I quickly lost interest. I turned on my laptop and updated my status on Facebook to *Bored and in class*. Ladi nudged me and pointed to Nikky, who was actually taking notes furiously during Dr. Potts's diatribe. We both snickered.

Chapter Thirty

Nikky

After the lecture, Sola invited me over to her apartment, and I was impressed by how beautifully decorated it was. I especially loved her room. Her sheets were gold and her comforter had a rich wine color with streaks of gold in it. There was a beautiful rug in the middle of the room, and she had chosen beautiful hardwood antique furniture pieces. She painted her walls wine-red also and neatly arranged golden picture frames with pictures of members of her family and especially her boyfriend around her room.

I picked up one of the pictures of her boyfriend and studied his picture.

Hmm, while he couldn't be described as good-looking, some of his facial features were somewhat pleasing to the eye.

Okay, fine. Pleasing to the eye was a euphemism for not so good-looking.

What! It was the truth!

I know fine boys. In fact, I should have a second degree in the art of good-looking men.

I knew how to spot good-looking boys, and Dare just wasn't it.

But Sola was so in love with him, so I guess that made it all right.

She saw me studying his picture and said, "That's my boo! My baby, Dare. Did you meet him in the white coat ceremony?"

"No, I didn't get a chance to."

She took the picture from me and smiled lovingly at it before she placed it back on her dresser.

"Wow, you are so in love with this Dare dude. I am happy for you, girl! Your story gives me hope that I will find my prince someday."

I flopped on her bed and increased the volume of the TV.

"How did you meet him?" I asked as Sola handed me the delicious-looking bowl of fried rice that I had asked for.

"Well, we actually knew each other since secondary school. We were probably like fifteen or sixteen, but I wasn't interested at all when he first started talking to me."

I laughed and said, "So what changed?

She suddenly looked sober and said, "Something changed...I don't know how to explain it to you. He helped me through a...rough period and I was able to see him for the person he truly is. Dare is my everything."

Watching her talk about him with that joy in her eyes made me envious.

Lord! When will I find love like that!?

I was tired of the bad boys like Tayo that I kept falling for. I wanted to talk about the man I loved like that, too!

"So how did you guys continue your relationship in America? You went to secondary school in Nigeria, right?"

"I moved first. We were still together, and we did the long distance thing for a while and it was hard. When he finished secondary school, he came here for college and made sure he applied to only Michigan schools so he would be with me."

"Awwww, so romantic!" I cried. "So you guys have been together for like five years?"

"Yes," she answered. "Five years."

"And no breaks in the relationship?" I asked incredulously.

"No, not really," she answered with a small smile. "Dare is all I know."

"Wow! I am so jealous, Sola! I want love like that, too."

I lowered my voice in case Tina was listening through the wall and said, "I like someone in our class but I don't know if he likes me."

She squinted her eyes at me. "Let me think...could this person happen to be Tayo Smith?"

What? Who told her? Then I realized that maybe I was too obvious with my feelings.

"No! You know! If you know! The whole class probably knows too! Have I been the desperate single girl?" I said, burying my head in her pillows.

Sola dissolved into laughter.

"Stop being dramatic, Nikky. Nobody knows. I am just good at observing people. It just comes across like you guys are very good friends. You don't look desperate."

I breathe a sigh of relief and said, "Thank God." I continued, "So what do you think? Do you think he likes me?"

Sola became quiet. She replied slowly, "It's not that I don't like him Nikky, but he seems to like a lot of women, like Ego. Then I saw him staring at Belinda Belfonte, the second year who organized the student elections for us, like she was a delicious steak. I just don't want you to get hurt."

My heart immediately sank.

"I know, but I think he likes me. He acts like he does. The way he watches me when he thinks I am not looking makes me think so," I replied.

"I don't know, Nikky, but...I won't say anything."

Gosh! I hated it when people did that. Why start saying something and stop?

"You obviously know I am going to beg you to continue with your statement."

So I did just that.

"What did you want to say Sola?"

"Just be very careful with him, Nikky."

"Okay," I answered. "I will try to be careful."

"Don't try Nikky. Just be careful," she said sharply. "You are like my younger sister. I have to take care of you," she added and winked.

I rolled my eyes at her. She knew I hated it when people teased me about my age.

I glanced at the TV and caught MC Hammer doing the hammer dance in the "U Can't Touch This" video.

I loved this video! This was my thing!

I jumped up from the bed and started doing the hammer dance.

"Oh oh, hammer time u can't touch this! Can't touch this! Can't touch this!"

Sola looked at me with amusement in her eyes and said, "Nikky! What are you doing?"

"The…hammer…dance," I said, pausing because I was out of breath.

"How old were you when this song was released? You had to be like, two? How do you know the hammer dance?" Sola asked, laughing.

"My cousins choreographed a song to it and I remember watching them," I said. "Get up, dance!" I said, pulling her up.

"Ohhh, Nikky leave me alone. I don't want to dance. Stop it," she said, laughing.

I ignored her and began singing along to the song while dancing, "Oh! Oh! Oh!" I watched the video, intently copying the dancers.

"Sola, do it! Just follow my moves," I said, laughing and dancing around her.

Sola needed to loosen up. She was too serious sometimes.

She self-consciously began to dance along with me.

"Go, Sola!" I screamed.

She quickly learned the steps to the choreography of the song and began mirroring my moves and those of MC Hammer and the dancers in the video.

"Can't touch this! Can't touch this!" we both screamed.

When the song ended, we both collapsed into her bed exhausted and laughing.

Chapter Thirty-One

Nikky

"Nikky, did I wake you up?" Tayo asked.

It was four in the morning. Of course he woke me up, but I wasn't going to say that. His usual calm velvety voice was strained, however.

"I had the nightmare again," he replied.

"Oh, it must be the stress of school. Those quizzes are getting more difficult. I got ninety-eight percent in the one yesterday instead of ninety-nine," I replied offhandedly.

Tayo had been having recurrent nightmares for the past few weeks. I don't remember exactly when they began, but I think they coincided with the beginning of our quizzes. I wasn't surprised. The quizzes (which were not really quizzes because they were worth almost forty percent of our grade cumulatively) *were* getting nightmarish. In fact, my academic career was in shambles right now. It all began when I picked up the grade of the first quiz from Dean Robert's office. I breathed a self-satisfied sigh of relief when I saw the *99%* on top left corner of the grade printout, then just as quickly, my feeling of self-satisfaction evaporated. On the top right hand corner, I noticed a phrase that I almost *never* saw. Under class rank, it said *second*.

I nearly passed out! I was never second in anything. Especially anything academic!

Tayo said I started hyperventilating right there, but I don't remember what I did. I just remember that I was distraught. You would think it would stop there, that the gods of academics would be merciful to me. It happened again and again and *again*! I was consistently number two, so much so that I barely glanced at my grade anymore and just looked at the class rank. To say I have been depressed the past few days is putting it mildly. I made it through only with support from Sola and even Tayo, who has impressed me with his staunch support and encouragement. Much like Anderson Cooper, my imaginary boo would have supported me if by some chance he answered my persistent emails to CNN for a blind date with him. Most days Tayo teases me about my current crisis by calling it imaginary, but he didn't even crack a smile when I broke down and cried in his apartment last week. Was I being a tad dramatic?

No.

I mean, when your whole life and identity is pretty much wrapped around being first and the best at all times and you fall short, you feel pretty *horrendous*. This was what made me Nikky. Being the best was an expectation I placed on myself and always fulfilled.

Sigh. Med school was already harder than I thought, and we haven't even had the first exam yet. My mind was constantly plagued with thought of who number one was. My first suspect was Daniel Masters, who always interrupted class with his persistent questions. I sometimes fantasized about slapping him whenever he made class run overtime. My second suspect was Lenny. Sometimes Tayo and I studied with Lenny and Thomas, and it was quite apparent that Lenny was extraordinarily smart. I did not let the fact that either of the two may be number one cloud my impression of them, but, trust me, it was hard not to let my *haterade* tendencies take over.

Anyway, everyone was pretty stressed out over the quizzes, even Tayo. And that's when his nightmares began.

"I don't think so, Nikky," he continued. "This has nothing to do with school. They are too..."

"Violent," I completed

He told me that the nightmares were always violent, but when he woke up he never remembered the exact content. I still thought it had to do with the quizzes, his unconscious mind somehow attributing violence to those quizzes. It had to be some psychological Freudian thing that was happening to him.

"Well, Mommy always said pray when you have a nightmare," I replied.

"No, Nikky. This is not a simple nightmare. This is…this is…serious. I don't know how to make you understand. Whenever I have the nightmare I always feel like it's a memory, that it actually happened."

His voice sounded strained and hoarse. I suddenly realized that this was more serious than I thought.

"Are you okay, Tayo?"

"No, not really. Can I come over?"

I hesitated before I answered. He did it the last time he had a nightmare. He came over to my place, and because we both lived in Morgan, it was so awfully convenient for him. Of course nothing happened because he slept on the couch *and* I am saving my goodies until marriage, but sometimes I felt like I was being used. He forced me to play the girlfriend role with requests like these, but he could still flirt with every female classmate of ours.

It wasn't fair, but I couldn't say no to him. The last time he came over, we spent the night talking about everything and nothing. That's how it was with us. I never remember what we do together, but I remember how he makes me feel and I am somewhat addicted to that.

The feeling.

Coupled with the little vision I had of being his future baby mama, Tayo Smith was a drug I couldn't refuse.

I found myself answering, "Yeah, sure you can come over. Bring extra pillows for the couch."

Chapter Thirty-Two

Sola

"I failed my quiz again," Irene cried, crumpling into tears.

"Oh, no," I replied then pulled her into the quiet section of the corridor.

I was heartbroken for her. Irene had consistently been failing the quizzes for a while now. She was petrified of failing the first unit.

"What do you think you might be doing wrong?" I asked her.

"I don't know," she answered. "It might be because I am so distracted by the divorce."

Irene was in the middle of a divorce from her high school sweetheart that definitely put additional strain on her. But I didn't think this was the reason for her failure. Whenever I came back home and crawled into bed around two in the morning, I would stop by Irene's room to say hi and she would be studying. She studied until the wee hours of the morning, but for some reason, she still failed the quizzes.

"I don't know what to do, Sola," she cried in the corridor. "At this point, I have failed forty percent of my grade. Now I have to get an A on the exam to even pass this unit."

The tears ran down her face freely.

I rubbed her arm and said, "It's okay. Maybe you could try studying with a group you know. When Ladi and I study with Nikky, we always go over the lectures at the end so if you haven't studied something, you can always fill in the gaps later."

Ladi and I had formed an easy study partnership and sometimes Nikky joined us.

"I don't work well with groups because I have to concentrate. It takes me a long time to go through the material. I barely finished studying all the lectures for the quizzes, and I am still failing!"

"I am sorry," I replied, because I didn't know what else to say

"Sola," she continued then edged closer to me. "I need extra help."

She lowered her voice and continued, "If we could sit together during the quizzes…"

I stared at her quizzically then almost immediately I understood what she was saying. She wanted me to allow her cheat by allowing her to get the answers off me.

I was genuinely shocked and confused by her suggestion. I knew she was desperate but not this desperate.

She must have noticed the surprise on my face because she quickly said, "Okay, Okay! Sorry, forget I said that."

She quickly walked away in the opposite direction before I could protest.

I really wanted to help her, but I didn't know how and cheating was out of the question. If we were caught we would go before the honor council of the school, and it could potentially destroy our careers as physicians.

But I had a feeling that if I didn't help her fast enough, Irene would get somebody else to help her cheat, and the consequences would be colossal.

As I headed towards the discussion room to study, I spotted Ladi through the transparent mirrors of one of the rooms.

He really was cute, in a sort of understated way.

Why hadn't I noticed it when I first met him during the interview?

He looked up from his laptop and smiled, his dark eyes lighting up. I liked his eyes, not because they were particularly beautiful but because there was something dependable, trustworthy about them.

"Hey," I said as we hugged. "How is studying going?"

He ran his hand on his bushy hair that was badly in need of a haircut and said, "It's so much stuff to study for! It really can't get much worse than this."

"Well everyone says it will," I said and pulled the chair next to him closer to the table. "So we better get used to it."

I removed my laptop, books, and pens from my book bag and arranged them on the table. My cell phone vibrated, and I glanced at it. It was a text message from my brother John. It read:

Are you busy? Can you call me?

I sighed and immediately prepared my mind for the worst as my heart sank.

What is it this time?

"I have to make a phone call," I said to Ladi and stepped out of the room to the quiet side of the corridor.

John picked after one ring and said, "Sola, Mother left yesterday. She didn't tell me where she was going. She just left." John sounded shaken.

"What do you mean she left?" I demanded.

"You know how she is. She has been talking about someone stalking her and trying to kill her. She just left yesterday."

"Did you see her leaving?"

"I think she left around three in the morning because I heard her," he replied.

I tried to control the boiling anger and frustration I felt. Why would this woman do this? Then I remembered she had done this many times before. The difference this time was I wasn't there to take care of my brother whenever my mother arbitrarily thought the CIA was stalking her and left the house for days. John and I would be blissfully unaware of her whereabouts and continue our daily lives as normal, counting down the days to when she would return, even making jokes about it.

It was our coping mechanism.

This was why I decided to stay home during college because John was much younger then, and I knew he wouldn't be able to cope with her alone. I left for medical school because I thought she had become somewhat stable, but apparently she had not.

This time John was alone; he couldn't quite cope and my heart bled for my brother.

Did I make a mistake by leaving my brother alone in Michigan?

I bit my lower lip tightly and felt the tears begin to fall slowly.

"Are you okay?" I asked

"Yes, don't worry, Sola. I know how you can get."

"Did she tell you where she was going? Did she at least leave a note?" I continued.

"Note? When has she ever left a note? She was restless before she left. She isn't quite used to you being away. Dare called her. She picked up her phone and said she was okay but couldn't talk long because she was being watched.

"Don't worry. I am good, Sola. I just wanted to let you know," my brother continued.

"I don't want you to be home alone," I replied. "Why is she doing this?"

"Sola, calm down. Dare spoke to her. He is trying to coax her to return. He said he will call you later today, and please, I am a big boy. I will be fine. I just wanted to let you know."

"No, I am flying back to Michigan," I replied.

"Sola, chill, she will come back. You know that's how she is. We just have to try to understand her and love her. She's ill and it's not her fault."

John's innate ability to love my mother despite everything she had done was frustrating.

I did not have that ability.

"I have to go Sola, I just wanted you to be aware of the situation. I will call back when there is news."

"Okay, make sure you keep in touch," I said. I quickly added, "I love you, John."

He chuckled and said, "Love you too, Sola."

When I hung up, I tried calling Dare, but his phone went to voice mail.

"Hey, Dare, call me back when you get this. I just spoke to John, so I need to know what is going on," I said.

I took a deep breath and physically had to stop myself from shaking.

I couldn't do anything right now. I contemplated going back to my apartment but realized I would lie in bed and cry or cut. I had to stay in school to study because studying took my mind off things. The guilt I felt was hard to fend off. John was still a teenager—he was fifteen. He really should not have to deal with this.

I wiped my tears, walked back into the discussion room and smiled at Ladi. "You probably have finished half of the Robbins biochem book."

"Sure, and I have written revisions for the publisher too," he said, looking up from his laptop.

"You are even smarter than I thought."

"Of course. Mother says I am the smartest person she knows," he replied.

"Your mom is hilarious. I especially liked her impromptu prayers for Nikky and me."

He laughed loudly, throwing his head back, "That's my mother for you. What about your parents? I didn't get to meet them. I met your brother who was pretty cool but he's nothing like you. He's more outgoing."

Here it was, the uncomfortable questions that I always got asked.

So I went to my default story. "Mommy was really busy and couldn't take time off work. My parents divorced, so my father isn't really involved with me."

Ladi said, "Well, it's your father's loss."

I continued, "How is your relationship with your parents?"

Ladi paused for a moment before he answered, "I guess good, normal. Why are you asking?"

"I am just curious, you know. Tell me," I replied.

He unplugged his headphones from his laptop and replied, "Pretty good. Close with my dad but my mother is…my rock."

Oh, I knew Ladi could not be perfect, I had stumbled upon his weakness. He was the quintessential Nigerian mommy's boy.

"Why?" I asked.

He paused for a moment again, almost like he was collecting his thoughts and said, "Because she is a woman of faith. She encourages me all the time. I believe I can do anything after I talk to my mother. I believe it because she believes it. Even when…"

"Even when what?"

He took a deep breath and continued, "Even when my brother died, she kept my family together. In a crisis, you really get to know a person's true character. I grew up thinking Daddy was the strong one, as most boys do. But Dad…Dad crumbled when Femi died. No one was expecting it, you know. Mom's strength encouraged us. She would get up and still go to church every day, when all I wanted to do was ask God why he took my brother. Femi, who was on his way to becoming a pastor."

He looked emotionally drained and I immediately regretted probing.

"I am sorry, Ladi. I am sorry for bringing it up," I said and pushed my chair closer to his and rubbed his back.

He sighed and replied, "It's not your fault. You didn't ask me for my life history."

He continued, "He is the reason I chose medicine; because he died in my arms in the hospital in Nigeria."

"Oh, no! Ladi! I didn't know that. That's horrifying. I am so sorry," I said in a rush.

I realized that you never knew what pain we all hid behind a façade of normalcy. I was a testament to that. I also realized my selfish motive too. I asked Ladi about his parents for my benefit, not his. What I really wanted to do was to unburden my heart to him by telling him a PG version of my relationship with my mother, complain while doing so, and finally accept his sympathy. In the process, I would fail to appreciate the fact that I, unlike him, still had a brother I simply adored.

"Yes, it was rough. Rough for us all," he said, looking away.

He continued, "What about your relationship with your parents?"

I did not want to talk about my nonexistent relationship with my parents after his revelation.

So I said, "Fine. My relationship with them is fine."

I was drawn to him at that moment. His devotion to his mother touched me profoundly. I realized he was an enigma to me, mostly because most of the times I had interacted with him. I was so wrapped up in my own issues and had not taken the time to actually get to know him.

"I really appreciate you sharing that with me, Ladi. Your strength is admirable," I continued.

He smiled and replied, "Thanks, Sola."

For me it began on that day.

But I was not going to acknowledge it.

I was not going to acknowledge it for a long time…

Chapter Thirty-Three

Tayo

Please, stop! Please!

I woke up in a fright, with my head pounding. Though my room was cool, I was drenched in sweat, and my sheets were soaked. I checked my cell phone on my night stand. It was four in the morning.

It was the same nightmare again. It was getting more and more disturbing to me. The intense panic that enveloped my body when I woke up bothered me, and the inability to remember the exact contents of the nightmare eerily mirrored my alcoholic blackouts. I wondered if memories from my blackouts were flooding my brain.

The whole episodes were so bizarre, and Nikky attributed it to stress, but I wasn't so sure.

Stress was not a factor in my life right now. I was smashing (doing well in) my quizzes with high nineties, and, unlike Nikky, I was satisfied with my scores and class rank.

My relationship with Nikky was complicated. Commitment was a foreign term to me. The last time I tried such nonsense, it was a disaster. My girlfriend at the time can attest to that. She still refers to me as the "worst heartbreak of her life that left her emotionally scarred forever." Well, what did she expect? She practically goaded me into a "committed" relationship. I was okay with our consistent hook ups and such until Lara started using words like "committed", "next level" and the worst: "relationship".

In retrospect, I should have run but Lara was a 5' 9" curvaceous beauty. I couldn't have run if I wanted to. I eventually cheated on her multiple times and it led to an unfortunate series of events. Lola discovering my cheating ways then a dramatic confrontation that got her locked up in jail for twenty-four hours, and finally a nasty breakup that led to my apartment being ransacked. All in the usually idyllic, upper-class campus of Oxford University.

Through that disaster, I confirmed one thing: I am incapable of being with one woman at a time. It's like eating oatmeal for breakfast, lunch, and dinner for the rest of my life. That's why I could not give Nikky what she wanted, and by the way she looked at me, I knew without a doubt she wanted me and only me.

I would not be able to give her that. I would end up hurting her and destroying our friendship. My friendship with her was too important to me and in a convoluted way, it proved I actually respected her.

I don't think Nikky understood my reasons for not giving in though, not with the way her eyes filled with hurt when she saw me with other women. We were in an all-too- familiar, dangerous place—the "undefined relationship."

Nikky tried to talk about it many times, but I was good at dodging issues I did not want to confront. Like when she tried to bring up the issue after a night of studying in my apartment at Morgan. She cleared her throat and began, "Tayo, I have to tell you something."

She looked so serious when she said that, I was convinced she was going to tell me she was pregnant, and I broke out in a cold sweat. Then I quickly realized that was impossible.

So I replied, "What is going on Nikky? You look so serious."

"I don't think I can take it anymore…"

"Take what anymore?"

She lowered her voice, bit her lip, and said, "I feel like I am being taken advantage of by you, Tayo."

Before I could raise my hands in protest, she said, "Wait! Let me finish.

"When it's convenient for you and when you need me, you treat me like a girlfriend. It's bothering me now because of how frequently you stay in my apartment after your…"

"Nightmares," I completed for her.

In the past couple of weeks, the nightmares had become so intense that I usually sought comfort with Nikky. I will admit that during these visits, the line between friend and girlfriend were blurry. She supported me emotionally after the nightmares, rubbing my back, making me hot chocolate, and staying up with me until I could sleep again.

I took what she offered without question. I needed her.

It never occurred to me that she felt used.

I could only stare back at her in silence.

She continued, "It's becoming...because my emotions...it's hard for me..."

She stopped and stared back at me.

"Everyone thinks we are together, Tayo. Tina is close friends with Mel, who lives on my floor in Morgan. She has seen you coming to my apartment late in the morning multiple times. She told Tina, and Tina told the whole class."

"Okay," I replied. "I'll stop coming so often."

Her face fell in disappointment because she probably wanted more than a promise to stay away, but that was all I could offer her for now.

She opened her mouth as if to say something, then shook her head before nodding in resignation.

We left things like that, but now, after this nightmare, I needed her again.

I tossed and turned in my bed before finally giving in and calling her.

"Hey."

"Hey."

"Nightmare?"

"Yes."

There was a long silence.

"Bring an extra pillow and your own hot chocolate this time."

"What! What is wrong with you people? Ladi is skipping, too. Do you guys realize we are in medical school?"

She paused for dramatic effect.

"We need the mentor's advice, and you are a part of the student council, Tayo."

The bored expression on my face only seemed to inflame her more.

We were at Mentors-Mentee meet-and-greet in 1007. Every year, each member of the freshman class was paired with a second year who became a mentor. According to Nancy, the enthusiastic second year in charge of the pairings, "the mentor's role was to provide invaluable advice, support, and books to the first year."

Considering that our first exam was days way and we already had a couple of really difficult quizzes, I thought this was a little too late, and judging from the empty chairs, so did the rest of my classmates.

"Tayo, this is serious!"

"I know," I replied dryly. "We are in medical school and so forth. I don't know why I need a mentor anyway. I just want to skip the stupid meeting."

"Everyone needs a mentor to navigate this jungle called medical school!"

"Oh, really?" I replied. "Do they also cook our meals and cut up our food? What does a second year know anyway? They just completed freshman year."

"A keyword is *completed*," she said, squinting her eyes and giving me what I had come to recognize as the death stare.

I chuckled.

"Sola isn't coming, either. I don't understand you guys," she completed with a pout.

"Oh, your best friend, Sola," I replied.

"What is that I detect in your voice?" she demanded. She moved closer to me and then said, "You don't like her!"

"No. It's not that I don't like her," I quickly replied, unconvincingly.

I did not dislike Sola, but I did not like her either. It was hard to like someone who always made an excuse to leave when you were close and could barely contain her distaste for you in the expression on her face.

"Hmm, spill, Tayo. What's up between you and Sola?"

"I don't know, Nikky. You're her friend. Do you know why she acts that way around me?"

"I don't know. It's so out of character for her. I really have no idea why she acts like that."

Nikky placed her hand on her cocked hip and asked playfully, "*Abi* she's one of your old girlfriends that you dumped and you don't remember."

"Who knows, Nikky. I have had so many girlfriends. Girls that thought they were my girlfriends, girls that I didn't know were my girlfriends, girls who told my mama they were my girlfriend without my knowledge!"

Nikky laughed and shook her head. "Tayo, you are a bad boy!"

But after that conversation, I started to really think about Sola and where I could have encountered her before. After a thorough examination of my catalogue of memories, I could not remember her. I knew her boyfriend was familiar, but I could not recall where I may have met him. My sixteenth through twenty-third years was a drug- and alcohol-filled blur. It might have been then.

The din of conversation in the class died down, and I turned my attention to the door.

Belinda, the regal goddess who introduced the student council during the election, led the sophomores into the lecture hall. Most of them were holding a bunch of textbooks, and Belinda was carrying a long list, which I assumed was the mentor-mentee pairings.

I groaned inwardly. I really hoped I didn't have to sit through Belinda calling the names of the mentors and mentees. We had already gotten an email with an excel sheet of the pairings.

"I am going to sit closer to the front," Nikky said.

In one quick motion, she packed her book bag and was sprinting to the front of class.

I shook my head at her retreating back and turned my attention back to Belinda.

If it was even possible, Belinda was looking hotter than usual with a black half top and red lipstick.

On second thought, I wouldn't mind if Belinda read out the names on the list. I could stare at her lips all day long.

I was disappointed when she said, "No. I will not be reading out the names on the list." She smiled and continued in her melodic Caribbean accent, "It's much more fun if you guys find each other." She gestured with her hands and said, "Now, mentors, find your mentees! Or vice versa!"

There was a flurry of activity in the class. All the freshmen, except for me, stood and went down to the sophomores standing at the podium. Soon the class was filled with the din of conversation and laughter as mentors found their mentees.

I had no intention of wasting my time to find my mentor, especially if it wasn't Belinda, so I turned my attention to the emails on my phone.

Nikky's irritatingly high-pitched voice indicated to me that she had found her mentor. "Hey, you are my mentor! I am so excited!" she screamed to the steps on my right.

"Hello," said a tall, bland-looking white guy.

"Sorry I am late. I am Robert. You are Nikky, I guess," he continued.

"Yes!" Nikky answered breathlessly. "So what advice do you have for me?"

He began to recite the same thing we had heard for the past two weeks: the first unit wasn't difficult, it's going to become very difficult when we started human anatomy and had to dissect the bodies, it was traditional in Stedman that 75% of the students failed the first exam in the Neurology unit because it was notoriously difficult, focus on the PowerPoint lectures, not on textbooks, etc.

However, Nikky looked at him like he had just invented sliced bread.

She slapped him lightly on the shoulder as she laughed.

Then Nikky and Robert walked down the stairs, deeply engrossed in an animated conversation. I couldn't hear their conversation anymore, but they were staring intently into each other's eyes. They were probably talking about biochemical principles.

My buzzing phone interrupted my assessment of the geek love connection unfolding before me.

It was from Ego and it said:

I haven't studied! We need to meet soon.

Well, duh! She had been MIA from class for a whole week! When she made an appearance in class, she was glued to Ben Odojie's side. However, I couldn't deny that I was a little excited that I would be meeting Ego again.

Sure, I texted back.

However, Nikky's irrational disdain for Ego stopped my enthusiasm cold. Nikky Abe was not going to be too happy with Ego joining our little study group.

I turned my attention back to her and watched her throw her head back and laugh. Her mentor responded by touching her lightly on the shoulder. Weren't they both getting a little too touchy-feely? Robert had probably mistaken the mentor-mentee relationship for a dating service. *I* didn't *like* the dude. Where was my mentor anyway? Why was I watching Nikky's mentor? I rechecked the email for mentor pairings, and mine was a guy named Brandon.

Nikky came over and said excitedly, "My mentor is awesome! He said he would email me the old exams so I could practice. He gave me the gift CD, and it has so many goodies: old exams, quizzes, advice, everything we need for first year! Anyway, do you know who your mentor is?"

"No, I don't think he showed up. Nikky, let's go."

"Oh no! Your mentor didn't come."

She made it seem like I was in kindergarten and my mother forgot to come pick me up after school.

"I will survive," I replied wryly.

"Okay," she said. "I have to organize the notes I took in class today, color code them, and send them to you guys. I'll do that here. Go get a discussion room for us, and I will join you."

I quickly left the lecture hall and followed Nikky's instructions because I knew there would be hell to pay if I didn't. I bumped into Ladi, apparently also looking for a room. Only one room was unoccupied and he said, "Let's share this room, man."

I hesitated before I answered. Every time I saw Ladi, Sola was not far behind. I was not in the mood for the awkwardness that came with my interactions with her.

I answered, "Nikky will be coming in a short while. Is Sola studying with you today?"

To my utmost relief, he answered, "No, she decided to stay home today,"

"Okay, cool, man. We could study together. How has it been going?"

"Good, I have been keeping up with lectures and everything and Nikky's notes are on point," he replied as we walked into the room.

"Yeah, she's good. The biochem stuff is pretty basic, you know, but, because this is the first exam, you want to start right."

"Yep, I am feeling like we could get overwhelmed soon, you know. Everyone is a little scared because this is the first exam but it should get better," I replied.

"Overwhelmed? I thought the general feeling of the class was that we were already overwhelmed," Ladi said and laughed.

He continued, "I am wondering if this class president thing is getting a bit much for me. It's getting more and more difficult to balance school and running that council."

I laughed. The class student council thing was getting very tedious and, if I could skip the meetings, I would. Ladi and Ronke had the good cop–bad cop/mommy-daddy routine down, quelling potential fires and generally forcing each meeting to end with a consensus. Everyone was generally cool but Joanna had to be the most irritating human being in the world, and she was the sole reason why the student council was so disruptive.

For instance, in the last meeting, I wasted sixty minutes of my life that I can never get back because they were arguing whether or not to take a vote on taking a vote about the traditional Stedman football game. It was Stedman tradition to have a football game that pitted the freshmen against the sophomores, juniors and seniors. The smack talk had been good natured at first until someone had the brilliant idea of making James the coach of the other team. Needless to say, the smack talk reached a fevered pitch, with bets, counter bets and counter–counter bets predicting who would win. The guys, especially Love, Thomas, and most especially Obi, were very concerned and rightfully so. They wanted to discuss the possibility of getting an outside coach for the freshman team.

However, the girls, especially Joanna, had a problem with the council discussing any item that wasn't in their precious agenda.

"This is not part of our agenda today!" Nneoma said passionately.

"According to the constitution we absolutely cannot discuss anything unless we take a vote!" Joanna chimed in.

"I don't know if you guys understand what is at stake here. We might as well kill ourselves if we lose this game!" Obi retorted.

I glanced at Ladi, who seemed to be nursing a headache.

Ronke immediately said, "Can't we discuss this in our next meeting?"

"No, we can't!" Thomas said.

"That's right, Thomas! Last time we had to sit through a discussion about what tablecloths we could use for the white coat ceremony, and that wasn't planned!" I chimed in.

"We need to take a vote to determine if we can add it to our agenda" soft-spoken and calm Uche said.

Sounds easy, right.

Well it would have been if Joanna did not open her mouth and say, "We need to consult the constitution to check if this is even allowed! I should have drafted the class constitution myself. I must say Love did not do a good job!"

Her statement was met with a long silence and Love's thunderstruck face. I was equally pissed with her statement.

"Joanna if you had any issues with the constitution you should have come to me first to discuss it personally," Ladi said coldly.

"I think we all need to cool down and discuss any other issues we have at the next meeting. Meeting adjourned? Any support for my motion?" Ronke quickly said.

"I second it," Nikky quickly replied before anyone could interject.

Nikky, who was usually passionately absorbed in the meetings, had stopped listening long ago and had only paused to second the motion by looking up from her color-coded notes.

There was serious tension between the student council and Joanna. Obi referred to her as "that crackhead."

"Yes. Joanna is getting a little bit out of control," I replied to Ladi.

He sighed and said, "I know, right. Sola keeps saying I should be patient."

"Yeah," I replied.

"So you and Sola are together right?" I continued.

"No," he said with his eyebrows raised. "Definitely not. She has a boyfriend back home."

"Hey," I said, raising my hands in protest. "It's just that I see you guys together all the time."

He laughed and said, "Just like I see you and Nikky together all the time."

I laughed too and said, "Okay, you got me there."

"So do you know her boyfriend's name?"

"I think she said Dare. Dare Martins, I think."

"Martins…I think I know that name," I replied. "I think I know his cousin."

"Okay," Ladi replied casually.

It made sense now. I finally had a reasonable explanation for Sola's boyfriend looking so familiar to me. I must have hung out with him during my secondary school days in Nigeria. My thought process was supposed to be reassuring but I still could not shake off the nagging feeling that there was more to him than that.

Chapter Thirty-Four

Nikky

Can Ego Boyo study with us? She had a huge fight with Ben Odojie and the poor girl is so sad. I think she found out he has a very serious relationship with someone from before we all started medical school.

I read the text from Tayo and bit my lip to keep from screaming!

He knew I did not like Ego! Why would he ask me for this and mess up our study routine so close to the exam!?

Why did I have to suffer because Ego was a fool? Everyone knew Ben had a real girlfriend outside medical school and, despite Ego's *hoe-ish* tendencies, he wasn't going to leave his girlfriend for her. Medical school was really a landmine for relationships. Tina told me that at least five people had broken up with their nonmedical student partners since medical school started. Still, I wasn't going to put up with Ego whether she had drama in her life or nor.

I was about to text *Absolutely not* to Tayo then got another text from him that read:

The girl is really sad. I couldn't say no so I will try and help her. You can join us if you want.

I shook my head in disgust at his text then stomped towards the discussion room, pushing past the short white coats of junior medical students heading to the clinical skills lab located right next to the rooms. I took short deep breaths as I walked across the concrete floors with purposeful steps.

Tayo's ability to switch allegiances so swiftly was annoying to me. Allegiances? Why was I acting like we were enemy tribes? I'll tell you why.

It was because I somehow got in entrenched in my puny brain that he was my future boo.

You are hopelessly daft, Nikky. A quintessential fool.

He really wanted to study with her instead of me!

I was seething with anger.

Ahh! The sight of that seductive temptress turned my stomach. How she looked attentively at Tayo while they talked at the party, casually brushing his shoulders with her hands with her perfectly manicured nails, and her trendy fashion-forward outfit irritated me. She probably was on one of those lucky women in the world who had no problems in the world and always got everything they wanted. She had Ben already, why did she want Tayo?

I realized that my disdain for her was surprising because I usually got on well with everyone but my aura-meter (what I affectionately nicknamed my gift for detecting bad auras) was never wrong. That girl was bad news, and I felt it.

I spotted Ladi and Sola through the transparent windows of one of the discussion rooms.

Sola looked up from staring intently at her laptop and said, "Hey, Nikky." Then she paused and added, "What happened? You look angry."

I couldn't exactly tell her why I was so angry without looking like a jealous girlfriend or non-girlfriend, and besides, Sola still had the weird thing with Tayo.

"Nothing," I replied as I dropped my book bag loudly on the table.

"Be careful, Nikky," said Ladi.

I rolled my eyes and replied, "Sorry, Ladi."

He smiled that reassuring manly smile of his and replied, "*Aburo…*"

I smiled that he had called me young sister.

"It's my duty to set you straight when you are wrong. By the way, where is your better half?" he added casually, almost too casually.

Sola tittered loudly and tittered even more when I gave her my do-not-mess-with-me stare, which Tayo had aptly nicknamed the death-stare. The death-stare had apparently lost it power because both laughed harder as I tried to increase the intensity of my stare.

"I don't have a better half, Ladi, so I don't know who you are referring to," I said innocently.

"Your neck will soon fall off with all this neck rolling," he said, chuckling to himself again.

Sola said, "Well, if you insist you don't have a better half, is Tayo coming?"

"Why, so you can escape again? You don't have to worry. He has found another study partner," I snapped.

Sola and Lade exchanged glances across the table. They were so annoying sometimes. They had a connection without using words, and they seemed able to communicate with one another.

Ladi asked, looking concerned, "Why are you upset, *aburo mi*? Do I have to go hurt someone? Was it Ego?"

I was shocked! How did Ladi know about Ego? I looked incredulously at the guilty culprit, Sola, who looked as guilty as Judas Iscariot as she motioned unsuccessfully to Ladi to keep quiet.

"Not that I heard anything. I saw her during orientation week," he quickly added.

"Save it," I said. "I know Sola probably told you everything. Is there no loyalty among girlfriends? Anyway if you must know, yes, he decided to study with her."

Right on cue, there was a loud knock on the door. I turned to see Tayo's face through the transparent doors, motioning for me to come over. Had he come to his senses and left that girl? I really hoped he had. My conversation with myself bothered me actually. I was somewhat obsessed with Tayo.

"Yes," I said rudely swinging the door open.

"Nikky, why are you overreacting? The girl just needed help. She wants to study with us just because she has fallen behind in her work.

"I still want us to study together. It's always been me and you, babe. You are the Bonnie to my Clyde. Can we can just allow a third wheel today?" He winked.

Dang it! Why was he so darn cute! He was impossible to say no to sometimes but *not this time*.

I *refused* to study with Ego. I would not suppress my disdain for her.

"Well, I don't know. We have other people in the study group, and I want to study with Sola and Ladi today. They might not be comfortable," I replied.

"Oh, we are very comfortable, Nikky," Ladi called from inside the room, tittering like a school girl with Sola.

I rolled my eyes and continued, "You know it's so close to the exam, we already have a dynamic going on. Maybe it's better the two of you just study together."

Did I just say that? I couldn't believe it.

He looked slightly hurt by my suggestion, and I quickly added, "Just for today."

"Well, if you say so," he said and walked in the opposite direction where the Jezebel, aka Ego, was waiting for him.

I felt sad watching him walk off with her, but I decided a separation would break the feelings I had caught for him. I did not think our feelings for each other were mutual. He treated me like a friend and then girlfriend when it was convenient for him. I treated him like… Well, I wasn't too sure. But I could not help feeling I had just handed him to another woman, a tempting seductress at that, as I watched him walk away.

The first examination was the easiest and the most exciting but soon the constant, bimonthly high-stakes examinations got old...and mentally grueling. I grudgingly admit that cramming Nikky's notes right before the exam saved me from summer school.

Ego Boyo
Class of 2012

Now looking back, the first examination was the first of many exams. We thought it was such a big deal, but it really wasn't.

Ben Odojie
Class of 2012

Chapter Thirty-Five

Sola

It was the eve before the first exam. I went over the notes Nikky had meticulously made for each of us while lying on my bed. Being in my room calmed my nerves somewhat, but I was still a little nervous. The crisis in Michigan wasn't helping my nerves at all. The text Dare sent me the night before and our lengthy conversation about my mother came to mind.

"Have you spoken to her?"

"Yes, she is fine, but she still hasn't told me where she is. She thinks her phone has been tapped."

I sighed. "Dare, I don't know what to do. Do you think we should get the police involved?"

"And say what? She's an adult. I think she's safe for now, just a little...paranoid."

"She is but she's...she's not okay. She's mentally ill. I cannot deal with this, Dare. I have a major exam tomorrow."

"I know, but she calls me on her cell phone every night, and I am keeping an eye on John. Everything is fine here, Sola."

"Are you sure?" I asked.

"Yes. I am sure, Sola."

"Thank you, Dare. I love you so much. What would I do without you?"

"What would you do without me, Sola? Not much," Dare said and chuckled.

I lay back on my bed, closed my eyes and tried to relax.

I drifted off to sleep and was suddenly awoken by loud music.

I groaned. It was Tina again playing the soundtrack of Rocky. She always played this before the quizzes, claiming that the music motivated her.

Irene and Tina had gotten into a fight over this particular tradition, and it hadn't been pretty.

Sure enough, Irene stormed into my room with her eyes flashing.

"What gives her the right to do this? She understands how important this exam is! I haven't even finished studying all the lectures!"

Irene flopped into my bed next to me and suddenly began to sob.

"It's okay," I said, trying to comfort her.

I put my arms around her as she sobbed even harder on the bed.

"I am sorry, Sola but I...I am...so scared. My average for all the quizzes is below 60." She burst into tears again.

Despite Irene's attempts to change her study habits, she was still consistently failing. It broke my heart to see her studying harder than everyone I knew and have nothing to show for her effort. I was somewhat relieved that she hadn't mentioned cheating again, but I knew she was getting desperate.

"Shhh, shhhh," I said, trying to calm her down. "You will pass the exam. We will all do well."

I ignored the anxiety in my heart and said a silent prayer that we would.

As the proctor handed out the exam sheets, I tried to control my shaking and sweaty palms. The stakes were so high because this exam was worth sixty percent of the final grade. Failing it was not a possibility, but there was still the neurotic side of me that was convinced I would fail.

I suddenly heard the words *Be still* and felt calm.

Where had I come across those words?

I think it was from the Bible somewhere. It was odd that I remembered a phrase I really needed at the moment from a book I had never read. I mouthed good luck to Irene, who was to the far right of me, and she smiled.

I turned the exam over, feeling confident.

Chapter Thirty-Six

Nikky

"Mommy, you don't know how difficult these exams are. I am really concerned," I screamed at the receiver to my mom.

"Nikky, you say that for every exam and you get a perfect score," she said, chuckling.

What was wrong with the picture here? I was the one usually chuckling at Mom's silly imaginary crisis.

"You will be fine baby. Don't worry. You will probably get a ninety-nine instead of a hundred," she said, dissolving into peals of laughter.

Why did everyone around me suddenly feel like Conan O'Brien and Jay Leno rolled into one and that making jokes at my expense was allowed?

"Mommy, you know what, is Daddy home? You are being awfully annoying right now," I replied sullenly. "Mommy, for the first time ever in my life! I am not number one! Don't you understand how that fact is affecting my psyche?" I screamed again.

"Okay! Pele!"

I huffed when she told me *sorry*.

"I believe in you, Nikky. I always have. Daddy and I moved from Nigeria to America because of your gift. You are an extremely gifted and intelligent young lady. You started to have intellectual conversations with me when you were two. You knew all the presidents and vice presidents in the entire world at two. I mean, you even knew the meaning of the equator. Nikky, you will call me tomorrow and sheepishly confirm you got a perfect score in the exam. I am used to it."

Now that's what I'm talking about, that's the kind of speech I needed. A tad bit over the top, but enough to get me pumped for the exam that afternoon. I had stopped going over my notes because I could recite them to myself, and it was a little disturbing. I wondered if it would be enough to get me the number one spot for the exam. I wanted…no, I craved that position.

"Okay, Mommy. Thank you for that. You are finally acting like a mommy should."

"Nike, you are a very naughty child. You must have learned that from your Daddy's side," she said, laughing. I heard the clanging of pots.

She must have been cooking again. I could almost smell the spicy jollof rice and *obe efo* and the assortment of goat meat, *shaki,* cow skin, and catfish that would be in the stew. It was Daddy's favorite meal. A wave of nostalgia came over me, and I glanced at the picture of Daddy and Mommy on my side table.

"What are you cooking, Mommy?" I asked, glancing at the clock on my wall. I had thirty minutes before the exam so I had better cut the conversation short.

"Jollof, *obe efo* and I am trying the recipe for one calabar soup. You know Aunty Adama from church, I got the recipe from her," Mommy said, the clanging of the pots almost drowning out her voice.

Was she cooking for the army? It certainly sounded like it.

"Hmm, okay, Mommy. Well, enjoy your new recipe. Say hi to daddy for me. I have to take my exam now. I will call you after it," I replied.

"Wait, Nikky!" Mommy interrupted. "So have you met any hot boys yet?" she added quickly.

No! Not the men/marriage conversation! I had a life-changing and important exam! And why was my mother using the words *hot boys*? Daddy had probably lost the remote again and the TV channel was stuck on *MTV*.

"Momsie," I said referring to her in the Nigerian nickname for mother. "No, I am not answering any questions about boys, men, or anything of that nature!"

"I am just trying to relate to your life because you are so far away, darling," she said, chuckling. "What about that very handsome young man you introduced me to in the white coat ceremony? He seemed so nice. Both of you fit perfectly. You will have fair-skinned babies together," she continued.

The young man she was referring to was Tayo. I inadvertently introduced her to Tayo during the white coat ceremony. I *say* inadvertently because I knew an introduction to an eligible Nigerian man would translate to marriage/engagement to my mother so I tried to avoid a meeting, but my mother's eagle eye spotted him speaking to me during the reception and demanded an introduction.

"Mommy, please! I don't have time for this conversation. I called you for support, and all you want to talk about is men."

"Well, I want to carry my grandbabies in this lifetime. This is just a preemptive strike. We have to start planning and finding you a life partner because you are still young. Your flower is still blooming. You don't want to be old and single, Nike," she said matter of factly.

"Mommy, can we talk about this tomorrow?" I quickly replied.

"Okay, darling," she said. "Good luck today."

"Bye, mom," I said, hanging up.

Even my mother wanted me to be with Tayo. Gosh! Well if a certain seductress would get out of the picture, maybe that would be possible! I kissed my poster of my imaginary boyfie Anderson Cooper goodbye then gathered my book bag, making sure I had a working pen, and headed to the examination hall.

I was early. The atmosphere in the examination room was quiet and tense. A few students went over notes while others studied quietly. The chairs were arranged in three long columns, which probably had a hundred seats. A stage with a podium was situated in the front of the room. The school probably also used the room for student awards nights and other academic events. The large grand piano on the stage confirmed my suspicions. Stedman College of Medicine was being prudent despite the hundreds of thousands of dollars I paid them. We still had a room that functioned as concert hall /event hall/exam hall. *Sigh.* The color of the chairs in the examination room was also very appropriate. It was fiery red, probably signifying that our brains were going to be fried in this room for the next four years. I quickly located my name on one of the chairs and sat down. I made sure my color-coordinated pens and pencil set was complete and arranged them carefully on the table. I glanced back when I heard the door open loudly and saw a group of students walk into the room talking loudly.

Well, I guess we all manifested our anxiety in different ways because this group didn't look the least bit worried or concerned. I spotted Tayo in the middle of the group with his arms wrapped around Ego.

Tayo spotted me from across the room, and his face lit up as he headed over.

"Ready?" he asked, and he sat on the table next to mine.

"I hope so. You probably are ready to kill this thing, Mr. Biochem degree from Oxford."

"Probably not as much as Miss Stanford School for the Gifted," he said, smiling. "I just want to get this over with, you know. The anxiety has been killing me. Ladi's anxiety might have rubbed off on me," he said, rearranging my carefully arranged pencils.

"Mr. Cool as Ice T is actually concerned. I never thought I would see the day," I replied, prying the pens from his hands and arranging them again.

The color of our skin was almost identical. Mom was right. We would have fair babies. *No! Stop it Nikky!* Now I was thinking about our babies, what next? I was a hop, skip and jump away from proposing to the dude. I blamed my mother and my overly *imaginative vision-having* mind for this line of thinking.

The room quickly filled up, and the quiet din of the room became a cacophony of different conversations. The man I assumed to be the proctor walked to the front of the room and announced, "I am Dr. Blum, the proctor for this examination. Settle down, all of you. Its nine fifty right now, and the exam will begin approximately at ten o'clock."

"Good luck, Nikky," Tayo said as he winked and hurried to his seat. I couldn't help smiling sheepishly back at him.

Dr. Blum continued when the room settled down, "Thank you. My assistant, Miss Flowers, will pass out the exam now. Do not break the seal until you are instructed to do so. Follow the instructions on the instruction sheet on how to fill the answer sheets."

There was a bustle of activity in the room as examination booklets were passed back and we filled in our names in the answer sheet.

Dr. Blum continued again when the room got quiet. "So, welcome to the first exam of your medical careers. This will be the first of many…many…many…exams in your professional career."

We all laughed at his joke then looked at him expectantly. I actually felt goose bumps on my legs. *The first exam for the Class of 2012!*

He continued, "Good luck. Start time is 10:05 am. Break the seal."

Chapter Thirty-Seven

Tayo

I bubbled in the last answer of the exam with relief coursing through my veins.

The exam was finally over! It was time to party like a rock star!

A small voice reminded me to look over the exam, but I shrugged it off. I really doubted I would get anything less than an A.

Besides, I had a party to plan. James, Ladi's roommate, wanted to collaborate with me and throw a party to celebrate the end of our first exam.

James had accosted me in the hallway one day. "Dude, Matt from the Ice Night Club says he knows you. He agreed to give us a discount for booze for the party."

Matt was an internationally known club promoter who had helped me plan many of my parties in America.

"Really," I replied.

"Let's make this party count!" James said, putting his hand out for a handshake.

"For sure," I replied.

"We might as well party before we whoop ya'll's ass in the football game!" he said and shrugged his shoulders.

"That won't be happening!" I called after his retreating back.

"Sure!" he called back. "I'll keep in touch with you!"

However, for the past few days, I avoided his persistent calls, insisting that we start planning. We both invariably ended up trash-talking each other about the football game and arguing about the party. Now that the exam was over, it was time to party.

I stood up abruptly and walked confidently to the front of the hall to turn in the examination to Dr. Blum.

There was an audible gasp in the room, and I chuckled silently to myself.

"Are you sure you don't want to look over the exam?" Dr. Blum asked before accepting the exam from me.

"No," I replied, shrugging my shoulders.

"It has just been fifteen minutes into the exam, Mr. Smith. Are you sure? There is no extra credit for turning in the exam earlier."

"No, it's fine," I replied, forcing the answer sheet into his hand.

What did everyone expect? That exam was ridiculously easy. I had a degree in biochemistry, for goodness' sake! Of course I was done with the exam.

"Okay," he said resignedly.

I walked out of the examination hall confidently, catching Nikky's eyes and winking at her incredulous expression.

"Freedom!" I exclaimed to myself at the entrance to the elevator.

"Hold it," I called to the shutting doors of an elevator.

A very attractive woman with a dazzling smile held the door open for me. "I'm holding, better try to make it."

I stepped into the elevator and said, "Thank you."

I glanced at the woman, and my heart almost skipped a beat.

It was Belinda Belfonte! The hotness known as Belinda Belfonte!

I immediately went into "Smith. Tayo Smith" mode.

I flashed my best smile, squinted my eyes slightly, and began my magic of seduction.

"Hey, I haven't met you. I am Smith. Tayo Smith," I said, extending my hand.

"I haven't met a lot of people in your class," she said, offering her hand. "I am Belinda Belfonte," she said as the colorful bangles on her wrist shook noisily. "You are a freshman, right? I haven't seen you around."

"We haven't met officially," I replied.

She smiled and said, "Well, that's because I usually study at home and stay away from medical school drama. How did the exam go for you guys? Ya'll had an exam today right?"

"Yes, we did. It was fine. It wasn't that bad actually." I said.

We both walked out of the elevator to the lobby on the first floor.

Even her walk was regal; she took small dainty steps, and I actually had to slow down to walk alongside her.

"Oh, that's good. So how does it feel to complete your first exam in medical school? I remember just one year ago I was in the same position. Time flies, doesn't it? Anyway, ya'll are probably going partying tonight, huh?" she asked, glancing at her watch.

"Yes," I answered. "I am having a party. You should come."

She laughed, "No, I don't think so...I told you I keep the drama to the minimum."

"Please," I said, making the motion of getting on my knees.

She laughed and replied, "Okay, sure, I will come."

"Well," I started to reply and was interrupted by a rush of bodies out of the elevators.

She glanced impatiently at her watch again. She interrupted me before I spoke saying, "Let me just cut to the chase. You obviously want my number. I obviously want to give you. So here it is."

She grabbed my forearm and scribbled her number on my palm.

"Oh, wipe that expression off your face, Tayo Smith. Don't tell me you have never met a girl who knows what she wants and goes for what she wants," she said.

Then she winked and walked away, swinging her hips back and forth.

I smiled. Belinda Belfonte was going to be a lot of trouble.

Chapter Thirty-Eight

Sola

"It's finally over!" I exclaimed.

I screamed at the top of my voice to be heard above the excited chatter of my classmates gathered outside the examination hall.

There was a universal feeling of relief in the Class of 2012.

"I am so happy! I feel like dancing!" Nikky exclaimed.

She began to do a dance and we all laughed.

"I don't even care if I passed! I am just happy it's over!" Lenny said.

"I care if I pass!" Irene interrupted. "What do you guys think the answer for the question about aldolase was?"

"Noooooo," Ladi groaned. "Can we not go over the exam? I already found I missed three questions already."

"Yeah! No going over exams!" TJ said.

"In fact, let's have a toast," Nikky said.

Almost like magic she was passing out plastic cups to everyone who stayed behind in the lobby. Soon she was pouring out a questionable-looking drink from a huge empty water bottle into the cups.

"It's pineapple juice. Mommy taught me how to make it," Nikky said.

When everyone had a drink, Nikky said, "Class president, a toast please!"

Ladi chuckled and raised his cup, then he said loudly, "To the end of the first medical school exam ever! And here's to smashing a lot more exams!"

"Yeah!" we screamed in response and clicked our plastic cups together.

Our celebration was interrupted by a man with grey hair who had an uncanny resemblance to Santa Claus, passing out CDs.

I groaned. The materials for the next unit.

We were not even given a chance to savor the completion of the first unit.

"Don't ya'll get too excited," he said, handing the CDs out. "You are not MDs yet. You are not anything yet. In fact, you all haven't seen anything yet. Ya'll haven't even seen a cadaver."

"But we are excited we are done! Shouldn't we be?" Nikky asked.

"Well, I guess you should," he said, forcing a CD into the hands of an unsuspecting classmate.

"But if the upperclassmen told ya'll about me, there's nothing to celebrate," he continued, rubbing his hands together. He threw his head back and laughed wickedly.

"I am not easy. But I promise you a lot of fun!"

I immediately knew who he was: Dr. Hines, the coordinator of our second unit, Human Genetics and Cell Biology. We had been warned that his bark was worse than his bite, but his exams were known to be extremely difficult. Great! More difficult exams for us.

"Please, I don't care about the exam. So what's the plan for after the exam? Are we hitting up Tayo's party? I hear this party is going to be legendary," Tina said.

Besides the fact that Tayo was the main organizer of the party, I really wasn't in the mood for partying. Part of me just wanted to go home, crawl under my covers, and talk to Dare on the phone; another part of me wanted to do something fun.

"I don't think so," Ladi said. "I am going to have sit this one out, guys. I have been putting off a lot of my student president duties. I just don't think I am in the mood to go out. I would like to go somewhere else."

"What?! You can't miss this party. Do you realize the location is being kept a secret because they want to limit the party to mostly first years and second years. Third and fourth years are begging for invitations! It's that serious! Tayo is sending our class an email one hour before the party to keep the location secret. This is huge!" Tina said, with her eyes almost popping out with excitement.

"Well, I don't have anything planned, and Tayo seemed so excited about this party. I guess I should go," Nikky answered.

"OK, I guess I'll go, too. Let's hope the party lives us to all the hype," Irene said.

"Sola, please come with us," Nikky said, turning to me with her large brown eyes, pleading with me.

"Nikky, I have a lot of things to do. I haven't spoken to Dare and..."

"No! You can be such a spoilsport sometimes, Sola," Nikky whined.

I laughed and replied, "I am sorrrrry! I am just busy! Call me after the party and give me all the jist."

"Oh, I can do a phone three-way with you guys so we can all jist," Tina interrupted.

We all erupted into laughter.

"Jist? I see Tina has spending too much time with you Nigerian women. Do you even know what just means?" Ladi asked.

"Yeah like talk," Tina said, looking quite pleased with herself.

"More like gossip," Irene said under her breath, and Nikky laughed.

"I don't have anything to wear! Maybe we should go shopping?" Irene said.

"Yeah, I don't have anything to wear, either. I haven't had time to straighten my room. Shopping in Georgetown is probably a good idea," Nikky said.

"Yeah! Maybe I will finally meet my ortho prince tonight!" Tina said.

"Ortho prince? Better give up on that dream, Tina, and listen to those nice internal medicine boys giving you attention," Nikky said as they walked away together.

"Which internal medicine boys?"

"Erm, I saw Bob Matterson giving you the eye...." Nikky said, winking.

"Ohhh, Nikky, stop that. I am not interested in him! He gives me the creeps," Tina said and shuddered.

"And he isn't going to be an orthopedic surgeon!" Irene and Nikky added, laughing.

Ladi and I watched them with amusement as they giggled and walked away.

He turned to me and said, "So what do you really have planned for today, Sola? You don't miss the party of the century for no good reason."

"I told you already! I want to have a full conversation with my boyfriend without having to interrupt him because I have to study.

"Look who's talking?" I added. "I am not the only one missing the party of the century. You are not going, either."

"No I am not. I am going to church."

Huh? Church?

Was that the name for a new club in DC? I mean, who went to church on a weekday? He had to be joking.

"You should come with me," he added.

"Why would I do that? I want to go home, cook, clean, get my life in order, and talk to my boyfriend. The last place I want to be after a stressful exam is church, especially on a weekday."

"It could be very relaxing, you know," he answered, looking amused.

"So God can ignore me in public like He does in private?" I answered half jokingly.

He watched me silently for a moment, raising his left eyebrow quizzically.

"Why would you say that Sola?"

"Say what?" I asked

"Your comment about God ignoring you in private. Why would you say that?" he asked, looking at me intently, waiting for my answer.

"I don't know, Ladi. It was just a joke."

"No, it wasn't."

"How do you know it wasn't?"

"You were not laughing."

There was a long silence.

"Ladi, please, enough with your interrogation. If going to church means so much to you, I will come with you!" I said, feeling slightly irritated.

He stared at me for a moment.

"Okay then," he said offering me his hand. "Let's go."

"Okay," I said, taking his hand.

Ladi's church service wasn't half as bad as I thought it would be. It was a mercifully short sermon in the local Stedman chapel. I recalled the long-winded prayers and sermons from the vice principal of my secondary school in Nigeria and shuddered. We were lucky if he finished morning prayers in three hours. But this was different. There was something hopeful, refreshing, and optimistic about being in this service. There were many young people in this church who listened to the sermon with rapt attention and genuinely seemed to believe.

I wasn't convinced as of yet.

But this church, this young crowd, was unique to me. I was intrigued.

I observed Ladi from the corner of my eye as I took my seat beside him. He carried himself with a self-assuredness in the church. It was almost like he had returned home after a long journey. The tension of the last few days seemed to seep slowly away from him as he listened attentively, taking notes in his Bible like his life depended on it. He seemed to be observing me too, because I caught him staring at me surreptitiously many times.

"Did you enjoy that?" he asked as we walked down F Street towards the Gallery Place, Chinatown, and Metro station.

"Well, I have to admit I did. It wasn't half as bad as I thought it would be. How did you find this place?"

"I just found it. I wanted to keep going to church like I did at home, so I was walking back from the grocery store after buying some groceries when I first moved into DC. I saw the cross, and I walked in. I found out it was the Stedman chapel later, though."

"Wow, that's interesting. The crowd is young, very relatable, and I liked the sermon. But I am a girl, I like any sermon about love."

He laughed and replied, "Not that type of love, Sola. Not the one you have with Dare. It's a more powerful kind."

"Hmmmmm," I replied. "If it's so powerful, how come I don't feel it or see it?"

"You don't. It's a love obtained my faith."

"You are getting a little too deep for me, Ladi. Let's just leave the religious talk alone."

He laughed and said, "Okay, but only if you promise that we can have this discussion again."

"Okay, Saint Ladi," I answered and smiled at him.

I was interrupted by my vibrating phone. It was a call from an unfamiliar number. Immediately after I glanced at the number, I knew something wasn't right.

"Excuse me, Ladi," I said clicking my talk button and walking slightly ahead.

"Okay," he replied.

When I was a safe distance away from him I answered, "Hello."

"Sola. It's me."

It was my mother.

I took a deep breath and said, "Where are you?"

"I am around."

"What do you mean around? Are you okay?"

"Yes."

"What is going on? Are you going to go back home?"

"Shhhh. Don't let them know I have left. They still think I am in the house," she said sharply.

I was confused, then I realized what her deluded mind was thinking. She thought someone was listening in on her phone conversations.

I groaned inwardly with exasperation.

There was no point in arguing with her once she had made up her mind in her deluded state.

"When are you going back home?" I asked quietly.

"I don't know. The people on the bus have also been giving me funny looks. I don't feel safe with them."

"Do you realize John is staying with Dare now? Mommy, when will you go back home? The phones are not tapped, and no one in the bus is giving you any looks! Go back home!"

"I can't. I will try when everything is in order. I just wanted to let you know that I was fine."

"Mother," I started again but gave up. I knew it was a lost battle. She would not come back until she wanted to. John and I would have to hope it was sooner rather than later.

"Okay. Just make sure you are safe," I finished.

"I will. Bye," she said and hung up.

That was how conversations with my mother went.

Simple conversations that left many things unsaid.

In some ways, I blamed myself for this mess. I watched her mentally deteriorate for years, hoping that she would get better, but she was never going to get better. When and if she came back, we would have to make some sort of arrangement for her. Maybe I could convince her to go back to Nigeria to live with my aunt. I would have to ask Dare if John could stay with him a little longer.

Transferring didn't seem to be a terrible prospect now. I would transfer to a medical school in Michigan so we could all be together.

It would all work out.

"Is everything okay?" Ladi asked, watching me closely and interrupting my train of thought.

"No…no I am fine," I answered distractedly.

"Are you sure?"

"Yes, of course I am."

I turned to him and gave him my brightest smile.

"Saint Ladi, leave me *jare*. I am fine." Then I changed the subject quickly, "But tell me: how does it feel being so perfect? Are you guys normal like us too? Do you breathe the same oxygen as we do?"

He laughed and replied, "I am not a saint, Sola. I have gotten into some pretty serious stuff also."

"Sure, like crossing the street without looking both ways, Ladi."

"I am not perfect Sola," he answered. "I am far from it."

Chapter Thirty-Nine

Ladi

If she only knew how imperfect I truly was, how I struggled daily to maintain the image of perfection that others had ascribed to me, she would not think I was perfect any longer. I struggled daily with my purity; even being this close to her was a struggle because I remembered how easy it was to give in, to fail and give in to one's desires. My mind wondered back to a time when, out of rebellion, I entered into a relationship that made sense at the time but cost me.

Even though I couldn't really say being with Sola was helping my convictions, at least with her there was the filter of her boyfriend.

The fact remained that Sola with her "little girl lost" eyes was dangerous. My ex-girlfriend, Naduah, always accused me of being "Captain Save-a-Damsel" and, though I would never admit it to her face, I think she was right. I couldn't resist trying to help Sola.

I glanced at her as we walked in companionable silence to the metro station, weaving past the local DC teenagers who clogged Seventh Street in Chinatown. She looked defeated after her conversation on the phone, and she sighed as we walked.

"What's up, Sola?"

"Nothing."

"Are you sure?'

"Honestly, no. But hopefully it will get better," she completed brightly with a smile, the smile that never reached her eyes.

This was why Sola was a contradiction to me. She could switch from being profoundly sad to happy in a matter of seconds. She seemed to embody polar opposites simultaneously. Vulnerability and strength, secretiveness and openness, and happiness and sadness. In short, Sola was a mystery, and I was drawn to her because of her ability to be so available yet an enigma to me. No matter how much I cautioned myself, reminding myself about her boyfriend, reminding myself that God would not be pleased with me, I couldn't help it. I knew I had feelings for her, and there was nothing I could do about it.

I regarded her silently and contemplated probing again, but her mouth was set in that stubborn line. I saw she wouldn't open up to me.

We fell into a companionable silence again.

We walked pass the billboards to the front of a movie theater, and I casually glanced at the movie showings that were listed.

"Look, they are playing *Pride and Prejudice*! It's my favorite movie in the world!" she exclaimed as her eyes lit up brightly.

She cocked her head to one side then said in a convincing British accent, *"It is a truth universally acknowledged, that a single man in possession of a good fortune, must be in want of a wife."*

Finally! A smile.

I laughed then said, "Let's go see it then."

She hesitated, "I don't know...I haven't spoken to Dare today, and I promised I would call him after the exam."

"You can always call him after the movie," I answered. "Come on, you can't miss *Pride and Prejudice*. This is the limited release, Sola."

She rolled her eyes and laughed. "You really want to watch *Pride and Prejudice* with me?"

"Yes, I read the book. I fell in love with Jane Austen when I read that. I love her ability to manipulate the English language."

"You read the book? I just watched the movie and loved it." She looked at me quizzically and continued, "You are so...different... You don't act like a Nigerian guy at all."

"Sola, is there a prototype for Nigerian guys that I am unaware of? Your statement categorically implies that you expect us Nigerian guys..." I stopped to make quotation marks in the air for the words *Nigerian guys*. "To behave in certain acceptable ways." I completed and smiled.

She laughed and said, "Okay, Ladi! No need to use all the words in the English language!"

I liked it when I made her laugh. I offered her my hand and said, "Take my hand and follow me to Pemberley."

She looked at me quizzically for a moment before I realized that she had no idea what Pemberley was.

I laughed and said, "Sola, were you paying attention in the movie or did you only care about Mr. Darcy and Elizabeth ending up together? Pemberley is Mr. Darcy's estate in the book."

She laughed and said, "I wasn't memorizing every single detail in the movie, Ladi, and, yes, all I cared about was that they ended up together."

"But I'll follow you to Pemberley," she completed, linking her hands with mine.

Chapter Forty

Tayo

Church? I thought.

I read the text from Ladi again: "Sorry, man, I can't make your party. I am going to church. You should try to make the service before the party if you can."

If I entered any church, I would probably burst into flames and personally be escorted out by Jesus for daring to show my face.

I chuckled to myself and shifted by concentration back to compiling the guest list for the party. I had thrown some pretty wild parties in my lifetime, but this party would be my crown jewel. Since word about the party had spread, I had been bombarded with emails, texts, and calls from people trying to get on the guest list. This did not include the insistent call from James instructing me to add yet another cousin of his to the guest list. How many cousins did he have anyway?!

"Finally," I said out loud and added the finishing touches to the mass email with the subject "Legendary Status."

Now that was done, the next order of business was money. The bubbly was costing more than I had an expected and, with paying for the club and the limousine we rented for the party, my account was in the red. I thought about the value-of-money lecture my dad would give me if I asked for money and groaned. That lecture would last thirty minutes to an hour, after which he would promptly transfer the money to me. I wondered why he even bothered.

Mom on the other hand was easy. She asked two questions. *When and where?* I made a mental note to remind her to transfer ten thousand to my account ASAP.

My ringing phone interrupted my train of thought, and I made it a point to glance at the caller ID before picking. I didn't want to be bothered with any more pesky requests to be added to the guest list.

I breathed a sigh of relief when I saw Nikky's name on the caller ID.

"Yo, Nikky," I answered.

"So how are you getting to the party?" she asked.

"We hired a limo. You coming with us, right?"

"Erm, I think I will just ride with Irene. It might be a little bit crazy for me. Your crew and James's crew will be too much for me."

"Please, Nikky! I want you to come with us."

"Well—"

"I want you there as my official date," I interrupted.

Why did I just say that? Belinda, the girl I met in the elevator, is coming to the party too, and I had given her the impression that she was my official date.

It must have been the shot of vodka I just gulped that was talking.

Nikky replied, "Oh, your official date? As in no flirting with all our other classmates type of date?"

"Look who's talking about flirting. I saw you with Robert, your mentor the other day. You were doing enough flirting with him."

She laughed and replied, "Robert is just cool."

"He spends a little too much time checking up on you to be entirely harmless. I don't see the other mentors checking on their mentees like that."

"Whatever, Tayo," she replied. "What time should I come to your apartment?"

"Come as soon as you are ready," I replied. "The party will start here before we head out to Ice."

As if on cue I heard a loud knock on my door.

"Open up! It's Lenny!" I heard.

"And James!" James piped in.

"Come here soon, Niks," I said then hung up.

Lenny, TJ, James and Earl all rushed into my room.

In a matter of minutes, we were doing vodka shots amidst loud music.

"Ehhhh! Another shot for the boys," James screamed as he filled the shot glasses again.

We gulped our glasses.

"You guys are quite loud," I heard Nikky say from the door.

We had left the door open and she walked in.

"OWWWWWWWWWWW!" James howled. "Miss Nikky Abe is looking mighty fine! That's why I love me some Nigerian woman!"

She shook her head and laughed. "You guys should stop staring at me. Can I at least have a drink?"

"Bring the bubbly out, Tayo!" Lenny said.

"I thought you said we had champagne! Bring it out boy!" said Earl.

"Sure," I said. Then I proceeded to fill six champagne glasses.

"Wait, a toast." I said, stopping James's pursed lips over the champagne glass. "To medical school and end of the first exam. Hoping we killed it!"

"Yeah!" they screamed, and we clicked our glasses.

"The limo should be here, right?" TJ asked.

"Yeah, it should," I said.

I glanced at my phone and saw the missed calls I assumed were from the now pissed-off limo driver.

"Ladies and gentlemen," I said before we headed out. "It's time to party like rock stars!"

With the exception of Nikky, we all got thoroughly wasted in the limo ride to the party. But this was what life was about: being young, free and able to do whatever you wanted. This was my domain, and I was king. We walked past the winding line of people trying to get into the club and were ushered directly into the VIP section, directly above where some of my classmates partying below.

Nikky whispered to me, "Hold on, Tayo. I am going to find Irene."

"Well, hurry back. You're my date, Nikky."

Because it was second nature to me, I winked at her.

She rolled her eyes and went off in the opposite direction.

Time to get cra cra crazy! James handed me a bottle of champagne, which I shook vigorously and opened. I began spraying the champagne on the crowd below. Then we all laughed loudly as the girls below shrieked.

An extremely hot body caught my attention, and I glanced down and saw Belinda in a form-fitting dress.

This girl wasn't playing!

She smiled at me and called out my name above the hubbub of the club music, "Tayo, baby!"

I smiled back at her and offered my hand to pull her up onto the platform. James immediately offered her a glass of champagne. I turned my attention back to my adoring crowd and screamed, "Let's get white boy wasted!"

The DJ must have heard my cue because he immediately began playing a song with a heavy bass and pulsating beat.

Everyone in the club screamed and went wild.

"Oh!" Belinda screamed. "That's my song!" She pushed her way through so she was standing in front of me and began dancing with me.

This was the life! Good music, alcohol, beautiful women, and me at the center of it all.

Belinda's lips were looking really sexy too. I wanted to make out with her at the moment.

Then I glanced up and caught Nikky's eyes looking directly into mine. She looked beautiful and vulnerable, standing in the middle of the dance floor and watching me.

In that moment, I only saw Nikky, and everyone else had become pale in comparison.

I knew what I wanted to do with Belinda here, who was moving her body like she wanted something. I was very ready to give in, but Nikky's eyes stopped me.

I held Belinda by her waist and pushed her away from me.

She looked back at me quizzically then she smiled naughtily.

She immediately grabbed my face with both her hands and began exploring my mouth with her lips hungrily. All thoughts of Nikky evaporated from my mind.

Chapter Forty-One

Nikky

I watched Tayo make out with Belinda for a moment then bit my lip and turned away. It was Belinda all along, while I was so preoccupied with his relationship with Ego. I tried to blink back the tears, but I couldn't.

Why did he go out of his way to tell me I was his official date if when I turned my back for five minutes, he was making out with somebody else?

I couldn't even deny to myself that I wasn't hurt.

Irene suddenly came to my side and shouted in my ear, "Nikky, let's go home. This party is getting a little bit crazy."

"Okay," I nodded, too exhausted to argue.

I was a little disappointed also because Irene, Tina, and I had spent hours shopping and getting ourselves ready for tonight. I looked pretty hot if I could say so myself. It was a pity all my hard work was going to be wasted.

She linked her hands with mine as we began to make our way towards the exit.

"Where is Tina?" I shouted into Irene's ear.

"Who knows? She is fine. I texted her, and she said she would meet me at home."

Irene suddenly moved her head to the side to avoid two huge men carrying an inebriated James above our heads to the exit.

"Hey, watch it!" she exclaimed.

"Let's get out of here," I said to her.

Partying and having fun after a stressful exam was one thing but total debauchery was another. This was totally unacceptable.

"Let's move faster," Irene said. She pulled my hands firmly towards the exit, pushing past the people who blocked our path.

We suddenly heard screaming from the direction of the VIP platform. I turned and saw the VIP platform buckling and swaying. My heart caught in my throat as my eyes searched frantically for Tayo. I sighed with relief when I spotted him jumping off the platform quickly, leaving Belinda standing on the swaying platform.

She quickly came to her senses and jumped off the platform before it collapsed.

The music suddenly stopped, and the lights were turned on.

We heard a man's voice over the intercom say, "Folks, the party is over! The building is filled to capacity and is in violation! Please head peacefully to the exits!"

"Boo!" someone shouted.

Soon a few others joined in with chants of "Not fair!"

"Boo!"

"Folks, the club is in violation of it capacity limit. It is time to leave or risk being arrested!"

Arrest what! I am too cute to be in jail!

My classmates must have the same thought, too, because they began heading towards the exits, making it more difficult for Irene and me to leave.

"Just make sure we keep holding hands," Irene said to me.

We finally made our way out of the warmth of the club to the chilly night.

I rubbed my hands to keep them warm and then quickly buttoned up my coat.

"How are we getting home?" I screamed above the din of honking cars and party revelers walking to the train station in droves.

Irene glanced at the traffic that had magically formed outside the club and said, "A cab will take forever. Let's take the metro."

I nodded in agreement.

We joined our other classmates walking towards the metro.

The crowd was certainly rowdy and rambunctious. Someone randomly began to sing the lyrics of the opening monologue of the *Fresh Prince of Bel-Air* show. I barely noticed when I joined them and began mouthing the words, too.

I made sure to ignore Tayo, who was walking or, more appropriately, stumbling in front of me, holding the hands of Belinda and another girl in our class. He laughed and talked loudly with them. I really could not believe I actually liked this dude. He looked so pathetic in his inebriated state. Irresponsible drinking was a trait I detested and would not tolerate.

Losing him to Belinda or Ego or whichever female he decided to suck face with wasn't such a tragedy after all. My stupid vision was obviously wrong!

I did not want a drunken hot mess for a boyfriend.

"That was a party! Girls! We literally shut the club down!" he screamed at the top of his lungs as we waited at a stoplight.

Both girls laughed and screamed, too.

I cringed inwardly with embarrassment.

Tayo screamed again, "Yo, I am tired of this light. Let's cross."

He began to cross the street when the light for pedestrian crossing was still red.

I watched horrified as a car sped towards the traffic light and Tayo.

"Tayo!" I began calling out with my heart beating wildly.

"Tayo!" I screamed again, making my way towards him, but Irene firmly held my hand.

I watched him helplessly, my head filled with images of him being hit and lying in a pool of blood.

I closed my eyes and opened them, expecting the worst.

The car came to screeching halt, just barely stopping where he stood.

"WHAT!" he screamed at the surprised driver and sauntered past the car.

We were all momentarily stunned, watching him from the other side of the street as the driver cursed loudly at him.

"Dude, do you realize you almost got hit!" Lenny called to him.

"Yes! So what!" he called back before laughing hysterically.

I realized then that Tayo Smith would never be good for me.

Especially because he was determined to give me a heart attack before I turned twenty.

Chapter Forty-Two

Tayo

I opened my eyes slowly and winced. It was cold and uncomfortable on the bed.

Why is my bed curved this way and so white?

I suddenly realized that I was in the bathtub, and I was stark naked.

How did I get here?

I wasn't even sure I was in my own bathtub. I crawled out of the bathtub and ignored my spinning head. I grabbed the towel on the rack and wrapped it around myself.

When the spinning finally stopped, I walked slowly into my bedroom using the wall to keep myself steady. My bedroom was turned upside down, my clothes were strewn on the floor, my flat screen TV and Xbox were smashed, and my mattress was missing.

The familiar humiliation and shame hit me like a ton of bricks.

The thought that I did something embarrassing yesterday and had absolutely no recollection of it made me feel powerless. The feeling was familiar. I had another blackout. I put my head in my hands and sunk to the floor of my bedroom.

I contemplated calling one of my brothers, but I realized there would be no comfort there. I searched my room for my cell phone then quickly dialed Nikky's number. Her phone went straight to voice mail. That was odd; her phone never went straight to voice mail.

I dialed her number again and waited.

"What do you want?" she answered.

"Nikky?" I asked.

"Yes, Tayo. What do you want?" she asked curtly.

"What's wrong, Nikky?"

"What's wrong? You don't remember what you did last night, do you?"

"Yes and no."

"Well, you made a drunken spectacle of yourself and humiliated me!" she screamed.

"How did I humiliate you?" I asked. My head began to pound louder, and I felt like my head was going to explode.

"After you told me I was your official date, I barely turned my head around and you were making out with Belinda!"

I kept silent.

"Well, what do you have to say for yourself?! You are an alcoholic, Tayo! I want nothing to do with you!"

"You are not my girlfriend, Nikky, and I can make out with whomever I please," I answered.

There was another long silence, and I immediately regretted my words.

"Nikky, I didn't mean…"

"Why did you call me, Tayo? What exactly do you want with me? If you are single, why call Belinda or Ego?"

"Nikky…."

"*What do you want from me*?"

"Nikky, please, I am so sorry. I didn't mean it like that."

"No, you did. I am done with you, Tayo."

"Nikky, please don't say that…"

"No. I won't allow you to use me as your clutch anymore. This friendship…this thing…whatever it is. It's emotionally draining."

"Nikky, please. Wait. Can I come to your apartment to talk to you?"

"No, Tayo. I don't think I want to see you."

"Nikky, please…"

Suddenly the idea of losing her as a friend scared me.

"Nikky?" I tried again.

"I don't think I want to see you, Tayo."

"Nikky, please."

"No, Tayo. Our relationship is becoming unhealthy for me. I want space away from you."

"Okay. I'll give you some space. I won't call you today."

"Tayo, I mean space. I don't want us to study together anymore."

I kept silent. At this moment, I wished I could take back my words.

"Okay. If you think we need space away from each other then I will give us space."

"Yes, I do," Nikky answered.

"Okay."

"Goodbye, Tayo," she said and hung up.

I hung up and sat quietly on the floor of bedroom, my brothers' words echoed in my mind.

I wonder how soon it will take you to mess medical school up? my brothers had both said.

Well, it didn't take me that long.

In the strenuously academic world of medicine, examinations were the stock exchange and grades were the currency.

Teddy Gray
Class of 1960

Grades were more than grades to us. Each pass put you one step closer to your dream, each failure pushed you farther away. Failure triggered a domino effect of emotions. If you failed the exam, you failed the unit, you failed the year, you were kicked out of medical school and still had to pay astronomical student loans.

Ranti Patel
Class of 2004

Chapter Forty-Three

Sola

After the post-exam euphoria died down, my classmates and I anxiously awaited the results of the exam. The lecture hall was unusually full today because Dean Roberts had sent an email the previous night announcing we could pick up our grades from the previous unit.

Dr. Ho was pleasantly surprised by the amount of students in class.

"Well, it seems like everyone wants a piece of genetics today!"

He proceeded to laugh loudly at his own joke, and a few students chuckled.

"I hope ya'll are ready for the hardest exam you will ever take, though. The biochem exam will be child's play compared to this."

We all groaned. He had been threatening to make the exam very difficult for the past two weeks, and we were tired of hearing it.

"Now ya'll know I heard about the last party, and Mr. Tayo Smith getting buckwild," Dr. Ho continued.

The whole class erupted into laughter. Nikky, who was sitting next to me, rolled her eyes.

Now, she rolled her eyes anytime Tayo's name was mentioned. Nikky had finally severed ties with Tayo because of his antics. I wasn't convinced at first because they were joined at the hip, but now I barely saw them together. I was relieved.

Although I planned to leave Stedman soon, I wanted to leave knowing Nikky would be far away from Tayo. My transfer was not final, but I had found some schools in Michigan that could accept me.

Dare had accepted John moving in with him temporarily until we found a permanent solution if and when my mother came back. Life was stable, and stability was good.

"Grades are ready, Sola," Nikky whispered to me excitedly after she glanced at her phone.

I gulped. The time I both dreaded and anticipated was finally here.

As if on cue, more than half the class got up and headed towards the exit, including Nikky, who practically sprinted out of class. I didn't want to leave class in the middle of the lecture, so I stayed.

"Why is everyone leaving?" Dr. Ho said mid-lecture.

"Grades," someone called back.

He laughed again and said, "I bet ya'll won't be so enthusiastic to see your grades after my exam."

I spent the next few minutes in the lecture hall thinking about my grade and hoping I didn't fail. I might as well have gotten my grade, though, because I didn't hear a word from the boring lecture

Nikky slipped back into her chair next to me, looking distraught.

I glanced at her and asked, "Nikky... Did you pass?"

"Yes," she answered in a strangled voice.

"So why are you crying?" I whispered to her and handed her a tissue.

"Sola, I don't know what I am doing wrong. I am still number two! I got a ninety-nine percent in the exam, and I am still number two."

I resisted the urge to roll my eyes.

"Nikky, it doesn't matter what your class rank is. You got a ninety-nine. You honored the exam! You did very well!"

She studied me for a moment then said, "You don't understand." She sank deeper in her chair then said, "I need to talk to Tayo. He will understand."

"Nikky," I warned. "I thought you made a resolution."

"Yes, I did, but I need to speak to him now. He's the only one who can understand."

"Don't call him, Nikky. He is not good for you. He is not as harmless as you think."

"What do you mean?"

I realized I had said too much.

"Don't worry. Stop crying, Nikky." I patted her on the arm. "I am going to get my grades," I continued.

"Okay," she replied resignedly.

She began to weep silently again, and I resisted the urge to laugh.

Chapter Forty-Four

Ladi

I sighed in relief when I glanced at the ninety-four on the grade sheet.

I walked back from Dean Robert's office and headed to the parking garage. Then I saw Sola sitting silently on the steps leading to Stedman.

She looked at me and smiled slightly, her lips barely curling up.

"What's up, Sola?"

"I am good, Ladi," she answered.

I took a seat next to her on the stairs and said, "What's really up, Sola?"

"I am probably just being a drama queen. I didn't do too well on the exam. I should probably be happy I passed, but I worked so hard for that exam! I wanted an A," she replied.

I watched her silently.

"I am sorry. Just keep trying. It will get better."

"Easy for you to say. You probably honored."

I had no reply for her, and we watched a car drive by silently.

"I am tired of struggling. I try to get it right for once in my life, but I just can't seem to."

I sensed she wasn't talking about the grades anymore.

"Come with me," I said.

"Where to?"

"Just come," I said, pulling her up gently.

"You have the football game. We have class. Where are we going?" she asked impatiently.

"Come," I said.

She followed me. We walked slowly at first then I began to increase my pace.

"Ladi! Why are you rushing? Don't go quite so fast."

But I paid her no mind and led her down the stairs, down the basement, and across the halls, running faster.

"Ladi! Stop going so fast!"

When we got there, I said, "Look at this."

She looked around gingerly with awe.

"It's so beautiful…How did you find this?"

"I like to take long walks, and I just stumbled upon this room."

"Does anyone know this room exists in the school? It's exquisite."

She was right. It was exquisite.

I discovered the rooms on my long walks pacing the school, during my short study breaks to ease the unbearable tension of studying for hours at end. The room reflected the rich history of Stedman. The golden carpets were threadbare and worn but held on to a dignified appearance. A grand piano stood opposite the empty doorway. There was a golden cross in the middle of the room. The most striking portion of the cross was the depiction of pain in the crucified Jesus' eyes.

A lone empty church pew was placed opposite the cross.

"I come here when I am stressed," I said to her.

"Was this the old Stedman Chapel? The one the founders used?"

"Yes," I answered.

She walked into the room and inspected the cross more closely. "You come here because it makes you feel closer to Him?"

"Yes, and because of the piano too."

She stared at the face of Jesus and placed her hand delicately on His face.

"Do you believe He exists? Do you believe in everything?" she asked seriously.

"Yes, I do."

She sighed deeply.

She switched her gaze from the cross to me and back again, like she was struggling internally with wanting to talk to me and wanting to end the conversation.

"Play me something," she finally said, wrenching herself away from the cross.

"How do you know I can play, Sola?"

"Because you wouldn't have brought me here if you couldn't."

I smiled slowly at her.

"Okay, I will."

We both sat on the chair next to the piano.

"I'll play *Heaven* by Vari Do you know that?"

"No! I don't imagine a lot of people would know Vari. Is that a band or are they Nigerian?"

I chuckled softly as I strummed the piano.

"My brother taught me how to play this song when we were younger. I found the song and learnt how to play it better It makes me feel closer to him."

"Oh…then please play it."

So I played her *Heaven*.

Chapter Forty-Five

Sola

The much-anticipated freshman vs Stedman football game was held in a public field across from Stedman College of Medicine. The stands were decorated with different posters in support of the freshmen. Ladi and the student council had sent a barrage of emails urging the class to participate. We were instructed to arrive at the field at least two hours before the upperclassmen to make sure the most of the banners were freshmen-friendly. It really was a testosterone-fueled event, and the guys were taking it a bit too seriously. But we obliged willfully because their enthusiasm was infectious.

In fact, I began to chant "2012 Rocks" as I took my seat on one of the stands with Nikky, Irene, and Tina. Tina brought out her multi-colored umbrella to shield us from the harsh sunlight. Nikky began to pour a yellowish-orange drink from a clear cooler into plastic cups.

"Mommy gave me this recipe for mango fruit drinks. You guys should try them. It's so 'delish'."

"Girl, it's good! Mmmmhh, you have to give me the recipe," Tina said, gulping her drink in one gulp and handing her cup back to Nikky for a refill.

"You see. I told you guys. Mommy's recipes are always good," Nikky said, refilling her cup.

We were interrupted by the guys chanting in response to Ladi.

"Twenty twelve! We in there!"

"WHAT ARE WE GOING TO DO?"

"WIN!"

"WHAT ARE WE GOING TO DO?"

"WIN!"

We all applauded as they dispersed from their hurdle and walked towards the stands.

Watching Ladi rally the guys, encourage them, and delegate tasks impressed me. He was charismatic and naturally good at being class president. I wondered why he hadn't deliberately run for class president instead of running on a whim. It seemed like the role suited him well.

We silently watched them as they began to stretch with Ladi, Tayo, and Lenny in a deep conversation.

"Ladi has a great body. He obviously works out," Tina said.

"How can you talk about Ladi when you see Tayo there? That boy is a god! He is just good to look at." Irene handed her cup to Nikky for another refill.

"You guys are lucky girls," Tina said, looking from Nikky to me.

"Why are we lucky?" Nikky asked with eyebrows raised.

"Aren't you dating Tayo?" Tina asked.

"NO! Absolutely not." Nikky answered

"Well, that's what I heard."

"Are you serious? People think we are dating?"

"Well, yeah, you guys are always together," Irene said softly.

"That doesn't mean we are together! Besides we have stopped hanging out together," Nikky said with her eyes flashing.

"But you are dating Ladi," Tina said turning to me.

"No, I am not! I have a boyfriend!" I protested.

"Well, you guys could have fooled me. You always seem to be together." Tina said, sipping her mango juice.

"That doesn't mean we are dating!" Nikky and I said at the same time.

"Well, then you must like him," Tina said, turning to Nikky.

Nikky hesitated before answering. "Not really. We just work well together."

Irene winked at Tina and me surreptitiously.

I was happy that Irene was in good spirits. I came back home to find her sobbing in her room earlier this week. She had found out she had failed the exam.

"I failed! Sola, I failed! What am I going to do?" She sobbed into her pillow.

It quickly put things in perspective for me. At least I had passed my exam; failure was a horrifying thought to me.

"It will be okay, Irene. Can you take the retake?"

"Yes, the retake is at the end of the semester, but can you imagine the pressure? If I fail one more unit, I will be kicked out of medical school."

I really did not know what to tell her, but I was worried for her.

"It will be fine. Go to the curriculum office. They can help you modify your study methods. It could help."

"Sola, I worked so hard! I am so upset! It's all the stress of the divorce that is getting to me."

"Hopefully, that will get resolved soon and you can focus on school," I said, trying to reassure her.

I suddenly realized that I wasn't the only one under tremendous emotional strain in medical school. We were good at keeping our problems hidden, and school distracted us from our lives.

"Well, you are off the hook, Sola. I'll go tell everyone you indeed are not dating Ladi," Tina continued, focusing the attention back to me.

"Who is everyone?"

"You know just a few people. We were talking about the couples in 2012 a few days ago, and your name came up.

"I hope you and your boyfriend are taking steps to make sure your relationship survives medical school," Tina continued.

"Survives medical school?" I asked, my heart beating slightly faster.

"Most relationships don't survive medical school. I was talking with Uche yesterday. She said most people come in with strong relationships with nonmedical school people but the strain of medical school breaks them up," Tina said.

"Did you guys hear that girl Ego broke up the relationship between Ben and his nonmedical school girlfriend?" Tina added with a smirk.

Tina could be very annoying sometimes. She almost always had unsolicited advice for everything.

"I think the couple may not have a lot in common anymore, you know. It's not medical school that breaks couples up," Irene said.

"I think it takes work on both sides. If the couple is committed to one another, I see no reason why they would break up," Nikky said, sounding uncharacteristically mature.

"Well, you are right, Nikky," Irene said.

"Hey, I was just telling you guys what the general consensus is," Tina said, throwing up her hands in protest. "Don't shoot the messenger."

There was a long silence as we all absorbed her words.

I could not imagine my life without Dare. My life could be divided into two options, life without Dare and life with Dare. Life without Dare was significantly bleaker than my life with him. He had the ability to make me feel better about everything. He was my existence.

However, as I turned my attention back to the guys on the field, the realization that Dare and I had not kept in contact as often as I would have liked hit me. He was attentive and caring when I first moved to DC, especially after I told him about Tayo Smith. But the calls soon tapered off, mainly because I wasn't available to take his calls. Studying had taken a higher priority in my life. I made a mental note to call him immediately after the game.

"Do you guys know who number one in the class rank is?" Tina suddenly asked.

"Who is it?" Nikky immediately demanded.

"I hear from very good sources that it's Dee," Tina said, cocking her head to the side.

"Dee!" we all exclaimed.

Dee was a nice enough girl, but with her baby face and child-like mannerisms she did not look like the smartest cookie.

"You have got to be joking! Dee is number one?! I may have a mild heart attack!" Nikky screamed. She clutched her heart and shook her head.

"Quit the dramatics, Nikky," Irene said.

"How did you find out, Tina?" I asked.

"Well—" Tina started, but we were interrupted by Ladi, Lenny, and, unfortunately, Tayo making their way toward us.

They stopped periodically to give hugs to other classmates seated on the lower stands. I felt the anxiety rising in my heart as they approached us, but I suppressed my emotions and quickly fixed a welcoming smile on my face.

"Hey, guys. We are just taking a break before we go back into the game," said Lenny as he hugged each girl in greeting.

I halfheartedly hugged Lenny and, when it was time for Tayo to hug me, he hesitated. For some reason, the lull of the conversation had stopped and everyone was staring at us. The negative feelings of disdain and hatred rose like bile from my belly. I suppressed those emotions, and I opened my arms out to him for a hug. He smiled and hugged me quickly. The physical action of touching him was more than I could bear. If anyone had seen what the action had cost me, they didn't seem to notice because everyone settled down in the stands with Nikky pouring out more of her flavored drinks.

I turned my attention back to the field and hoped the game would start soon. I wanted Tayo back on the field and away from me as soon as possible.

"FRY THE FRESHMEN! LET THEM BURN! GO UPPERCLASSMEN!"

We all turned our heads to a loud commotion and chanting coming from the entrance of the field.

The group was made of mostly upperclassmen guys playing in the football game. I watched in amusement as James and members of the "Unholy Alliance" led the chant. Most of them rushed into the field while others took seats on the stands opposite to us. Gradually the stand right next to ours was crawling with overzealous upperclassmen.

"Girls, can you see how the upperclassmen girls are screaming? I should hear your screams on the field, too," Tayo started.

He was interrupted by an extremely pretty girl I had seen walking in with the upperclassmen.

She plastered her curvy body on Tayo as she hugged him.

"Hey, stranger," she said slowly, almost whispering into his ear, her mouth dangerously close to his ears.

It also looked like the girl would need a group of highly trained firefighters to help her remove the extremely tight skinny jeans and crop top she had on. How long had it taken her to force herself into it?

"You know the fresh men are going down ya'll. Don't even bother," she said with a slightly melodic Caribbean accent.

Lenny had a foolish grin on his face and replied, "I wouldn't be so sure."

"Yeah, sure! The freshmen have never won the football game! Ever!"

"And since you are making such bold statements, can we know your name?" Irene asked.

"I am sorry," Tayo said, interrupting. "This is Belinda, guys. Belinda, meet my medical school crew."

"Hello, medical school crew," she said, smiling.

Nikky had pointedly ignored the girl and Tayo throughout the conversation, and I chuckled inwardly to myself. The ensuing drama was going to be interesting to watch.

Chapter Forty-Six

Nikky

"Hi, Belinda," I answered, barely glancing at Tayo and his *new friend*. She looked like the girl he had been sucking face with at the club, but I didn't care. I turned my attention back to the guys practicing on the field.

The girls had created some type of invisible division between Belinda, the guys, and us. We all edged away from them unconsciously and ignored their conversation.

My eye caught a tall figure walking purposefully up the steps towards me, and I smiled in greeting. It was Robert, my mentor.

"Hey, you," he started as he sat beside me. "How did the exam go?"

Sola glanced at me again, but this time it was a different type of teasing glance. I knew I was going to get an interrogation from her immediately after Robert left. I could practically see Tina's brain recording the scene so she could relay it verbatim to whomever she wanted.

"It went okay. I did pretty good."

"So that means you got an A? Great job, Nikky."

I laughed. "It doesn't mean anything Robert, but your advice and tips helped."

"Glad I could help. So did you go partying after the exam?"

"Yes, but I wish I hadn't."

"Well, maybe you will have more fun next time," he said, catching my eye.

His eyes were light brown. *I liked them.*

"Well, I can tell you the partying is getting old."

"Well, anyway, I wanted to ask…"

He was interrupted by Tayo nudging me—rudely I might add—on the shoulder.

"Hey, Nikita, I am about to go back into the field. Wish me luck."

Why is he touching me?

I ignored the fact that he had arbitrarily given me a new nickname and replied coolly, "Okay, good luck."

He hesitated, almost like he was waiting for me to add something and then said, "Well, okay…see you."

He walked off with a perceivable slump of his shoulders. I immediately felt a little annoying tug in my heart but ignored it. It served him right for all he had put me through. I was determined to wean myself off any feelings for Tayo Smith.

I turned back to Robert and said, "You were saying?"

I caught Tina's face. Her eyes were practically leaping with joy at the scene unfolding. I was slightly annoyed that my life was providing her with such amusement.

Robert appeared a little flustered and caught Tina's eyes as she leaned forward to listen to the conversation.

He continued, "Let's take a short walk."

I wondered what he wanted to talk about, but I accompanied him down the steps and walked alongside him next to the field.

"Are you free this Friday?"

"Well, yeah."

"We could go catch a movie and dinner then if you would like."

Mommy's lecture about appearing unavailable to the opposite sex immediately came to my mind. I could almost hear her telling the story I had heard over a thousand times.

"I made your daddy wait!" she would say, cocking her hips to the right.

"Well, I am not sure…"

He watched me closely as I spoke.

"But, okay, dinner and a movie would be fine," I answered finally.

He smiled at me.

Hmmm. I could work with Robert Downing. He was cute so that was a good start.

I couldn't wait to get on the phone with Mommy and tell her! *I just got asked on a date! Not just any date but one with a cute and intelligent guy! A future ortho prince!* He would definitely help me forget that Tayo Smith even existed.

"Okay, great, Nikky. The game is starting," he said pointing to his classmates running into the field.

"We should better head to the stands," he continued.

I glanced back at the field, and my eyes caught the 2012 players getting into position. I watched Tayo taking his position as the quarterback and could not help thinking, *Yes, I have a date but with the wrong man...*

With the limited pool of choices for dates in medical school, medical students invariably ended up dating one another. This usually led to disastrous love triangles, rectangles, squares and even love pentagons.

Melinda Allaya
Class of 1989

Everyone that came into med school with a boyfriend or vice versa more than likely ended up breaking up with the significant other or cheating on them. It wasn't necessarily always in that order too.

Samantha Asare
Class of 1965

I remember Robert was crazy about Nikky, much like I was crazy about my African queen, Ronke. Pity that Nikky had eyes only for Tayo. She was so obvious about it. We all knew and talked about it behind her back.

James Potter
Class of 2012

Chapter Forty-Seven

Nikky

"Wow," Robert said as I opened the door to my apartment.

I laughed and said, "I can take that as a compliment. I look really good?"

"Wow," he repeated again.

He changed the expression on his face to appear more serious and said, "You look okay. I mean you just look like a cross between Gisele and that other blonde model. So you just look okay. You will have to excuse me for staring at you."

I laughed and replied, "Now stop lying. I am not tall enough to look like Gisele."

"You are certainly beautiful enough, though," he said and smiled at me.

I smiled back and slipped into his car.

Maybe Robert and I being together wouldn't be such a bad idea after all. He certainly would be a welcome distraction from my darn kryptonite, Tayo Smith.

Sola was very excited about Robert, and she had only good things to say about Robert. She even helped me get ready tonight by doing my makeup.

My mother on the other hand was not enthusiastic. When I called her about the date, she immediately put me on a three-way call with my Aunty Nike.

"Thank God!" Aunty Nike started. "So when can we expect an engagement?"

"Where is he from? I hope he is a good Yoruba boy from a nice Christian home," my mother added.

I rolled my eyes and answered, "Aunty Nike, this is our first date so we really can't start planning a wedding now. Mommy, he is…"

I paused. This was the hard part.

My mother was traditional, and she would not be too pleased with me dating a white guy.

I could imagine her scrunching her face up with distaste and saying "An *oyinbo* boy? No, oh! We don't want oh!"

"Well, he is not…he is from…" I stammered.

Nikky, just say it, I said to myself. "He is actually a Caucasian."

There was a long silence on the phone.

"A CAU-CA WHAT!" Aunty Nike screamed.

"He is white," I said dryly.

There was another long silence.

"Well, you can still have fun when you are young, but don't waste too much time," my mother began.

"What about that guy I met in the white coat ceremony that we were talking about? Tayo… What was his last name again? Smith. Yes. What about him? Doesn't he like you?" she continued.

Why did my mommy insist on asking embarrassing questions?

I quickly cut the conversation, mentioning something about needing to study in spite of their protests.

I glanced at Robert's handsome profile as he drove.

I hoped we both had a good time tonight.

"So have you decided what you want to specialize in?" Robert asked before he took a sip of his drink in the quaint steak restaurant he took me to.

"Well," I answered. "I am actually thinking of cardiology. Interventional cardiology."

He laughed and said, "Wow, you are very specific, Nikky."

"I like to be," I answered and took a bite of the delicious steak.

Robert got a check mark for the restaurant selection.

"So why did you choose orthopedic surgery? What do you even know about it except most of the alpha males choose that specialty? " I asked.

"I shadowed a doctor when I was in high school, and I really liked it. When I found out that they worked with a lot of athletes, I was sold. I love sports."

"Just like every other guy in the entire world," I answered and bit into the steak again.

This steak was delish! I had to get the name of the restaurant; maybe Sola and I could come back.

I recalled the steep prices on the menu and realized my budget couldn't afford this place. Hmm, that meant Robert had pulled out all the stops for me.

He got another check mark again.

When the check for the meal was brought to the table, I smiled with approval as he paid and tipped the waitress quite nicely.

Generous, too? Robert Downing was the perfect gentleman.

After he drove me back to the Morgan apartment complex, he walked me to my door.

I gave him a hug and said, "I had a great time Robert."

"It was my pleasure, Nikky. I certainly had a great time too," he said, accepting my hug.

He chuckled and said, "You are so short, Nikky. I feel I could carry you."

"Noooo! Don't say that, Rob! I am not short! I am petite!" I insisted.

He laughed and replied, "Okay, sorry. Petite."

I smiled too and waved one last time at him before I closed the door to my apartment.

I dropped my bags on my couch and kicked off my heels before flopping on my bed.

The date with Robert was close to perfect, but I wasn't really excited. I didn't feel any butterflies in my stomach nor did I feel giddy. I wasn't going over every single detail of the date like I usually did.

He had gotten all my check mark requirements but...he wasn't Tayo Smith.

What was it with me and bad boys? This reminded me of the time I fell in love with a guy in my high school who was later caught in an affair with one of the female teachers. This caused the scandal of the decade in my school, and I was just glad I had escaped being the Casanova's ex-girlfriend, but trust me, it wasn't due to my lack of trying. Sigh. Me and my penchant for bad boys, it seems like my aura-meter doesn't work where they are concerned.

Tayo wasn't good for me. I knew that, but here I was pining over him. I really just liked what I liked. Robert was perfect and all, but he was...boring. He was just *blah*, but with time I could probably grow to like him very much.

This line of thinking got me a tad bit depressed, so I dialed Mommy's number, hoping a conversation with her would lift my spirits.

"Nike, my daughter, how are you doing? How was your date?" Mommy answered.

"It was okay, Mommy."

"You don't sound excited, my dear. Why?"

"I don't know, Mommy. It was a great date with Robert and all, but I don't know."

"Hmm, you don't have the hots for him like you do for that Tayo boy," Mommy completed.

Mommy had that uncanny ability of hitting the nail right on the head sometimes. I would ignore her use of the words "hots" because she sounded so appropriately sympathetic.

"Well, I can't say I am disappointed, Nikky. You know all those white boys won't understand our ways."

I rolled my eyes.

"Anyway, what is wrong with this foolish Tayo Smith? He must be a fool, a big one!"

I heard a click on the phone and my father's baritone voice added, "A fool indeed. What man dares to not like my daughter? He is an idiot or he is blind."

What! Why was daddy on the phone? No, Mommy did not put me in a three-way conversation with my daddy!

"Mommy! Why is Daddy on the phone?"

"Because my girls are talking, and I have to know what they are talking about. I'm thankful I picked up the phone. Elizabeth, I told you to stop filling my princess's head with these thoughts. Let her focus on school. All this husband-boyfriend talk is unwarranted. She is only nineteen."

"No, Ayo, you don't understand these things for women. She better start looking now."

"But who is this young man? I have on my mind coming to your school and beating the living day lights out of him. Who is the moron? How dare he not like you? Don't waste your time over him, princess. He obviously doesn't recognize a jewel when he sees one."

Come to my school? Oh no! I better put a stop to that! I knew my daddy was certainly capable of doing that. My mind immediately filled with images of my father pulling Tayo's ears in 1007.

"Daddy, better make sure you don't do that," I quickly said.

"Your father is right, Nikky. That is not the way it works. You are not supposed to fight for any man's attention. It doesn't work that way. If he can't see you for what you are then let him go. They are plenty of men who will. Nikky Abe, know your self-worth. You are my child."

That's was why I loved my Mommy! She always had these encouraging speeches for me to stand by.

"Your mommy is right. I worked hard for your mother because I knew what she was worth. I knew I wasn't getting a woman. I was looking for my queen, and if this idiot cannot see that, cut him loose before I come to your school and box his ears!" my daddy added.

I laughed and said, "No thanks, Daddy!"

Then I spent the next fifteen minutes trying to convince daddy that he didn't need to fly across the coast to "box" Tayo's ears.

Chapter Forty-Eight

Tayo

"Open the door, Nikky! "I screamed outside Nikky's apartment—or at least I thought it was her apartment.

The alcohol definitely had me buzzed. I wasn't drunk yet, but I probably was getting there. I did not realize how much Nikky's friendship had meant to me nor did I expect her departure to turn me into a miserable mess. Just a few weeks prior, it seemed like I had gotten this med school down. I was popular, well liked, and respected, *smashing* my classes, and I had Nikky.

Now my life was spiraling out of control, and I needed her back. I wasn't doing as well in the quizzes. This probably had to do with Dr. Ho's constant threats that we would fail his classes. It was a prophecy.

Now I half dragged myself to school to study with Lenny and TJ, pushing myself to study until the wee hours of the morning so I wouldn't have to go home and face the loneliness and isolation. But long after TJ and Lenny had left, the loneliness hit me like a ton of bricks, carrying with it the fear of closing my eyes because of my nightmarish dreams. So I drank because passing out was a better alternative to sleeping and having a nightmare. When I woke up in the morning, I always felt guilty about drinking, so I would drink again to alleviate my guilt. The alcohol wasn't affecting my grades so it didn't bother me. I just needed the alcohol to get through this rough patch.

When Nikky and I resumed our friendship, I would be fine. I had to have her back.

No, I wanted her back.

I wanted her playful smile, her childish tantrums, her fiery personality, her child-like innocence. I wanted all of her back, and I was determined to get her back.

Tonight, I had come back from studying to resume my routine. But with my lips poised over my vodka bottle, I stopped. It occurred to me that if I had her back, I would simply stop drinking. The constant updates from Tina about her relationship with Robert also pushed me over the edge.

"Nikky! NIKKY! I know you can hear me! Open the door for me!" I screamed.

The door remained stubbornly closed.

I took a deep breath and was prepared to scream her name again when she opened the door.

"Shh! Keep quiet! Have you gone crazy! What is wrong with you?"

She pulled me into her apartment in one swift motion and stared at me in disbelief.

Then she turned up her nose in distaste and said, "Have you been drinking?"

"No."

"Don't lie to me, Tayo. You have been drinking."

"Okay. Yes, I have. It's because of you. You are making me miserable."

"No. You are making yourself miserable."

She paused to observe me again then said, "Come, sit down on the couch. You look like a hot mess."

I allowed her to pull me into the couch and said, "Nikky, please. This no-contact thing is killing me. I want...no, I need your friendship, please."

She sat down next to me and asked, "Why do you want my friendship, Tayo?"

"Because...because...I think we work well together, and we are a good team," I spluttered out

"Really? Don't you work well with Lenny and Thomas Jacob?"

"Nikky...It's pretty obvious. We both have feelings for each other."

"Don't be so sure about my feelings, Tayo," she snapped back.

I stared at her, unsure of how to continue, then I saw her face soften.

"Tayo...I can't do this...undefined thing. It's difficult for me. I honestly want us to be together or be friends from afar."

"We can be together. I want us to be together," I quickly added.

"So then what would we be?" she asked carefully.

I couldn't say what she wanted. I knew what she wanted, but I couldn't say it. It wasn't because I thought I would invariably mess up and hurt her that stopped me this time. It was the fear of hurting her with revelations from my past that stopped me.

"We have to go slow, Nikky. I know you want a relationship, but you are not ready for a relationship with me. I am...I am not what you think I am. I am a horrible person."

She rolled her eyes and said, "You are still being selfish, Tayo. You still want to have your cake and eat it, too. Well, I am not doing this with you."

"No! Nikky, listen, please." I moved closer to her on the couch. I *had* to make her understand.

"I know you want a relationship, and I know I want a relationship. I know it will eventually happen, but I want us to build our friendship exclusively first. I need to know I can trust you."

"Build our friendship exclusively? What? You mean like an exclusive friendship?" she asked with her eyebrows raised quizzically.

"Yes." I answered, gauging her reaction.

"Can we date others in this exclusive friendship?"

"No."

"So you want me to stop dating Robert?"

"Well...yes."

"Can we make out with others in a club?" she asked giving me the side eye.

"No."

"So basically a relationship that you want us to refer to as a friendship?"

"Yes," I answered sheepishly. "Aren't we friends?'

"Yes. Yes, we are friends," she answered intently.

She edged closer to me on the couch and kissed the top of my head then she gently turned my face to kiss each cheek before she found my lips.

"Why do you feel you can't trust me, Tayo?"

"Because…" I couldn't make her understand my past, not now. So I said, "I will tell you when it's time."

"But, Tayo!" she protested.

"Nikky, I will tell you when it's time and hopefully you will still want to be with me."

"Of course, I will want to be with you!"

"Are you sure, Nikky?" I edged closer and looked directly into her eyes, "Can you forgive me for anything?"

"Yes," she answered cautiously.

"Promise me then. Promise me that you will forgive me for anything I have done in my past."

"The past is over, Tayo. I can forgive you. And if I can't forgive you, Mommy always said Jesus and God forgive us for all our transgressions. If He can, I should be able to," she added with a laugh.

I laughed along with her but wondered if even God would forgive me for my past.

"So are ya'll telling me you can't tell me the topoisomerase's role in the DNA cycle?" Dr. Ho asked the class.

"Well, I think…" Daniel Masters called out.

"Think? I hope ya'll know *all* the functions of topoisomeirase, or ya'll are gonna fail the exam!" he exclaimed with joy. "My questions are no joke."

I dutifully accompanied Nikky to class and sat in front with her in my role as her new "exclusive friend." Even the word exclusive friend made me break out in a cold sweat.

I knew I would find a way to mess this up. This exclusive friendship thing made me "exclusive" to Nikky and, to be honest, was an odd arrangement. But it was the only way I could get her back without using the word "relationship," and it gave me leeway to maneuver. The word "relationship" was scary; it meant potential disaster.

Nikky hissed to me under her breath, "Honestly, I am tired of this. His quizzes are hard enough and now this constant threat of failure is annoying. We are already under enough pressure."

"In fact, I think I might just add another question on Topoisomerase," Dr. Ho said then burst into laughter.

Dr. Ho's joke was getting old and annoying. I soon lost interest.

I turned to Nikky and said, "Nikky, I'll come back to school to study. I don't think this lecture thing is working."

"Okay," she replied, barely looking up from her notes.

I walked out of class with relief, already dreaming about my warm bed, but I was accosted by Belinda at the doors leading out of the lecture hall.

Remembering my "exclusive friendship" commitment to Nikky, I pointedly ignored her, but she stopped me.

"Hey, I haven't seen you in a while," she said, searching my eyes.

"Yes. I have been very busy."

I tried to walk around her, but she stopped me again.

"What are you doing tonight? Are you down for happy hour?"

"No, I have to study."

"So what else is new? Come on. A few of the sophomores are going for happy hour at five at Jetty's to celebrate taking our first exam."

I reminded myself about my decision to cut back on drinking and said, "I don't think I can."

"Come on!" she insisted.

Well, a drink or two wouldn't hurt me.

"Okay…only for a short while, though" I replied.

"It will be fun," she replied then winked.

"Take the shot man!" Renee, a second year and Belinda's friend, was forcing a shot glass into my hand.

"We killed that exam!" James said and downed his glass

Belinda starting chanting, "Take the shot! Take the shot!"

Soon everyone joined her with the chanting, hitting their hands on the table and chanting in unison.

Well one shot wouldn't kill me. I downed the shot to cheers and screams.

Joseph, Belinda's classmate, immediately replaced our shot glasses with new ones.

"One! Two! Three!" we all shouted then downed the glasses.

After the fourth or fifth shot glass, I had lost count. I felt the familiar buzz, and it felt good. I caught Belinda watching me, almost like I was a piece of meat, and smiled back at her.

"Let's go get a drink at the bar," I said.

"Sure," she answered.

I got up and almost stumbled out of our booth in the lounge.

"Hey, steady there," she said and held me up.

"I am sorry," I mumbled.

"Two Long Islands," I said to the bar man.

When the bar men gave us our drinks, I clicked glasses with her and downed the drink in quick succession.

I opened my eyes slowly, unsure of where I was. The room was foreign to me. The sheets were pink, and the fan was also painted pink.

Where am I?

I felt something move beside me then I glanced to my side.

Belinda was sound asleep beside, and I immediately shrank back from her, wrapping the sheets tightly around me.

It had happened again, another blackout. I did not remember anything from last night.

Before I could wallow in my humiliation, a wave of panic hit me. I wanted to get as far away from Belinda as possible.

Then a quick survey of the room answered my next logical question.

I slept with her and I have no recollection of it.

In total horror and humiliation, I quietly gathered my clothing, careful not to wake her up, and practically ran out of the room, ignoring my pounding headache.

When I finally got to my apartment, I checked my phone and was immediately confronted with guilt. Nikky had called me three times.

I called her back and gulped when she answered.

"Where have you been? I thought we were supposed to study yesterday."

"Yeah… I just overslept," I answered hating myself for lying to her.

"Are you okay? You sound tired? Should I come over?"

"No!" I quickly answered. "I'll come join you in school."

"Okay, bye," she answered then hung up.

I lay back on my bed in disbelief. How did this happen again? I thought I was over this, that if I controlled my drinking, there would be no more blackouts.

I immediately began to go over the events of last night in my head. I remembered the happy hour, some vodka shots, and then having drinks with Belinda at the bar. I racked my brain, but I didn't remember much after that.

What had I done last night? *What did I do?*

Just accept that you are a mess up, I thought to myself.

I was definitely going to lose Nikky's friendship if she found out what I did.

The scariest part was that I wasn't even sure of what I did.

I decided to take one last drink right now. I needed something to make me feel a little better, then I would empty and discard all the bottles of alcohol I had.

I half dragged myself out of bed and poured myself a glass of alcohol from a bottle I kept. I gulped quickly then filled another glass. Two glasses of alcohol wouldn't hurt me.

I could control my drinking if I really tried to. I wasn't so bad after all.

I wouldn't lose Nikky. I *couldn't* lose her.

I would have to talk the second years at the happy hour, find out exactly what happened then tell them to keep it quiet. Yes, that would work.

I would not drink anymore. It was as simple as that.

I began to empty all the alcoholic bottles in the house into the kitchen sink.

"I will not touch alcohol again," I said to myself, after the last bottle of alcohol was emptied.

I am not an alcoholic.

Chapter Forty-Nine

Sola

Rough hands, many voices.
"What is going on! Where am I?" I scream.
No words, they don't answer.
Pushed, shoved, carried.
I open my mouth to scream again.
Gagged.
Laughter.
"Why are they laughing? Please make them stop!"
But they don't...

I try to scream again, and this time I hear my voice.

I woke up with the sounds of my own screams unrecognizable to me as Irene's soothing voice said, "Shhhh. You are fine, Sola. You are fine. It's just a bad dream." She climbed into the bed next to me and held her arms around me protectively.

"Oh, no! Oh, no! No!" I screamed repeatedly.

Irene began to rock me back and forth in her arms, "Sola, it's okay. You are here, safe in your own room."

I finally stopped screaming, but I couldn't control my crying. Every time I tried to control the crying by telling myself, *"Sola, stop, control yourself. You look odd."*

I could hear myself screaming.

I could hear myself sobbing but could not control my emotions.

The pain in my heart was like a pot boiling over, always threatening to come to the surface and, when it did, I could never quite put the tight lid back on. Irene continued rubbing my back as she let me cry.

Tina rushed into the room, looking harried and tired. She quietly observed the scene then she said softly, "Are you all right, Sola? Do you need anything?"

Irene answered for me, "I think we all need some coffee or hot chocolate."

Tina rushed out of the room, seemingly relieved to be away from the uncomfortable situation. I felt so embarrassed for causing a scene. I disentangled myself from Irene's embrace saying, "I just had a bad dream, Irene. I am okay now. I think some hot chocolate will do us some good."

Irene regarded me for a moment before she replied, "Sola, I think that was more than a dream. Are you sure you are okay?"

"I have been going through some stress lately."

"Well, if you are sure you are okay."

I quickly glanced at my alarm clock. It was four in the morning, and I was annoyed at myself for creating such an uproar in the house. The whole episode was puzzling to me. I never behaved like that, even during the worst time of my life. I always made sure to disguise my emotions. In fact, I prided myself in being inscrutable.

I needed the blades to ease the pain again.

I knew what had pushed me over the edge tonight: physically touching Tayo Smith at that football game while suppressing everything I felt for him culminated in this breakdown tonight. The constant worry about my brother and my mother certainly did not help matters.

I immediately dialed Dare's number.

"Please pick up!" I pleaded to the ringtone. I ended the call with irritation when I heard his familiar voice mail message.

I needed to talk to Dare. I needed to talk to someone, and if I didn't, all I could do to relieve the tension was the blades. I really didn't want to do it, not tonight, but I was in pain. I lay in bed tossing restlessly and then impulsively dialed Ladi's number.

"Hello," he answered groggily. "Sola, what's up? Why are you calling so early?"

"I couldn't go back to sleep, and I decided to call," I lied.

"Are you sure everything is fine? It's that trouble maker, Nikky, right?" he asked.

I laughed and replied, "No, it isn't. I was just stressed and tired. I needed someone to talk to."

There was a lengthy silence on the phone. I could almost hear him thinking, "Why are you speaking to me instead of your boyfriend?"

I continued quickly, "Dare is busy. I couldn't reach him."

"No problem, Sola. What was stressing you out? Grades? Don't worry about that. You will do better next time."

"It's not the grade, Ladi. I was upset about grades in general, but, Ladi…Ladi, do you think mental illness runs in families?"

He paused before he answered, "There could be a genetic component, but I believe that an individual is different from a family and, just because you might have that in your history, it doesn't mean you have to manifest the traits.

"Sola…what happened?" he added.

I wanted to tell him everything at that moment but knew I couldn't.

I trusted Ladi enough to share parts but not all of myself.

"Remember that day I started the conversation about my mother but stopped?" I started

"Yes, that day in the reading room."

"My mother and I…we have a complicated relationship. So many things…so many things have gone wrong, and it affected my brother and me. I am…I am so angry with her. She…she changed after we moved from Nigeria, over the years. She became irrational…a little bit paranoid and depressed. Her mental health is fragile. I was…my family is struggling with so many things."

I felt the tears in the corner of my eye as memories began to flood my mind.

I continued, "Do you know how it feels to be perpetually angry? I am angry at her. I am angry with God. I am angry at life. I am always angry, Ladi! I am angry because she didn't even consider trying to help me in Nigeria after…"

Ladi asked gently, "After what Sola?"

This was the part I could never tell him, or at least not yet.

"I can't tell you now, Ladi. Maybe I will later. I feel so guilty sometimes about leaving John on his own to deal with her. She left the house in Michigan some months ago. We don't know where she is."

There was another silence on the phone, and I began to question my decision to open up to Ladi.

"Sola...it will get better. Life is not a fairy tale, but I have learned to trust God in all things. I have learned to trust no matter how I feel and, trust me, life has been difficult."

"You don't understand, Ladi. You have perfect parents."

"Your mother has tried all she can, Sola, but she is a flawed human being just like you and I. Does the past affect you? Yes, it certainly does, but it does not have to affect your future. Your future is in your hands."

His words made perfect sense but didn't abate the anger.

"What do you do when life is falling apart and you feel so lonely and isolated, even when you have friends?" I asked, abruptly changing the subject.

"Do you really want to know?" he asked.

"Yes," I answered.

"Well, I turn to God. He is all I have and has always been there for me."

"Honestly, God and I are not on speaking terms."

"Why not, Sola?"

"He abandoned me when I needed Him the most."

There was a long silence.

"I felt He abandoned me when my brother died. I did everything right, Sola. Femi did everything right, but he still died. Sometimes when we feel abandoned by God is when He is the most available to us."

There was another silence.

"If you say so, Ladi," I replied, unconvinced.

I glanced at my alarm clock. It was five thirty in the morning, so I said, "I am so sorry for keeping you up, Ladi. I should let you go now."

"No problem, Sola, anytime. Thank you for sharing this with me."

"Thanks for listening, Ladi."

I hung up the phone, replaying Ladi's words in my head: "When we feel abandoned by God is when He is most available to us."

B cells keep in touch with the helper T cells
Like Jay and B
B cells become plasma cells
Antibodies not far behind the plasma's

I watched the scene with a mixture of distaste and amusement. I found myself laughing despite the fact that Tayo was the source of the amusement. We were in the lecture hall of 1007 for what Dr. Ho had aptly named the "American Immunology Pop Idol of 2008". It was traditional that for ten percent of our grade, we were divided into groups, and each group had to perform a certain immunology concept. No PowerPoints, lecture notes, or talking to your audience was allowed. As a result of this, all sorts of hilarity ensued.

Nikky had dressed up as Janet Jackson and led her group to a choreography of "Rhythm Nation" to explain killer T cells. Even Ladi had performed with them. I was beside myself with laughter. My group had performed prior to Tayo's, and we had performed a version of *The Maury Povich Show* with DNA dispute to explain genetics. I played one of the baby mamas. I had to bite my cheeks so I would not burst out laughing.

"Tayo Zeezee! In the HIZZHOUSE!" Tayo exclaimed when he finished performing his song with his backup singers, Ego and Tina.

The whole class erupted into applause.

"Thanks! Thank you! I love you, Chicago!" he screamed to the microphone, mimicking rappers in award shows.

I watched him calmly. He looked so confident and happy, like he had no care in the world. He probably didn't. He and Nikky were studying together again, and all was dandy in the world of Tayo Smith.

Well, all wasn't well with my world. My world was in shambles. I dug my nails into my chair tightly and watched him dance back to his seat, high-fiving the guys along the way.

Don't worry Sola, your transfer will soon go through, I reminded myself.

The dean of the school in Michigan had emailed me and reassured me that my application was being reviewed. But I was sill torn. I wanted to be a part of this till the end, the annual football games, the late night study sessions with Nikky, the Stedman traditions, and Ladi. I thought my home was with Dare and John, but as I looked around and saw Nikky talking animatedly to Ladi, Irene giggling with Thomas at the back of the class, and Tina whispering what I was sure was the latest bit of gossip to Lenny, I wasn't so sure where home was anymore. I wanted to stay. I really did, but I couldn't...

And it wasn't fair.

Life isn't fair, honey, I reminded myself.

Well, it didn't have to be unfair to me.

I packed my laptop in resignation and quietly exited the hall with the sounds of my classmates' laughter, completely oblivious to my pain, replaying in my head, mocking my sadness.

My plan was to take a nap at home, but sleep eluded me. It was early in the morning, and I was still wide awake. I had been crying since I got back from school. I locked myself in my room, and I wept softly. What I really wanted to do was to wail loudly. I wanted someone else to at least hear my pain if they couldn't feel it. I wanted to know I wasn't the only person in the world who felt like this. But I cried silently because private pain could not be shared in the open. No one could be trusted with it.

So I cried and cried and cried and used the pillows to muffle the sounds so my housemates wouldn't hear me, when all I really wanted was for someone to hear me.

Then when I couldn't cry any longer, I found a new unopened blade I had purchased and did my self-destructive dance again.

Same hand, same direction of cutting, same scars, then finally the physical pain taking my attention away from the emotional pain. It was my temporary fix. My very own personal poison.

I looked at the scars on my hand and picked at them. All that was left of the physical pain was my sore arms. I still couldn't sleep though, and soon the tears began to fall again.

Why don't you end this? Do you want to be in pain all the time? I heard a voice ask.

"I don't want to be in pain anymore, but I can't do that. What about John and Dare?" I answered back.

You can end this pain. Isn't it unbearable to you?

It is.

Then just end it.

I can't.

Why? You don't have the courage to. It takes a certain amount of courage to do it. Be courageous, Sola.

"I can't. My brother. My boyfriend," I pleaded.

Then you are a coward.

"I am not," I halfheartedly answered back to myself.

You are a coward.

"No!" I protested as I drifted off to sleep.

I went to bed with the same words replaying over and over in my head,

You are a coward, Sola. You don't have to be in pain anymore. You can end this.

Chapter Fifty

Ladi

As I headed to the discussion rooms to study, I shook my head in frustration.

It was hard to believe that we were all back in the rooms studying for another exam.

Sola and Lenny were already in a room studying.

"Hey, guys," I said casually.

"Hey," they all replied, barely raising their head from the laptop.

I quietly settled down beside Sola and brought up my laptop.

Today is going to be a very long day, I thought to myself and glanced toward Sola and Lenny, who were concentrating on their laptop screens.

I watched Sola as she ran her hands down her hair and stretched her neck. Her motion accentuated her long lashes. I liked the way they curved upward, almost at an angle. I had never really noticed them until today.

Get a hold of yourself, Ladi, I admonished myself.

Sola caught my eye and smiled at me.

"Somebody is bored already. The lecture notes are that way," she said pointing to my laptop.

My reply was interrupted by Lenny saying "What are the characteristics of the paramyxovirus? Go."

"Well, they are negative sense single-stranded RNA viruses," Sola replied.

"And picornaviruses: what is unique about them?"

"An icosahedral capsid," Sola replied.

Lenny then proceeded to mercilessly quiz us about the fifty or so viruses we somehow had to memorize before the exam.

"I am exhausted," Sola finally protested. "I need a break."

"I could use a break too," I echoed.

"Didn't you just start studying, Ladi? You don't need a break," she said, wagging her finger at me.

There she was, being the Sola that I enjoyed being around, the playful and witty one. But I knew it wouldn't last; one phone call, and she would become melancholy again.

She continued, "Let's go to the room with the cross. Play me *Heaven* again."

"Okay," I replied.

"You guys better not take a three-hour break. I expect you all back!" Lenny called from the room.

"Yes, Dad," I replied, meeting Sola's laughing eyes.

We walked out the door into the corridors and bumped into Tina carrying a pile of books.

"Hey Tina," we both greeted.

"Hey, guys," Tina answered, fixing a puzzling gaze on both of us and emphasizing the word *guys*.

I turned to Sola and asked, "What was that look for?"

Sola answered, "Well, apparently, everyone is convinced we are dating."

"Dating? Why would anyone think we were dating?" I asked.

"Well, because according to her, we are always together," Sola said, shaking her head.

Tina did have a point, and if Tina noticed this, my whole class probably did, too. But we were study partners, and we had to spend a lot of time with each other. But I failed to convince myself that was the reason I spent so much time with Sola. My complicated feelings towards our deepening friendship and the existence of her boyfriend were probably indications that we had to cut back on the time we spent together. But our relationship has always been purely professional, so it didn't warrant any drastic measures.

Yes. I had feelings for her but I would not act on those feelings, so we were safe.

We walked down winding stairs leading to the basement rooms and walked into the room with the cross.

"It's amazing, right? Stedman is a school filled with so much history and steeped in so much tradition. This building must be like…what? A hundred years old?" I said as we walked in.

She walked to the grand piano and ran her hands over the keys.

"Yes, rooms like these are cool," she replied distractedly.

I sat next to her on the piano and began to play. She watched me silently for a while. She gingerly placed her small hands on mine, strumming the keys with me.

"Your hands are cold!" I exclaimed. "And soft also."

She smiled and tried to keep up with me as my hands moved from key to key. She couldn't, so she repeatedly pressed the wrong keys. The melodic and soothing sounds of Vari's *Heaven* now sounded like a cacophony, no thanks to Sola.

"Sola, stop it," I said, smiling at her and swatting her hands away.

"I want to learn, Ladi!" she said. "Stop it, Ladi, and teach me how to play!"

"Well, darling," I said, putting on a fake British accent. "You are positively and absolutely hopeless, and I don't have all day. I will teach you some other time when we don't have an exam."

"You, sir, are not a gentleman," she replied, laughing.

"Frankly, my dear," I started and moved inches away from her face. "I don't give a damn."

"*Gone with the Wind*!" she exclaimed. "Let me guess. You read the book?" she asked, hitting me playfully on the shoulder.

"I read the book, of course."

"How many girly books do you read, Ladi?" she asked and dissolved into laughter.

"Excuse me, Sola. There is no such thing as a girly book. There are just books. I read voraciously, that's all," I answered.

She continued, "Well, it just doesn't seem like the type of book a typical *naija* guy would read."

She paused to gauge my reaction and then laughed.

"So we are back to this conversation again. So, Sola. Tell me: what is a typical Nigerian boy?" I asked, amused.

"Well, you know, probably more into hip-hop, Nigerian music, chasing girls, that type of stuff…" She trailed off with that wicked smile in her eyes.

"Wow, I don't even have a suitable reply for that grossly inaccurate assessment, Sola," I replied, shaking my head.

"You don't have a suitable reply because you know I am right," she said.

"Is that what your boyfriend does?" I asked.

"Well, apart from the chasing girls part. I would hope not," she replied and then smiled.

"Ladi," she started, suddenly becoming somber again

"What?" I asked.

"I wanted to let you know first. Please, don't let anyone, especially Nikky, know," she started.

I was immediately curious. Was she going to tell me the secrets she kept behind those closely veiled eyes?

She started, "I am leaving Stedman after this first year. I just started the process to transfer medical schools."

I stopped playing the piano and looked at her quizzically.

"Why? Aren't you happy here?" I asked.

"I am, but I want to be close to my brother and Dare."

My heart sank. She had a very plausible reason to transfer schools, but did she realize how insanely difficult the process was? Plus, I had to admit to myself that I didn't want her to leave.

"Sola, the process is extremely difficult. I think I read an article that said the deans of both schools have to be involved."

"I know, but I have to go," she said and set her lip in that stubborn line.

"Sola, I know you miss your life in Michigan but it's rare for medical schools to accept transfers in the first or second year. Why don't you try in the third year? It's more plausible."

"I know all that, Ladi, but I can't stay here. I have to leave."

"Sola..."

"Ladi..."

"You have really made your decision? It's final?"

"Yes, I have."

"Then we better make the most of the time we have together then," I replied.

"We will," she replied, looking directly at me.

But I think we both had different interpretations of the statement. She wanted to enjoy her time with her study partner turned friend, while I wanted to spend time with the woman that had taken over my thoughts.

Chapter Fifty-One

Sola

Ladi looked so upset after I told him. He concentrated on playing the song on the piano and didn't speak to me

I wanted to tell him the truth, but I couldn't.

It would be painful to watch Ladi's eyes, that always regarded me with respect, to fill with pity. I detested pity. There was a sting to pity; pity was insulting.

"I wish things were better. I do," I said and lay my head on his shoulder.

He stopped playing, and I felt him relax his shoulders.

He said, "They are better, Sola. You just have to think like it's better and soon it will get better."

Ladi always knew the right thing to say to me, but I wasn't always certain of his convictions. He was a product of his experiences. Loving parents, plus a Christian home, equaled a well-behaved son. The fact that he had such a positive outlook on life wasn't rocket science.

For this very reason, he fascinated me. I had never met anyone so uncompromising about his Christianity. It wasn't a religion to him; he really believed with all his heart.

I was used to the superficial Christian culture of Nigeria. You went to church on Sunday because everyone did. You sang the hymns in class because you were required to do so. You prayed because everyone was praying, and you looked bad if you didn't.

I have never been around anyone so passionate about his beliefs.

I had also never met a Nigerian man who read *Gone with the Wind* and *Pride and Prejudice.*

Or maybe I had to change the caliber of Nigerian men I exposed myself to, I concluded and chuckled out loud.

He glanced at me, amused, and said, "Share the joke, please."

"Nothing," I replied, smiling.

We sat in comfortable silence for a while.

Ladi broke the silence by saying, "We should head back up now, Sola. We don't want Lenny to call the campus police to search for us."

Lenny was the unofficial taskmaster of the bigger group, always making sure we were at our A-game for studying. Anytime I didn't make it to the discussion room on time, I could trust Lenny to blow up my phone with texts and phone calls insisting that I better come study.

I laughed and replied, "For real. I can't endure another fifteen minute lecture about my study habits."

We walked back to the discussion room in silence, and Ladi suddenly said, "I will really miss you when you leave."

I couldn't meet his eye when he said that because I knew I would burst into tears.

I really didn't want to leave! Life was so unfair!

Then I spotted the reason for transferring medical schools, the person who had caused me many sleepless nights, who was the reason my left arm was bandaged under my long-sleeved shirt.

Tayo Smith.

He looked like he had no care in the world. He walked towards us and smiled in greeting.

My heart began to beat wildly.

This was what I went through every time I saw him, every time someone mentioned his name, every time he had the audacity to smile at me. I wasn't going to play this game today. I was done with it!

"See you in the discussion room," I said quickly to Ladi, ignoring Tayo's raised hand of greeting.

I heard him ask Ladi, "What was that about?"

I paused in front of the door to the discussion room and wiped tears off my face.

God, I am so tired, so tired.

I walked into the discussion room, grateful to find it empty.

I sat on my chair and buried my face in my hands in frustration. I could feel myself losing control again. I could feel the emotions, especially the rage, bubbling to the surface.

Soon tears began to fall down my face. *Stop it, Sola! Stop it!* I admonished myself.

But I couldn't stop.

I had to control myself before Lenny and Ladi walked back in. I picked up my cell phone and headed to the bathroom. There were six missed calls from Dare.

I immediately called him back. He answered after the first ring.

"Why haven't you been picking up your phone?"

My heart immediately sank. He sounded angry.

"I was away from my phone. I am sorry."

"Whatever Sola. We haven't spoken to each other for over two weeks and you don't seem bothered by it at all," he answered gruffly.

I don't need this right now, not in this emotional state. But I knew Dare and there was no way I was going to get out of this unscathed. When Dare wanted a fight, Dare got a fight.

I chose my words carefully and said, "Dare, I have an exam. I have so much to study."

"Isn't the exam on Monday? You have three whole days to study. If I were your priority, you would keep in touch with me."

"What do you mean? You don't even understand the amount of work I have to do. Three days isn't enough!"

"Oh, medical school has made you too arrogant to keep in touch with your little minions in Michigan? Tell me, Sola, have you even spoken to your mother?"

I didn't trust myself to respond.

I whispered into the phone, "Why are you saying this, Dare? What is really going on?"

"I am here in Michigan, taking care of your brother, keeping tabs on your..." he trailed off.

"Finish it. Say it! My crazy mother! You cruel bastard! How dare you think of saying such to me!"

"Do you think I like having to schedule phone conversations with you? I would like to have my house to myself, but I have your brother with me! I am sacrificing a lot for you, and a phone call from you every now and then is not too much to ask!"

I immediately felt guilty.

"Dare, stop acting like this. You don't know how busy I am. I am trying my best!"

"Whatever, Sola. When you are ready to be a girlfriend, then give me a call. Otherwise, goodbye."

"Dare! Dare!" I screamed into the phone, but he had hung up.

I immediately tried calling him back, but his phone repeatedly went to voice mail.

"I don't need this! I don't need this," I repeatedly said to myself.

But I needed Dare. I couldn't do this without him.

I tried calling him one last time, but his phone went straight to voice mail again.

Why was he being so stubborn?

I immediately sent Nikky a text.

Nikky meet me in the blue bathroom next to the discussion rooms ASAP please.

I walked into an empty stall in the bathroom and locked myself in, rocking back and forth on the toilet seat.

I refused to think, because if I did I would get angrier. If I got angry enough, I could do anything to myself. I was safe in the bathroom. In the bathroom, I couldn't hurt myself.

Soon I heard Nikky's purposeful steps walk gingerly into the bathroom. "Sola, are you here?" she called out.

"I am here," I called out. My voice sounded muffled, even to me.

She swung open the door slowly and squeezed herself into the bathroom.

"Sola, what's wrong? What happened? Oh, you look so sad. Come, let me give you a hug," she said, and she stroked my hair.

"Dare and I just had a horrible fight!" I said and then burst into tears again.

"Sola, it's okay. It's okay."

She managed to sit down beside me on the tiny toilet seat, and she wrapped her arms around me, enveloping me in a hug.

"You guys will make up soon. Don't worry," she added.

"He thinks I don't call him enough," I continued.

"Please! Dare doesn't understand how medical school is!" she scoffed.

"But now he is not picking up my phone calls! I am so mad right now."

"Sola, don't worry. This is what we are going to do. Tina and Irene are coming over to my house so we can study. You can pick your favorite ice cream, and we can have a girls' night in–man-bashing study session."

I cracked a smile in spite of myself.

Nikky grinned widely and said, "You see! Girl, there's no point crying over guys. They are from a different planet!"

"Give me a little more ice cream!" Nikky complained as Irene dished the ice cream into big bowls on the center table in the kitchen.

"Gosh, Nikky, that will be enough for you. You've already finished the first carton of ice cream that we bought," Irene answered firmly, taking the serving spoon from Nikky.

"No, I didn't! Tina helped me with that!" Nikky exclaimed.

"I took only one spoon," Tina answered from the living room where she was lying on a couch with her eyes buried in a past question booklet.

I half listened to the conversation with amusement. I really did not want to be here at this moment, but I came at Nikky's insistence that it would make me feel better.

"What do you want to do? You want to spend the rest of the night crying in your bed and calling him every thirty minutes?" she asked.

That was exactly what I intended on doing.

"No," I answered unconvincingly. "I just want to go to bed."

"You are not fooling me, Sola. You want to go and cry in bed, and I won't allow you to do that."

"Okay," I answered resignedly.

But I had to admit as we sat in the living room going over the past questions, the fight with Dare became a distant memory. I was still hurt though, and my mind replayed the conversation again and again in my head. Dare, of all people, understood that my sanity was hanging by a thread. Any major disruption was enough to tip me over the edge. Throwing such baseless accusations at me was cruel and uncalled for.

Besides Dare knew everything about me, and there were no secrets with him.

I turned my attention back to the conversation the girls were having, I would deal with Dare and his accusations after the exam. Failing the exam and consequently, the unit, would ruin my chances of transferring to another school, and that would be my worst nightmare come true.

"I haven't seen that girl. What's her name…Ego? I haven't seen her in class for a while," Tina said.

"It's close to another exam. She will probably come back and ask Tayo for help with studying again. I don't know why she can't study with her *boyfriend,* Ben," Nikky said with her eyes flashing.

"You seem bothered by the fact that Tayo will be helping her," Irene said teasingly.

"And spending lots of time with her," Tina chimed in, not taking her eyes off her past question booklet.

"Please, I trust Tayo."

She cocked her head to the side then said with sass, "Let's keep this between us, but Tayo and I will soon be official."

My heart stopped when I heard her. No, I didn't want her to date him. The close study-buddy relationship was bad enough, but for her to be his girlfriend was inconceivable to me.

"What! Girl, you've been holding out on us. Tell us what's really going on," Tina said and edged closer to Nikky.

"Well, we are exclusive friends for now. We are going slow until it becomes official."

"Exclusive friends?" Irene asked.

"Yes. We don't want to move to fast, or he doesn't want us to move to fast."

Nikky sighed then clutched her heart dramatically, "Gosh, guys! Is this how love feels!? I am so in love with him, and he's so gorgeous! I think I am going to marry him."

Tina chuckled then said, "Nikky, I don't think you should start planning a wedding anytime soon. How do you even know that he's the one?"

"Because I had a vision the first time I saw him," Nikky answered.

We all stared back at her blankly.

She continued, "I saw a vision of him and our first child, a girl."

I exchanged quick glances with Tina and Irene. Tina tried to hold back laughter but burst out laughing. Irene soon joined her.

"You guys!" Nikky protested. "Stop laughing!" she insisted then she began to laugh too.

I couldn't even crack a smile. Nothing Nikky said was funny to me. If I was previously unsure about transferring medical schools, I wasn't anymore. I did not want to be here to witness Nikky and Tayo together as a couple. But if for some reason I stayed back in Stedman, I would not allow a relationship to develop between them.

I would do whatever was in my power to stop it.

"Let's go back to studying," Irene said after the laughter died down.

We went over the past question swiftly, pausing to explain questions that were unclear.

But my mind kept drifting back to Dare, and I could barely concentrate. I repeatedly checked my cell phone, hoping for a phone call or text from him.

My phone stubbornly remained silent.

I quickly suppressed my anger and concentrated on studying.

Everything that was wrong with my life at this moment was one man's fault.

Tayo Smith's.

Chapter Fifty-Two

Tayo

"Nikky, please stop talking on the phone so we can go over these flash cards!" I shouted at Nikky for the umpteenth time that day.

The exam was days away, and this kid insisted on talking on the phone, which was annoying, especially because she was the one who set up the study session.

"Mommy! I have to go now," she said and hung up.

I was lying on the floor of her bedroom, going over the flash cards while listening to Asa's new album on my iPod using only one ear of my headphones.

Nikky lay beside me on the floor and said, "Give me a few flash cards."

She snatched them from me and began to flip through them also.

"What are you listening to?" she asked, grabbing the headphones.

"Asa."

Nikky listened to the music with one half of the headphones and then said, "Oh, I like her. She sounds really good! I love her."

I smiled at Nikky. We lay on the floor for a while in complete silence, but you could trust Nikky not to keep quiet for more than five minutes.

She said, "Tayo, don't you think it's time we move from the exclusive friendship zone to the relationship zone?"

I groaned inwardly. I had managed to dodge that conversation until now. I absolutely was not ready for the title of relationship, not after the disaster with Belinda.

I finally got the nerve to call Belinda, and I asked her exactly what had happened that night.

"Nothing much," Belinda answered with a chuckle. "You got very touchy-feely when you got the alcohol in your system. Then we went to my apartment."

"So I didn't do anything else embarrassing," I probed.

"Well, I was pretty wasted too, but I don't think so."

I breathed a sigh of relief then said, "Okay...please, Belinda, can you keep this between us?"

She laughed and said, "I should be asking you the same thing. Gossip spreads in Stedman. If it gets out, everyone will call me the slut that hooked up with a first year and you will be the player that hooked up with a second year. Trust me. I want this to be kept a secret."

I ended the conversation feeling slightly more confident that Nikky would never find out what happened. I really did not want to hurt her.

I had feelings for her, but I knew that I wasn't ready for a committed relationship with her. It would not work.

"Nikky, can we have this conversation after the exam? I am not ready yet." I replied.

"But we have to define our relationship. I am not a let's-hang-out-and-see-where-things-go type of girl. I need us to have a definition to our friendship."

"Nikky, what we have is great. I think pressuring ourselves to define it will destroy what we have."

"Tayo, I don't understand your reasoning. We are practically in a relationship already. All your reasons for this 'exclusive friendship' sound like excuses. First it's 'we need to ease into a relationship', then it's 'you don't trust me enough'."

She gave me a pointed look and added, "What's really going on?"

"It's not that I don't trust you, Nikky. Honestly, I don't want us to get too deep into a relationship then you withdraw from me when you find out more things about me."

She turned off the iPod then said, "Find out more things like what?"

"I am not ready to talk, Nikky. Please can we just drop the subject?"

My past was not something I particularly enjoyed dwelling on. Most of my memories were fragmented because I was usually under the influence of something, whether it be cocaine or alcohol. But the memories that came to me at the most inopportune moments were frightening, like my nightmares. I sometimes hoped they were figments of my imagination and not actual memories.

She studied me for a moment then said, "I will drop it for now, but we have to talk after the exam."

"Sure," I answered, half distracted by my beeping phone. It was Hassan, an old friend from my teenage years. We were both mutual friends of Dotun, who was a cousin of Sola's boyfriend, Dare. After Sola's cold behavior towards me in the corridor that day, I called Hassan on a whim. I couldn't dismiss her behavior any longer. There had to be a reasonable explanation for it, and I was determined to find out.

"Hey, my guy! Longest time," I answered.

I quickly walked out into the living room so we could have some privacy.

"Hey, what's up?" he answered back. "I heard your message about Dare Martins."

"Yeah, so he's Dotun Martin's cousin, right?"

"Yes, he is," Hassan answered.

"So did we hang out with him at all? There's something about the guy that bothers me."

There was a long pause before Hassan answered, "Tayo, it's better if we let sleeping dogs lie. There's no need for us to be having this conversation."

So I was right. I must have encountered Dare somewhere in my past. Hassan's clipped answers proved it.

"I am not asking for his social security number, just how I met him." I said.

"Well, you know the answer to that one. He is Dotun's cousin, and we were friends with Dotun."

"Is there anything else?"

"No," Hassan answered curtly.

There was a long silence then he said, "*Abeg*, my guy, can I call you back? I am kind of busy."

"Wait. Do you know his girlfriend? Her name is Sola. She's my classmate."

Hassan's sharp intake of breath answered my question.

He knew her.

"Tayo, listen to me carefully. Let things be. There is no need to ruffle any feathers."

"Hassan, I am not sixteen anymore. You can't protect me by keeping secrets about my mistakes from me just like you did that night."

I was talking about the events of the night recorded in the blue folder in Nigeria. Hassan had kept in touch over the years, but we never referred to that night. We always acted like it never happened. I think we both convinced ourselves that it didn't happen. "Shut up," Hassan hissed sharply. "What night? Don't ever talk about that to me."

"Hassan, look man. We haven't spoken in a while. I am just trying to piece together my puzzling thoughts."

There was a long silence on the phone.

"See the girl, Sola, she acts so odd around me, like she's afraid of me. Sometimes she acts like she hates me," I said in a rush.

"You said she's in your med school," Hassan asked.

"Yes."

There was another long silence, and I added, "Please, Hassan, tell me what you know."

"I can't tell you over the phone," he finally answered. "I can come down to Stedman in about five months. Work has got me in Europe, and this is not a conversation we should have on the phone."

"Okay," I answered, finally relieved that I would get the answers to my questions.

"Tayo, listen…just be careful," Hassan added.

"I will."

"No, really. Don't do anything stupid until I come to see you."

"Okay. I guess we will keep in touch then," I said.

"Okay. Bye," he said then hung up.

I walked back into the room and lay on the floor next to Nikky.

She offered me some flash cards and placed one side of the headphones on my ear.

I tried studying the flash cards, but I couldn't concentrate. I almost felt like this was the calm before the storm, that my conversation with Hassan would turn my life upside down.

I wondered if it was indeed true that human beings could be forgiven for anything.

"Nikky," I started.

She turned to me and said, "Yes, Tayo?"

"Nikky, do you really believe we can be forgiven for anything we do in life, no matter how bad?"

"Oh, no," she started. "Whose heart did you break this time?" She laughed.

"Nikky, I am serious," I replied.

She regarded me for a moment and then said, "I think so. I guess so. I mean the Bible says so, so it must be true."

"No matter how bad?"

"Yes, no matter how bad. I barely paid attention in my Sunday school class, but there were no exceptions. It said you could be forgiven."

"Because, Nikky..." I started and then sat up.

"What?" she asked.

"Nothing. I did a few wild things in my past, you know, and sometimes I am weighed down by guilt. The worst part is that I can't remember everything I did because I was so drugged up."

She paused, searching my eyes with hers and then asked, "When did you stop using drugs?"

"I just stopped one day. I was bored with everything really. It was getting repetitive. The partying, the women, everything." I massaged my temples as my head flooded with memories

"Then I broke my leg and came here," I completed with a half-smile.

"But it's the past, Tayo, so you've moved on from it. But I do have to add that you need to ease up on the liquor," she said, fixing a stern glare at me. "I was embarrassed for you after the drunken stunts you pulled during that party."

"I know," I replied somberly.

"Aww, it's okay," Nikky said, and then she grabbed my cheeks like one would do a child's. "At least you know it's a problem now," she continued.

She suddenly stood up and started singing along to the song playing on the iPod, "No one knows tomorrow!"

She started doing this odd dance where she twisted her waist from side to side.

"Get up," she said, grabbing me and pulling me up.

"Oh, Nikky," I groaned.

"Get up!" she insisted.

She held my hands and proceeded to force me to dance with her to Asa's song "No One Knows."

"No one knows tomorrow. Forget the past!" she said in a sing-song voice. I laughed and moved along with her to the music.

Nikky was right: the past was done with. All that mattered now was the future. But what if the past had somehow managed to rear its ugly head now and consequently affect my future?

"Ben, please, I need you. Don't leave, let's not end our relationship like this!" Ego pleaded.

Why did I always find myself yet again in these positions? I was going to the discussion rooms like a good "exclusive friend, not boyfriend" as ordered by Nikky. The corridor was uncharacteristically empty, but then I caught Ben Odojie and Ego in a heated argument in the corridor. I did not want to interrupt them, thereby creating an embarrassing situation for me, so I quietly stayed out of their sight in the doorway, hoping the lover's tiff would be short.

"I cannot continue in this relationship. What you did was unacceptable, Ego," Ben replied, disentangling himself from Ego's embrace

"What's so good about her? Why won't you choose me? I love you. I need your help to study," she replied with a rising edge to her voice

"Ego, please don't make this harder. You don't need me to study. You called Tayo Smith the last time. You can do that again,"

Ben replied coldly, before walking away and leaving Ego crying in the corridor.

I winced when he mentioned my name. Why did trouble always find me? Even when I wasn't looking for it. She kept crying in the corridor then turned to face me directly. I gave her a tentative smile then said the first thing that came to my mind, "Let's go to McDonald's for lunch. I am in the mood to splurge. We could catch up with studying, *jist* about life."

Her small laugh told me I had said the right thing.

"The truth is that these girls don't know me. They don't understand my life and they make these harsh judgments about me," Ego said, then dipped her fry slowly into the ketchup.

She looked so vulnerable when she spoke.

I reached out to her poised hand over another fry and said, "It's not like that."

"It's true. They don't know half my story. You wouldn't understand, Tayo. Your life is perfect."

When we first got to McDonald's I carefully avoided talking about her argument with Ben. We talked generally about life in medical school before the conversation led to Nikky and her animosity towards Ego.

I laughed then said, "No one's life is perfect, Ego."

"Well it can't be as messed up as mine, Tayo."

"Ego, stop crying. It's okay."

"It's not okay," I replied. "Tayo, you don't know the half of it. I am a *side piece* to a man with a fiancée. To put it bluntly, I am a mistress. I didn't plan on being in this situation. It just happened..."

Her words shocked me into silence.

Then I said, "Your life isn't that bad. If we are playing the 'my life is more messed up than yours' game, I have something to share. Alcohol makes me do stupid things."

I leaned closer to me then said, "I slept with a chick, and I have absolutely no recollection of it. Can you imagine?"

"That's bad. Okay, maybe you have me beaten in this game."

"You see! Your life isn't that bad!" I said then laughed.

"So who was the lucky woman?"

"Ego, promise you will keep this between us."

"I promise."

"It was Belinda. She's a second year."

"You and Nikky are somewhat of an item, right? Does she know?"

"No. So let's keep this a secret," I reiterated.

"I understand," she replied. "Thanks for sharing," she added then linked her hands with mine over the table.

"Everyone in medical school has so much drama."

"Tell me about it," I replied dryly.

That had to be the hardest exam I had taken in my entire life.

The temperature in 3019 was comfortable, but I kept wiping perspiration from my brow.

I glanced at the clock, and my heart sank. I had only five minutes left!

I quickly bubbled in the answer of the last question with barely enough time left.

Dr. Ho collected the packets from us and then chuckled slightly in front of the hall, "I told ya'll I was going to get ya'll."

I walked out of the examination hall like I was in a trance.

I am really going to fail this exam and Tayo Smith does not fail exams, I thought to myself.

My classmates around me echoed my concerns because I heard bits of conversation around me.

"What was that?"

"That was horrible!"

"I know he said it was going to be hard, but wow."

"Question forty-five was wrong and I tried to tell him…"

"Question sixty-five had no answer in the answer choices…"

"I am going to fail this unit."

Well, there was no need crying over spilt milk. I had done my best to study for that exam. Now it was time to party, without alcohol of course.

Failing an exam was worse than death to me. In fact, in med school I would have preferred to die than fail an exam.

Nikky Abe
Class of 2012

Failure was not just failure. Failure was domino effect. It meant failing the unit, then failing the retake, then failing summer school then failing ultimately out of medical school with no way to pay back your student loans.

Robb Sanderson
Class of 1974

Chapter Fifty-Three

Sola

"Ladi, that was complete disaster. I failed that exam."

"It's okay Sola, you probably didn't. The exam was really rough, but I spoke to Dr. Ho, and if enough students fail the exam, the grades will be curved."

"I need to honor the exam! I have to honor every exam! If I don't, I won't have a chance of transferring schools. Which school would want a student who messed up their academic record?" I said, hearing my voice shake. "I am in trouble," I said then buried my face in my hands crying.

He pulled me to him and hugged me.

"It's okay, Sola. Don't worry. You will do fine. One bad exam won't stop you from transferring. Stop crying," he said then stroked my hair. "If you have a strong letter from the dean and other supporting letters you should be able to transfer," he continued.

I felt a glimmer of hope. Maybe it wasn't so bad after all. I would have to wait and hope I didn't do too badly.

I held on to him for a moment and tried to calm my frayed nerves. I knew I was a hop, skip and jump away from an emotional breakdown. Nothing in my life seemed to be working right now.

Dare still wasn't speaking to me. I called him several times crying and left numerous voice messages, but still there was no response from him. Just a cryptic text message informing me that my brother was okay and still staying with him and that my mother's whereabouts were still unknown.

The mental and emotional turmoil was becoming unbearable and the simplest of actions supported me, like Ladi's hugs. This was comforting because I ordinarily hated any casual physical contact, but when Ladi held me, he really held me.

I felt safe with him.

This did not mean I had any sort of feelings for him. It meant we were really good friends. I realized my relationship with Ladi was still the source of much gossip in Stedman even after I repeatedly told Tina we were not dating.

She would cock her head to the side and say, "Are you sure? Because you guys are so perfect together!"

Then Nikky would say, "They are not dating, Tina. Stop that! I just call them the non-couple that spends all their time together."

Both of them would then burst into laughter.

It had gotten particularly irritating this week becomes it seemed like everyone wanted to know or just assumed we were a couple. Ladi and I could never be a couple. No man would want damaged goods like me, especially not someone like Ladi.

I was good enough for Dare so I would stay with Dare.

I detached myself from the embrace and then Ladi asked, "Is the boyfriend speaking to you now?"

"No," I answered. "He is being so stubborn! Ladi, he doesn't understand how much studying I have to do. It's so stressful!"

"Try to make him understand, Sola," Ladi said.

He continued with a small smile on his face. "I don't think anybody can really understand this med school thing. It's something you have to experience."

"Well, that doesn't make it less hurtful. I was looking forward to having fun this weekend, but I feel miserable."

"We have to have fun. It's my birthday!" he said.

"Really? Are you planning anything special?"

"Yes. Dinner at my house."

"Aww, that's so thoughtful of you, Ladi. The girls could cook for you. I will ask Nikky, Irene, and Tina. We could ask the student council, too, like Ronke and the rest."

He laughed and replied, "Sure, Sola. I was thinking of a very small dinner, but apparently you have other plans."

I laughed then was interrupted by my vibrating phone. I rummaged in my purse for it.

"Speak of the devil," I said after I glanced at Dare's name on the caller ID.

"Good luck," Ladi mouthed and gave me a thumbs sign before he walked away.

"Hey," I answered cautiously.

"Can you talk?" he replied gruffly.

"Yes," I said, walking into the quieter part of the school lobby.

"Sola, you really hurt me."

"Dare, you didn't even give me a chance to explain myself."

"Okay. Go ahead. Explain yourself."

"Dare, I am overwhelmed here. I am trying to do well in school despite everything. I am dealing with the transfer and worrying about you guys in Michigan. I apologize for not keeping in touch as much as you want to, but I am just overwhelmed with life."

"I understand, but it still hurts you know. I didn't hear from you for over two weeks. We went from speaking everyday on the phone to barely speaking at all."

"I know. You placed all the blame on me, and that was unfair. We both should make an effort to make our relationship work."

"Well, I am here taking care of your family. I *am* making an effort. You are not at all…" He started again, "Sola, I don't know if this is working…"

My heart sank.

"Dare please, let's just end this. There is no reason for us to be fighting. I need…" I broke down crying. "I need you. I really need you. Don't do this to me, not now. I can't lose you now."

There was a long silence then he said, "Sola…stop crying."

"I really tried to stay angry, but I have been counting down the days till we made up," he completed.

"So we are cool, baby?" I asked with my heart skipping a beat.

"Yes, we are," he answered.

He sighed then continued, "Okay. I do want you to know I am committed to us, and I want to make us work."

"Thanks, baby," I replied. "I am committed to us, too."

I felt relieved that our fight was over and the threat of a break up had been averted.

"So is everything cool in school? Tayo Smith has stayed away?"

"Yes," I answered, feeling the familiar tension creep back slowly into my heart. I did not want to talk about him, so I said, "I am in school right now. Let me call you back, Dare."

"Okay. I'll wait for your call. Stop worrying. Everything will be fine. When you are back in Michigan you will forget you were ever in the same vicinity with Tayo."

"Okay," I answered

But somehow I knew that it wasn't going to be that easy.

"I failed that exam, Sola!" Irene said immediately after I walked into our apartment.

She followed me into my room where I dropped my book bag on my bed and turned to face her.

"Irene, that exam was really hard," I replied.

"No. I know I failed," she replied resolutely "I am preparing myself to take two retakes and possibly go to summer school."

"Don't worry. Ladi said Dr. Ho will curve the grades."

Irene shook her head and said, "Sola, you don't understand. I didn't finish. There were hundred questions. I was on number sixty when time was called."

She sank into the floor of my bedroom crying, "I can't fail out of medical school! I just can't! How will I repay the student loans I took? The divorce is already costing so much. This is horrible."

I sat next to her on the floor then put my arms around her.

"It's okay," I said.

She was right. She could not afford to fail any more exams.

She looked at me, then said, "Sola, please, I really need your help… We could sit together during quizzes and exams. Be a friend to me and help me."

I froze. She still had not given up this notion of cheating. The implications of getting caught while cheating in medical school were dire. With my impending transfer, I could not risk messing up my academic record.

My phone rang on the table, saving me from having to answer her question.

"I have to pick this up," I said apologetically to her before I answered.

She watched me for a moment then walked out of my room, looking downcast.

"So what are you cooking for Ladi's birthday?" Nikky asked immediately without bothering to say hello.

"I could make some fried rice," I replied.

I heard some background noise and then some laughter

"Nooooo... Stop that, Tayo. Help me chop the onions, just stop that."

She was with him again.

"Maybe we should invite the other student council members, too, like Joanna," I continued.

"Yes...no, don't do that Tayo. Tayo, no, no!" I heard Nikky scream.

She began to laugh hysterically and scream into the phone, "Sola, tell him to stop tickling me!"

I hissed in irritation.

"What are you doing, Nikky?"

"Tayo is supposed to help me to cook dinner and he isn't helping! Tayo, come say hi to Sola!" she continued before I could protest.

"Sola, what's up!" Tayo screamed into the phone.

"Hey," I answered coolly.

"Anyway," Nikky said on the phone again. "So dinner it is then. I'll invite some other people."

"Okay," I replied. "Hey, I will talk to you later," I continued then hung up.

I suddenly felt very tired.

I hung up the phone and lay on my bed silently.

It was becoming more and more difficult for me to believe that Tayo did not remember me.

He really had to be acting and the thought of that made me even more worried.

I wondered if I was so inconsequential to him. I wouldn't be surprised if he couldn't remember, though. In high school, I had been treated like a nonentity both in school and with my family.

No one ever noticed me.

The excruciating anger began to bubble up to the surface again then I felt the familiar taut tension.

Why don't you just end this? You don't have to be in pain any longer.

It was the voice in my head again.

This time I lay on my bed, sobbing, unable to muster enough strength to even reply.

You are a coward. Sola, you don't have to feel like this any longer. Why don't you just end it?

"Stop it!" I said out loud.

I wanted to scream, but I couldn't because Irene was home, so I tossed and turned in my bed hoping that this would distract me from the voice in my head that repeatedly called me a coward for refusing to take my own life.

Then the moment came, the same dance. I became very still and got out of bed.

I made sure the door to my room was locked then went to the bathroom.

Sola, you don't have to do this...

I have to. I had no choice. If I didn't do this, I would kill myself. My pain would choke the life out of me.

With the blade and my finger poised over my arm, I paused and looked at my reflection in the mirror. I really looked at myself this time without flinching. It was then I realized the depths of my mental instability, my insanity.

I need help and I need it fast.

I decided it was time for me to see a mental health professional.

So I calmly cut myself and bandaged my arm like I usually did.

But instead of lying back in bed, I began to think of who could help me.

Ladi mentioned to me that his ex-girlfriend was in town and she was a psychology intern.

I would make an appointment with her. The issue of confidentiality immediately crossed my mind, but I realized that she was professionally bound to keep my secrets.

Yes. I have to see someone. It is definitely time for me to see someone.

The fact that I decided to speak with someone did not stop the tears from falling, did not abate my anger, did not extinguish my pain.

And so I did what I've done every night for the past few years.

I cried out to the God that I had tried but failed to convince myself did not exist.

Am I not worth something to you? Do you not love me?

Chapter Fifty-Four

Ladi

"So, tell me about this Sola girl. The girl that seems to have done the impossible," Naduah said, moving swiftly around my kitchen. She looked right at home in yet another colorful kaftan as she stirred the *obe efo* bubbling on the stove.

"Come on! Tell me the full story!" she demanded again, offering me a piece of chicken from the stew to taste.

"Well," I began wiping my eyes as fumes of the spicy stew escaped from the pot. "We are in the same class. We interviewed together...wait, before I continue, she has a boyfriend."

"No!" Naduah exclaimed. "The plot thickens! Who is this imposter that has taken over Ladi? The Ladi Adeoti I know doesn't develop feelings for random women, especially not ones with boyfriends."

"Naduah, you see now why I need an intervention," I said and laughed.

With one swift motion, I popped the piece of chicken in my mouth.

It tasted just right, soft and seasoned correctly. Naduah's cooking was just like I remembered. In true Naduah fashion, she had texted me out of the blue weeks ago to tell me she had gotten a much sought after psychology internship, and she was coming when it was closer to my birthday.

The exact text read:

I am going to call you later tonight. I got the psychology internship in DC, so you will be seeing me soon, probably on your birthday. Excited? I will need a ride from the airport!

Naduah and I are a dangerous combination, and I wasn't entirely excited that she was coming back into my life. Naduah Ibrahim is a tornado and tsunami all wrapped into one.

Naduah is interesting, to say the least. Part German, French, Italian, Caribbean and Hausa, she is as eclectic as her heritage. She is also the most strong-willed woman I know. Defying her wealthy parents, she had converted from Islam to Christianity and was promptly disowned by her father. We met at that pivotal moment in her life, when she had an emotional need for me. I also needed her to exorcise the demons of my brother's death, and together we supported one another, growing together in our Christian faith. Naduah, with the voracious appetite of a beginner who had accepted Jesus, seeking justification for her decisions, sought me out for guidance because in her words, "I was a veteran Christian." I could hardly describe myself as a veteran anything, but it brought me closer to this exquisite creature. I provided what little guidance I could and from that, our relationship grew. But no matter how much we tried, Naduah and I could never maintain a pure relationship, and we always gave in to our desires. The relationship could never quite work because of this. The guilt was unbearable to bear; I was supposed to help her grow in Christ but here I was doing with her what I knew was clearly a sin. We made sense at the time, but most times I felt trapped in that relationship.

But Naduah's penchant for stubborn impulsive decisions soon ended our relationship because she decided to complete her collegiate career in Paris, then Sweden and London.

I was somewhat relieved, and vowed to myself not to get so emotionally involved with any woman—especially one so vulnerable—that deeply again, except when I was ready for marriage.

I couldn't exactly describe myself as being excited that Naduah was going to become an almost permanent fixture of my life in DC. I know how easy it is to fall back into a relationship with her and then fall.

Naduah switched the heat off and sat on the cabinet chair opposite mine, then said gleefully, "A love triangle...this is getting too good!"

"Will you at least show less excitement?" I asked.

"Absolutely not!" she said. "Please continue."

"Anyway, I don't think there is much to say. I'm developing…I think…I don't know. Naduah, I don't know…I feel like I can help her…that she needs help that only I can provide."

Naduah listened in silence and replied slowly, "Ladi you are a Captain Save-a-Damsel. You attract damsels in distress. It was the same with us, remember?"

I ignored her Captain Save-a-Damsel comment and replied, "She has a boyfriend for goodness' sake! It makes no sense."

"Aha, you have hit the nail on the head. It doesn't make sense, so it's wrong. Everything doesn't have to make sense, Ladi. Sometimes life throws us curve balls, and we have to deal with them. Sometimes I think God allows those curve balls so we can learn from them or grow from them."

I really couldn't believe she had just said that.

"So, Naduah, what you are saying is that God threw me a curve ball so I can make a girl and her boyfriend break up."

She laughed and replied, "No, Ladi. I am just saying that sometimes your need for order is a defense mechanism. You are only comfortable in life when things make sense. If it makes sense, you go for it, but sometimes that's not how life works. We made sense, but we didn't work out. Get out of the box of making sense and just go with the flow."

"Stop psychoanalyzing me," I answered curtly. "Naduah. First, you're telling me to go with the flow and break up a relationship, and now you keep mentioning our long dead relationship, which ended because you were bored as usual and moved away."

She remained silent for a while as she regarded me. "Ladi, we ended because we stopped making sense to you. We got together because I was searching for my meaning in Christianity and God and when I found that, you unconsciously checked out. I just moved on before you ended the relationship like I expected you to."

I also regarded her in silence.

"You are just annoyed because as usual I am right," she continued.

"You are not right, Naduah."

She smiled before she replied, "You know I am."

"Anyway, you will meet her tonight at dinner," I said, quickly changing the subject.

"And I am excited!" Naduah said, her eyes lighting. "Will I get to meet the rest of your classmates?"

"Yes, you will get to meet the whole crew. It should be interesting."

"Won't that be exciting? Ladi's crush is cooking for his ex-girl-friend," she said with a smirk.

I shook my head in amusement and answered, "Yes, it will."

She yawned loudly and said, "I am going to take a nap before the party. Come to think of it, you could serve my stew in the party. My stew is delicious…as usual."

"Whatever, Naduah. Aren't you going to help me tidy up for tonight?"

"No, not really. I have to take a beauty nap," she said and gestured to my bedroom. "Have fun cleaning," she added before she chuckled and shut the door to my bedroom.

I shook my head at her and headed to the storage room for the vacuum cleaner.

I cleaned my apartment but I couldn't get Naduah's words out of my head.

Life sometimes throws us curveballs which God allows.

What if God had allowed a curveball I was ill-equipped to handle?

A curve ball I wasn't expecting. Love.

"Hey," I said after swinging the door open. Sola was standing at my doorway.

"You are quite early," I continued and let her in.

"I am? Anyway, Happy Birthday, Ladi!" she said quietly with a little smile. "Here," she said, offering me a small wrapped package.

I accepted the gift and gave her a quick hug.

"Open it," she urged.

I opened the gift and chuckled when I saw it.

It was the Vari CD, the classical musical group I had introduced her to.

"I am into classical music now. Soon I'll be playing complex musical pieces."

I chucked and replied, "Yeah, right. Let me play it now." I slipped the disc into the CD player.

We both listened in silence in the living room. She sat opposite me on the couch.

She looked really beautiful sitting on the couch quietly and concentrating on the music.

She caught my eye and smiled, "Classical music is all good, but we really can't dance to it. How about we play something that the birthday boy can dance to?"

I smiled then replied, "Fine."

I stopped the Vari CD and slipped in one of James's pop CDs.

We listened for a while then I said, "I thought the reason we changed the CD was to dance."

"Yes. I am not dancing. You should dance if you want to."

"I do," I said then stood and began to dance along to the music.

She dissolved into peals of laughter.

"Ladi, please, please, stop! Is that what you call dancing?"

"Of course it's dancing! Did I mention it's my birthday? I demand we dance together," I said, offering her my hand.

"Wow, you are pulling the birthday card! Fine. All right. I will dance with you Ladi, but don't expect me to be good at it," she said getting up from the couch.

I continued with my best dance moves or what I thought were my best ones.

She laughed and moved along with me to the music then she really got into it, moving her hands in front of me and then shaking her hips from side to side.

"Oh, I see you can dance!" I exclaimed, pulling her closer to me by the waist.

That single motion changed the mood from fun to dangerous for me with her body pressed so close to mine.

She didn't stop dancing though, and she laughed playfully, unaware of my discomfort.

Then I think it changed for her, too; she stopped dancing.

Without even thinking, I inched my mouth closer to hers. I could feel her breath on mine, my mouth barely touching her yielding, parting lips before I heard, "Am I interrupting something?"

It was Naduah standing in the doorway of my bedroom. Her arms were folded across her chest, and she had a self-satisfied smile on her face.

I quickly let go of Sola who looked stunned. She moved back from me quickly and sat back on the couch.

There was a long and uncomfortable silence, then Naduah said, "You must be Sola. You definitely need no introduction."

She walked to Sola and offered her hand, giving me a sideways glance.

I groaned inwardly. What was I thinking? How could I lose control of my sanity like that? This was ludicrous! And for Naduah to be the one who interrupted us, that was embarrassing. No, it was worse. It was humiliating!

Her expression all but said what she thought. "I told you so!" was etched on her face.

I was grateful when she took Sola to the kitchen area so they could unpack the food Nikky had brought earlier.

I, on the other hand, was stunned into silence by my foolish actions.

"Dr. Ho really got us with that exam! It was Ladi's fault," Nikky said at the dinner table before she took a big bite of a chicken drumstick.

"It wasn't my fault!" I exclaimed and shook my head.

The party could only be described as raucous. Everyone that I invited showed up. There was Irene, Tina, Nikky, Tayo, Ego, Lenny, TJ, James and, of course, Sola. A few of my other classmates in the student council had stopped by also, including Uche, Love, Harrison, Obi, Nneoma and Ronke, who was trying but failing to ignore James. Unfortunately, James had not given up his fantasy about becoming Ronke's boyfriend.

He showed me a random quote last night: "A woman's heart has to be so hidden in God a man has to find God to find her."

"I think that's what I am going to do," he said resolutely. "I am going to find God then find my African Queen, Ronke."

I suppressed my laughter and nodded at him. I did not take his statement seriously until later that day when he asked me why he couldn't find the book of Matthew in the Bible.

He had been looking in the Old Testament.

I glanced at James.

He was deeply engrossed in a conversation with Ronke. Well, maybe his new strategy was working.

I was having a good time despite the incident with Sola.

When I repeatedly tried to catch her eye across the table, she refused to even glance at me. I was deeply ashamed by my actions. It was time to make a tough decision about my friendship with her and this was a decision that I wasn't even ready to contemplate yet. However, I had been down this slippery slope before with Naduah. It always started with seemingly innocent kisses, but if I didn't nip this downward spiral in the bud I would find myself falling back into past patterns of sexual impurity.

It was apparent I could not keep my feelings hidden any longer and things would get potentially awkward between us. I made up my mind to set things right with her before the evening was over.

I turned my attention back to the conversation.

"The second years already warned that his questions were hard!"

"Well, you didn't have to goad him. I feel he wanted to make that exam especially hard for us." Irene said then she dished some salad into her plate.

"I definitely failed," Ego chimed in "It was a disaster."

Although she wasn't really part of my circle of friends, Tayo had persuaded me to invite Ego because she was going through a rough patch with Ben and needed the support.

"Didn't my study tips help?" Tayo asked, turning to look at Ego.

"They did. Instead of absolute failure like forty percent, a sixty-five percent may be possible. I will be glad if I can fail with a sixty-five," Ego finished.

The table erupted into laugher.

"I am so worried about how my residency application will look if I fail that exam!" said Nikky, anxiously pulling on her hair.

"Please, Nikky, don't start with residency applications aggaaain!" Tayo groaned.

"But—" she started and was interrupted by Naduah.

"Do you guys talk about anything other than school?"

"Yes, we do," I answered.

"Like what?" she replied.

There was a long silence on the table then we all laughed again.

"Excuse me," Ego suddenly said, getting up from the table and answering her phone.

Nikky made a face behind Ego, and Tina giggled.

I shook my head at Nikky and wondered what Ego had done to land on Nikky's bad side.

"Well, give me Dr. Potts' inappropriate dressing and mini-skirts any day. Dr. Ho gives the hardest exams!" Tayo said again.

"YES!" we all exclaimed.

We continued debating the pros and cons of both professors, and we were interrupted by Ego slipping back into her chair.

No sooner had she slipped back into the chair did her phone ring again.

"Ego, why don't you go and have your phone conversation outside? It's hard to concentrate on the conversation I am having with you interrupting so frequently," Nikky said.

"Oh, really?"

"Yes, really."

"Why don't you go jump off a bridge?" Ego completed coolly.

There was silence on the table

Oh no, there was going to be trouble.

Chapter Fifty-Five

Nikky

Did this girl actually say that to me?

Was I mistaken?

But it seemed like I wasn't because everyone had stopped talking. Tayo stared at Ego open-mouthed.

"Yes, I just said that," Ego continued. "I have been watching you say things to me, and I have kept my cool but if you open up your mouth and say nonsense again to me, you little rat, I will make sure you regret it."

"Watch your mouth! Don't you ever open your mouth to talk to me like that again," I spluttered, standing from my chair.

"Nikky…" Tayo started then he tried to hold me back.

"Stop it." I wriggled away from his grasp and said, "Don't touch me, Tayo!" "What exactly do you have against me, Ego?"

"What do I have against you? You must be joking! I have done nothing but try to be nice to you! Yet you have treated me with scorn from the moment I met you."

"Do you know why I treat you with scorn? You are a manipulative human being! You use people for your own selfish gain. I don't like people like you."

"You guys stop this!" Irene interrupted.

"Selfish gain? Oh, you are talking about your precious Tayo Smith. The Tayo Smith you want to die for," she said in a mocking tone. "You know nothing about me, Nikky, absolutely nothing. I eat girls like you for breakfast. I can destroy you. You are a child."

"Oh really!"

"You guys, this is my birthday," Ladi interrupted.

I felt a pang of guilt for creating a scene at Ladi's dinner, but I wasn't going to let anyone speak to me like that in public, ever!

Not even my mother had ever spoken to me in that manner!

"Yes, really. Nikky Abe, I pity you. You are resentful and jealous of me because of the attention Tayo gives me. You are obsessed with a boy who regards you as nothing."

"Ego, don't say another word," Tayo commanded.

"At least I am not pathetic enough to be a side piece to Ben Odojie, who clearly has a girlfriend he loves and respects. Two things I doubt any man will ever feel for you," I retorted.

"What about you, Nikky? Tayo Smith couldn't care less about your existence. You are nothing more than his little pet, like a puppy. You are the amusing thing he keeps around to stroke his ego. You really think he will make you his girlfriend? Do you know what he did right under your nose?

"Ego, please..." Tayo started.

"He slept with Belinda Belfonte!"

There was a long silence. My heart began to beat wildly, and I quickly found Tayo's eyes. I asked him without speaking, "Is she correct?"

He wouldn't even meet my eye. He turned away quickly.

Then in one swift motion, I was standing right in front of her.

I struck her hard across the face.

She put her hand on her now reddening cheeks and looked surprised. Then almost immediately, she raised up her hand as if to strike me.

"No. Stop this nonsense, both of you," Sola said, catching her hand from behind.

Sola's intervention seemed to spur everyone into action, and Tayo and Ladi quickly separated us.

My eyes began to smart with tears, but I held them back.

I wasn't in control of my body. All I could think of was her accusation about Tayo. I felt so embarrassed. Now everyone knew I was the desperate best friend and secret "exclusive friendship" partner who was in love with him.

I just wanted to die. I wanted the ground to open up so I would sink into it. I wanted to crawl into bed, kiss my imaginary boo Anderson Cooper, then call Mommy and cry.

If what she said was true, Tayo Smith had hurt me beyond repair.

I turned to Tayo's booming voice saying, "Why would you say such a thing?"

He was confronting Ego near the doorway while the rest of us were in the dining area.

"Well, it's true. Isn't it? And honey, your personal business isn't so personal. The whole school knows," Ego replied defiantly.

"Who do you think you are, Ego? Nikky is right about you. You always call me four days before every exam expecting me to help you. You think I don't know you want to use me."

"Well, it's help you are more than willing to give," Ego replied snidely.

"You know what Ego? You are not even our friend. I told Ladi to invite you because I felt sorry for you. You have no friends. Why are you even here?"

There was a long silence.

Then Ego raised her shoulder slightly and turned to Ladi.

"I am sorry for ruining your birthday dinner, Ladi, but apparently I am not wanted here. I don't stay where I am not wanted."

With that, she retrieved her coat and walked out of the apartment silently.

No one tried to stop her.

Chapter Fifty-Six

Tayo

I opened my apartment door and groaned. Before I could slam the door, Ego stopped me by saying, "Wait. Tayo, I came with food."

She held a box of pizza and a bottle of vodka in her hand.

I raised my eyes quizzically at the vodka, and she said, "It was the only bottle of alcohol I had at home. I just ordered the pizza, grabbed it, and came here on a whim."

"Okay," I replied then shrugged my shoulders. If she thought a pizza and some cheap alcohol would make me forgive her for creating a scene at Ladi's birthday last night, she was mistaken. I had mentally dismissed her in my mind.

She must have sensed my nonchalance so she said, "Tayo, please let me try to explain last night. Please, will you at least let me in?"

I reluctantly held the door open for her and walked into my apartment.

"Ego, I don't really want to speak with you," I started. "I don't have anything to say to you."

She rushed into the apartment and placed her gifts on the center table in the living room then said, "Please, Tayo. I feel terrible after the way I acted."

I flopped on the couch then said, "Yeah, well, you should have thought about it."

"Please," she pleaded again. "I really want to make this up to you."

"Well, what about Nikky?"

"I already apologized to her," she replied.

"Really? She didn't mention anything to me."

"I said I apologized. I didn't say she accepted my apology."

She sat next to me on the couch then said, "Tayo, I am a complicated person. I didn't mean to hurt anybody at that party. Nikky said some pretty mean things about me and, when she mentioned my relationship with Ben, I just lost it."

She wiped tears from her eyes as she spoke, and she looked a little genuine, but I was still pissed with her. I pointedly avoided Nikky after the disastrous dinner because I wasn't ready to tell her the truth about Belinda. Of course, Nikky wasn't going to let me get away with that. When she asked me point-blank, with eyes blazing, if Ego's statement was true, I categorically denied it.

"Ego, I told you about Belinda in confidence. We were opening up to each other, and you betrayed that trust."

"Tayo, I am so sorry. It's because of all my problems with Ben. How can I love a man who's so cruel to me? He makes me feel pathetic, like I am nothing. When Nikky mentioned his name..."

Her voice cracked, and she broke into sobs.

Dang, I was angry with her but not angry enough to watch her cry without feeling a little bad.

I put my arms around her and let her sob. It seemed like she needed it. When she finally calmed down, she smiled then said, "The pizza is getting cold. Let's eat the pizza at least and maybe do some vodka shots."

"Well, I am not too sure about vodka shots, but I will eat the pizza," I replied.

"Please," she pouted. "I don't want to drink alone!"

Well, vodka shots wouldn't hurt. I was in my apartment, so it was safe.

She smiled then opened the pizza box, and then I noticed how attractive a woman she was. Ben Odojie was an idiot.

It was apparent she wanted comfort tonight. She kept talking about her complicated relationship with Ben and, as we did more shots, we both became more open with one another.

"Ben and I are so complicated, but I know he loves me," she said with her eyes glazing.

I was on the border between tipsy and buzzed, too, so I laughed at her statement.

She laughed, too, then slapped me on the shoulder. Then I hit her back. She exclaimed then hit me again. Soon we were play-hitting one another on the couch. Then it changed.

I don't know who kissed who first, but I know I made the biggest mistake of my life on that couch that day.

This time I couldn't blame it on the alcohol.

Anatomy was the dark ages. It was one of the toughest periods of medical school.

Ann Francis
Class of 1997

I almost forgot I was working with a human cadaver by the second week. I would leave the anatomy lab and go to McDonald's to eat burgers without a moment's thought.

Pyong Hong
Class of 2003

We all thought we had this med school thing down until anatomy hit and we were not so sure anymore.
Thomas Jacob
Class of 2012

Chapter Fifty-Seven

Nikky

"Mommy, I am so sad!" I whined to my mother.

It was a few hours before the first anatomy lecture, and I was having a much-needed powwow conversation with Mommy. After all the horror stories we heard from the seniors about how difficult anatomy would be, especially the neuroanatomy section, I was both anxious and excited to get the ball rolling.

I was anxious about everything nowadays. Who could blame me? After that soap opera-ish birthday dinner with Ladi, anyone would be stressed out. I had been quite close to having a cardiac arrest this week.

It had been terrible.

The exam results were released, and I did better than I expected considering how difficult the exam had been. I honored the exam, but I was still number two. I got a ninety-eight while the number one got a ninety-nine.

I walked past the dean's office with my head spinning. As I crawled away from the dean's office in dismay, I spotted Dee with a couple of her friends.

Then I heard Dee laugh and say, "I got a ninety-nine. Does that mean I am at the top of the class? They always put number one on that corner of my result slip. Does it mean I have been number one in the class all this while?"

I stared at her open-mouthed. How could Dee with her child-like voice, baby doll features and all around *mugu* tendencies be number one? Tina's rumor was now confirmed.

Nikky Abe, your humiliation is complete!

How was I going to get into the national Alpha Omega Alpha honor society if I couldn't beat Dee Masters, of all people? Only the top one percent of medical students across the nation were admitted into this society. I had seen the names of the juniors and seniors admitted into the exclusive society prominently and proudly displayed on a plaque in the lobby of 1007 and vowed to myself I would get my name on that plaque.

How would I achieve this feat if I couldn't beat Dee Masters in class?

I almost had a cardiac arrest right there, but I began to practice the breathing techniques I learned from watching my imaginary boo Anderson Cooper's show the previous night.

At least things were going great between my imaginary boo and me. He didn't give me any reason to distrust him unlike Tayo "exclusive friend" Smith.

Mommy's next words reminded me of all the drama with Tayo.

"Nikky, I am so disappointed in you. I think it's that Tayo boy that is influencing you. He is not good for you at all!" Mommy completed her statement with a loud hiss.

"I am so disappointed in myself. I actually hit her, Mommy. How embarrassing is that?"

"Nikky, you have been raised better than that," Mommy replied somberly. Then she added, "What came over you?"

That was the question I asked myself over and over again. The party pretty much ended after the altercation, with everyone saying their goodbyes and parting ways. Tayo ran out of the party like his pants were on fire, and he refused to meet my probing eyes. I was so angry with him, so hurt by his antics. I couldn't even mention his name without my eyes filling with tears.

He came to my apartment immediately after the party.

"Nikky, please..." he started.

"Just tell me the truth, Tayo. Was Ego lying?"

"Nikky...nothing happened. Ego is lying."

I observed him for a moment then said, "Why would she just randomly think of a lie like that? She did not sound like she was lying."

"She wanted to hurt you. She heard the stuff you said about her."

I looked at him quizzically.

"She said you called her a slut, that she was a loose girl."

I might have said a few things about Ego, but I hadn't said anything out of the ordinary. The whole class called her a *side piece hoe* behind her back anyway, and the things I may have said were nice compared to my other classmates. I reasoned that if she overheard the conversation, maybe her statement about Belinda was Ego being spiteful.

Tayo looked so broken in my living room, so extremely gorgeous in his button-down shirt. He also looked so contrite and distraught. I would have forgiven him for anything.

Well, except if the whole Belinda thing was true, but I was convinced that it wasn't.

Ego was a mean girl, and I would not take her word over Tayo's.

After I told Mommy the whole story she said, "Are you sure you can trust his word? Nikky, I know your Aunty and I always encourage you to meet young eligible bachelors, but I really don't think I like Tayo anymore."

"Mommy. He is not that bad. He is just a little complicated," I replied.

I even failed to convince myself with that statement.

"Ohh," Mommy groaned. "It's worse than I thought. You don't just like him."

I winced and braced myself for what Mommy would say next.

"You actually love this man."

"Yes, mommy," I answered softly "Unfortunately, I love the most inappropriate men."

"But, Nikky, you haven't told me why you do. All I have ever heard you say about him is that he is gorgeous. Apart from that, why are you so in love with this man?"

"I don't know, Mommy."

And that was the truth, I didn't know why I loved this womanizing, no-good, wild-partying but adorable man-child.

We filed into the anatomy lab solemnly. I heard a few nervous giggles here and there, but for the most part the class was silent. After a short "introduction to anatomy" lecture by a white old man with gray hair called Dr. Bean, a lab practical where we would actually get to dissect the bodies was scheduled.

I was beyond excited! Now was the time to get our hands dirty with human anatomy.

We had been instructed to dress in scrubs or laboratory coats and everyone followed the instructions to the letter. Of course, people like Ego still managed to make a fashion statement with pink scrubs and matching pink sneakers. I glanced at her and felt guilty. Mommy had ended our conversation by commanding me to apologize to her for my behavior. I knew I had to, but I wasn't quite ready yet. She had said some pretty mean things to me.

I turned my attention back to the anatomy lab. I was slightly worried about working on actual human bodies, but, hey, I was in medical school. I would get used to these types of things soon enough.

The anatomy room was cold and slightly dingy, with tiled floors. About thirty bodies were in zipped-up plastic bags on tables that were referred to as tanks. Each tank was a metallic bench with a curved top. The bodies were placed on the curved top. Connected to each tank were huge tubes which were part of the central air system that ensured that the stench of the formaldehyde was not overwhelming. The tanks were lined across each side of the wall in a row and there were two neat rows of tanks down the middle of the room. Each tank had a clear label with the word "MEDICAL" on the top. We were randomly assigned to groups and fortunately or unfortunately, depending on the perspective, Tayo was in my group.

I quickly joined my group members and the professor around my tank.

The professor leading my group was Dr. Zee. Dr. Zee was an older man with graying hair and a handlebar moustache which made it difficult to take him seriously. Tayo was standing next to Dr. Zee and mouthed a quick hello to me.

Dr. Zee began, "Do we have everyone?"

Then Dr. Zee cleared his throat and held the blade poised over the zipped body, "Now I remember while hiking on Mount Kilimanjaro, I thought of the absolute perfection of the human body. The well-formed and perfected gastrocnemius, the soleus, and then we move up to the biceps and triceps in all their glory that marks the arms. I thought anatomy is God's perfect gift to us."

I met Tayo's eyes again and suppressed a giggle. Janice, who was next to me, was trying really hard to suppress her laughter.

Dr. Zee closed his eyes and continued, "Dark muscle, white muscle, the brachial plexus, the aorta. Every single organ is part of the synchronized musical orchestration of the likes of Mozart or Beethoven." He waved his arms like he was playing a violin as he talked.

He finished his speech and looked at us expectantly.

Gabe immediately began to applaud and said, "Bravo, Dr. Zee! Bravo!"

Dr. Zee smiled and said, "Now, my future doctors, a moment of silence before we start working with the cadaver, Nancy. If Nancy had not donated her body to the pursuit of science, ladies and gentleman, boys and girls, I would have to say your medical education would be quite delinquent."

We all obeyed and bowed our heads for a moment.

"Now," Dr. Zee continued, "Who would like the honor of zipping the body bag down?"

No one volunteered themselves, so I said, "I will do it."

I placed my hand on the zipper of the body bag and slowly unzipped the bag. My tank group mates all leaned in to see the body. Nancy looked almost like she was sleeping. I had no immediate emotional response to seeing a dead body for the first time in my life, but I was taken aback by how young she was. She was a thin woman who looked to be in her mid-fifties with specks of grey hair and a huge imposing nose. The body had been doused with the chemical formaldehyde, and the stench was overpowering.

"Wow, she's so fat!" I heard from the tank next to mine. The other students giggled.

I turned my head to see who spoke and it was Tina. Apparently, some people were not taking this as seriously as our tank and Dr. Zee.

Elsewhere Dr. Irina, the small and stocky Russian professor who I was a little afraid of, screamed at her terrified tank, "All of you. Quick! Turn the body over now! We starrrt woking on dee back! Fast! Don't be stooooopid!"

I shuddered. Thank God my group didn't have Dr. Irina as the tank instructor until the next semester. Things were done differently in the anatomy unit. Dr. Bean explained that instead of having one principal lecturer, we would be taught by ten or twelve professors throughout the year. For the lab practicals, the professors spent two weeks on each tank group and rotated so they would get to work with all the students.

Dr. Zee said, "Okay. We are going to turn the body over now so we can start working on the muscles of the back.

"Come on," he commanded again because we all looked hesitant.

We all put on our plastic gloves and turned the body over with some difficulty.

"Now, since we are working on the muscles of the back, we will cut superficially," Dr. Zee said and made a cut on Nancy's body.

He began to explain the different layers of the tissues that lined the human body then he expertly isolated the first muscle. Soon I was engrossed in his words, trying to learn all the muscles he pointed out. He later allowed me to isolate some of the muscles and, like all things academic, I was very good at it. I liked the feel of the blade in my hands and differentiating the different textures of the human tissues as I worked with them.

I was momentarily distracted by a big crowd who seemed to follow Dr. Bean around as he moved from tank to tank.

Dr. Bean said, "I have some fans! Well, fans, make sure you remember the nerve that innervates each muscle!"

"Why are they all following him?" I asked, turning my head and hoping to catch a glance of the muscle he was pointing to.

"Apparently, Dr. Bean is very good at dropping hints for the exam," Janice replied.

"Gabe has abandoned our tank for his," Tayo said, gesturing with his head.

I followed his gaze and spotted Gabe listening intently to Dr. Bean at another tank.

"Such a sell-out," I said.

I turned my attention back to separating the connective tissue and fat. It became a little more difficult as the fat became more dense. My tank members soon lost interest in what I was doing and wandered away to other tanks. Soon it was only Tayo and I who were left.

"Wow, everyone has abandoned ship," I said then shook my head at Tayo.

Tayo smiled then said, "Let me take over."

I handed him the blade and smiled at him.

When I caught his eyes, I immediately became convinced that Ego was lying.

Tayo was a lot of things, but this gorgeous man would never lie to me so blatantly.

Chapter Fifty-Eight

Tayo

"While surfing in the Atlantic Ocean, it dawned on me that as the surfboard balances on the waves delicately, so also is the human body's delicate balance," Dr. Zee said.

He looked around the table expectantly, waiting for the usual giggle or laughter. The table was completely silent. Gabe would have laughed, but he was taking notes as he followed Dr. Bean around the anatomy lab like a little puppy.

"That's interesting, Dr. Zee," Nikky replied. "But we have to finish dissecting all the abdominal muscles next! We are far behind!"

The truth was everyone in our tank was feeling frustrated and a little scared. Dr. Zee's stories, which had previously been sources of amusement, were now tedious. Our tank trailed sluggishly behind the class with the dissection schedule while tanks that Dr. Irina led were ahead. This put us at a significant disadvantage for the quizzes. The quizzes in the anatomy weighed more so the stakes were higher, and everyone was not in a joking mood.

"Okay, do that, Nikky," Dr. Zee said.

He moved on to the next tank, hoping to gain a captive audience for his stories.

Nikky sighed and said, "I am so happy I have you, Tayo. You are the only one who sticks with me in this tank. This anatomy thing is getting so stressful! I was so excited when we started, but I am not so sure anymore! I barely sleep anymore! The only time I sleep is after a quiz."

"At least you are honoring the quiz. I barely passed my last quiz, and it wasn't like I didn't study. I *have* been studying!" I replied.

"Yeah, I am so glad I have you though. You are the best anatomy partner and exclusive best friend ever!" Nikky said.

She turned back to dissecting the body with a determined look on her face.

I did not reply but bowed my head silently. The last couple of weeks had been hellish for me. Even sleep eluded me.

The nightmares had become worse, like I was being punished for my actions. In some ways, I was glad anatomy was so demanding. If I could study twenty-four hours a day I would, but I couldn't. When I shut my eyes, I would soon be awakened by fragments of violent images and my brother's words that I was a mess-up. I felt isolated and afraid.

Nikky was so engrossed in Anatomy that she didn't notice I was deteriorating. But Nikky couldn't help me this time, since she was the reason I felt so guilty.

Whenever I looked at her big brown child-like eyes, I was reminded that I was a cheat and a liar. Especially when Nikky made statements like "she was glad she had me."

I hated myself for lying to her.

I made up my mind to eventually admit my mistake with Belinda to her. But now I made matters worse with this "thing" with Ego. After the "incident" with Ego, I made a promise to myself never to touch alcohol again. It wasn't like I went out of my way to find it. Ego kept insisting I drink something so I become more relaxed. I obviously drank a little more than I intended too. My problem wasn't alcohol itself; it was just the amount I consumed. I would soon have that under control.

"Ohhh! I can't believe I can't find the splenic vein!" Nikky suddenly said. She threw her hands up in frustration and said, "I am tired! Let's go study the x-rays for a while then come back to this."

I smiled then nodded my head. As if learning all the parts of the human body wasn't hard enough, we also had to know how to identify them on x-rays. Let's just say x-rays were more than difficult to decipher because everything looked like a lump or shadow or nothing.

We shoved past the students trying to cram the x-rays and silently studied an arteriogram of the blood supply of the abdomen.

"Hey, mister," I heard close to my ear.

I jumped back in alarm then my heart began to race widely. It was Ego.

Nikky gave her a sideways glance and avoided eye contact with her, but I knew she would be listening to any conversation I had with Ego.

"Hey, Ego," I replied coolly, praying silently that she would go away.

"So we need to talk about that night—" she started.

"Ego have you seen this new x-ray?" I quickly interrupted. I maneuvered her to the x-rays on the other side of the room, far away from Nikky.

"What do you want?" I hissed in her ear.

She looked a little taken back then said, "I was just being friendly. I mean, you have been avoiding me and haven't picked up my phone calls for the past weeks."

"Well, I am busy," I said curtly.

She glanced back at Nikky, who fixed a pointed "what are you doing with her?" look on me then said, "Oh, you don't want your precious Nikky to find out about our night."

She squeezed my arm again and then said, "Don't worry. I can keep a secret. I don't want Ben to find out, either. Please don't tell anyone."

"Ego, just stop bothering me. I regret ever meeting you. All I have experienced is trouble since I started hanging out with you. No wonder Ben stays away from you too."

I regretted the words when I said them because she immediately shrank back with a hurt expression on her face.

"Ego, I didn't mean…"

"Whatever, Tayo. You meant what you said. You better be nice to me because if not I might get angry at you. Who knows what I might tell Nikky?"

"She won't believe you. She didn't believe what you said about Belinda and she won't believe this. It will be your word against mine."

"Really? Don't be so sure, Tayo," she said then walked past me.

I watched her as she walked away and shook my head.

"What did she want?" Nikky demanded soon after Ego left.

"Nothing. Just help with anatomy," I lied.

Nikky squinted at me then shook her head in disgust, "I still don't like her."

I nodded silently and quickly pointed her attention back to the x-rays.

But I was a million miles away and nothing I tried to memorize stuck in my brain.

I had to tell Nikky the truth.

I could not stand the guilt anymore. I was so afraid of losing her. The way she looked at me in awe, with so much respect, it was addicting. I didn't want to lose that.

When I looked into her eyes, I saw myself as the man I had the potential of becoming, not the man I was. I could not cheapen her any longer.

I decided to tell her about Belinda but not about Ego. She may forgive me for Belinda, but she would never forgive me for Ego. I would let her know the truth even if it meant losing her. I loved her that much.

Chapter Fifty-Nine

Sola

"*Ring!*" the bell went.

I had barely finished writing down my answer for the labeled cranial nerve in the exposed skull before I had to move immediately to the next tank.

It was our first cumulative anatomy lab practical. Fifty bodies were labeled, and we were given one minute at each tank to correctly identify then write down our answers on the exam sheet. When the alarm clock went off, we switched position and moved to the next tank. I gave a backward glance to what I thought was the trigeminal nerve, marveling at how quickly I had become desensitized to working with human bodies. The whole human bodies we started with had become a collection of parts, with a leg placed on one exam tank, a quarter of an exposed skull in another, an abdomen with the entrails taken out to expose the arteries on another tank. I had quickly gotten over any misgivings I had about working with human bodies when I realized the inordinate amount of material we would have to study in the short time we had.

For the past couple of months, I had lived my life like I was in a trance. I didn't have time to think. I just moved. Although I had been teetering close to the edge of a mental breakdown for a while, the puzzling almost-kiss with Ladi did not push me over the edge like I expected it to. After the debacle of the dinner party ended, I went home and sat on my bed, expecting to feel guilty. But I didn't.

I didn't feel the least bit guilty, and that was puzzling.

Even when Ladi called to profusely apologize, I didn't feel anything. It was only when he mentioned that we stop studying together did I feel any sort of alarm.

"So I guess we have to stop hanging around each other as often," he said.

"No!" I answered. "We just can't dance together anymore."

He laughed and replied, "No, we can't." He paused for a moment before asking, "Will you tell Dare?"

"It was just a little mistake, and we both got carried away," I replied firmly.

The almost-kiss was just that, a mistake. I didn't have to tell Dare because it meant nothing. I would not even allow myself to fantasize that someone as perfect as Ladi could possibly want me. He would probably drop me like a hot potato when he got to know my secrets.

The demands of anatomy and my barely passing grades had taken my mind of all thoughts of the kiss. My grades had gone from bad to worse in anatomy. I recalled how upset I had been with eighty-four in the first unit and sighed. An eighty-four would be better than the consistent seventies I got in the anatomy quizzes.

All this weighed down on me and I found myself falling deeper and deeper in my despair.

Now I stood over another tank, and I shook my head in frustration. I did not know what was labeled.

I moved over when I heard the alarm clock with my answer sheet bare.

My greatest fear was going to become a reality. I would not be able to transfer because of mediocre grades and would be forced to spend the next three years with Tayo Smith.

I bit my cheek to keep from bursting into tears in the exam, then I was distracted by a loud hiss I heard. It was Irene.

She gestured to my answer sheet with pleading eyes. I looked back at her in confusion then immediately understood what she wanted. She wanted to see my answers.

I had successfully avoided Irene since she last mentioned cheating. Now it seemed I had to make a clear choice. I glanced at Dr. Bean and Dr. Zee, who were deep in conversation and barely paid any attention to the students.

I wanted to tell Irene she was better off copying someone else's answers, but I saw her pleading eyes and felt sorry for her. I surreptitiously gave her a full view of my answer sheet when the bell rang again, and we moved on to the next tank.

She quickly glanced at my sheet and mouthed *Thanks*.

I wanted to tell her not to thank me yet. I might just have given her all wrong answers.

"Let me start with the question I always ask my first-time clients. Why do you think you need to see me? What is the current state of your mind?" Naduah asked, looking very much like a Grecian goddess dressed in a flowing boubou and chunky earrings.

How much time did she have? Because she had just asked me a loaded question.

The current state of my mind was confusion mixed with the usual feelings of angst.

I finally made the appointment with Naduah after much rumination and procrastination and after I got over the embarrassment of her catching the almost kiss with Ladi. Anatomy was a welcome distraction because I focused so much on studying and came back home so exhausted from studying that cutting did not even occur to me anymore. However, I realized I still needed help. In my quiet moments, I was still consumed with thoughts of suicide, and I couldn't stop.

I was also in a constant state of anxiety. I was anxious about the results of the last exam, the transfer, my relationship with Dare, failing anatomy, getting caught cheating with Irene, and that Tayo would suddenly remember who I was and my life would be over. I was constantly on edge, and Ladi noticed.

It was my last conversation with him that finally convinced me to make the appointment with Naduah. As I sat opposite her pondering her question, I wondered if I made the right decision.

"Because if I am losing control of my emotions and myself," I answered then the tears started. "I am sorry."

"It's okay. Take your time, Sola," she said.

She watched me for a moment and then handed me a box of tissues

She continued, "What do you think is making you lose control?"

What really made me lose control was the constant reminder of Tayo in Stedman. I didn't want to tell her that, at least not yet.

"Just the presence of someone from my past."

"Is this person so important in your life to cause an emotional breakdown?"

"He is not important. He…apart from that, things are not going okay in my life right now. I worry constantly about my little brother. I don't know where my mom is, and I haven't spoken to her in months. She just left the house abruptly, you know. She has mental issues too."

"Why do you use the word 'too'? Do you think you have mental issues?"

"I know I do, that's just how I am."

"Why say that, Sola? Have you been clinically diagnosed with anything?"

I kept silent, wondering if I could open up to her.

She sensed my vacillation and said, "For this to work, you have to be completely open with me, Sola. Everything you say here is confidential."

I was tired of holding all these secrets. She was probably used to hearing these type of things anyway.

"I haven't been clinically diagnosed, but I cut myself…I cut myself with a blade when I feel overwhelmed with my emotions."

I watched her face for any reaction, but she looked concerned and asked, "When did you start cutting?"

Tear welled up in my eyes when I remembered the first time.

"I was about sixteen and I was going through a bad time. I don't know why I did it the first time. But I was in so much pain, and I just wanted the pain to go away, and I just found that cutting made me feel better. I did it less frequently as I grew older but now…now I cut all the time."

"What first gave you the idea to cut?"

"I don't know…I started with pinching myself really hard and then one day I had a blade in my hand, and I just cut."

"I don't have to tell you that I don't want you to do that because it's not safe. I know you know that. What we can talk about later is better coping mechanisms when you feel pain."

I nodded my head.

"Did something trigger the first episode?"

"Yes, yes something did."

"What was it?"

I did not want to tell her, but I knew if I wanted help I had to open up to someone.

I felt that I could trust Naduah. I felt safe with her.

So I told her the biggest secret of my life. The secret that changed everything for me.

Chapter Sixty

Ego

"I know I promised. But I won't be able to spend Thanksgiving with you," Ben said.

He had the decency to look contrite.

"I really tried, but I have to go…home."

I knew he meant he was going home to be with her. It was the same old tune Ben sang and it shouldn't have hurt me, but it did. After the disaster with Tayo, I was so distraught and confused. I called Ben and begged for a reconciliation. It was ironic, really. He was cheating with me on his girlfriend, yet I wanted to be faithful to him even when we were apart. We did reconcile, but he still refused to break things off with his girlfriend back home. He said things were too "complicated" for that now. He continually shut down any suggestion of a breakup with his girlfriend, but his stern rebuffs carried the undertone of a threat of breaking up with me again. He knew I loved him more than he loved me so he exploited it. So, as usual, I took what he offered me.

"It's okay, Ben," I replied. "I still have some studying to do. So it wasn't going to be much of a break anyway."

It was true. The Thanksgiving holiday was not a break; it was more like a pause because we had another major *quizamination* soon. Ladi had nicknamed the quizzes quizaminations because the quizzes were as hard and weighed as much as any exam. After I apologized for disrupting his party, Ladi seemed to be the only friend I had left in Stedman. Dee had gotten back with Lenny and hardly noticed that I wasn't talking to her. Tayo avoided me like the plague, and Nikky shot daggers at me with her eyes. LD, as I called Ladi, regularly checked up on me via text. He had become the unofficial class motivator in addition to class president ever since anatomy began. He sent inspirational quotes and Bible passages to the class on a weekly basis.

"Okay. I will see you soon," Ben replied before he kissed me on the cheek.

I watched him go with a half-smile on my face then settled down on the couch to study, slipping headphones on my ears and ignoring the pang of disappointment and loneliness I felt.

I sighed and turned the page of the Gray's Anatomy textbook.

Anatomy had hit the Class of 2012 like a head-on collision with a high speed train. It was generally frustrating to everyone to work so hard and not have that reflect in your grades. Then there was the "ninety-eight percent failure rate disaster" in the first neuroanatomy quiz. Dr. Bean had come in to the lecture hall looking quite somber and proceeded to show the class a PowerPoint of our downward trending grades before announcing we all failed the quiz. The class reacted with grave silence. Some dramatic people like Nikky proceeded to create a scene by fainting. I really think she was acting because she came around rather quickly. Anyway, class morale, including mine, was at an all-time low.

I sighed again then closed the book in frustration. I did not want to spend the Thanksgiving holiday alone! I impulsively decided to go to the Thanksgiving potluck Ladi had invited me to. I had previously declined because he said the whole "crew" would be there, and I was trying to avoid Nikky and Tayo. However, Nikky's hateful stares and the fearful please-keep-my-secret glances Tayo cast my way were better than spending Thanksgiving alone. I got dressed and headed to Ladi's apartment, armed with my contribution to the potluck: an apple pie.

I braced myself at the door of Ladi's apartment and even contemplated going home when I remembered what happened the last time I was here. But I quietly knocked on his door and waited.

The door swung open quickly. It was Nikky.

"You guys better not try to cheat," she said loudly to someone in the apartment.

The big grin on her face disappeared when she turned to face me. She quickly recovered then swung the door open more widely so I could come in.

I passed by her silently and was glad when I spotted Ladi's welcoming smile.

"Hey, you made it," he said as he offered his arm out for a hug.

I accepted his hug and said, "Where should I put the pie?"

"There," he replied and gestured to his dining table which was packed with food.

There was jollof rice, corn bread, turkey stuffing, mac and cheese, bread rolls, salsas, grilled chicken, samosas, meat pie, sausage rolls, pink lemonade, soda and sweet wine. In the center of the table was a huge half-carved turkey.

"Ladi, we are waiting for you!" I heard from the living room.

Ladi shook his head and smiled. "I am coming!" he shouted back.

"We are playing Taboo and let's just say some people are taking the whole thing a little too seriously. Fix a plate for yourself and come join us in the living room."

"Sure," I answered. I soon became absorbed with not picking too many fattening foods and picking more protein.

Nikky soon joined me in the dining area. I ignored her, concentrating instead on my food.

She broke the silence and said, "I wanted to apologize for putting my hands on you. It was very wrong of me."

I was taken aback by her direct approach. I studied her for a moment and contemplated how to respond.

She did not sound the least bit contrite to me. I also noted she was careful not to apologize for her words.

"Okay," I replied.

There was a long silence then she said grudgingly, "I hope you are staying for the game?"

"Yes, I am," I answered. "I am sorry too," I added, not because I meant it but because it was the most appropriate thing to say at the time.

She nodded silently then walked into the living room. I followed behind her, holding my plate of food.

Sola, Irene, Lenny, James, Naduah, Thomas, Ladi and even Tina said hello to me enthusiastically. Harrison, Ronke, Nneoma, Love, Uche and Obi of the student council were also in the crowded living room. This *had* to be the entirety of Ladi's network of close friends. The living room was already crowded enough.

The greeting was a little too enthusiastic for my liking. I reasoned Ladi had spoken to them about making me feel welcome. I gave him a grateful smile. I also noticed Tayo wasn't there.

"Where is Tayo?" I asked Ladi who was sitting next to me.

"He decided not to come. He wanted to catch up on his studying," he replied.

I nodded politely and turned my attention to my food, but Ladi interrupted again. "He was going to come, though, but he asked specifically if you were coming then decided he wanted to study."

Ladi shook his head and continued, "Sola was the opposite. She absolutely insisted she wasn't coming until I told her Tayo decided not to come. It's hard to keep up with you guys. You guys are complicated."

I smiled back at him and inwardly sighed.

"Steeple? How was Christ born in a steeple!" Love exploded.

"Well, I thought it would be a good clue for the word," Uche replied.

I turned my attention to the game of Taboo in progress and quickly suppressed all thoughts of Tayo.

After I got over the initial awkwardness with the group, I kicked back and enjoyed the good food then played a round of what was supposed to be a friendly game of Taboo. Nikky did not get the memo because we spent half of the game arguing over the rules with her.

But, after I said my goodbyes and crawled into bed that night, I lay in bed with a smile on my face. I realized Ben was not the only human being in the world. For the first time in a long time, I was part of something bigger that myself. I couldn't have chosen a better group of people to spend this time of my life with.

Well, maybe not Nikky.

I think every med student reaches the point where you question your career choice and ask yourself if it's worth it.

Mauricio Ebert
Class of 1965

By the end I was burnt out. It went from *I have to get an A* to *please God let me just pass.*

Rashad Mohammed
Class of 2012

Chapter Sixty-One

Sola

"How do you read this? I can't even identify the stupid bone!" I said, edging closer to the x-ray in the anatomy lab.

It was two in the morning and TJ, Ladi, and I were reviewing the x-rays we needed to know before the exam.

It was bad enough that we had to memorize countless muscles, their insertions and origins, nerves, blood vessels, bones of the spine, we also had to be able to identify these structures on x-ray.

I didn't just dislike anatomy.

I hated it!

On the other hand, for people like Nikky, it just came naturally. Nikky's eyes lit up with excitement when she isolated a particular nerve or muscle. She would go on and on about how interesting it was while I could not contain my boredom.

"Sola, that's the cuboid bone. Just try to remember its position and its shape," Ladi said, squinting at the x-ray.

He pulled me closer to the x-ray and said, "Don't get frustrated, Sola. It's right after the calceneous. Just try to remember that."

"Okay," I answered, resigned to the fact that I just wasn't good at anatomy. I nodded my head as he pointed out the bones to me on the x-ray, but I knew nothing would stick.

"Are you listening to me?" Ladi asked, trying to shake me out of my reverie.

"I am not, Ladi. You know what, this is not working. Can we continue tomorrow?"

"Sure. Sola is everything all right? Not just with anatomy, I mean everything," he asked, with his eyes searching mine.

"No, Ladi, everything is not all right," I said, trying to keep my anxiety-laden voice low.

"Sola. Come on, let's take a break," Ladi said, leading me out of the wooden double doors of the anatomy lab. "Sola, what is it?"

"Every single aspect of my life is messed up right now! I won't be able to transfer because I can barely pass, my mom still hasn't come home, and I am worried about my brother!"

"Wait, let's sit and talk here," Ladi said, pulling me down to sit on the steps of the stairs we were climbing.

"I am tired, Ladi. I am constantly on edge, and I feel anxious about everything. I don't even like being by myself any longer because…"

"Yes?"

"I am worried about…what I am capable of doing to myself."

"Sola…are you still seeing Naduah?"

"I am, but I am so overwhelmed. Ladi, I literally want to escape my life, but I can't. I am stuck in it."

"Don't talk like that, Sola. There are some bright spots in your life, you know. Your boyfriend loves you and, in spite of everything, your brother is doing well."

"Yes…" I replied.

"And you have us, your medical school crew!" he said and then he hit me playfully in the shoulder.

I smiled and said, "I guess…"

"You can relax after the Christmas break. This time it will be a real break, not like Thanksgiving," he replied.

He continued, "Don't worry, Sola. You always have God."

"Stop saying that," I hissed.

"Sola…"

I interrupted, "Please, Ladi, I don't have to have this conversation with you again. I am not in the mood."

I didn't want to listen to meaningless platitudes I had heard all my life: "God will provide", "God will take care of you", and the one I hated the most, "God loves you".

If he existed, He had to be blind. Did he not see how much I suffered?

My life was enough evidence that He couldn't care less about me. Or Ladi's convictions were wrong: this God did not exist.

Ladi opened his mouth to say as if to say something, but then he kept silent.

We sat silently together on the stairs for a moment, lost in our thoughts. Mine were turbulent, his may have been peaceful thoughts about his God.

Then he turned to me and said, "You know, Sola, He really does care about you."

I didn't reply and turned away.

If He indeed cared about me why was I hurting so badly?
Was I not worth something to him?

"How are you feeling today?" Naduah asked soon after I sat opposite her in the office.

"I had a rough night. But I think I am better now," I answered.

"Did you get a good night's rest?"

If crying in bed and using the pillow to stifle the sound of my wailing was a good night's sleep, then yes, I did.

I answered, "No, not really. I was up late studying and cried throughout most of the night before I came here."

Naduah regarded me for a moment then said, "Why were you crying?"

"You already know why, Naduah. Stop asking me silly questions," I snapped.

There was another long silence, and I immediately felt guilty.

"Naduah, I am sorry. I am just irritable nowadays."

"I understand, Sola." She continued, "Sola, I think in the context of this setting you should refer to me as Dr. Ibrahim so the lines of professionalism don't get blurred."

She always reminded me of that, but I always felt so comfortable with Naduah and I slipped back to addressing her by her first name.

"Sure, I understand. I feel anxious about everything Nad...sorry, Dr. Ibrahim. I feel anxious about my grades, you know. I don't think any school will accept me as a transfer because I am mediocre."

"Sola, what did we speak about the last time? I told you to stop being so negative and for every negative word you had to give five dollars to a charity of your choice."

I nodded my head sheepishly because I had lost count of all the negative words I had used to describe myself. At this point I owed my battered women's charity about five hundred dollars.

"How was the exam?"

"I did okay. I didn't fail but I didn't get an A either."

"Don't be so hard on yourself, Sola. Hold yourself to the standard of giving your best at all times. That's all that matters."

"But you know, I won't be able to transfer and avoid you-know-who," I said, with my voice breaking as the tears began to fall.

"Sola, I have a suggestion. Just listen to what I have to say…your protection is the most important to me. "

"Yes…" I replied, hoping she wasn't going to meddle in my life, when I told her my only intention was to experience the freedom from keeping everything bottled in.

"Can you get someone…like the police involved? Is the issue over the statute of limitations? Do you know where you stand legally? Wait!" she said, before I opened my mouth in protest.

"I am concerned about your safety, Sola. I understand if you don't want to get anyone else involved. But please, regardless of what happens with your transfer, I want you to take the next year off. I can write a letter to the school you want to transfer to in Michigan explaining your extraneous circumstances. I don't think you can function in Stedman for another year."

"Please…please I didn't even tell my boyfriend I told you. I will deal with this on my own."

"You can't deal with this on your own, Sola. I am not telling you to make a decision right now but think about it."

"Sure," I answered, thankful that she was off the subject.

"What else is making you anxious?"

"The usual. I am worried about my brother and my relationship with my boyfriend. My brother is all alone dealing with all this and he's too young," I said, breaking down into tears.

"Is there any update about your mother's whereabouts?"

"No. I am so tired, Naduah."

"I understand," Naduah replied, ignoring my slip.

I wanted tell her the other anxious thoughts that kept me up late at night.

"I am scared, Naduah."

"Scared of what?"

"I am always filled with thoughts of suicide, with thoughts of killing myself and ending all the pain right now. Yes, I know the consequences. I know how everyone thinks that Nigerians don't commit suicide for some odd reason, but I am consumed with thoughts of ending it all."

"Have you had these thoughts previously in your life?"

"Yes, I have, but not as strongly as this. I feel like I am being taunted. I hear in my heart, *Kill your self, Sola. End it now. Or you are not courageous enough to do so*? Then I feel excruciating emotional pain that even cutting cannot stop. It makes me feel anxious. Now I don't like being alone at night because I fear I might give in."

Naduah stood up from her chair and grabbed by hands, "Sola, look at me. Promise me that you won't hurt yourself in any way."

I could promise her that but the problem was I wasn't sure I could keep that promise.

"Yes, I will try."

"Don't tell me you will try, Sola. Tell me you *will*."

"Okay, I will."

"Have you ever thought of a definitive plan?" she asked.

"I don't know. I am not sure." "I would probably just cut an artery. I could put my knowledge from anatomy to use," I joked morbidly.

Naduah wasn't amused. She sighed deeply then said, "Sola, we have to do something today. I want us both to sign a no-suicide contract. It's not a legally binding document. It's an agreement that you will not under any circumstances end your life by suicide. It will also contain a list of instructions you have to follow anytime you are suicidal. I just want you to be aware that there is help for you whenever you think of committing suicide."

"Okay," I answered softly.

"We will come up with a list of people you may call when you have these feelings. I will also give you clear instructions about calling the suicide hotline if at some point you feel confused."

"Okay."

"Who are the people you trust enough to be on the list?"

"My boyfriend…"

"No, he's in Michigan. He is too far away. I want someone who can come to you at a moment's notice."

"Okay," I tried again. "You and maybe Ladi."

"Okay, that's a good start. I will make two copies of the contract so you can keep one, and I will keep the other."

The no-suicide contract made me feel calmer—at least I knew I had a plan now if things got out of control…

Naduah typed out the contract and then handed it to me. I signed my name where it said, *I, Fadesola, hereby agree that I will not harm myself in any way, attempt suicide, or die by suicide.* The contract also outlined actions I could take if I were ever suicidal, which included reminding myself of the commitment to the contract, calling 911 if I was in any immediate danger of harming myself, and the contact information for Ladi and Naduah.

"Okay Sola, this is an agreement that is binding even when you are away during the Christmas holidays. In that case, your boyfriend would be your contact person."

"I don't think I will need the contract at home. It's all the pressure of being in medical school that must be getting to me. I will be safe at home."

Or I hoped I would be. At least when I was back home I would have Dare and John, and Dare had a way of taking care of me.

"Just in case, Sola. Don't be hesitant to call or text me when you are in Michigan," Naduah said.

"Okay, Naddy," I said using Ladi's nickname for her.

"Sola!" she warned.

"Okay, I am sorry! Dr. Ibrahim. How do you like your new apartment?" I added.

To Ladi's relief, she had finally moved out of Ladi's apartment. But I knew he enjoyed her company more than he let on; they had a cute brother-sister camaraderie I envied.

"I am enjoying the independence. But Sola, we should try to focus on you during these sessions. Did you notice you just went from suicidal ideation to talking about my new apartment like that?"

"My emotions change easily sometimes," I replied and shrugged my shoulders.

She watched me for a moment, almost like she was forming an opinion about me and then she said, "Just remember that statement anytime thoughts of suicide come to your mind. Remember that your emotions change easily; because you feel a certain way in one moment doesn't mean you have to act on that emotion."

"Okay," I replied. Her words certainly made sense to me, but I knew myself. My fleeting but volatile emotions were capable of choking the life out of me.

Chapter Sixty-Two

Ladi

"Aha!! Ladi, how was your break!" I turned in the direction of the voice and, sure enough, it was Nikky sprinting towards me for a hug. This was our first class after the much needed Christmas holidays and I was glad to be back with the crew.

"Nikky! How are you?" I said, leaning down to accept the hug from her. "What did you do during the break?" I asked.

"I spent one half of the holiday eating, the next half I spent avoiding Mommy and Aunty Nikky's shopping sprees. What about you?"

I laughed and replied, "Just chilling. I was exhausted after anatomy. We all needed that break."

"Well, buckle your seat belt," Nikky said. "Because I have heard cardio and respiratory is no joke! The next exam is going to be bloody."

"Men, I am not looking forward to it."

"Hey!" Nikky screamed again and made a beeline for Tina.

I felt a tap on my shoulder and then turned. It was Ego.

"Hey, Ego," I said.

"Hi, Ladi," she replied then hugged me.

"How was your break? You were in DC right?"

"Yes," she replied.

"So did you have fun during the break?"

"Yes, I was alone for most of the break though, so that was difficult."

"Don't you have family around?" I asked, alarmed with the prospect of anyone spending Christmas alone.

"No. I don't," she answered with a sad smile on her face.

I replied, "I am sorry to hear that, Ego. You should have come home with me. My mom would have been so happy to pamper you right after she tried to convince you to become my wife. She actually spent this holiday trying to convince every eligible bachelorette in church that I was husband material."

She laughed and said, "For real? She would have said something about you being a young doctor. That's hilarious. Maybe next year I will take you up on your offer."

"Yes, really," I replied shaking my head.

My mother's antics during the holidays were hilarious.

Her subtle hints urging me to settle down had turned into downright confrontations.

I told her that was out of the question till medical school was over. I also jokingly reminded her of what she told me right before I left, that I would meet the love of my life in med school.

"I haven't met anyone yet," I replied, suppressing all thoughts of Sola from my mind.

My mother replied like only she could, "You have. You just don't realize it yet or you are not being truthful to yourself about her."

Needless to say, I steered clear of any wife conversations after mom's uncannily accurate statement.

I turned my attention back to my classmates in 1007 as they screamed greetings to each other and hugged me like they hadn't seen each other for years. I spotted Irene and Sola walking in to the lecture hall and smiled in greeting. Sola's face lit up.

 She made her way towards me, weaving past our screaming classmates.

"Ladi, hi!" she said, accepting my hug.

She looked much happier now. I was really concerned for her and became even more concerned when Naduah specifically asked me to make sure I kept in touch with her during the holidays. I called her a couple of times and she sounded upbeat. She told me her mother had finally come home and things were going well with her boyfriend. I didn't know whether I was thrilled about the boyfriend part, but at least I was happy she was happy now.

"Hi, Sola. You are looking so much—"

I was interrupted by Dr. Bean. "Yeah, yeah, yeah, I know my fans missed me! Settle down."

The class laughed loudly.

Lenny called out like a crazed fan, "We love you, Dr. Bean!"

Dr. Bean shook his head in amusement then said, "Ya'll have probably heard how difficult cardio and respiratory is, how everyone fails the exam, how you have to learn a million things and yada, yada..."

He paused then said, "You have heard wrong. It's even more difficult than you can ever imagine! You think Neuro was bad, wait for the cardio-respiratory exam. Traditionally, only five people pass the exam."

My heart sank when I heard this.

Then Dr. Bean burst into laughter and said, "Don't worry, guys, I am just messing with you. If you study, you will pass the exam. It's honestly not that bad."

"Boo, Dr. Bean," Joanna called from the back of the lecture hall. "You almost gave us a stroke!"

"I kid. I kid," he said, raising up his hands in protest.

"The upperclassmen want to speak to you guys." Dr. Bean said, handing the microphone to a second year, Belinda Belfonte.

"Hey 2012!" she began. "I am here to speak to you about a Stedman tradition, the Smo-KER! The Class of 2011, my class, will be throwing the smoker this year, for the Class of 2009! If you don't know what the smoker is about, well, after the seniors' 'match', meaning finding residency positions, the sophomores throw a big celebration or party for them, which we refer to as the smoker. It's basically a skit night. Each class has to produce a video making fun of the medical school experience. You can poke fun at each other, your professors, even the upperclassmen. After that, we party like it's 1999! We all are very excited! And we decided to give you a sample of what to expect this year!

"Go 2009! It's all about class unity this year!" she screamed. Then the lights went dim and the words SMOKER 2009! THE REMIX! flashed across the projector screen. Loud hip hop music began to blast from the sound system then a group of about twenty girls I recognized from 2011 began to dance to music down the stairs of the lecture hall. They were all wearing the same black shirt

Belinda had on with SMOKER 2009-THE REMIX written boldly on the back of the shirt.

"Is that James?!" Sola asked. Her head was turned towards the back of the lecture hall.

I turned my head and saw James with a group of 2011 guys dancing to the music and getting the class hyped by screaming, "Yeah! Twenty-ELEVEN! Smoker 2009! The remix!"

He ran to the front of the lecture hall where Ronke was seated and planted a wet big kiss on her cheeks. She shrank back in dismay, but I noticed she couldn't help laughing.

The class erupted into applause, and we all got up on our feet. I craned by neck to see the girls' choreography because my classmates below were blocking my view.

In one moment, the atmosphere of the class had turned from serious pre-cardio unit mode to party mode. That was Stedman College of Medicine for you!

The choreography ended with the girls pointing to the projector screen, then music that I can only describe as movie trailer music began to play.

On the screen big and bold words flashed across the screen, matching the tempo of the music:

THE YEAR 2009!

SMOKER 2009!

THE REMIX

HOSTED BY THE BEST CLASS OF STEDMAN

2011

ON MARCH 18, 2009!

BE THERE!

The class erupted into applause again with James grabbing the microphone and screaming, "Yeah, lets get the party started! Smoker TWENTY O NINNEEEEE!!!"

Then my attention went back to the screen again, because apparently the presentation wasn't over.

On the screen were the words:

2012

BEWARE OF THE IDES OF MARCH!

The presentation ended with the sound of maniacal laughter.

Oh, no, what did that mean? I glanced at James who had a self-satisfied smirk on his face amidst his laughing classmates.

"What does that mean?" Sola asked me.

"I think 2011 is going to play another prank on us," I said then shook my head.

Sola laughed and replied, "This semester is going to be very interesting!"

Yes, it would be and no thanks to the Class of 2011.

Chapter Sixty-Three

Tayo

"What do you think 2011 is about to do?" Nikky demanded as her eyes lit up in amusement.

"I have no idea," I replied, trying to keep up with her as she walked briskly down the corridor of the discussion rooms.

It was barely two weeks into the new semester, and we were back on the studying grind again. We had to. After neuro-anatomy, everybody was on top of their academic game.

"Here, this one is empty," Nikky said and opened the door to an empty room. "The *smoker* is a big deal! And the sophomore prank is a traditional thing. We really have to find out what James is up to," Nikky said.

I watched in amusement as she arranged her laptop, her colored pens, notes and pencils neatly on her table as she talked.

"We should ask Ronke to find out. He is in *luv* with that girl," I replied then chuckled.

Nikky laughed then quickly turned her attention to her notes.

We settled into companionable silence before she said without taking her eyes from her notes, "Tayo. You said you wanted to tell me something when we got back to school?"

My heart sank. I almost convinced myself that this unpleasant conversation would not take place. Every time I tried to tell Nikky about Belinda, I would look at those big brown eyes of hers that gazed at me with pure admiration, and I would stop. I couldn't bring myself to tell her. All through the last semester, I tried countless times to start the conversation but each time I would stop. Then I became complacent in my cowardice, and I forgot altogether. I became accustomed to the guilty feelings that usually confronted me and simply ignored any of my misgivings and threw myself into school. But immediately after I went back home for the Christmas holidays, without the demands of school to distract me, I was raked by my guilt again.

I really shouldn't have bothered going home for the holidays because my break couldn't be described as restive. My father had the not-so-brilliant idea of the family touring Europe in the family private jet. So instead of heading to Lagos, like I usually did for every Christmas break, I headed to the family home in West Virginia.

My mother was ecstatic to see me but after she embraced me, she said, "I have won a bet against your brothers and father. They bet you would not last a semester in medical school, and you have proven them wrong! Try to stay in school for the next semester because I had another bet with your father and this time, he promised to get me the Chopard diamond I have had my eye on if I win!"

I hardly had time to respond to her when my father walked in and said, "Your mother is cheating! You are not supposed to know about the bet."

I prostrated before him in the traditional Yoruba way of greeting. I closed my eyes for a moment so my parents wouldn't see my tears. I knew they had low expectations of me, but when I heard them jest so casually about my career, it hurt me. After the support they showed me during the white coat ceremony, I thought that I finally won their respect but apparently not.

My father then said, "Don't worry. You only have to do this med school thing for one year then you can help your brothers with one of my businesses in Nigeria. Your mother would have won enough diamonds to fill two vaults by then."

I didn't bother with a reply.

Any hope I had of an iota of respect or even love from my brothers was destroyed when Teni greeted me with the words, "You are home? You haven't messed up yet? Well, it's only a matter of time before you do."

I thought that he was just being the usual mean-spirited Teni but later that day he and Temi ordered me to their office for a meeting.

"What are you doing?!" Teni demanded as soon as I walked in.

"What are you talking about?" I asked tiredly. I was particularly exhausted that day because we had just flown in.

"I just got a call from Hassan, and he said you are asking questions about that old blue folder. The one that was made because of your stupidity," Temi replied.

With my brothers' eyes boring into me with hostility and impatience, I couldn't even register the hurt I felt at Hassan's betrayal.

He told my brothers? I was still expecting the call he had promised me

"I wasn't asking specifically about the blue folder. There is someone in school who looks familiar, and I asked Hassan if she was a mutual friend."

My brothers exchanged quick glances.

"Now, look here—" Teni started.

Temi interrupted saying, "Calm down, Teni."

He continued again after sighing deeply. "Tayo. Teni and I have done all we can to protect this family. We both genuinely love you and we do what we do to protect you."

He sat down directly in front of me and continued, "Trust me. I want you to stop asking questions and stay far away from that girl. It will be...better for everyone. After this year, you can join us in the family business. You have pursued this medical school thing far enough."

I nodded quietly, but I made up my mind that I would never drop out of medical school, and I would resolutely find the connection that Sola had to the blue folder. My brothers' actions proved my suspicions were right.

The implications of my thought process immediately occurred to me, then I quickly dismissed the thought.

There was no way it could be her. Perhaps, Sola had some connection to that night but she couldn't be the *girl. I refuse to believe that.*

I half listened to the rest of their boring lecture until I crawled back into bed.

Needless to say, the holiday was more of a living nightmare than a holiday. I avoided everyone in my family and made myself scarce during family outings. I found comfort in the long-distance phone calls I made to Nikky. It did not matter what obscure location in Europe my family had dragged me to, I always called Nikky, even just to hear the sound of her voice. We usually stayed on the phone for hours, and she would regale me with tales about her parents and her very dramatic aunt. Her mother even demanded to speak to me during one of our conversations and asked me not so politely what my intentions were for her daughter. Nikky was beyond mortified and quickly hung up after she wrestled the phone from her mother.

After one of my long conversations with Nikky, I decided to tell her the truth. Every time I hung up the phone, the guilt weighed heavily on my heart. I didn't want to tell her over the phone so I told her to remind me that I had to tell her something when I was back in the States. This was the first time she reminded me, and it crossed my mind to postpone the conversation.

I glanced at her big brown eyes and knew this would be the last time she would ever look at me with respect. Her eyes would soon regard me with scorn like my parents and my brothers.

I was very scared. No, I wasn't scared.

I was petrified of losing her.

I remembered what happened to me the last time Nikky and I took a break from our friendship. Without even realizing it, I had fallen in love with her and needed her like oxygen. I could not bear the thought of a permanent break from her.

I sighed and glanced at her again. She caught my eyes then smiled.

I had women problems before, but this one really took the cake. How was I going to tell her I "cheated" on her with two people? If I really analyzed the situation, I didn't really cheat on her. I mean we were not in a defined relationship.

Who was I kidding? Nikky would not let me go scot free on a technicality.

There would never be a right moment to tell her.

I had to tell her now.

I cleared my throat and began, "Nikky…"

Chapter Sixty-Four

Nikky

"I made a mistake. I went out for a happy hour with a couple of second years...there was a lot of alcohol," Tayo started.

I squinted my eyes at him. He looked so wonderfully adorable today. I really missed him during the holidays. Every time I spoke to him on the phone, I wanted to fly across the Atlantic Ocean and give him a hug. He always sounded so lost and broken on the phone. I hated the way his family treated him. I know he made mistakes, but he had a good aura. At the core of Tayo Smith's being was a good man.

It didn't hurt that he was so gorgeous!

"What's up? Tell me," I replied to him.

He probably got drunk and broke his flat screen TV again. He did that the last time he got drunk.

"I slept with someone, Nikky."

I heard the words, but I didn't understand them.

What did he mean by 'he slept with someone'? Did he mean fell asleep with someone on the same bed?

Then it dawned on me. He slept with someone.

He had cheated on me.

"Oh, my goodness," I began because those were the first words that came out of my mouth.

I think I was crying because he immediately rushed over to my side of the table and put his arm around me.

I shrank back immediately.

"Don't you dare touch me! Don't you put your hands on me!" I screamed.

He quickly withdrew his hands and folded his arms across his chest.

"Nikky...it was a drunken mistake. I don't even remember what happened. I know I woke up, and she was next to me."

He paused then got on his knees.

He cautiously put his hand on my knee then continued, "I don't know what to tell you. I am so sorry, Nikky. I regret my actions with every fiber of my being. I was drunk. I don't remember what happened."

"Who was she?"

"Belinda Belfonte, the second year."

I knew her. She was the one who came to him at the football game. The one with the body-hugging jeans. She was the one he kissed at the first post-exam party.

I wondered if he had been sleeping with her then.

"So you have been cheating on me for a while with her? Even before the football game?"

"Nikky, it wasn't...I wasn't cheating. It happened one time. It was after the football game."

I stared at him for a moment then my vision became cloudy because of my tears. I wondered if desperation had gotten me into this mess, that the raised eyebrows of Sola, Irene and Tina at our undefined relationship were warranted, that my mother's disapproval and concern was warranted.

Then I remembered what Ego had said in Ladi's dinner party. She had not been lying after all. I was thoroughly humiliated; just like the proverbial wife, I was the last to know.

Probably everyone knew and had kept it from me.

"You lied to me at Ladi's dinner party. You looked me in the eye and told me Ego was lying."

It was then that I realized I loved a man who had room only for himself in his heart.

"I was so scared. I tried to tell you so many times, but I couldn't. I didn't want to lose you and have the nightmares again," he said. "I didn't want to go through that again."

His words now hurt me more that the revelation of his actions.

"Do you realize that all you keep talking about is you? All you care about is how losing me would affect YOU, not the consequences of your actions, not how you would hurt me, but how losing me would HURT you!"

"Nikky," he began then he tried to clasp my hands in his.

"No! No! Don't touch me! Just let me be!"

I put my head on the table and wept bitterly while he looked at me helplessly.

He had hurt me more than he would ever imagine. Tayo wasn't just Tayo, the gorgeous one; to me, he was the one I had seen in the vision.

Now the memory of that vision taunted me because as I wept, I saw myself holding that beautiful girl and Tayo looking at both of us with love that could only be reserved for a wife and daughter. Love that could only come from a husband's and father's eyes.

I wept because I finally accepted that the vision was a figment of my imagination, that it would never be.

I glanced up at him after a moment. He was still kneeling in front of me with his head bowed. He glanced up and caught my eye, and I gazed back at him.

I felt a mixture of hate, betrayal, hurt, anger and…love.

Yes, even at this moment, I realized that I still loved him.

But that wasn't good enough any longer. My love could not hold us together.

This thing me and Tayo had. This undefined-crazy-love relationship we had.

He was too selfish for that.

I wiped my tears then said, "This relationship, exclusive friendship or whatever it was, is over. Go get help for yourself, Tayo. You are obviously an alcoholic."

With that, I calmly packed my belongings and walked out of the room.

I made sure not to glance at him once because I knew I would falter if I did.

It was cruel, but it had to be done.

Tayo Smith and I were done for good.

But as I walked away, I wasn't too sure because his question to me in my apartment last semester immediately came to my mind.

"Nikky will you forgive me for anything?" he had asked.

Well apparently not, because I definitely wasn't going to forgive him for this.

"You guys get it! The alveoli says to the bronchioles, 'How are you doing?' And they say, 'ALL VE you later!'"

The whole class watched the spectacle silently.

Dr. Moore continued, "You get it. You get it! AL-VEo u later!"

He still did not get the response he hoped for because you could hear a pin drop in the class.

I sighed and shook my head. It was another painful class of Dr. Moore of the respiratory unit. I knew it would all go downhill when I saw him for the first time. He was a tall gigantic man with a huge imposing nose. In fact everything about him was huge: his eyes, his mouth, his ears even his huge hands. I wondered if he suffered from gigantism. We had been told about his bad jokes, his inability to teach, and his notoriously difficult exams, but seeing was actually believing.

"Let me try this one, guys. What did the pussy cat say to the terminal bronchioles?" Dr. Moore asked again.

I sighed and immediately logged on to the Internet to check my email, tuning out Dr. Moore and his bad jokes.

I clicked on the one with the subject heading *Congratulations,* and ignored the fifteen or so emails from Tayo. He had tried calling me, but I didn't answer his phone calls. He had resorted to trying to speak to me after lectures, but I always ignored him. I would not speak to him. Then he began sending emails to me. I read the first one a few days ago

It said:

You have become my life, the very essence of my being. Without even realizing it, Nikky, you have captured my heart and my soul.

You say I am selfish.

Yes, I know I am.

I messed up really badly, but it was because of the alcohol.

I do genuinely care for you, and I am going to get help to cut back on alcohol.

Nikky, you and I cannot deny the facts.

I love you with all my heart and my soul.

You are the love of my life.
I think you love me, too…

I stopped reading his emails after that. I knew if I allowed him back into my mind, then he would invariably get back into my heart. I couldn't risk that with him again.

But he didn't stop. Now he slipped notes under my apartment door and left flowers at my door. He had done this every day for the past weeks.

I ignored all his gestures and concentrated on school. I would never let him back in to hurt me again.

I wiped the tears that always seemed to be in my eyes when I thought of him.

"Are you okay?" asked Sola, who was sitting next to me.

"Yes," I replied then quickly turned my attention to the email.

Sola had been my rock in the past few weeks. I had told her everything, and she had listened sympathetically. She never once told me "I told you so". She just listened and held me when I cried.

I will always respect and cherish her for her nonjudgmental attitude. I had been ashamed to tell any of the girls because they had all warned me about Tayo, but I refused to listen.

I clicked on the email and quickly scanned it.

It was the school's Academic Awards Night. The top ten of the class would be recognized and given cash scholarships. I was one of them.

I was supposed to be happy, but I wasn't.

I wasn't happy about much of anything these days, thanks to Tayo "Heartbreaker" Smith.

"I thought this class would never end. Thank God," Sola exclaimed.

I glanced up and noted with relief that Dr. Moore's lecture of sorts was over.

"Ladi already has a room. Are you studying with us today?" Sola asked.

"No. I have smoker practice," I answered.

This was another activity that took my attention away from Tayo. I was dancing in the smoker and also helping out with the class video skit.

"Everyone has been going on and on about the smoker! I hear this is the event of the year. It's the biggest fashion parade, concert, celebration and drunk fest of Stedman all rolled into one!"

Sola was right. The preparation for "Smoker 2009 the Remix" had taken over Stedman. From the sophomores' constant promotion with large posters around the school to the t-shirts they practically forced all the freshmen to buy, to the constant dance practices in 3019, and the impromptu film crews of each class filming the video skits, Stedman had full blown smoker fever.

I laughed and replied, "Yeah. I am excited, girl!"

"Okay. Have fun, babe," Sola said before she headed in the direction of the reading rooms.

I nodded, but I knew fun wasn't something I was going to have.

Tayo Smith had made sure of that.

Chapter Sixty-Five

Sola

I wanted to march to the front of the class and rip his head off. Tayo Smith's head, that is. Dr. Zee was using him as an example of a "perfect anatomical specimen" to Tayo's delight and that of half the female population of 2012, judging from the catcalls and whistles.

Dr. Zee said, "Class of 2012, behold the Vitruvian man! Perfect in all angles and proportions…"

Dr. Zee paused for effect and then said, "During my hiking trip in Venezuela, I met such a man like this." He gestured to Tayo, who was smiling broadly.

He continued, "Now to hear the heartbeat of such a man."

He placed a stethoscope on Tayo's heart and listened.

I hissed then stomped out of the lecture hall, bristling with anger.

It was obvious his brief remorseful countenance after the breakup with Nikky was over.

I even had to admit to myself that he looked terrible on the days following. His usual clean-shaven face was unkempt, and his eyes looked tired and bloodshot. I looked at him on those days and thought to myself, *Good. Now you know how it is to suffer. You deserve it.*

Now he was back to his jovial self, and I hated him for it.

I have never hated anyone in my life like I hated Tayo Smith.

The reason for all my pain was him having a good time with his life while I suffered.

I really thought I was getting better. So much so that I stopped keeping my appointments with Naduah. I came back to school in a better, more hopeful mood—two rare emotions for me—and for a while, I was okay. Despite Dr. Moore's and Dr. Zee's best efforts, my grades were getting better. Two medical schools in Michigan had indicated that they were interested in admitting me as a transfer student, and I was ecstatic.

My relationship with Dare was waxing stronger. There were no more fights or disagreements and I made it a point to call him every day. Mother came back from her "trip" of sorts like nothing happened and was seemingly stable. She resisted our attempts to make an appointment with a psychiatrist for her, insisting she was okay.

She called me when I was in Dare's house while in Michigan. "Sola. It's me. It's me, your mother."

I was momentarily confused and kept silent for a while.

Where was she calling from?

She answered that question next.

"I am home. I came back this morning."

There was another long silence. I realized that I had come to accept her absence. She had been gone for six months. When I went home to Michigan and saw that John was actually doing very well with Dare, I stopped worrying about my mother or wondering where she was.

In some ways, I was glad she was away. If she wasn't around, she couldn't have any of her episodes of depression, anxiety or whatever psychiatric demon she was fighting that threw poor John into disarray and made me seethe with anger.

Now she was back and with her, she would bring her demons.

I should have been happy, but I was not.

I was angry and disappointed even.

"So where have you been?" I asked dryly.

"I went to a women's shelter and moved around because..."

She moved around because in her paranoid and deluded mind, the FBI, the police or even the mafia was stalking her.

Something snapped in me at that moment. The situation was both pitiful and funny.

"So you are home now?"

"Yes, I called John and he came home straight from school."

Poor John would have to nurse her back to some semblance of stable mental health.

I did not want to continue the conversation with her any longer. It was pointless. We had been down that road before. She would never admit she needed help; to her, she was right and our reluctance to believe her paranoid tales was all part of the grand conspiracy. I suddenly realized my previous plans were fantasies. She would also never agree to see a mental health person nor would she agree to go back to Nigeria. She couldn't bear the thought of her society friends seeing what she had become.

I quickly ended the conversation by saying, "Okay. I am glad you are back home. I will call John later."

I hung up before she could protest. So my mother was as stable as she was ever going to be. And although it broke my heart to watch her heart break, Nikky's breakup with Tayo made me deliriously happy. Tayo and I had even reached some sort of stalemate regarding each other.

We avoided interacting with each other.

I don't know why he suddenly started making a conscious effort to avoid me, but I was too resentful to even begin to care. I did not want to fill my head with fearful thoughts.

My greatest fear was that he would remember who I was.

So I ignored and functioned the best way I could. There was no pain and no cutting.

The only thing that threatened to rain on my parade during the idyllic first days of this semester was when Irene told me she would be repeating the year.

She had failed every unit prior to this unit. I shudder every time I remember her tear-strained eyes and her desperate voice, weeping in my arms when she first got the email from Dean Robert's office. I was heartbroken for her.

Besides that, my life was better than it had ever been. But something snapped in me as I watched Tayo with a self-satisfied smile on his face, standing with Dr. Zee.

I kept hearing Naduah's advice: "Because you feel a certain way does not mean you have to act on that emotion."

If it were that easy, my life would be much simpler.

His display in the lecture hall, basking in all the attention after almost destroying my life and breaking my friend's heart, was too much.

I walked briskly past the lobby of 1007 and headed to the room with the cross. I needed a place to think. I swung open the door slowly and then sat on the pew opposite the cross. I always found the room oddly comforting, even without Ladi to play the piano.

Then without knowing what I was doing or why I was doing it, I knelt before the cross and closed my eyes. I don't remember when I last prayed or if I even knew how to, but I found that no matter how much I tried to deny the existence of God I somehow always found myself seeking answers to the questions that plagued my heart from this entity.

How do I talk to you?

Then it came to me: talk to Him like you would a friend.

So I started, "God, please help me, if you truly exist I need your help right now. Why do you ignore me? Am I not worth something to you?"

I rocked myself back and forth in my kneeling position, repeating the same words over and over again.

As usual, no profound answer came to me but being in that room, kneeling before that cross, I felt oddly calm and comforted.

Then I heard somewhere from the deepest recesses of my heart, I heard the words, *Be still. Still.*

So for that moment my emotional disquiet was finally at peace, albeit temporarily.

After my prayer of sorts I stayed back in the room with the cross, ignoring texts from Thomas ordering me to come to the discussion room to study. The room gave me solace, and I liked fantasizing that I could play the old piano. I strummed the keys of the piano slowly and tried to remember the first bar of *Heaven* that Ladi had tried to teach me.

It seemed like the harder I tried, the worse it sounded and I finally gave up.

"I had a feeling I would find you in here."

It was Ladi at the door. He was the only one that came to this room.

"Thomas Jacob is about to send the police to search for you. You are supposed to be studying," Ladi said and then walked into the room. He sat beside me on the stool opposite the piano, "Scoot! Give me some space!"

"Ladi, I was here first," I protested, but I moved a little so he could sit beside me.

"I discovered this room, Sola," he replied dryly. "So I can sit wherever I want."

I laughed and replied, "Whatever!"

He regarded me for a moment then asked, "Sola, are you okay? I mean, are you really okay?"

I looked at him then sighed. He really did get me. Despite my best efforts to hide my emotions, he always knew when I was in emotional turmoil. I wasn't ready to let him in yet. He was just a friend.

"Yes, I am fine."

I quickly changed the subject.

"So how are things in the student council?"

Ladi shook his head then said, "We spent the next hour or two arguing about our smoker skit."

I laughed then replied, "Have you guys thought of a theme yet?"

"I don't know, I tuned off while they were arguing."

I laughed then said, "Well, that's what you get Mr. President."

He smiled at me then began to play on the piano.

At that moment, I wished I could play the piano. The music was evocative and moving.

"What do you see when you hear this music?" I asked Ladi.

He stopped playing and then said, "I see my brother."

I put my arms around him and squeezed his shoulder.

"What do you see?" he asked.

I replied, "I see love. The piece is moving. I hear the tune over and over again in my head some times. It's the soundtrack in my head during exams."

He laughed and said, "The soundtrack in my head for my exams is 'Let Me Get Out of This Alive'."

We both laughed and then there was a long silence, no words with both of us staring into each other's eyes.

He is my friend, I quickly reminded myself. We were really good friends who almost kissed once but didn't. We got carried away that day, and I don't think it meant much to him anyway because he never mentioned the incident to me again. He was just more careful around me now.

I noticed he only gave me perfunctory side hugs now.

I quickly continued the conversation. "It reminds me of love and...loss."

"Why love?"

"Because that is what I see in my head when you play."

He eyes looked amused, "So tell me how love looks."

"I don't know how to describe it to you, but that's what I see," I answered matter of factly.

He laughed and then said, "Okay, let's see love together, shall we?"

Then he began to play, and I saw shades of gray because to me, love was never black or white or the colors of the rainbow. Love to me was always in shades of grey.

I am sorry to inform you that after careful consideration we will not be accepting you as a transfer candidate to our school.

Sincerely yours,

Dr. Heckenbottom

Dean of Academic Affairs
Michigan State University

I read the email again to make sure I wasn't mistaken.
Okay, Sola, don't panic. Keep calm.
I was in my bedroom trying to do some late night studying when I got the email from Michigan State University.

But I could already feel the emotional angst beginning to build up inside of me.

This was the worst possible news I could receive because, out of the two schools that replied to my inquiries, this was the school more likely to accept me. The other school, Bayarn Medical College, had only accepted two transfers in the past five years. Michigan State had accepted ten, and I had been optimistic I would get accepted.

Why was Tayo Smith in Stedman!? If he wasn't here, my life would be blissful!

The bitter tears began to fall, and the searing emotional pain in my heart became physical. I could actually feel it this time.

I had to be realistic with myself. Bayern would not accept me. I had failed yet again.

Naduah's constant reminder that I stop allowing negative connotations came to my mind, but I was simply stating a fact. I had failed.

I would have to stay in Stedman...with Tayo Smith.

Though my heart had made a decision with certainty, my heart bled with anger and pain.

"I really have to torment myself for three more years with him?" I asked myself.

Then I heard in my head, *You don't have to. Why don't you end it? You know your life is never going to get better.*

"I can't. I am too tired," I replied back.

It will end the pain. It will end the hurt. Just do it, Sola, for once in your life take control or are you still a coward.

I glanced at the fan and imagined hanging myself from it, but where would I find a sturdy rope? Besides, I was too tired and too exhausted to go through the trouble of finding a rope.

What about something easier? You could just take some pills.

I glanced at the pills of acetaminophen on my dressing table. I could gulp a few of those pills but I knew it would be a slow painful death, if it killed me. What if Irene came into my room and found me? She would take me to Stedman's emergency room right next door, and they would pump my stomach. I would have to deal with the embarrassment of being "the girl that almost committed suicide."

Then you can cut. You know where the most important blood vessels are, the voice said again.

Too dramatic and painful, I answered back.

What about benzodiazepines or barbiturates? You will simply drift off to sleep, there will be no pain.

That could work but where would I get the pills from? If I acted anxious enough, maybe Naduah would get a psychiatrist to prescribe me some.

What about your brother? What about Ladi? I heard in my heart.

There it was again. The greys of love that prevented me from hurting myself, knowing that if I did, I would not only take my life but my brother's too and that of everyone who loved me.

Then I heard quietly in my heart, *Be still, Sola. Your life is not yours to take.*

"But I am in pain. When will all the pain end? I can't take the pain anymore," I answered back.

Although *I* was not in any immediate danger of killing myself, I remembered the no-suicide contract I signed with Naduah then searched for my cell phone. I needed to call Ladi, my contact person.

As I began to dial his number, my phone rang, and it was Ladi.

That's odd.

"I was thinking about you," he started.

"Are you okay? I had a premonition that you were in danger."

His statement shocked me into silence. How did he know?

I wanted to answer with the usual but untrue statement, "I am fine." But I couldn't.

Instead I said, "Ladi, I…I don't know…Can you come over? I don't want to be alone."

I was asking a lot because it was one in the morning, but I needed him.

"Okay," he answered immediately. "I will soon be over."

And he was true to his word, he was in my room fifteen minutes later with a bag of junk food and a DVD of *Pride and Prejudice*.

"I come bearing gifts," he said.

I laughed and, for the first time that night, felt tension seep through my heart slowly.

We spent the most of the night eating junk food, with me laughing at Ladi's reenactments as Mr. Darcy in scenes of *Pride and Prejudice* like it was perfectly normal for him to be in my house at one in the morning.

Chapter Sixty-Six

SMOKER 2009: The Remix

The truth is that no one ever really remembers the events of the smoker in Stedman, especially the graduating seniors who are smashed to oblivion.

For those who were not sober enough to remember, here are a few highlights.

The invitations always say six but everyone shows up at seven thirty and the show starts at eight or even nine. This timeline has been consistent for forty years of Stedman history.

This year the sophomores had chosen the theme "the remix". No one really understands what it means but goes along with it to show support. They keep insisting that it is an ode to the past smokers of Stedman, a tradition that began forty or more years ago.

The show begins in 3019 promptly at eight. The usually quiet examination hall has been transformed into a festive party hall. Balloons are strewn around the windows, there is a DJ blasting music at the back of the hall, and huge posters with SMOKER 2009: The Remix decorating the room. The atmosphere is electric and rowdy. The room is packed to the brim and some people resort to standing at the back.

The host Belinda comes on stage after the DJ is able to convince the seniors to return to their seats. They climb onto the stage and dance, block the projectors and sing along to every *popular song that comes along. No one questions them. After four years of hard work, they have earned the right to climb onto stages.*

The first video is a montage of all the smokers past. From afros to Jerry curls, it seems like only the hairstyles of these future doctors have changed in the past smokers. The audience applauds appreciatively. Then a video montage of the seniors opening their match envelopes (the envelope with the name of the medical residency) is played and this earns a tear or two from the graduating class. Everyone notes that, so far so good, the sophomores are putting on a good show this year. They make sure to play the montage with heartfelt I-will-miss-you music.

The choreography proper starts, and that's when the shows gets a little crazy. The excitement and anticipation for the performances is palpable, The audience is treated to Salt-n-Pepa's "Push It", performed by Nikky and Tina. Michael Jackson' "Beat It" and Prince's "Kiss" performed by a very Jerry-curled James, TLC's "Waterfalls", Destiny's Child's "Survivor" and Tayo Smith surprising the crowd with an energetic performance of MC Hammer's "U Can't Touch This". The audience now begins to grasp the theme, its music and smokers through the era.

The video skit begins and, as tradition dictates, it starts with the freshman video. The freshman video has traditionally always been the funniest so there is a high level of expectation from the student body. The freshman class watches the video with bated breath. Every freshman is thinking "Please laugh. I hope you like our video!"

The video begins with a tired-looking Irene in the anatomy lab, guzzling energy drinks then falling asleep. She wakes up and all the bodies in the anatomy lab are dancing to Michael Jackson's "Thriller" around her. Of course, "the bodies" are played by individuals in the freshman class including the most talented dancer of all, Nikky. The crowd roars with laughter, and the president of 2012 breathes easier. The video ends with Irene running to 1007 where Tayo is rapping. He has changed the lyrics of popular song "In My White Tee" to "In My White Coat." The members of his class provide backup dancers for him with each wearing the short white coat. He raps about the pressures of first year, the late nights, the hookups. Then he stops momentarily, looks directly into the camera and says, "Please forgive me Nikky Abe, I want you back."

The audience is stunned into silence and look at each other in confusion. Nikky shakes her head and wipes a surreptitious tear from her cheek. Sola bristles with anger and abruptly walks out. Ladi looks confused, and wonders how Tayo pulled that off.

No one really remembers the rest of the smoker after that because all other videos paled in comparison to that romantic gesture.

Everyone does remember the sophomore prank, though. The show ends with a montage of memories the seniors made throughout their four years in medical school. Again the seniors shed a tear or two basking in nostalgia. Then a hundred and twenty freshman students head to the parking lot and find empty parking spots. Slowly and surely, each freshman remembers handing their keys to a sophomore who reassured them that this was a complimentary valet service.

Every freshman collectively groans, with some using more colorful language than others. And so Smoker 2009 will always be remembered for Tayo Smith's desperate gesture of love in the Class of 2012's skit video and the inconvenient prank that Class of 2011 played on the Class of 2012.

Chapter Sixty-Seven

Tayo

"So will you forgive me?" I asked Nikky from my kneeling position outside her apartment door.

I waited with bated breath for her response. She sighed and ran her fingers through her hair then she fixed those big brown eyes on me.

I could tell her resolve was weakening. I knew then that I didn't just want her back because she was one of the only people that made me feel good about myself, but because I loved her.

After my public plea in the smoker video, I retrieved her car from the parking lot where the sophomores had stashed our cars. She accepted the keys wordlessly from me and, when I held her hand a moment longer than necessary, she did not protest nor did she snatch her hand away. I was encouraged by all this but knew it wasn't going to be that easy to win her back.

Nikky avoided me for the next few weeks after the smoker. She made excuses to disappear when I was in her vicinity and studiously avoided all eye contact with me when we were forced to work together in anatomy lab. Today, I decided to wait for her at the entrance of her apartment.

"Tayo," she started.

"Nikky, please? Let's just talk. All I want is to talk with you."

She sighed then unlocked her door, and I quickly stood.

She dropped her book bag on her couch and turned to face me with a resigned look on her face.

"Tayo, answer the questions I ask you truthfully. Don't you dare lie to me anymore."

"No, I won't lie," I answered and gulped.

"Have you been drinking since we separated?"

I shook my head slowly and replied, "No."

I was glad she had started with an easy question. After our breakup I had steered clear of alcoholic drinks, even turning down invitations to parties. The weeks had been hellish without Nikky and without alcohol, but I had survived by focusing solely on demands of school and the smoker video. Slowly, some semblance of normalcy came in to my life. I pushed myself hard in school and replaced alcohol with energy drinks. By the time I crashed into my bed each night, I was too exhausted to have nightmares or think of Nikky, who occupied my thoughts during the day. Of course, Ladi and the rest of the guys teased me for my cheesy romantic move in the smoker video.

I had to do it. I was desperate.

"So you have that under control?" Nikky continued.

"Yes, I do," I answered.

"How do I know you won't slip then cheat on me with another person because you are drunk again?"

"Nikky, technically I didn't cheat. We were not in a defined relationship."

"You better shut up, Tayo. Stop that foolishness!" Nikky interrupted sharply with her eyes flashing.

With my ill-advised words, the old Nikky was back. Nikky the fire cracker, the one always ready for a fight.

You are a fool, Tayo, and better do as the woman says, I cautioned myself.

"Okay, I am sorry for that statement. I am really trying to stop drinking. I can control it if I really try," I answered, immediately becoming contrite.

"Hmmm, I think you need medical help. I know it's hard to hear but the things you tell me are not normal. You have alcoholic blackouts. You drink alcohol to a point where you do things and later have no recollection of them."

I did not need any type of medical intervention, but if agreeing to medical intervention would help me win her back, I would agree to it.

"Okay, if you say so," I answered.

I crossed over to her side in the living room, cutting the distance between us.

I held her hand firmly then slowly pulled her to me.

"Nikky. Please. You have to understand. It was a bad mistake. I am crazy about you. I admit I was being stubborn and didn't admit it to myself earlier. That's why I was idiotic enough to suggest the exclusive friendship thing. Why do you think my world is turned upside down whenever you are not with me?"

"Tayo," she began, her eyes pleading with me.

I knew then that I had won, that she would come back to me.

"You hurt me. You hurt me very badly. I don't think I am ready to let you waltz back into my life."

"Nikky, you don't understand," I began.

She really did not understand how much I wanted and needed her. How much her smile meant to me. What her eyes did to me. I had to make her understand.

I turned her chin upward with my hand so she was facing me, but she looked away and tried to escape from my embrace.

"Tayo. You hurt me. I can't allow you in again. I won't. I am not ready," she replied and broke free.

"Nikky, I will not stop. I can't stop. I have fallen in love with you. You have become like oxygen to me. I refuse to live without you."

"Tayo, sometimes love just isn't enough," she replied.

She walked over to her couch and sat down then said, "I won't forgive you now. I am not ready.

"This thing," she said and gestured with her hands. "Us. We are too intense and too complicated. This whole love thingy is so dramatic! Why is my love life so dramatic?!"

She lay back on the couch and massaged her temples.

I chuckled. I was glad to see the drama queen back in her.

"Let's take a pause on this. I have to call Mommy to remind her to buy the plane ticket."

Before I could protest, she was speaking to her mother on the speakerphone of her cell phone.

"Mommy, have you bought the plane ticket!?" Nikky started.

"Nikky, my child, I told your father last week to buy the tickets. Oh! He hasn't!"

"Mommy!" Nikky protested.

"Don't worry. I will make sure your daddy buys it today. Come to think of it, I think he has. He mentioned this morning that he got reasonably priced tickets from AirAero."

Nikky sighed then said, "Okay. Thank God."

Her parents were coming for Awards Night, and I was a little anxious about meeting them again.

"We are so excited for this Award Night! My incredibly smart and gifted daughter! Top of her medical school class! I know you got those genes from my side and not your father's. They are not smart in his family."

Nikky rolled her eyes and gestured that I should sit beside her on the couch.

"I hope you now have a suitable young man for us to meet, not that useless Tayo boy," her mother added.

Nikky glanced at me then quickly took the phone off speaker.

"Mommy, please, I don't want to talk about it," Nikky said.

"Let me just call you back, please."

"Yes, I love you, too. Why have you become so lovey-dovey all of a sudden?"

"No, you are not always lovey-dovey."

"Okay, bye, see you soon, Mommy. I love you."

Nikky hung up the phone and turned to me.

"Tayo, before I consider forgiving you, tell me the truth. Were there other girls? Was it only Belinda?"

There it was. The nagging, troubling thought that kept me up at night. That I was still yet to tell Nikky about Ego and, if she forgave me for Belinda, she would never forgive me for Ego. I was so close to having her back. I did not want to lose her now. I could not bear the thought.

So I lied, "No. There were no other women."

"I will be so glad when this is over," I whispered to TJ and yawned.

"Yeah, men, Dr. Moore is horrible."

"And the vital capacity of the lung is like a taaaaaaunt elastic baaaaand!" Dr. Moore screamed.

I made a rare appearance in the lecture class to put myself back in good graces with Nikky. It was also the last official lecture of the academic school year. We were close to the finish line of first year, and my classmates and I were eager to cross it.

Nikky had not exactly forgiven me, but at least now she was talking to me. And though I was still banned from studying with her, she sat beside me during lectures. But after ten minutes of trying to listen to Dr. Moore's bad lecture and cringe-inducing jokes, I was wondering if even Nikky was even worth this torture.

Dr. Moore was trying to demonstrate the physiology of the respiratory system using a computer program he had forced us to download. The problem was the class didn't understand half of the terms he used. How were we supposed to pass the last exam of medical school with horrible lectures like this? Even Dr. Moore's PowerPoints were difficult to study. Like most of the class, I had given up listening. Only Nikky seemed to listen, and she typed furiously on her laptop.

I turned on my laptop and began to check the NBA scores, ignoring Moore's lecture, but I couldn't stop surreptitiously glancing at Nikky in class.

She was so beautiful!

Then I said to her softly, in was almost a whisper, "Will you forgive me?" I ran my hands through my hair then said, "To be honest, I messed up and made mistakes but every—"

She opened her mouth to interrupt me but I continued. "Every time we are not together because I messed up, my life falls to pieces."

She stopped typing then rolled her eyes, "Tayo, stop. We can't have this conversation in class. I am still not ready to forgive you."

"You may deny it Nikky, but I know you have feelings for me too," I replied.

She did not answer, but she had a little smile on her face when my eyes met hers.

I knew she had forgiven me.

Chapter Sixty-Eight

Sola

I watched Nikky smile at Tayo, and my stomach turned.

I hated him. I hated them both.

He whispered something in her ear again and she hit him playfully on his leg.

Ignoring the stares of my classmates, I abruptly stood up in the middle of the lecture hall and headed toward the exit.

I was in a dangerous mood, and this time I allowed no interruptions of my rumination. When I got home I drowned out Naduah's advice, Dare' warnings to keep silent, and Ladi's religious platitudes.

I lay in bed; blinking back tears as painful memories came flooding into my mind.

Take yourself back to that night. Don't dream. Don't think. Take yourself there so you remember what he really did to you, the voice said.

So I did.

It was the twenty-fourth day in June in the year 1999, at 11:15 pm.

I was in the wrong place at the wrong time.

Mary, my best friend at the time insisted I come for a party I had no interest in attending. "Sola, baby," she started. "Everyone is going to the party. Stop acting like a fool. See, I will tell my mother that I am sleeping over at your house and you can tell your momsie that you are sleeping over at mine."

She grinned mischievously, "It's a fool-proof plan. No one will ever find out."

With that, I was convinced by Mary to go to the party, inadvertently setting a chain of events that would leave me emotionally destroyed. The three people I knew prior to the party each had a role to play. Mary left me to my own devices, leaving me vulnerable. Dare, who came to my rescue at the last moment and saved my life. And last but certainly not least, Tayo Smith, who did the exact opposite, destroying it.

I remember feeling very uneasy, but there was nothing to feel uneasy about. The party, although loud, was relatively calm. No one was doing anything out of the ordinary, except there was inordinate amounts of alcohol in the party and I wasn't used to that...but my uneasiness became an urgency soon after we arrived.

I knew I had to leave the party.

But neither Mary nor Mary's driver was anywhere to be found.

I sat still on the couch in the dark room with my hand gripped tightly around the cup of alcohol that Mary had handed to me shortly before she disappeared.

Dare sat on the couch next to me, and I winced because at that time Dare was not my Dare. He was the older guy from the neighboring secondary school who would not take no for an answer.

"Sola, how are you doing? Have you thought about my question?"

Before replying, I remembered Mary's advice to me, "Boys like Dare need to be told off firmly unless he will never leave you alone. Stop all this nice girl nonsense and tell him to leave you alone!"

So I said, "Get out of my sight, Dare. I have told you numerous times. I will not nor will I ever go out with you."

It was dark so I couldn't make out his face but saw his eyes glistening.

He stared at me for a moment then said coolly, "Okay."

Then he walked away, disappearing into the darkness.

I sat down silently on the couch, observing the rowdy party with boredom for what seemed like an eternity. The middle of the living room, which served as the dance floor, was filled with gyrating couples. A group of guys loudly passed drinks to one another and laughed loudly at their crude jokes. One of the guys was knocked over and he came flying onto the couch, making me spill the drink I was holding on my lap. He apologized profusely to me then continued laughing with his friends like he hadn't just ruined my dress.

That was it! I stood up from the couch, pushing past the bodies that blocked my path, and headed to the bathroom.

Where was the bathroom? I turned around swiftly, changing direction, and bumped into a tall guy who steadied me.

"Hey, watch it," he said.

"Oh thanks," I replied.

He stared at me for a moment then said, "Are you trying to leave?

"Yes," I replied. "I am trying to find the bathroom. Do you know where it is?"

He held my hand very firmly. He said loudly to me over the music, "Come with me. It's this way."

Before I could answer, he began pulling me roughly in the opposite direction and I knew immediately that something was very wrong.

I tried to wrestle my hand from his grip, but he wouldn't budge. "Leave me alone! Where are you taking me to!?"

But he didn't stop.

He half dragged me by the hand towards a large door and I remember thinking Don't let him take you behind that door, Sola. *So I tried to draw some attention to myself by screaming, but the music was too loud or the party revelers ignored my screams. I would never know.*

He got me behind the door then he shut the door firmly.

"What do you want with—"

I was not allowed to complete the sentence. Someone hit me on the back of the head with a blunt object, and I fell to the floor with my head feeling like it was going to explode.

At this point, I was too confused to be afraid. But the fear would come soon enough when I realized that there were four other men standing over me.

I opened my mouth to scream again, but one of the guys immediately stuffed a piece of cloth into my mouth and taped my mouth firmly.

I couldn't move my mouth to scream, so I tried pulling myself up by grabbing onto the man nearest to me.

He hit me hard across my face with the back of his hand, and I fell to the ground again.

"Please stop this," I screamed again but my words came out mumbled and unintelligible.

"If you scream again when we are done with you, I promise you I will personally break your neck. Keep quiet and you may survive this."

The casual but menacing tone of his voice made me realize that that wasn't an empty threat. I was paralyzed with terror, but I nodded in helpless acquiescence.

If I did exactly what I was told maybe I would survive this.

I looked up at the man who had promised to kill me, wondering if I recognized him.

I didn't.

He stared back at me boldly, lazily even.

I moved my eyes to scan the room and saw the others guys watching me, then I noticed one who looked familiar. He placed his head against the wall and rocked his head back and forth. Where had I seen him before? Then the realization suddenly hit me. It was Tayo Smith. He went to a different high school, but everyone knew Tayo Smith. I had seen him many times before in social events at my school. I looked directly at him hoping for some sort of acknowledgement that he recognized me and he would stop this madness. He stared back at me with bloodshot menacing eyes, and I knew there would be no saving me.

The man standing to my left tipped his head towards Tayo and said, "We shouldn't have allowed him to come with us. He is high on every drug under the planet."

The man over me said, "Even better."

The man on the left shook his head but his action was imperceptible to everyone except for me.

I turned my eye to the right and stared at the man standing there.

He was breathing deeply and almost smiling with anticipation.

I didn't recognize that I had peed on myself until the man said, "Look at you, how disgusting of you."

Tayo began to laugh hysterically then began to hit his head violently and loudly against the wall.

"What are we doing?! Are we going to play?!" he screamed.

"Shut up!" the man who was apparently the leader said.

"We are supposed to let her go," the one on the left said. Although this man would participate fully in the terrorizing events to follow in that room that fateful night, I will always remember that the only mercy that was showed to me came from him.

None of the men responded and the only sound inside the room was Tayo hitting his head against the wall violently and laughing.

"We shouldn't have brought the crazy dude here. He is gone. Let him go," the one on the left said again.

"No," the leader commanded. "Nobody will be allowed to leave this room. If you stepped in here, you knew what you were getting yourself into. Don't worry about him, this won't be his first time doing this."

"But he's from here," the one on the left hissed. "What if she recognizes him?"

"That's not our problem. And besides..." He looked directly at me then said, "She will be a good girl."

Then before I knew what was happening, Tayo Smith grabbed my left foot and then unceremoniously began dragging me.

"No! No! No!" I screamed but my word came out muffled.

"This can not be happening! This cannot be happening!" I screamed in terror to myself, hoping that I would wake up and realize this was just a nightmare.

But I had no such luck: this was real, and it was happening to me.

I couldn't figure out where I was being taken to but saw furniture passing before my eyes as I was dragged past them, so I grabbed on to the legs of a dining table with my right hand and held on to it with the desperate hope that escape was possible if I wasn't taken past this room.

Tayo immediately stomped over my fingers with his heavy boot. I screamed in pain and watched helplessly as he relentlessly continued to crush my fingers with his boot. But I wasn't ready to give up, so I tried to reach across with my left hand and grabbed the leg of the dining table again

The guy who had been sympathetic to me firmly removed my hand and said, "Stop it. Don't make it any worse for yourself. It will be over soon."

He was wrong. It wasn't going to be over soon. It was going to be the longest and most agonizing night of my life.

I let go and allowed myself to be dragged into another room where the door was firmly locked.

In that room, I was brutally raped five times by five different men in quick succession with each goading the current rapist with lewd praises. The moments when I lost consciousness were blissful, but I regained consciousness many times and at those times I was acutely aware of the nightmare. At those times, the fear left me, the terror left me, even the pain left me.

All I could think of, as I was used as a sexual plaything, was my survival.

How exactly would I get out of this alive?

When they were done, I was left for dead but not before I was warned by their leader, "Fadesola Cardoso, remember this was not random. If you speak of this to anyone or do anything silly like reporting to the police, I will kill you."

Then they all walked out of the room casually. The sympathetic man glanced back at me as if to apologize for his role. I don't know how long I lay there, completely still, in my own pool of blood, too paralyzed with terror to scream for help.

But someone came for me.

I don't know how he found me, but Dare came to me alarmed and visibly disturbed by the scene in the room.

He quickly removed the gag from my mouth. I don't remember much after that. My memories came to me in fragments: someone giving me new clothes, someone driving me somewhere, someone in a white coat speaking to me, then the pain and tears afterwards. I will always remember that I didn't cry until after it was over. That always stood out to me. Sometimes we have a mental picture of how we will react to terror, but I did not react like how I thought I would.

I did not cry until it was all over, and I haven't stopped crying ever since.

Armed with the potency of the memory, I decided not to live in terror any longer. I was going to confront Tayo Smith for what he did to me regardless of the consequences. I would turn his life upside down just as he had done to mine five years ago.

Chapter Sixty-Nine

Tayo

"With that, Class of 2012, you have just sat for and hopefully passed the last exam of first year of medical school!" Dr. Moore said with a wide grin on his face.

The class erupted into applause, wild cheers, and hoots!

I handed my examination to Dr. Moore with elation. It was finally over! We made it through! Well, pending a passing score in the examination, but it hadn't been that difficult and I expected to pass.

I joined the excited chatter of the students in the lobby outside of 3019.

All around us, my classmates were in groups, hugging and kissing one another in congratulations.

"We should all go to the barbecue the third years are throwing in our honor," Tina said excitedly.

"I am so happy! It's over. We did it!" Nikky screamed and skipped around the group. "Where is Sola? I want to hug her!" Nikky exclaimed again.

I glanced around for Sola, but she wasn't around. I had seen her turn in her exam and rush out of the examination hall. Her eyes were puffy, and she looked tired. Sola was a boatload of drama, so I quickly focused my attention back to the celebration.

"Ladi, you should give a toast! And a speech!" I said loudly.

Then I quickly planted a wet one on Nikky's cheek after she finally stopped skipping around.

She shook her head at me and smiled.

"I am not sure about a toast. But I am glad first year is over! Second year is up next! We came, we saw, we conquered first year!" Ladi raised his voice loudly and soon everyone in the lobby was clapping excitedly.

The excitement was infectious, and I got swept up in it despite my usual nonchalance to everything academic. This was a big deal, especially for someone like me with a family who expected me to fail. I could not help but feel a sense of accomplishment.

I did it. Temi was wrong. I did not and will not mess medical school up.

But the pessimistic part of me, the part that has given up on myself, answered back, *Give yourself time. You will fail sooner or later.*

It was the Saturday afternoon after the last day of first year and I winced when I saw Ego's name on my caller ID.

Oh, what did she want now?

I did not have time for Ego's antics, especially because I was getting into full "perfect boyfriend mode" for Nikky's parents, who were both flying in today for the Awards ceremony tomorrow. I had plans to meet them for dinner. They already had a bad opinion of me, so I was pulling out all the James Bond swag in my arsenal. I was going to make them love me even if it killed me!

Every time Ego came in to my life, she messed something up. She knew I hadn't forgiven her for opening her big mouth about Belinda, so why was she calling me?

Against my better judgment, I answered my phone.

'Hello," I answered dryly.

"I am sorry for calling, Tayo. Thank you so much for answering."

Well, that was a good start. Her voice sounded so small on the phone, and I didn't have the heart to be mean to her, but I was still cautious.

"Yeah, no problem. What's up?"

"I know you don't want to talk about it, but Ben found out we slept together. Did you tell anyone we slept together?"

I winced and answered dryly, "No Ego, I did not tell anyone we slept together. Why would I do that?"

Just when I was about to make a joke that it wasn't my proudest moment, a small voice from my unlocked apartment door stopped me, I turned and saw Nikky at the door, staring at me with tears in her eyes.

"Nikky," I said immediately, dropping the phone and rushing towards her.

She recoiled from me.

"My parents are dead. I came to you immediately after I found out. You weren't picking up your phone. You were on the phone with Ego. There was a plane crash, and my parents are dead."

Chapter Seventy

Nikky

I spoke to Mommy and Daddy last night.

"Good bye, Mommy. Good bye, Daddy," I said.

"Good bye, baby. See you tomorrow. We are very proud of you!" they replied.

That would be the last time I would hear their voices.

There was no premonition, no warning, no harbinger.

Just a breaking news update rudely interrupting my regular Saturday morning program on CNN. AirAero airlines flight 134 from California had crashed shortly after takeoff.

There were no survivors.

The word *AirAero*. Mommy had said last night that there were flying AirAero.

The flight number, *134.* Daddy had made sure he mentioned the flight number at least twice because he didn't want to wait forever before I located their departure gate and found them.

Then *California,* my beloved California, my home.

But I still refused to panic. Maybe they somehow missed the flight, maybe they were actually survivors.

Aunty Nikky's hysterical screams on the phone when I called confirmed my worst fears. Daddy and Mommy were gone.

Even then, I still refused to believe it. I held on to stubborn hope that they were still alive. I refused to call Tayo and tell him because, if I did, I was confirming the impossible to myself.

I did not know how to exist in a world where my parents were not alive.

The phone call from the AirAero customer service grief team killed whatever hope I stubbornly held on to.

I nodded in acquiesce to the airline's employee's question, "Miss Nike Abe, do you understand what I just told you?"

I knew that her words did not register to me, that I was still expecting Mommy to fuss over me and stock my fridge with food. I was still expecting Daddy to get a scolding from Mommy because he had done something funny again. So I sought Tayo out, because maybe if I told him I would believe it.

So I went to his apartment in Morgan and found him talking on the phone with Ego and heard a sentence that would haunt me: "Ego, I did not tell anyone we slept together."

I felt so utterly alone and broken. He betrayed me again. The day I needed him the most, he was not there for me, and for that I would never forgive him.

Chapter Seventy-One

Sola

I woke up on Saturday morning with a singular thought in my mind: confronting Tayo Smith. All the reasons why I should not immediately came to me. Dare had made me promise that I wouldn't directly confront him because he was concerned for my safety. He was concerned that the threats that were made to me five years ago still held, that if I revealed my secret in any way, Tayo and his gang would harm me. But this was America, and I no longer lived in a lawless country where I was forced to endure a façade of normalcy whenever I saw Tayo Smith. Yes. I did see him many times after the ordeal in Nigeria, and he did not appear to recognize me. I was forced to act like everything was normal because of fear. It was like being violated over and over until I decided to stay away from the social events that would bring me in close proximity with him. When I moved to America, I thought I was free of the agony of being fearful of my attackers, like I was the one who did something wrong. I wasn't. After spending a year in close proximity with him, I realized that he genuinely had no recollection of me. All my encounters with him over the year came flooding into my memory: his guileless hello to me the first time he was introduced to me, his genuine greetings of hello to me when I saw me passing the hall, and his hurt expression when I ignored his greeting in the hall that day.

He did not remember me. The harrowing ordeal that drove me to the precipice of suicide was not important enough to be stored in the annals of his memories.

I was nothing.

I was inconsequential.

That day was just another commonplace event in the life of Tayo Smith.

I know what kept me silent for the whole year. It wasn't Dare's concerns or my fears that there would be consequences if I spoke up.

I now know undoubtedly that it was shame.

I disdained the shame.

I rejected the pity.

I did not want to be "that girl" so I kept silent and died slowly each day.

Well, I was tired of dying today.

There was no gang now. The threats had become powerless to me.

Chapter Seventy-Two

Tayo

"Nikky, please you don't understand."

"Don't touch me," she hissed. "Leave me alone."

"Nikky," I tried again and then grabbed her arm. "Nikky, please…"

"No. Let me be, Tayo. I can't and will not deal with you today. You never loved me. You are incapable of the emotion. The only person you love is yourself."

Her words pierced the deepest recesses of my heart because I knew she was wrong.

She walked out of my room and headed to the door.

"Nikky, please, you have to believe me," I said again in close pursuit of her.

"Let me be, Tayo. My parents are dead. I have a burial to plan."

Her words made no sense to me. I heard her say previously that her parents were dead but I was confused. How could her parents have died? They were flying in today.

"What do you mean by your parents have died?" I asked.

She shook her head slowly and said, "Don't worry." She paused before she walked out my apartment, "You know, Sola was right. You don't deserve me."

Chapter Seventy-Three

Sola

His door was open so I walked into his apartment. He was sitting in his living room with his face in his hands. He almost looked like a decent human being.

I wanted to kill him.

I didn't want to talk to him or even ask questions.

I wanted to take a knife and slice his throat right then.

He looked up and said, "Oh, Sola, what are you doing here?"

The candid way he said my name enraged me further.

"You really don't remember me?" I asked quietly.

He stared back at me quizzically.

Without even knowing what I was doing, I smashed my hand into the glass coffee table opposite his couch.

"Sola, what are you doing?"

I ignored my bleeding hand and picked up a piece of glass from the broken pieces of the table. He stared back at me in alarm, frozen on the couch.

"I am going to kill you! I am going to kill you!" I screamed and lunged towards him with the glass.

"What!" he screamed in alarm.

He caught my swinging arm in mid-air with the jagged edge of the glass just inches from his face. I tried to wrestle out of his grip, but he was stronger than I was.

"Let me go! Let me go!" I screamed.

"Let you go so you can kill me? What is wrong with you?!"

"Let me go!" I screamed again.

"Okay. I will let you go but drop the glass."

I dropped the glass in one quick motion when I felt him relax, then I hit him across the face with all the strength I could muster. He was knocked backward by the force of the blow.

He screamed, nursing his head with one hand.

Then, exactly as he had done to me five years ago, I stomped hard on his splayed hand.

"Sola, for goodness' sake. What have I done to you!?" he screamed and then tried to stand to his feet.

I hit him hard across the face again. He fell down to the floor again on his knees.

"You raped me with four other men when I was sixteen."

"What do you mean I raped you? What are you talking about?"

I swung my hand back to hit him again, but he caught my hand.

"Stop this! What are you saying?!"

"Remember the party Jubril had in his house in Victoria Island? Remember you took me into a room with your friends you threatened me then raped me?" I screamed, trying to wrestle out of his grip.

This time he didn't let me go.

"Yes, I think I remember the party. Jubril had many wild parties, but I don't remember you."

"You don't remember me! You destroyed my life, and you don't remember me! I am going to kill you!"

I tried to free my hand from his grasp, but he wouldn't let me go.

"Let me go!" I screamed at him then I tried to force my hand out his grip.

We struggled like that for what seemed like an eternity, but he would not let me go.

"Sola, please tell me what exactly are you talking about," he asked, raising his voice higher than mine.

"You killed me five years ago. You took my dignity from me. You took everything from me."

I suddenly felt very tired and began to cry. All the anger that fueled my energy suddenly evaporated from my heart.

"Let me go, please. Let me go," I cried.

He did and he stood watching me while I cried and crumpled to the floor.

I cried, "Five years ago you killed me. You don't understand what you did to me, what you took from me."

He stared at me with a deer-in-headlights expression on his face and I knew in that moment he finally remembered.

"Maybe you have me mistaken me for someone else."

"No, I don't. You are Tayo Smith! Your brothers' names are Teni and Temi Smith! You went to Kensington. You, Tobi, and Chris were close friends. I know who you are. I know who raped me." I added with finality.

He looked visibly shaken, but he continued to stare at me helplessly. Then he absentmindedly began to straighten the overturned furniture in the living room. Finally he sat on his couch with his head buried in his hands, weeping silently.

I don't know how long we both stayed in that position, me on the floor sobbing and him on the couch crying silently, rapist and rape victim bound by the horror of one fateful night.

He finally said to me, "I am sorry."

But it was not enough. It would never be enough.

It was too late, and the damage had already been done.

So I told him simply, "It's too late now."

Then I walked out of his door silently and the only sound in the room was his loud weeping.

Chapter Seventy-Four

Sola

I thought confronting him would make me feel better. It doesn't.
It just makes me feel empty.
The voice says to me again, *End it now. You can end the pain now.*
I can. Irene and Tina are not home. But what about my brother?
He will understand."
What about my friends?
They will understand. Write a note.
So I wrote,
I am tired
the agonizing torment of bitterness and rage
I am tired
Of the cruel life
I am tired
Of the misery
There is nothing left to live for.
My life is worthless.
So I'm going to end it now.
I am sorry. So very sorry
I dropped the note on the side table.
I made sure the door is locked.
Do not think. Do not think. If you think, you will not go through
with it.
I filled the bath and got the blade.
I waited for the bath to get filled.
Do not think of Dare. Do not think of John. Do not think of Ladi.
The bath is filled. I turned off the tap.
I climbed in.
Then I slit my left wrist on both sides.
 I watched the blood gush out slowly, too slowly.

I must have hit a vein.
I tried again and made a deeper cut this time.
The blood gushed out faster. Good.
This time I think I got the artery.
Then I waited.
I slipped into the darkness.
And I await a blissful death.

Chapter Seventy-Five

Ladi

"Sola!" I shout after being abruptly awoken from my sleep by an uneasy premonition, like the same premonition I got the night I went to her house, but this time it is stronger.

Then I hear a voice very clearly in my heart saying, *Go to her right now.*

I knew something wasn't right, so I immediately called her cell phone. But it kept going to voicemail.

Then I called Naduah who answered her phone with a groggy, "Hello."

"Naddy, I think something is wrong with Sola. Have you spoken with her recently?" I bark into the phone, not bothering with the preamble of a greeting.

"No, not since you guys started the new semester. Why do you say that?"

"I had a premonition, Naduah. Something is very wrong, and she needs help."

"Then why are you on the phone with me? Go to her apartment right now. I will keep calling her cell phone but go to her right now."

I was already out of the door before she completed her instructions, and all I kept hearing in my heart as I frantically backed out of my parking spot was, *She needs you, Ladi. She needs you.*

My heart raced wildly as I took the stairs leading to Sola's apartment two at a time. I frantically looked for her apartment and fumbled with dialing her number on my cell phone at the same time. I found her apartment door wide open.

That is odd, I think to myself.

However, I don't waste time thinking. I gingerly walked into the apartment and called out, "Sola! Sola!"

There is no answer and the apartment is eerily quiet. It seems like both Irene and Tina have gone home for the summer break. I cannot hear Tina's obnoxiously loud music or Irene memorizing anatomy flashcards from her bedroom.

"Sola, are you home?" I call out again and make my way towards her bedroom door but it is locked.

Then I hear in my heart, *The bathroom.*

I rushed into the open bathroom, knocking over the lamp on the side table in my haste. I flipped the light switch in the bathroom on and gasped in surprise, "Oh no! Sola what have you done?" At first glance, she looked like she had simply dosed off in the bathtub but the distinct slightly pink color of the water told me otherwise.

I plunged my hand in the cold water, splashing water on the bathroom floor and pulled her out, "Sola!" "Sola, please be okay. What's going on?" I managed to pull her almost lifeless body onto a mat on the floor, almost slipping in the process.

The abrupt motion seemed to jolt her awake and she moaned softly then said, "What is going on?"

"Sola, are you okay? Did you fall and slip in the bathroom?" I asked her frantically. I pulled her towards me to examine her more closely then noticed the blood trickling down her cut wrists with horror. "Oh my God! Sola! What have you done?" I gently lay her down on the floor, frantically grabbed some towels and wrapped it around her wrists as a tourniquet. Then I draped another towel on her to cover her naked body.

Sola moaned then said, "I am so tired...so thirsty. Where am I?"

I slipped into a tight space between her sprawled body and bath tub then propped her up. "You are in your apartment."

"What happened?" Her eyes met mine and she opened her mouth as if she is going to say something. Then the veil of secrecy drops again and she keeps silent.

"Fine," I said resignedly. "You don't have to tell me. But..." I pause to examine her wrists. The makeshift tourniquet seemed to have stopped the bleeding. "You have to go to the emergency room to get stitches for that."

"No!" she exclaimed softly. "I don't want anyone to know."

It was then I realized that I had just interrupted a suicide attempt. I didn't know exactly what to say to her but I realized she needed support now more than ever, not my judgment or questions. So I said, "Sola, you need to get stitches. You have lost quite a bit of blood. It will be kept confidential in the hospital."

"It won't be, at least not in the Stedman College of Medicine emergency room." She shrugged her shoulders and continued, "If you insist I go to the hospital, then take me to Riverdale Hospital."

"Okay, Riverdale is fine then. Will you need help getting dressed?" I replied.

She chuckled then replied, "I am not an invalid, Ladi. I may be slightly off mentally but I can get dressed by myself."

I ignored the macabre dig at her and replied, "We need to get to the hospital as soon as possible, Sola."

"Well, please can you get off me so I can stand?" she replied with a small smile on her face.

"Oh, sorry," I apologized, suddenly realizing that my arms are wrapped around her and she is pinned under me. I stood up and awkwardly helped her to her feet.

"The towels are not helping," she said with a chuckle. "Thank you," she added.

The irony of the situation is not lost on me. Sola is smiling and joking around me, almost as if this "situation" was normal, like she was trying to prove to me that she was okay.

But I knew she was not. I would not be so easily fooled. From the moment I saw her weeping on the night of the freshman party, I knew something was not right. Now I was determined to find out what exactly triggered her pain and protect her.

"I will wait right outside for you," I replied. She attempted to close the bathroom door but I stopped her. "No, keep it open." She opened her mouth like she is going to protest, then quietly nodded.

As I kept a watchful eye on her in the bathroom, I said a silent prayer of thanks to God for helping me to get to her on time. In that moment, my purpose in Stedman became crystal clear to me.

I was to protect Fadesola Cardoso with my life.

And as much as it scared me, I was to love her with all my heart.

Chapter Seventy-Six

Sola

"The physical examination in the emergency room showed that you did not sustain any significant nerve or muscle damage. You are one lucky woman. You somehow missed the major nerves so you will retain dexterity of your hands. However, we have to wait and see if there are any residual effects.

"You will be discharged after seventy-two hours," the psychiatric doctor continued. He chuckled at my alarmed expression and said, "It's standard procedure in the psych unit."

"Okay, I suppose this is going to be my home for the next three days," I said resignedly.

"I will be back later in the morning to speak with you. In the meantime, get some rest," he completed then walked out leaving me alone in the silent room. I immediately tried to reach for the remote control on the side table but my bandaged wrists and stiff fingers made it difficult. Then I tried using my elbow to push the remote closer to me but finally I gave up in frustration.

Sola, why did you do this to yourself?

No! I did not want to think about that now. I could not think about it now. I wasn't ready. It was already humiliating enough that Ladi had found me. I wasn't Sola his friend anymore, I was Sola the basket case. I heard someone chuckle at the door and turned.

"How long have you been trying to turn on the television?" Ladi asked. He was holding a bag of Chinese takeout. "I thought you would be hungry," he said and gestured to the food. "Let me help you." He picked up the remote and turned on the television.

The solemn voice of the local reporter's voice filled the room. "Wow, everyone is talking about the plane crash that happened. It was a direct flight from L.A. to DC. I hope we don't know anyone on the plane," Ladi said.

I immediately thought of Nikky's parents.

"I don't think Nikky's parents were on the flight," Ladi said.

"Are you sure? She said they were coming for Awards Night," I replied, eyeing the Chinese food.

"I don't think so. I thought they were arriving later in the week. I tried calling her but she didn't pick up," Ladi began to set the food out of the table. The aroma of General Tso's chicken filled the room.

"Well, I hope she's okay." I tried to reach for the food and almost tipped the carton over.

"Doing anything with bandaged wrists is so difficult!" I exclaimed.

Ladi laughed and picked up the carton. "Just stop. I will help you." He picked up the carton and a spoon and commanded, "Open up."

I laughed then complied. In between bites, I started, "Ladi, I want to thank you."

"For the Chinese? Don't be, I was hungry too." He did not skip a beat and shoved another spoonful of rice into my mouth.

"No, wait." I moved my head slightly back and raised my bandaged wrist. "You know it's more than the rice. It's for everything Ladi."

"It's fine, Sola," he replied then smiled.

"No it's not fine," I insisted.

He replied, "Oh, it isn't?"

"Ladi stop teasing me!" I exclaimed.

He laughed then put the spoon back into the carton. "Okay! I will stop teasing!"

"Ladi," I continued. "I may never tell you what pushed me to this. We may never talk about it but I want you to know that…I am grateful that you are my friend."

He replied, "I won't ask you to tell me why until you are ready, but I will always support—"

"Aww, look at us being mushy," I interrupted.

"No wait, listen to me. I want to say something that I have known for a long time. What I meant to say is that I will always love you." He paused and our eyes met, then he continued, "I love you, Sola. I believe God led me to Stedman for a reason and that reason is you."

And because it felt right, because there seemed to be no other adequate response, I moved closer, within inches to his mouth and kissed him. He was stiff for a moment then relaxed. He kissed me insistently, almost possessively.

Then in that moment of passion, the most inappropriate thought came to me.

Maybe God sent someone to take care of me.

Maybe I am worth something to God, after all.

THE END

If you enjoyed Still *book one* , you will love book two of the series

Coming in 2015, Still book two.

Sign up at eniolaprentice.com to download a free excerpt of book two, pre-launch specials and notifications about the series.

Website :www.eniolaprenticewrites.blogspot.com

Still two excerpt

Nikky

I wasn't picking up any phone calls.

It knew it was Aunty Nikky, and I knew what she wanted to do.

Scream in my ear and ask me over and over again why this happened, if this was really happening.

I would say, yes, this is really happening. My parents were dead.

The whole conversation would make it absolute to me, would make it real to me.

So I avoided speaking to anyone in those first hours and lay quietly in my dark room, afraid to even sob because if I started I would not stop.

My cell phone rang relentlessly and persistently, but I lay frozen in my couch, too devastated to muster the strength to even switch it off.

I glanced at the caller ID for each call, though, and not once did I see Tayo's number. The plane crash was all over the news, so he had to know. He didn't even call me to even apologize about cheating on me with *her*.

I was thoroughly heartbroken. I would never forgive him.

So for the first time in my life, I prayed.

Not using the words I learned from Sunday school or boring Catholic mass or from my Mommy's prayers, I said simple words.

"Please, God," I said over and over again until my voice became hoarse, not knowing exactly how God could help me, but knowing I needed Him now more than ever.

Tayo

In one very short moment, my assessment of myself and my life had changed. I had gone from "young and promising future physician" with a wild but fun past to rapist. I still could not or would not allow myself to remember the incident but I knew her words were true. She was the subject of the blue folder my brothers hid from me.

I had to travel back to Lagos and find out the exact contents and perhaps finally find out Dare's connection to that night.

From the moment those nightmares began, my subconscious knew it was her. When my brothers and Hassan warned me to stay away from her, I knew it was her, but I unconsciously suppressed any thought of it. I knew what they told me happened on that night really happened but when you have no memory of something, no face to remember, it becomes easier to convince yourself that it didn't happen. But I knew my payback would come and it had come today.

What kind of human being was I?

What kind of man did this sort of thing?

I have always imagined that people who did this were uneducated, sex-deprived illiterates who no woman in her right mind would sleep with.

Apparently, I was wrong. I had never had a problem obtaining sex in my life; it was offered to me on a daily basis like candy and to think I forcefully took it from somebody was inconceivable.

It destroyed my mind.

There had to be some sort of reasonable explanation. Maybe somehow she was mistaken.

I couldn't have participated in this horrible act.

But my heart knew she wasn't mistaken. I was only trying to convince myself of my own humanity, that I wasn't a monstrous beast.

Having failed to convince myself of that fact, in my prostrate position in my living room, I searched for redemption in the only place I assumed could still love me.

"God can you forgive me for this?"

Acknowledgement

While I am prone to forget significant people in my life who helped in the process of writing this novel, let me start with a blanket statement by saying I sincerely thank all my family and friends who supported me in every step of this process. As you supported my medical career, you supported this novel.

I would like to specifically thank my family, my aunty Bisi Akanwo without whose support medical school would not have been possible, my sister Fola for all her love and support and being an unwilling atm machine for me when financial aid had not come through, my mother for giving her all to support my education and get me to this point, my aunt Joy for her support with scriptures in my dark moments, my grandmother for raising me to become the woman I am today.

My friends, the material of this novel came from our collective stories. To the girls of 426 who compelled me to Christianity not with words but with the way you led your lives I thank you for your unwavering support. To Ronke Adefisayo, one of the first and biggest supporters of this novel, my *besto* and the friend I confidently say I speak to everyday, thank you. To Olamide Jegede for support and understanding and for teaching me about patience, thank you. To Nneoma Okoronkwo for being my "medical school sibling" a relationship filled with equal parts love and squabbling, thank you for your advice, love and support. To my other circle of friends, that became my family in medical school that inspired these stories in me, Love and Uche Anani, for making me believe in love, Thomas Jacob, my Indian brother from another mother, for being my official medical school *boo,* for taking care of me and scolding me when you needed to, Harrison Ajeh for being my older brother in medical school, to Supo , for a quite unique friendship and being a support system for me. Having you all as my friends makes me feel like I am truly blessed. A big thank you to the Howard University College of Medicine, for giving me a chance when no one else would and providing the setting for some of the best memories of my life.

To my church family, I thank you for your love and support. To Pastor Nike for fanning the flames of my destiny and being the words and encouragement of God to me on the days I had lost hope. To pastor Tayo Thycus for reading and giving me feedback of an embarrassingly unfinished version of the novel. I am sorry for the torture. To Enaruna Tychus for your support over the years and knowing I have an encourager that is a phone call away.

To the other independent authors, I thank you from the bottom of my heart, Eric Swanson for being a beta reader, Mirandah Uyeh for giving me advice freely without conceit and helping me feel less alone in lonely terrain of independent publishing. A big thank you to other independent authors too numerous to name who posted reviews, promoted the novel, gave invaluable advice and shared their work with me.

A big thank you to all the bloggers that supported me in this journey by posting reviews and hosting me on their blogs. I appreciate your support because after inundated with "nos" your "yes" means so much more to me. Thank for showing me that social media can lead to meaningful and genuine relationships.

Finally and most importantly to Jesus my confidante, my roll dog and best friend there are no words to encapsulate your love, encouragement, your patience and kindness during this process for making your Teflon princess. There are no words for everything you have done for me and the things you are yet to do. I thank you for your unfailing love.

Authors note

Still like most ideas started with a little spark. My friends and I would spend all day talking about medical school and its nuances. We gossiped about professors and attendings, about the ever changing mine field of who was dating who in medical school, about how fair or unfair examinations were, about the step scores of upper class men and our class mates, about what we loved about school and what frustrated us. We talked about everything and gradually I realized that the collection of stories being written in my life and my friend's life against the back drop of medical education was compelling. I said to myself someone has to write about this. I wasn't really sure it was going to be me.

So God reawakened gift of storytelling that I had almost forgotten and after a few false starts, I officially started writing in January of 2011.The story of Sola, Ladi Tayo and Nikky developed organically without much of a thought process. However, I wrote with the conviction that my characters' experiences was not unique-there were people... mothers, daughters, sisters, brothers, who experienced the same isolating dark emotions.

Still, from conception to actualization, took three years, as a result the final manuscript differs slightly from the original manuscript. I originally had five major characters including Ego. But I realized that her story made the manuscript weak because her storyline did not merge as seamlessly as the others. I altered the plot of the novel and included only one chapter of her point of view However, I believe her storyline with Ben deserves to be told, and because there is something I like about her, I saved the material so it can be published later as another novel tentatively named *Art of Completion*.

The portrayal of medical school and the medical school experience in this novel is tongue in cheek, nothing should be taken seriously. It was my opportunity to poke fun of our collective experience. As a result, most of my actual medical school friends are featured in the novel as minor characters. For a more realistic portrayal of medical school, I broke the series into four novels, for each year of medical school.

As I move on the next level of my medical career, where free time to write will be a luxury, I am hopeful that God will complete the work He has started in me. Although I know exactly how the story ends because I wrote down the general plan for the series, I am still curious to learn how the story actually ends for the characters. I know how plans and though processes change during the novel writing process and I know the characters' stories may end up starkly different from what I envisioned three years ago.

As I said before, I don't exactly know why I choose to write about the darker parts of human emotions however I hope my imperfect story is the word of God to a wounded heart and in some way recognizing yourself in the novel brings some comfort in knowing that you are not isolated, someone is listening to you, someone understands you and most of all God loves you.

If you would like to learn more about the *Still* series and the author, please visit www.eniolaprenticewrites.blogspot.com. You can also download a free excerpt of *Still* 2 the next book of the series and get updates by subscribing to the website.

www.ingramcontent.com/pod-product-compliance
Lightning Source LLC
Chambersburg PA
CBHW020222180626
46810CB00006B/2018